A Distant Technology

J. P. Telotte

A DISTANT TECHNOLOGY

TECHNOLOGY

Science Fiction Film and the Machine Age

Wesleyan University Press

Published by University Press of New England

Hanover and London

Wesleyan University Press
Published by University Press of New England
Hanover, NH 03755
©1999 by J. P. Telotte
All rights reserved
Printed in the United States of American 5 4 3 2 1
CIP data appear at the end of the book

Contents

Illustrations

Acknowledgments

A number of people have contributed their time, resources, and general knowledge to the creation of this book and deserve special note. As every film student knows, one of the greatest difficulties in doing historical research is simply locating copies of the films. Ken Landgraf came to my rescue several times, helping me find much of what I needed. I also owe a large debt to my colleague Bud Foote who, I continue to believe, knows far more about science fiction literature than any human should be allowed to know. His passing commentary on science fiction is a resource I value even more than I do access to his large library of the genre. As in the past, another colleague, Robert E. Wood, has been an invaluable sounding board for many of the ideas here and contributed to the crafting of several arguments. No less important are my students at Georgia Tech, especially those in my Film and the Machine Age course. Their reactions to the films have proved an invaluable check on my own enthusiasm, and their comments have often been insightful. My largest debt, though, is to two of the foremost commentators on science fiction film, Vivian Sobchack and Brooks Landon. Their readings of the manuscript helped give point to my argument and to flesh out a social dimension I had only vaguely sketched. Finally, I want to thank my editor at Wesleyan University Press, Suzanna Tamminen. Her early interest in and enthusiasm for the project encouraged me at a time when I was unsure whether, in the midst of the digital era, there was any audience for a Machine-Age study. I appreciate the help of all of these people and apologize for not singling out many others whose comments on various paper presentations in which much of this work first appeared also contributed to its final formulation.

J.P.T.

A Distant Technology

1

Introduction

Technology and Distance

I

For this was the triumph of the machine—that in its capacity to produce imitations it could supply everything from entertainment to necessities in virtually unlimited quantities. But to the more thoughtful observers of change, it was precisely the machine's capacity to imitate that raised the knottiest issues. And the question first posed by industrial technology in the nineteenth century would become the question we are still trying to answer: how has the machine, with its power to produce replicas and reproductions, altered our culture?—MILES ORVELL, *The Real Thing* (36)

The Machine Age, that period which stretches roughly from the time of World War I to the start of World War II, is a watershed era for both American and world culture. It marks, as Richard Guy Wilson has offered, the coming "dominance of the machine in all areas of life and culture" and the emergence of a "special sensibility" that informs the twentieth century. It is also, many would argue, the moment at which the modern world first discovers its specifically modern character. Furthermore, and probably far more significantly for us today, it is the point at which the modern establishes the terms for the emergence of a contemporary, postmodern culture—one that draws much of its character from the technology that seems to be constantly reshaping our world, reworking our culture, even modifying our very humanity.

As the epigraph from Miles Orvell hints, the Machine Age is also a most crucial period for the movies. For film is itself one of those machines—indeed, for most of this century, the preeminent one—whose "power to produce replicas and reproductions" has "altered our culture" in ways we are only beginning to assess. During this era the way in which film functioned changed tremendously. From its earlier status as a curiosity or simple entertainment for the lower classes, from a "cinema of attractions," it became a worldwide medium of general communication and artistic expression. In this period too technology abruptly changed film's form, as the various apparatuses for sound recording, synchronization, and amplification converged, forcing a medium that had developed a highly conventional and effective practice of silent communication to shift gears, to acquire a voice, and in the process to explore new approaches to narration. In addition, the era saw the development of various technologies for color reproduction with the introduction of first the two-strip and later the three-strip Technicolor process.[1] The Machine Age thus becomes a special historical marker for film, a point at which it pushes definitively in the direction of André Bazin's "myth of total cinema,"[2] while also foregrounding, in an incipiently postmodern way, the very technologies involved in its efforts at reproduction, at actuating that "myth."

The resulting tensions, as film strives for a new level of realistic representation, for what has been described as a "transparent realism," while struggling with its own technological development, become particularly obvious in those films that clearly respond to and reflect the Machine Age. Specifically, the science fiction films of the era—which, in focusing on the technological, invariably foreground the machine, even the machinery of the cinema—can help us sketch the tensions involved in that "special sensibility" of which Wilson speaks as it resonated in modern culture and in the cinema. In this period most of the major industrialized countries that were struggling with the new dominance of the machine and its accompanying sensibility also produced significant science fiction texts. Of course, I do not mean to suggest that there is a massive body of film work to rival the explosion of pulp literature in the era, much less to approach the great flood of science fiction movies that would appear in the early Cold War years. Still, the major industrialized countries, particularly the Soviet Union, Germany, France, the United States, and England, produced films that are often cited as key works in cinematic history, as well as classics of the genre. Yet while films like *Paris qui dort (The Crazy Ray,* 1924), *Metropolis* (1926), and *Things to Come* (1936) have figured substantially in discussions of the cinematic avant-garde *(Paris qui dort),* the expressionist movement *(Metropolis),* and the influence of literature *(Things to Come),* few of the period's other science fiction films, when they are mentioned at all, have received more than cursory critical attention.

Because they seem so central to that question Orvell poses, reflect so fundamentally the machine's subtle alterations of our culture, and look so obviously toward our current technological world—having helped to construct it—these films beg more careful consideration, and in some cases *a first* contemporary examination. In them we can find a catalogue of the various technologies that were already shaping the modern world and a forecast of those that would influence or become commonplace in our own time: the setback skyscraper, the automobile, the long-range airplane, the helicopter, high-speed trains, the radiotelescope, television, rocketships, robotics, and atomic power, among others. With these elements the films echoed the visionary work of established writers like Jules Verne and H. G. Wells, brought to life the highly popular pulp fiction of the period, found in the pages of publications like *Amazing Stories* and *Astounding Stories*, and drew into the cultural mainstream the imaginings of such figures as the avant-garde planner Le Corbusier, the architect Hugh Ferriss, and the industrial designer Norman Bel Geddes. They provide us with a telling record of our machine imaginings in the first half of this century, and thus rich material for beginning to study the ongoing cultural construction of the technological in America and other industrialized countries. From such a beginning, we might also better understand how that construction of the technological has shaped our contemporary world, which seems to live and breathe through its technology.

The period's science fiction films offer us more, however, than just a catalogue of appealing images and traces of various other cultural movements. For in them we can also begin to detect a curious ambivalence about the technological that seems to run counter to the supposed cultural embrace of a Machine Age ethos and to strike a rather different chord than we find in most of the technology-romanticizing pulps. As we shall see, the films tend in various ways to appear detached from and at times even skeptical of the very machines on which their narratives focus, and in some cases far more aware than mainstream movies of their own status as cinema, as products of a technology of reproduction. The tensions involved in the development of film technology and narrative in this period thus seem to intersect with those implicit in a Western world that was struggling with its own transition into the modern, into a Machine Age culture.

I want to look at the science fiction films of this period, then, as key cultural texts—texts that speak simultaneously about the nature of film, about the science fiction genre, and about our sense of the technological, particularly about the ways in which we were engaged in the cultural construction of the technological. That "special sensibility" of which Wilson speaks, and which he ties to the very meaning of the word "modern," is the key link here. For in this period, as he explains, "modern" implied "a complete break with the past," the abandonment of "outmoded" traditions and traditional styles in favor of a thoroughly contemporary aesthetic based largely on the properties of the machine—speed, regularity, efficiency—and its powers of reproduction, the implicit notion that "a whole new culture . . . could be built as readily as the machine" (23). Certainly, films, as the key aesthetic product of what Walter Benjamin has termed "the Age of Mechanical Reproduction," were engaged in all of these tasks. And along with the literature of science fiction, which found its name if not quite its origin in this period,[3] they often looked to the future, visualized various utopian possibilities, offered us schemes for building "a whole new culture." In effect, these films seem to have been involved in another kind of distancing project that was also a key part of Machine Age culture: detaching audiences from the familiar or traditional world, as well as from its associated values.

Yet as we shall see, that project was problematic, since the machine technology that was proving so pervasive came with its own problems. Mechanisms such as the airplane and the tractor, which promised so many benefits to modern life, also, as bombers and tanks, contributed massively to the slaughter of World War I. The introduction of Henry Ford's assembly-line techniques met with violent resistance in England and elsewhere. Literature of the early Machine Age, as Cecelia Tichi has shown, repeatedly evoked the image of technology "to represent uncontrolled, destabilizing power" (52). While such an attitude partly followed from a simple distrust of change, another factor was the sense that, as Tichi explains, "a dominant technology" effectively "redefines the human role," even threatens to redefine human nature (16)—a problem with which we continue to struggle today. Science fiction films from the Machine Age consequently faced the difficult task of fashioning an acceptable view of the technological, of presenting technology not as a distancing or alienating force, but as a means of bridging the distances that gaped all the more obviously in the modern world—distances between different nations and peoples, between the different classes in every nation, between men and women, between the individual and that natural world from which all of us were increasingly estranged. And they had to do so, as I have suggested above, while confronting their own distant perspective, their own skepticism about this technological work. As we shall see, the task was a rather paradoxical and difficult one, and in its ambivalences perhaps a revealing mark of modernism itself.

II

Of course, in order to begin exploring these tensions and that sense of distance from which they emanate, we do not have to look solely at the science fiction film. The Machine Age provides us with ample film texts that attest to the power, allure, and pervasiveness of the technological in this era, and that reflect the dynamic of its construction. The very appearance of certain other film genres, after all, testifies to one dimension of this technological development. The musical, most obviously, could find its voice only with the coming of sound technology. And the excitement of the gangster film relied on its characteristic combination of technological images and violent sounds—speeding cars, squealing tires, and chattering machine guns. On a thematic level, the biopic (biographical picture) explored the new appeal of the scientist and his struggles with science and technology, as films like *The Story of Louis Pasteur* (1936), *The Story of Alexander Graham Bell* (1939), *Young Tom Edison* (1940), and *Dr. Erlich's Magic Bullet* (1940) suggest. But even prior to these developments the silent comedy had demonstrated the appeal of certain technological imagery. Particularly, it showed that the automobile—or flivver—made a most apt prop for all sorts of humorous situations. If, as Henri Bergson claims, laughter commonly proceeds from the "encrustation" of the mechanical on the human,[4] then comedy, particularly under the guiding hand of Mack Sennett, could make great capital by depicting humans trying to conform to the logic of the auto and, in some cases, by attributing human characteristics to that same mechanism, as well as by repeatedly rendering characters as the offspring of machines.

A more complex response to the Machine Age shows up in the work of the three key comic filmmakers of this period, Harold Lloyd, Charlie Chaplin, and Buster Keaton. In both his shorts and early features, most notably films like *Get Out and Get Under* (1920) and *Hot Water* (1924), Lloyd works his own variations on the Sennett pattern, with his glasses character struggling to cope with Model-Ts that seem to have minds of their own. But Lloyd's greatest successes were never so much when his character is at odds with technology as when he embodies the very spirit of the Machine Age, as the title of one of his best features, *Speedy* (1928), implies. In fact, most often Lloyd's films chronicle his reckless exploits in the big city: driving various vehicles at breakneck speed through crowded streets, chasing runaway cars, buses, or trollies, climbing the sides of setback skyscrapers. Certainly, he is most remembered for the iconic image of his glasses character dangling from a clock face many stories up in *Safety Last* (1923), as he tried to emulate a key popular culture figure of the era, the human fly. It is an image that Lloyd knew would appeal to period audiences, since he had put his character into that same precarious situation in several of his most popular shorts—*High and Dizzy* (1920) and *Never Weaken* (1921)—and when trying to adapt to the new technology of sound, he naturally returned to this formula for success in *Feet First* (1930). In every instance Lloyd sought to offer his audience a reassuring image, that of a thoroughly modern man, able quite literally to "rise" to the challenge of the modern technological world, to master one of its foremost emblems, the setback skyscraper. And at least for his silent films, his audience responded with enthusiasm to that image.

If the Machine Age posed a challenge to the individual, then, it seems to have been a challenge that, Lloyd's films reiterate, the "speedy," optimistic individual could meet. Still, nothing came easily to the Lloyd persona. The modern world, as his movies depict it, is clearly marked by a sense of distance—the great heights his character must climb or cope with, the distances he must cover in various mad dashes to the rescue, the seemingly insurmountable obstacles that separate him from the success he both desires and deserves. But no distance or obstacle ever defeats this figure, in great part because Lloyd is so much a part of that Machine Age world, so driven by its spirit, as if he were himself a machine—or at least a construct of the times.

For Charlie Chaplin, whose little tramp character was by nature always shut off from the cultural mainstream and always seemed to be at odds with that spirit of the times, there was far less possibility of such accommodation. In his first film, *Kid Auto Races at Venice* (1914), the lines are not drawn so starkly. For here he happens upon a sure emblem of the era, a motion picture camera filming a local soap box derby. The comic confrontation that follows, as he repeatedly draws up close, studies the mechanism, and constantly positions himself between the camera and its erstwhile subject, suggests less the sort of conflict to be found throughout his feature films and more of the Sennett-like encounter between man and machine designed to make comic capital from human curiosity or vanity.

In his later films, with his tramp persona more elaborately drawn and thoroughly established with movie audiences worldwide, Chaplin turns that Machine Age world into a far more active antagonist. As its title implies, *Modern Times* (1936) offers probably the best gloss on this relationship. Here Chaplin's tramp is, from the start, out of step with the machine world, as he works on an assembly line, performing a mindless, repetitive

1. *The little tramp at odds with the assembly line in* Modern Times.

task, tightening bolts. He becomes so much an extension of the line, so machine-like in his motions, that when given a break, a moment to become human again, he at first cannot control his body's near-automatic twisting motions. The assembly line has produced a physiological fallout, a twitch that makes it practically impossible for him even to eat during his lunch break. And when offered the solution of being fed by a product of the period's much-trumpeted efficiency movement, an automatic feeding machine, the tramp fares no better. Battered and beaten by the machine as it runs amuck, the tramp at one point even has bolts pushed into his mouth — perhaps the most appropriate food for someone who has become little more than an extension of the machine. By the end of the day, as the line has gotten faster and faster, it also produces a psychological fallout, as the tramp, just like the feeding machine, goes haywire, tightening everything on which his wrenches can be fitted: the noses of his coworkers, the bolts on a fire hydrant, the buttons on prominant parts of a woman's dress. And in both this scene and a later one, first the tramp and then a mechanic he is assisting are swallowed up by the factory machinery. In the first of these swallowings, we see the tramp stretched over cog wheels, impelled by the great gears of a machine, looking very much like a piece of film caught in

2. Modern Times: *The tramp becomes like a piece of film in a camera.*

the sprockets of a camera or projector, as he evokes the movie apparatus not as an object of curiosity, as in *Kid Auto Races*, but rather as yet another threatening machine.[5] The larger implication is clear; for Chaplin the world of the Machine Age is ultimately at odds with human nature, even destructive of that nature, and we should keep our distance. Thus he would end his last film of this era, *The Great Dictator* (1940), with his little tramp, here in the character of a Jewish barber mistaken for the Hitler-like dictator Hynkel, surrounded by storm troopers as he makes a passionate speech warning the people against "these unnatural men—machine men with machine minds and machine hearts."

Neither wholeheartedly embracing the spirit of the age, as did Lloyd, nor quite as alienated from it as Chaplin, Buster Keaton offers a more complex response to this modern, technological world, a kind of middle ground. For his persona is, apparently like Keaton himself[6]—and, we might assume, like much of his audience—almost invariably curious and even enthusiastic about the machines that provide the backdrop or become the central props in many of his films: steamboats, trains, cars, cameras, projectors, ocean liners, and so on. Often, the Keaton persona even acts like a machine—fast, efficient, thoroughly predictable—as if he were one of those very "machine men" against whom Chaplin inveighs. The opening scene of what is probably his most famous film, the Civil War epic *The General* (1926), amply illustrates this character. As Johnnie Gray, the engineer of the locomotive "The General," he leaves his train to visit his girl, Annabelle Lee. On the way, he picks up two young admirers who fall in behind him as he walks; unnoticed, Annabelle Lee too joins the procession, picking up the rear of this human train. After reaching her house, Johnnie finds that to be alone with his girl, he must first get rid of the two boys, so he pretends to leave, they rise to follow, he marches them through the door, and then he falls back, shutting the door on them—effectively uncoupling several cars from the human train. His train-like behavior seems all the more fitting when we see a present Johnnie has brought Annabelle Lee—a photograph showing his face low in the foreground and "The General" in the background, dominating the composition and looking as if it were driving *through his head*. More than just an indication of how important the locomotive is to him, this picture tells us precisely what is on, or in, his mind, in fact, how much his mind is guided by a kind of machine model. He thinks in a very simple cause-and-effect, linear, train-like way, and he acts accordingly.

And yet a troubling undercurrent always threatens that characterization. In her discussion of the Machine Age in America, Cecelia Tichi describes a key shift that occurs in the era. While in the nineteenth century, she suggests, "machine technology, like the forces of nature," often came to represent instability, to suggest "horrific, destabilizing energies loosed in the universe," "chaotic natural energies" against which the individual seemed practically helpless (52, 53), with the coming of the Machine Age those same images were often transformed into ones of stability and efficiency, typically linked to the machine itself. In the Keaton world, there is no possibility for such easy demarcation. Machines are as tricky as they are efficient; instability and chaos are constant potentials in both the natural and the mechanical worlds. Hence Keaton's films offer the war setting of *The General*, the deadly feud of *Our Hospitality* (1923), the cannibal attack in *The Navigator* (1924), the cyclone of *Steamboat Bill, Jr.* (1928), and the great rock slide in *Seven Chances* (1925). As this last film illustrates, though, that instability and the energy involved are elements that the Keaton character can often turn to profit. In *Seven Chances* he is being pursued by a mob of women—all dressed in wedding gowns and veils—who have heard he will inherit a million dollars if he is married before day's end. In trying to escape this capitalist love connection, Keaton tumbles down a mountainside, dislodging several boulders, which, in turn, start a massive rock slide

3. *Buster Keaton copes with the outsized machinery of a steampship in* The Navigator.

from which he must run for his life. As he runs from the rocks, he plunges headlong into the army of pursuing brides and momentarily freezes, trying to decide on the better of the two terrible fates—being crushed or married. As an alternative, he heads back toward the rocks, dodging them and letting the boulders chase off his female pursuers. He has simply turned that natural instability to his own end, using one chaotic element to negate another.

That same imaginative and transformative spirit underlies Keaton's relationship to the machine, which, for all of its often daunting power or puzzling character, remains a source of attraction, and at times even a vehicle of salvation. In *The Navigator*, for example, Rollo Treadway and his girl, attacked by cannibals, abandon their steamship and sink beneath the waves, only to be saved at the last moment by a passing submarine, which just happens to surface under them. In *The General* Johnnie Gray uses his train to rescue Annabelle Lee from her Union kidnappers, to warn the Confederate forces about a surprise attack, and to win this battle if not the Civil War. *Steamboat Bill, Jr.* (1928) concludes with Willie Canfield maneuvering his father's steamboat through a cyclone- and storm-swollen river to rescue his father, his girl, her father, and a drifting preacher who, we assume, will perform the expected marriage. And in *Sherlock, Jr.* (1924) we see another sort

4. *Keaton fascinated by the mechanical reproduction of the movies in* Sherlock, Jr.

of rescue, as Keaton, a film projectionist, turns to the movie he is then showing for help when his girl suddenly shows up and suggests marriage. By sneaking quick glimpses at the film, he figures out how to hold her hand, embrace her, offer her a ring, and then kiss her, while he is also warned of what will surely, if rather inexplicably, follow—a hoard of children. Serving in such a supporting role, the machine never seems a true menace in Keaton's films. While it often signals his detachment from others—in *The General*, for instance, the train is one of his "two loves" and all too easily substitutes for his girl—and points up the folly of acting *too* machine-like, the machine more generally helps to measure his characters' gradual maturing and involvement in the modern world.

Keaton seems to have gauged better than any of his fellow comedians the very nature of the machine. While it may be fast and efficient, it is never totally reliable or free from its own instabilities, in part because of the larger instability of this world and the unpredictability of everything in it. What is probably his most representative Machine Age work, the two-reeler *The Electric House* (1922), well illustrates this view. In this film Keaton plays a recent college graduate—his degree is in Botany—who is mistaken for an electrical engineer and asked to convert the Dean's old house to a modern, totally electric residence. This narrative premise obviously echoes Wilson's description of the period's belief that everything "could be built as readily as the machine" itself. And the character's acceptance of the project, with a manual titled *Electricity Made Easy* as his only aid, seems to affirm that notion. However, when the Dean returns from vacation to inspect his "electric house," he finds it not only wired and equipped with multiple mechanical conveniences, but also a place of constant surprise. The escalator, for example, never seems to run at the same speed twice, and when he first tries it out, the mechanism vaults the Dean through a second-story window into the pool below.[7] The lights flicker off and on, and the train Keaton has rigged to serve meals jumps its track, dumping the main course in the lap of the Dean's wife. Further compounding this unpredictability is the appearance of a real electrical engineer, jealous of Buster's work, who tinkers with the wiring to make the entire house appear as if it had a mind of its own. The chaos that results, as all the household mechanisms run amuck and make the inhabitants think the place is haunted, drives home the film's key point: that modernizing the world—or a house—does not make it any less capable of surprise, any less challenging, any less human.

Outside of the comic world, that rather mixed view of the age's technological thrust seems all the more common. In that bellwether of an emerging Russian cinema, *Battleship Potemkin* (1925), the modern steel warship is a site of oppression and dehumanization in the hands of the Czar's officers, as well as a sign of the people's power and revolutionary spirit once it is commandeered by mutinying sailors. René Clair's social commentary *A Nous la liberté* (1930) on the one hand presents the modern manufacturing system, complete with its Fordian assembly line, as the surest sign of its escaped-convict protagonist's successful movement into the modern world and attainment of wealth and social standing. On the other, it suggests that such a status—and the conditions that make it possible—is something else from which he needs to escape, something from which we shall all eventually need "la liberté." In numerous films on World War I, that testing ground for "mechanized" warfare, the machine—whether airplane, dirigible, machine gun, or tank—becomes the key image of both human power and human destruction. Thus such works as *Hell's Angels* (1930), *All Quiet on the Western Front* (1930), *The Dawn Patrol* (1930, 1938), and *La Grande Illusion* (1937), among many others, use exciting aerial and combat sequences in large part to set the stage for antiwar and at times anti-machine messages. And in a host of period cartoons, perhaps most notably those of Max and Dave Fleischer (such as *Ko-Ko's Earth Control* [1928], *Come Take a Trip in My Airship* [1925, 1930], *Sky Scraping* [1930], *The*

Robot [1932], *Crazy Inventions* [1933], *More Pep* [1936], and especially the various Betty Boop and Grampy pairings) we repeatedly see a fascination not only with the latest technology, but also with the ways in which that technology plays tricks on people, renders them comic figures, component parts in an unpredictable Rube Goldberg machine.

Probably the most telling text in this regard is the air epic *Wings* (1927), a film historically renowned for winning the first Academy Award for Best Picture. Blessed with a large budget and an unparalleled level of assistance in both men and machines from the army,[8] director William Wellman fashioned a tribute to the pioneer aviators of World War I and the fragile machines in which they flew, drawing largely on his own experiences as a pilot with the Lafayette Flying Corps. More than just a film about the war, though, *Wings* explores the technological spirit that moved those early aviators, that spurred them to flight. Thus the film begins with a title card offering a tribute to Lindbergh, who had only recently accomplished his great transatlantic crossing, and quoting his praise for the fliers of World War I when "feats were performed and deeds accomplished which were far greater than any peace accomplishments of aviation." With that epigraph, the film links its recollections of the decade before to current events, indeed, to one of the signal events of the era, and in the process affirms its own Machine Age sensibility.

The narrative that follows further places its tale of mechanized warfare by framing it with two extensive home-town sequences. These not only introduce the key figures—Jack Powell, his neighbor Mary Preston, and David Armstrong, who is both Jack's rival for the love of Sylvia Lewis and also his best friend—but also establish what another title card terms "the dreams of youth," which inspire these people and have helped quicken the pace of modern life. Those dreams are all about speed and flight. After staring up at the sky, Jack turns to working on his car, stripping it, souping up the engine for more speed, all with the help of Mary, who also graces the car with an emblem, a shooting star. It is a vehicle with which, we learn, he has already "left the ground several times"—in accidents. More to the point, it is a kind of dream machine, a device that makes him dream of being up in the clouds, far away from his small-town home and its suggestion of a rural, agrarian America of earlier times. This dream leaves him so detached from this world that he hardly notices Mary, who has a crush on him, as he races off to show Sylvia his car. And this mad rushing about—"Life marched at the double quick," a title offers—prepares us for the speed with which, as war is announced, both he and David jump at the chance to sign up for the Army Air Corps and go to France.

5. Wings: *Friends united by their common love of flying.*

That dream of distance and detachment from this world, though, is repeatedly punctured as Jack and David enter service in the Air Corps. The more experienced Cadet White, with whom they are first billeted, dies in a crash on a routine training flight right after introducing himself and promising that they "will be seeing a lot of each other." On their first combat sortie, nearly the entire flight is shot down; Jack crashes in no-man's land and David is narrowly spared after his machine guns jam. During the big offensive thrust at St. Mihiel, Jack accidentally shoots down and kills David, who had been flying in a captured German plane—who had *become*, in Jack's eyes, that enemy machine. On this note, with the machine as emblem of alienation and destruction, the war narrative ends and we return to Jack's hometown, where he is lauded as a hero but must also face David's parents and return his effects. To complete the framing effect, the narrative shows Jack uncovering his old hot rod and encountering Mary. But instead of speeding away in the car, as he did in the opening sequence, now Jack treats it like a park bench, sitting on it with Mary, watching a shooting star in the night sky, and finally pledging his love to her. After his great dreams of speed and flight, of being much like that distant shooting star, he has definitively returned to earth and to life. These framing scenes thus acknowledge what we might term the special sensibility of the Machine Age, even define it as a dream of distance, speed, and power, but also trace its possible consequences and draw its dreamers back to reality.

III

That dream of distance chronicled in *Wings*, of a kind of transcendence available through the machine, and the eventual devastation of that dream compose a story hardly limited to the period's narratives of air warfare. It is, in fact, the driving pattern at work in the science fiction films of this era; yet that pattern and this whole body of work have largely gone unexplored. As we have already noted, most of the major industrialized nations, and thus most of the major film-producing countries, turned out in this era not only a number of texts *about* technology and its shaping power, but also a variety of science fiction films that parallel, in focus though not in the volume, the science fiction stories then appearing in the pulp literature. And with but a few notable exceptions, this segment of our cinematic and cultural history, as well as a potentially resonant element of the science fiction genre's history, has largely escaped critical notice.

Certainly, the science fiction literature of this era suffers from no similar lack of attention. As Edward James notes in his history of the genre, the period between the wars saw the science fiction genre become "fully recognized," having developed a readily identifiable set of concerns, "its own specialist magazines and its own specialist readership" (53), along with an enthusiastic and organized fandom.[9] As a result, no examination of the development or impact of the literary genre has been able to overlook the remarkable convergence in this time of a traditional speculative literature, such as that of H. G. Wells; of the pulps, particularly Hugo Gernsback's *Amazing Stories, Astounding Stories* (especially under the editorship of John W. Campbell, Jr.), and *Wonder Stories*; and of what James terms "a boom in 'futurology'" (43), which produced a body of essays, pamphlets, and books attempting to assess the direction and future development of our culture and its institutions. Indeed, as Howard Segal reminds us, the "extraordinary final outpouring of faith in technological progress" (132) in the late Machine Age occurs across a broad range of texts, often blurring distinctions between fiction, informational text, and polemic, and all converging in their speculations on how technological development and planning might begin to reconstruct modern culture. These developments have all been seen as crucial to defining the literary genre and to placing it in our cultural history.

However, the films of this period have seldom been brought within that larger generic vantage and, with a few exceptions, have often become little more than footnotes to both film history and our speculations about technology in the era. Among many others, this relatively neglected body of Machine Age science fiction films includes works like France's *Paris qui dort (The Crazy Ray)* and *La Fin du monde* (1930); Germany's *Metropolis, Die Frau im Mond* (1929), *F.P. 1 Antwortet Nicht* (1932), *Gold* (1934), and various, largely forgotten films by Harry Piel, such as *Der Herr der Welt* (1934); Russia's *Aelita* (1924); the United States' *The Mysterious Island* (1929), *Just Imagine* (1930), and *The Invisible Ray* (1936); and England's *The Tunnel* (1935) and *Things to Come*. Of this group, only *Metropolis*, partly because of director Fritz Lang's auteur status and partly because of the film's standing as the earliest utopian/dystopian film, has previously received much detailed attention. Others draw only cursory consideration at best. *Paris qui dort*, for example, is at times mentioned in the context of early avant-garde filmmaking; *Just Imagine* has become little more than an object warning about merging genres, in this case the musical and science fiction; and *Things to Come* is cited for H. G. Wells's singular participation in the project. The rest of those mentioned above, since they are generally difficult to locate today and appeared at a time when film was in transition between the full flowering of the silent aesthetic and the awkward emergence of sound narrative, tend to be ignored and are practically absent from all standard histories of film.[10]

Of course, one reason for this relative neglect is that these are all essentially border films, and as such create difficulties for historians, who, because of the very requirements of their task, tend to focus on more definitive works. Yet precisely because of that border status, these films stand to reveal much about technologies, cultures, and indeed a cinema all in transition. Certainly as a group these films speak revealingly and perhaps surprisingly about Western culture in this period, as well as about its embrace of technology and even of the movies themselves. In these works, for example, we find a remarkable cultural convergence on technological issues, which were already perceived as remaking our world. Yet in that convergence, as we noted above, we can also sense a curious ambivalence about the technological, which, for the most part, runs counter to the supposed cultural embrace of a Machine Age ethos, and which certainly strikes a rather different chord than does the popular pulp fiction. In them too we find constant intersections with other popular genres of the period—for example, the disaster film, the horror film, even the musical and the western—that suggest a rather fluid and developing sense of these formulas.

These border works thus promise to shed a revealing light on the cultural work of this genre.

To collect on that promise, we might first consider our conventional views of both the science fiction film and of the very mechanism of genre. As Susan Sontag has emphasized, the science fiction genre, especially in its American incarnations, has typically focused on a triad of elements: technology, science, and reason.[11] Perhaps its key semantic element—and thus one of the most basic signposts indicating we have entered science fiction territory—is the technology we typically encounter, the spaceships, robots, ray guns, futuristic architecture, and so on, which mark the form. That technology derives from a scientific world, typically from a culture that is intent on exploring, understanding, and codifying our world, as well as any others we might encounter. Behind that effort is a rational perspective, a thoroughly modernist view of the world, and indeed the universe, as essentially knowable, reducible to cause-and-effect terms, and thus accessible to human manipulation. Yet Sontag also reminds us how often that effort fails, how typically calamity or "disaster" follows from the application of this triad, as we see in the numerous alien invasion films of the 1950s, the atomic mutation movies of the same period, the post-apocalyptic works of more recent times, and the rather questionable portrayal of the scientist throughout the genre's history. Following her lead, yet arriving at a different end, Bruce Kawin has described the genre, in its best incarnations, as intent on vanquishing the unknown, overcoming limits—"it opens the field of inquiry, the range of possible subjects, and leaves us open" to wonder as well (321), he says. In contrast to Sontag, he views those films that cast our technology or the science behind it in a threatening light, films like *The Thing* (1951), *Invasion of the Body Snatchers* (1956), or *Alien* (1982), as horror, not science fiction films, concerned mainly with the dangers that attend such openness. Of course, both of these vantages have at their heart a fundamental tension between the professed aims of science/technology/reason and their cultural products—a tension which each critic tries to resolve by pushing what may seem an absolutist view of the genre. In fact, this effort at resolution may be at the root of Sontag's ultimate dissatisfaction with the form; she finds that it usually offers "an inadequate response" to our more pressing cultural problems (211).

And yet the genre has, as have our other popular formulas, often served us well in doing the work of culture, that is, in providing the imaginative constructs we need—in this case, those revolving around technology, science, and reason—to cope with the problems of our culture. They offer, as Barry Grant simply puts it, "contemporary versions of social myth" (115).

Those myths help us by imaginatively resolving the seemingly unresolvable problems with which we wrestle. Thus, even as our culture has struggled recently with issues of cloning, genetic manipulation, and artificial intelligence, our science fiction films have repeatedly offered up a central and multiply resonant image, that of the android/robot/cyborg, the image of human artifice, as a means of narratizing those concerns and rendering them less uncanny, less menacing, and, in the case of the *Star Wars* trilogy's almost cuddly robots, even comforting.[12]

I emphasize this cultural work because it may offer another clue as to why these films have generally received so little attention. Certainly in the Machine Age, with its pervasive machine culture, we might expect a genre whose very focus is the technological to be prominent in this "mythic" work of constructing a friendly image of technology and a comforting narrative of its place in our world. Western culture at every turn confronted signs of this new industrial civilization: new processes of production (Fordism, Taylorism), the prominence of the automobile, high-speed air travel, widespread electrification, the introduction of various labor-saving household appliances, an architectural emphasis on the setback skyscraper, literature in which, as Cecelia Tichi observes, machine metaphors were becoming pervasive, even a music that, Richard Guy Wilson reminds us, increasingly incorporated "nontraditional sounds that reflected the machine" (34). And yet the genre that seems best equipped for addressing these dizzying developments never fully rises to the occasion, never manages to become the sort of prominent formula we might expect, certainly not to the extent that the musical, gangster film, or comedy did in the same era. The absence of a large body of work to match that literary outpouring of the genre is itself an interesting symptom to consider.

Of course, as William Johnson has argued, we should not expect to understand the science fiction film simply by seeing it as an extension of the literary genre (2). The film form develops together with the cinema itself, and consequently is more fundamentally invested in the technological, more implicated in its cultural construction than the literature; it has more at stake. With this history in mind, Garrett Stewart suggests that "science fiction in the cinema often turns out to be, turns round to be, the fictional or fictive science of the cinema itself" (159), a form haunted by "the spirit of fabrication" (162)—technological, cinematic. As a result, the form's examinations of machine technology or its impact always evoke an element of reflexivity or self-consciousness from which a cinema, driven by an emphasis on seamless narrative and transparent realism, might inevitably recoil.

What I am suggesting is that on some level the science fiction *film* genre always seems to find its very subject matter—science, technology, or more generally, fabrication—challenging, even a bit troubling. Of course, in the Machine Age there were added anxieties with which our films and their audiences had to cope. A testing ground for much modern technology, World War I had also left a terrible fallout from the mechanized destruction that technology brought, as a film like *Wings* demonstrates. And later, with the Great Depression, as we see in Chaplin's *Modern Times*, technology was often associated with those cultural forces that seemed antithetical to labor, that seemed intent on eliminating the individual from the workplace or reducing him to a part in a machine. But while other films managed to dissolve those anxieties in their generic formulas (*A Connecticut Yankee* [1931], *Modern Times*) or blunt them with romantic or other compensations (*Wings, Dirigible* [1930]), the science fiction film seems, throughout much of the Machine Age, to have been almost too close to its subject, too marked by the same sort of tensions that typified modern culture, tensions that came with technology itself. What we find, consequently, is a form simply unable to fully or satisfactorily accommodate the very values associated with its subject, to solve the problem of distance.

IV

Yet what is this problem of distance? For much of my thinking about the position of technology in modern Western culture, I have drawn on the philosopher Robert Romanyshyn's analysis of the technological, which he describes in very nonmaterial terms—as a kind of "cultural-psychological dream of distance from matter" (194). That dream, he suggests, has at its core our desire for detachment from this world, for freedom from our human limitations. Jean Baudrillard, with his almost ahistorical perspective, describes that sort of distance not only as possible but as the inescapable condition of our postmodern, electronic culture, wherein the individual has come to resemble an "orbital satellite in the universe of the everyday" (*Ecstasy* 16), always removed from the world and thus never able to determine what is "real" in it. As Mark Dery has more recently assessed, ours is a culture longing to achieve "escape velocity," the technological expertise necessary to escape from our very humanity, weighed down as it is by an environment and a mortality that clearly have their limits.[13] In line with these views, Romanyshyn argues that technology is "a matter [not just] of measure but of attitude" (21)—an attitude that represents a most telling "symptom" of all technological culture, both in its formative stages during the modern era and in its state of seeming exhaustion in our postmodern time. Ultimately, these two metaphors, of "dream" and "symptom," encompass his explanation of our modern-day technological condition.

Romanyshyn suggests, in a way that recalls the work of Martin Heidegger[14] and seems particularly fitting to a consideration of film, that we might think of technology not so much as a thing, but as "the enactment of the human imagination in the world." In its various manifestations, technology demonstrates how we have tried to "create ourselves" and the world we inhabit (10). In effect, he says, we "dream" through the technologies we produce; we dream of ways to alter material reality, including our own bodies, to make it correspond to our desires, and to banish our sense of limitation. Thus he describes the technological in a rather conventional way as "a work of reason," but reminds us that it is "reason lined with desire" (10). That description not only invites us to do a bit of dream analysis—examining the dream of technology according to its own logic, searching for any "repressed" significances it may have, while trying to access a kind of cultural unconscious—but also implicates the movies themselves as products of a "dream factory," as we still commonly describe the film industry.

At the same time, Romanyshyn views the technological as a key *symptom* of the modern—and indeed the postmodern—world. A symptom, he says, is "a way of saying not only that something is wrong, but also how that something can be made right" (13). Technology as symptom, then, speaks about that desire we share for what Stewart terms "fabrication"—for remaking the self, reshaping our world, overcoming our human limitations, or as Dery offers, simply escaping from those limitations—but in doing so it reveals the objectification, detachment, and distance built into that desire, attitudes that have become all the more obvious and troubling in the contemporary world, where, says Baudrillard, they have come to seem practically unavoidable. At the same time, the technological suggests a route back from or an alternative to those attitudes, what Romanyshyn would call a "recovery" from those symptoms. For through a mindfulness of our technological culture and its implications, through facing the doubleness of our technology and ourselves, he suggests, we might reenter a world from which we have become distant, alien, astronaut-like.

Of course, the science fiction film in general offers a natural field for exploring this pattern, for examining the traces of distance that mark the form and assessing the symptomatic status of these cultural texts. But by generally limiting our focus to the science fiction films of the Machine Age, I hope to stake out an especially revealing bit of territory. Their generic fore-grounding of the technological brings into sharp focus this pattern of distance at a particularly formative time, when the modern world was preparing for the emergence of our contemporary, postmodern, and thoroughly technologized culture. In her study of the era, Cecelia Tichi notes how, by the turn of the century, popular culture and serious literature alike had already begun to reflect a whole new, Machine Age sensibility, particularly through the pervasive use of machine metaphors, even in the least likely places, such as descriptions of natural phenomena. The implication, she says, is that "knowledge of the workings of nature is . . . knowledge of machines"; that at least in Machine Age America our art had begun to suggest there was no easy "distinction" (40) to be drawn. While that same argument is a difficult one to make for many films of this period—indeed, a film like *Wings*, in both its title cards and images, repeatedly resorts to *nature* metaphors to describe the machines and mechanical endeavors it depicts—at least the science fiction films allow for no easy retreat, no way to draw back from a technological world, from an environment shaped by machines and machine attitudes. Instead, they confront us with the fact of fabrication, bring the technology itself up close for our inspection, and in the process hold our own, at times hesitant embrace of the technological up for examination as well.

What we repeatedly see in those Machine Age confrontations is a complex story of distance and detachment. For as we range across the science fiction films of several countries, trying to sketch the different contexts in which they confront the technological, we shall consistently encounter narratives about great physical, cultural, or epistemological distances and the struggle to overcome them—to move from the Earth to the moon, to span this world's barrier oceans, to unite different cultures or classes, to gain some great knowledge or distinction. And those narratives typically turn on technological devices—rockets, submarines, radio-telescopes, tunnels, aircraft, and various sorts of rays—for bridging these gaps, or, in some cases, for coping with a threatening distance. While those efforts sometimes fail (as in *La Fin du monde* or *The Mysterious Island*) and sometimes succeed (as in *The Tunnel* or *Die Frau im Mond*), the tension that hangs over the narratives, another sort of distance that haunts the point of success or failure, seems most telling in terms of what these films together reveal about attitudes toward the technological.

Even beyond this tension, the narratives themselves are obviously symptomatic, suggesting a modern culture that is intensely aware of a problem of distance. That problem is in part indicative of the more general modern sensibility, what Orvell terms "the central problem of the machine age," that "of man's alienation from the concrete world of experience" (*Real Thing* 172). It is also fallout from what Walter Benjamin in his landmark essay "The Work of Art in the Age of Mechanical Reproduction" describes as our modern detachment "from the domain of tradition" (221), from all that formerly carried authority or meaning—what he terms "aura." But it is also the problem of the technological sensibility itself, of the fact that technology, along with the great power it offers, intervenes between the self and the world, placing us, as Romanyshyn puts it, behind a "window on the world" (31). There we may feel in control of the world, but we also come to feel like something less than participants in it; we become observers and manipulators essentially *displaced* from the world. Orvell puts this attitude in more concrete terms when he describes a shift in the very function of machines in this period. In the nineteenth century, he argues, "the machine was used predominantly to create consumer objects that enthusiastically mimicked handcrafted things"—objects like clothing and furniture that retained a link to the natural world and a traditional way of life. However, in the twentieth century, the machine increasingly was employed "to manufacture objects that were themselves machines—telephones, phonographs, coffee makers, toasters, vacuum cleaners" (*Real Thing* 142); those machines, in turn, marked an ever greater distance from the natural world inhabited by previous generations. More subtly, they began to fashion a world that was fundamentally *defined by distance*, from the beliefs and values of those earlier generations, from the "aura" of things, even from each other.

As machine-made products themselves, the films we will study bear the marks of this problem, which we can begin here to trace. While they find their central attraction in technology and its power, in the constructs of reason that they visualize, that imagery always represents, in Romanyshyn's phrase, "reason lined with desire," in effect, a kind of wish fulfillment—just what we would expect from a dream factory. Yet it is a wish fulfillment that inevitably falls short. Thus while these films offer us images that emphasize the power and potential of technology—power and potential that modernism would claim as our birthright—they also typically reveal the shadow of technology, the problems that desire would overlook. When seen in the context of genre, the era's science fiction films do seem intent on carrying out the usual work of genre: helping audiences troubled by the rapid pace of technological development and the embrace of the machine in all areas of life find some accommodation with this modern situation, by offering them strategies for distancing themselves from their anxieties, by constructing the technological in accord with their desires. So while a film like the Will Rogers *Connecticut Yankee* offers us images of airborn destruction, of tanks, machine guns, and mechanized soldiers—all nightmarish leftovers of World War I and hints of wars yet to come—it marshals those images in defense of Western culture, as signs of how Yankee mechanical ingenuity can triumph over a barbaric spirit, here embodied in the treacherous figure of Morgan Le Fay.[15] Yet even as such films offer comforting strategies, they seem almost inevitably haunted by that sense of distance, as if it were built into the technology itself—hard-wired, to use a contemporary image. Thus, for all of the affirmations of the technological they offer, for all their reminders that, as cultural historian David Gelernter offers, "technology had accomplished breathtaking things" (262) and promised to do far more, the era's films also leave us strangely unsatisfied, never fully convinced, still apprehensive.

V

Before turning to the films themselves and measuring out their dream of distance, we might pause for a brief comment on methodology. This study aims to explore that ambivalence noted above, those abiding tensions in modern industrial culture and its films, by drawing both on Machine Age and postmodern assessments of the impact of technology. Thus, while it attempts to ground its speculations in the history and attitudes of the Machine Age, to draw as much as possible on the era's own ideas, it also hopes to suggest an element of continuity, one in which the Machine Age appears as an early development of patterns we would now identify as postmodern. To better identify this continuity, the study also adopts certain postmodern critical assumptions. Most important, it assumes Baudrillard's notion of seduction to suggest the subtle way in which the technological has always wielded its power. As he argues, "technology . . . doesn't push things forward or transform the world"; it very simply "becomes the world" (*Baudrillard Live* 44). And that "becoming," I would suggest, is essentially recorded on these science fiction films. At the same time, this study takes its central conceit from a complementary and more historically grounded view, Romanyshyn's study of how the technological has functioned in Western culture as a powerful distancing device, something that places us at "a distance from matter," including *human* matter. This view especially helps us describe a central pattern at work in the texts we encounter—a pattern of distance and detachment that affords these films a kind of double vision, as they both embrace and critique the technological and its growing hold on our lives. It also offers a new perspective on ways in which the technological has been implicated in oppositions between classes, races, and genders throughout much of this century.

More broadly conceived, then, this examination is situated in both contemporary cultural criticism and film history. On the one hand, it is concerned with the ways in which our technological consciousness has evolved, both empowering us and distancing us from the very world over which we would exercise that power, even distancing us from each other. That development in the modern era, in what we have come to call the Machine Age, has dramatically set the stage for our postmodern encounter with the technological, and particularly for our own conflicted attitudes toward an electronic, computer-driven technology that promises one day to "download" us into a machine. On the other hand, this examination tries to fill in a large gap of film history, a gap primarily in our study of the science fiction genre but also in film's encounter with its own technological base. As we have noted, the science fiction films of this era, with very few exceptions, go unmentioned in our histories, despite their implications for film in a crucial, formative period. Yet as Garrett Stewart puts it, in their technological thrust, our science fiction films can help us "peer into the mechanics of apparition that permit these films in the outermost and first place" (161). By at least partially filling in these gaps and grappling with that reflexive potential, we might better understand how a kind of cinematic imagination became so powerful in and symptomatic of modern life.

This simultaneously cultural and cinematic vantage could easily focus solely on the American cinema, providing a filmic complement to Tichi's examination of the Machine Age's literary impact, *Shifting Gears*, or a prologue to Vivian Sobchack's study of more recent science fiction films, *Screening Space*. To limit the focus in this way, though, would miss an opportunity for cross-cultural study to which this material readily lends itself. For despite the cultural differences we expect to find in films from countries such as the Soviet Union, Germany, France, the United States, and England, their science fiction films converge enough in their key images, concerns, and attitudes to suggest what Stuart Hall terms a cultural "conventionalization" (30) of technology's presentation, which helps show us how a broad technological perspective was being constructed. These films allow us to gauge both similar and different responses to the technological in different countries, as well as to glimpse the international circulation of meaning in this era. While the discussion that follows is organized on the basis of national origins, then, it also proceeds in a roughly chronological, if at times overlapping, way in its discussion of the films. With this vantage we might better observe the process of change — even radical transformation — that the industrialized cultures that produced key science fiction texts underwent as they tried to address the seemingly irresistible power of the machine and machine principles.

Finally, we shall carry out this investigation by assuming a fundamental dynamic that should be endemic to most cultural criticism. In genre study we often begin from the notion that every film represents a combination of *convention* and *invention*. The work draws on a vast pool of readily recognizable components — character types, objects, settings, attitudes, narrative turns, and so on; to this relatively stable base it adds its own particular developments, its own coloring, its own narrative trajectory, with which it addresses its specific temporal and cultural circumstances. For the purposes of this study we might consider another, similar dynamic at work, one of *reflection* and *construction*. Certainly, the films we shall consider are themselves historical artifacts and reflect their times and their societies, yet seeing them only as historical records can produce misperceptions and misconstructions. For even in their own times and places these films represented particular constructions of a cultural reality, constructions that at times drained technology of value, linked it to colonialism, or even ascribed its more negative elements to the feminine.[16] To better gauge the function of our science fiction films in this era, particularly as they helped accommodate the technological, we need to keep this reflection/construction dynamic in focus.

In the process, we shall be triangulating film, science fiction, and modern technological culture to reveal the significant reshaping that was underway, as the modern world, through its embrace of technology and its powers, was just beginning to point the way to a postmodern world. This is the point when, as Walter Benjamin has so neatly codified it, we were beginning to notice a fundamental shift in the way in which we viewed our world. As he formulated this change, the "cult value" we once saw in our world and especially its artistic products was being replaced by "exhibition value"; a world that assumed a certain essence or "aura" (221) in each work of art, in each act of reproduction — and indeed, in all that was the model for reproduction — was giving way to one that detached production from tradition and traditional meanings, and in the process asserted a whole new function, a materialist and political one, for the process of reproduction. Thus our art, and preeminently the cinema, according to Benjamin, would find its fundamental concern — and source of value — in our world's "reproducibility," as it set about chronicling or reproducing real events in order to make visible the relations governing that world (223).

What the Machine Age brought, in all aspects of modern technological culture, was a new dominance of the machine that effectively *re-placed* the human, that is, it put us in a *new* place. It shifted us from among the many creatures of nature, particularly of a divinely ordained natural order, to the movers and manipulators of that order, operating from a position outside of it—at a great psychological if not physical distance from it. Thus Orvell, following Benjamin's lead, has argued that one of the era's key manifestations was the "discovery of new ways of looking" at things (*Real Thing* 222), ways that, it was thought, at least in America, might restore our "contact with reality" (241) and replace a cultural fascination with imitation with a new access to authenticity itself. Our technology—the technology of the movie camera most certainly, but also the work of industrial construction, architecture, processes of manufacture, and so on—provided us with "a new 'screen' or 'filter' through which the world was experienced" (*After* 10), and that new experience could conceivably enable us to rework our world in ever more productive and efficient ways. Through our technology, in other words, we might begin determining the function and teleology of all things, even the human, and manipulating them in accord with the values inherent in this new, technological way of seeing.

The key factor in this new positioning, as Romanyshyn observes, is that the individual is placed not at the center of the world, but rather *outside* it, there to become a kind of "spectator self" (117) or moviegoer, viewing the world as if through a window or screen—that of the technological—and thus seeing the self as separate from and unconnected to the fate of the rest of that world. Of course, instead of simply providing us with power over the world, the conditions of existence, and our own bodies, as our "technological dream" has long and seductively promised, that attitude of distance has opened the way for ecological abuses, estranged people from one another, and even promoted what Romanyshyn terms the "abandonment of the body" (20), an ongoing effort, which Dery describes, to distance ourselves from the frailties of the "human machine," from the conditions of our very humanity.

Yet another, perhaps more personal sort of problem also attends this Machine Age sensibility and repeatedly surfaces in the era's films. A felt separation or difference from the world, such as both Romanyshyn and Baudrillard describe, could well leave us unmoored in a traditionally conceived reality and prone to see the self as simply another sort of "invented . . . created . . . manufactured" thing (Romanyshyn 17). We might come to seem like the product of a far less efficient system than that which Frederick Winslow Taylor championed in his popular *Principles of Scientific*

Management in 1911 or that Henry Ford demonstrated in his production techniques, or perhaps just one more of those "component parts" which, Tichi explains, were central to a developing aesthetic of the period (173). When exaggerated, the basic principles of what came to be known as Taylorism and Fordism, championed—and reviled—by many in this period can easily suggest what Carroll Pursell terms "a hegemonic culture of modernism run amok" (117). Certainly, those principles often enthroned by the Machine Age—motion and time studies, emphasis on efficient management, assembly-line techniques—contain attitudes that not only linked workers to the technology of the assembly line, but also subtly conflated them with the very products of that line—as Chaplin so well illustrated in the factory scenes of *Modern Times*. Such linking and conflating threatened to make workers not just the manipulators but the manipulated, not just contrivors but contrivances, not just the masters of the machine but the mastered as well. In that threat, we can begin to see the foundation of a typically postmodern anxiety, as our efforts to deploy the latest technological advances seemed to render us more and more "technologized," and our creation of all varieties of artifacts seemed to draw us further toward the artificial and further from the human.

And yet, our science and technology, particularly in the Machine Age, also have at their core our own desire to locate a place for the human—to put us in a position to better deal with our world, our situations, our selves, in effect, to construct a *better* place for us and our machines. In the Machine Age, we were already congratulating ourselves on "A Century of Progress" and planning out "The World of Tomorrow," as the themes for the two most significant World's Fairs of the era underscore. These fairs should remind us, Gelernter argues, of the extent to which in this era, despite all forebodings, when "people turned their minds to the future, what they saw was *good*. Technology in particular was good" (25). Our films of this period were employed precisely in doing the generic work necessary to accommodate these attitudes toward the technology of "progress" and "tomorrow." Yet that was hardly an unproblematic task, for before we could enter this "world of tomorrow," we had to distance ourselves from our anxieties about the machine—quite reasonable reactions for a period sandwiched between two great mechanized wars—while we also embraced a technological attitude that subtly fostered its own disconcerting sense of distance and detachment. As we shall see, the inevitable tensions and rather forced accommodations that resulted are a hallmark of this era's films, as well as of the troubled emergence of modern technological culture.

2

Revolution as Technology

Soviet Science Fiction Film

I

[In Russia] more than anywhere else, people are forced to look to the future.
—ALEXANDER BOGDANOV, *Red Star* (42)

Writing in 1908, on the heels of the first, abortive uprisings against the Czar, Alexander Bogdanov, one of the most important Russian science fiction authors, expressed both the plight and the hopes of his people. With no assurance of immediate change in their social conditions, Russians had no choice but to look toward the future, to dream of other, better possibilities for their lives. And Bogdanov contributed significantly to those dreams through such popular science fiction novels as *Red Star* and *Engineer Menni* (1913). In those stories he highlighted his country's plight by contrasting Russia with Mars, on which he described a successful socialist revolution that had already radically altered society and provided a model for change that the countries of Earth might one day emulate. But also, as his writings, or later, those of such futurists as Yakov Okunev, Innokenty Zhukov, or Alexei Tolstoi clearly suggest, Russia in both pre- and immediately post-revolutionary periods seemed practically *compelled* to look ahead, possessed by a conviction that radical change was near. Reflected in a flood of science fiction and utopian literature, this hope—and its attendant compulsions—was bound up in the very nature of modern industrial society, as it was then emerging on a global scale. As Richard Guy Wilson explains, in this period of intense cultural change, "the machine in all its manifestations—as an object, a process, and ultimately a symbol—became the fundamental fact of modernism," and seemed for many almost "to mandate an art and culture" with a correspondingly machine-like nature (23). However, between plight and hope, circumstance and compulsion, there exists a tension that reflects tellingly on Russia's ability to envision such a new culture, as well as on the construction of a machine technology that might sanction or promote that culture.

Perhaps "tension" seems a problematic term for describing Soviet Machine Age films. For we might suppose there should have been a natural fit—the Russian revolution and technology, the story of the Revolution and science fiction narratives. I do not want to suggest, of course, that the Revolution was itself something of a fiction, although there are certainly some similarities; rather, I simply want to emphasize the congruent and even symbiotic forces that were at work here. We might recall one of the key and most celebrated symbols of the revolutionary spirit in this era, Vladimir Tatlin's proposed *Monument to the Third International* (1919). Inspired by Picasso's three-dimensional constructions in various materials, Tatlin applied engineering and architectural principles to sculpture, fashioning in this his most famous project a spiralling metal and glass framework, projected to be twice as tall as the Eiffel tower. Suggesting simultaneously the dynamic, constructed spirit of a technological age—one hinting, as Wilson says, that "a whole new culture . . . could be built as readily as the machine" (23)—and the aspiring spirit of the Revolution itself, his projected tower seemed to embody a widely felt link between a revolutionary style of art and the sweep of social revolution. At the same time, it was a projection never to be realized. Tatlin's *Monument* was never built and its model destroyed in 1920.

That link between art and the Revolution was further emphasized in the constructivist movement that developed in pre- and immediately post-revolutionary Russia. Led by Tatlin, the painters Wassily Kandinsky and Kasimir Malevich, and the filmmaker Dziga-Vertov, among others, the constructivists generally followed the European futurists, with their emphases on speed and the aesthetic beauty of the machine. Never quite as unified as the futurist vision, however, and certainly not as prone to glorify the violent potential that also attended this modern age, as was the latter's chief figure, F. T. Marinetti,[1] constructivism subscribed to a relatively simple basic principle: "the ideational juxtaposition of different materials to produce a more meaningful structural whole" (Petric 4). For some, that "meaningful . . . whole" was a political statement, referring precisely to the construction of a new society: the bringing together of different cultural elements to produce a social structure. It thus pointed to a commitment throughout the arts at this time to "being politically responsible" (ix). For others, constructivist art simply reflected, according to Vlada Petric, "the dynamism of a technological age" (8); it recognized art as one of many active and invigorating social forces in this time of ferment. In either case, the movement speaks to the widespread sense in this period that the avant-garde was inseparable from the larger cultural revolution, one mixed with both political change and a new appreciation of technology's key role in modern culture.

Symptomatic of this appreciation was the standing accorded to the technological art of film itself in this era. While a constructivist art could underscore the links between social change and technological development, it might not provide the best means of reaching the masses and communicating the Revolution's ideology. As Trotsky offered, "Futurism proclaims the revolution in Moscow cafes, but not at all in the factories" (quoted in Constantine and Fern 7). To bridge this distance, to reach those in the factories, as well as the peasants on the newly collectivized farms, a more accessible, yet still thoroughly revolutionary sort of art was needed. A Machine Age art such as film fit the bill; Lenin himself said that "of all the arts, for us the cinema is the most important" (Leyda 161). To effect this policy, the Bolsheviks nationalized the film industry in 1919 and, shortly thereafter, placed it under the ideological control of the Commissariat of Enlightenment (Youngblood 2). With this appropriate ideological guidance, the Communist government assumed, the new Soviet films could better than any other medium of communication answer "the questions of the main body of Soviet citizens," especially those regarding "the revolutionary-historical background of the new society" (Leyda 190), which was then under construction.

A second sort of "natural fit," so we might assume, was that of the Revolution and science fiction. As Edward James notes in his history of the genre, "in the former Soviet Union, particularly during the 1920s," this sort of literature — "nauchnaia fantastika," as it was labeled — "appears to have had a stronger presence and identity than anywhere else" in the world outside of the United States (39). That popularity followed in large part because this body of science fiction talked of possibilities, speculated on what might be, even in the face of a seemingly intransigent reality, and so seemed congruent with the Revolution's forward-looking nature and its efforts to enact new social possibilities consistent with an emerging, technologically shaped world. A figure like Bogdanov emphasizes this logical connection, for even as he wrote science fiction novels depicting successful social transformations, he also sought to encourage the revolutionary spirit in practice, through his theoretical treatises such as *Tektologiia* (1913–

1929), which detailed the materialist and technological bases of modern culture, and his commitment to, and even personal involvement in, scientific experiments, one of which—on blood transfusion—eventually cost his life.

This same revolutionary spirit manifests itself across a broad range of science fiction in both pre- and post-revolutionary Russia. While Russia, compared to America and the major European powers, was rather backward in its technological development, there was apparently a similar widespread enthusiasm for Machine Age ideas. As John Griffiths offers, Russian writers of the period shared and even exceeded "the Western fascination with gadgetry and technical marvels" (44). As evidence we need only note the great popularity of the literary genre, as marked by a significant body of novels and the rise of a pulp literature, which parallels that found in the West. Inspired by the first uprisings against the czarist regime in 1905, a flood of science fiction, and especially utopian works appeared, taking the potential of social revolution and reconstruction as their central focus. Probably the most famous work of this early group is Bogdanov's novel *Red Star.* It was soon followed by other tales that would gain international attention, such as Michael Artsybashev's *Sanin* (1908), Bogdanov's *Engineer Menni* (1913), Konstantin Tsiolkowski's *Beyond the Planet Earth* (1920), and Alexei Tolstoi's *Aelita* (1923). Many of these novels chronicled a double revolutionary dream, that is, the simultaneous victory of the socialist revolution and the emerging scientific-technological revolution, as they promised both to reform and, indeed, to remake the modern world. Repeatedly, the triumphant march of the Revolution was depicted as naturally accompanying, and even following directly from, the triumph of technology itself—the latter affording not only the appropriate context for the Revolution but also the tools and power it would need to sustain itself, compete with the industrialized Western powers, and spread its gospel beyond the Soviet borders. Thus, in the wake of the Revolution, in the 1920s alone more than two hundred works of Soviet science fiction appeared, marrying technological development to social change and translating the basic themes of the Revolution into a futuristic or utopian context.

Alexei Tolstoi, who was both a widely popular novelist and a trained engineer, typifies this development. His most famous novels, *Aelita* and *The Hyperloid of Engineer Garin,* seem inspired less by the pure possibilities of technological development than by the Revolution itself. But to say, as John Baxter does, that stories like these "depended excessively on revolutionary doctrine for their impetus" (19) is to put the case a bit too harshly and simplistically. Admittedly, a work like *Aelita* includes as one of its central figures a near-professional revolutionary and member of the proletariat, Alexei Gusev, whose first thought when he lands on Mars is how he might begin to spread the benefits of the Soviet revolution among the downtrodden Martian workers for whom "there was no hope" (116). However, on Mars the seemingly inevitable victory of the proletariat fails and Gusev, along with the novel's central figure, the engineer Los, barely manages to escape the planet alive. That distant voyage, though, brings a boon to humankind, in the form of the technological knowledge the voyagers gain on Mars. Once recovered from this experience, Los sets his engineering skills to work on Martian ideas, as he begins "constructing a universal power plant of the Martian type" that promises to "revolutionize all the principles of Mechanics and solve all the problems of the world's economic system" (173). Through his interplanetary voyage, Los has, in effect, gained a great secret, one that the Machine Age in general but Russia especially seemed quite ready to embrace: that the technological revolution might hold the key to real social revolution, that scientific change would ring in social change as well.

And yet despite such works, that "fit" of science fiction with the Revolution seems never to have been wholly comfortable, the leaders of the new Soviet society never fully ready to embrace a form that *always* dreamt of the future, that kept what "might be" at the sort of distance we have found invariably linked to the Machine Age view of the technological. Even as the new society announced its desire to move forward, even as the Soviet leaders' "rush to industrialize a largely peasant society" initially led to, as Carroll Pursell puts it, "the hopeful embracing of any formula that promised to bring order out of chaos" (112) — especially such influential technological philosophies as Fordism and Taylorism — and even as they virtually enthroned such technological icons of collectivism as the tractor and harvester, those leaders also found it necessary to rein in some of that activity. One way in which this tension manifested itself was in the establishment of the New Economic Policy (or NEP), with its practices that uncomfortably recalled those of the capitalist enemy. In its "relaxed attitude" toward reform, as Denise Youngblood explains, the NEP encouraged economic experimentation and profit consciousness in a way that made doctrinaire Bolsheviks uneasy and eventually set the stage for the new rigidities and ideological purification of the cultural revolution of 1928–32 (4).

Another instance of that tension appears in the shifting attitude toward art and its place in the Revolution. While this era's avant-garde, technologically oriented turn in the arts was, as we have noted, initially seen by the new Soviet leaders as a potent ally against the old order, against the political, social, and even aesthetic status quo, there was also a worry that a technological "attitude" or even art for art's sake might crowd out or substitute for the ideology which art, even the art of an "age of mechanical reproduction," should promote. The larger "institutional restructuring" (Youngblood 171) of this period, consequently, eventually encompassed the arts as well, reining them in, affirming the line of socialist realism to which all were expected to conform, and in the process, as Petric reminds us, "inevitably and ironically" branding some of the most innovative Soviet avantgarde artists of the era, notably Dziga-Vertov, as "'counterrevolutionary' and 'reactionary'" (69). As evidence of this turn, we might note that by 1930 even the many Soviet counterparts of the prolific Western pulps had all been suppressed (Griffiths 45).

Probably the most pointed example of this tension occurs in the work of another of the country's foremost science fiction writers, Yevgeny Zamyatin, author of the acclaimed dystopian novel *We* (1924). Dedicated to science and technology through his training as a naval engineer and early career as a ship designer and builder, Zamyatin was also fully committed to revolution. He was, in fact, an early enlistee in the ranks of the Bolshevik party and took part in the revolutionary activities of 1905—partially chronicled in Eisenstein's *Battleship Potemkin* (1925)—for which he was eventually imprisoned and then exiled to his native province. After his reprieve in the general amnesty of 1913, Zamyatin, one of those real-life engineer-heroes of the sort Cecelia Tichi describes in her history of the era,[2] returned to his engineering activities, to a world of "iron, machines, blueprints," as he describes it (13), designing and building icebreakers and warships for the Czarist government. With the advent of the Revolution, though, he quickly abandoned that work—"practical technology dried up and fell away from me like a yellowed leaf" (14), he says—and turned his attention to helping engineer a new society.

That distance from the world of "practical technology," though, presaged another sort of distance or detachment. It was, eventually, one from the very revolution that he had long advocated. For philosophically, Zamyatin was fully committed to the sort of Machine Age values Tichi describes, to acceleration and constant change, and thus to the notion of a revolution that never achieved stasis, that would constantly renew itself. Along with the Scythian movement of which he was a member, Zamyatin argued that "dogmatization in science, religion, social life, or art is the entropy of thought. What has become dogma no longer burns; it only gives off warmth—it is tepid, it is cool" (108). In an effort to preserve what he saw as the true spirit of the Revolution, therefore, he spoke out against its perceived "entropic," stultifying tendencies, its enforced embrace of "dogma," arguing that there could be "no final revolution, no final number. The social revolution is only one of an infinite number of numbers" (107). As a result of such pronouncements, he was eventually compelled to resign from the Soviet Writers' Union, his books were banned, and in 1931 he was forced into permanent exile in France.

As Zamyatin came to recognize, there was a danger built into the very nature of the Revolution, a tendency to disguise or deny the sort of distance that needed to be traveled in order to accomplish its social goals. The Revolution came to represent not a continuing subversion of the status quo, an ongoing challenge or, as Zamyatin says, "a means of combating calcification, sclerosis, crust, moss, quiescence" (109), but rather a mechanism or technology itself, some*thing* that might be used to maintain the *new* status quo, which would, in its turn, have to be protected from subversion. The consequence for the cinema, as Leyda notes in his history of Russian film, was that every filmmaker had to confront one basic issue: how he was "to reach the social goal that was the understood base of every contract to work for a Soviet studio or to produce a Soviet film" (191). And in doing so, that filmmaker also had to be wary of his methods, conscious of, as Petric offers, "the danger of engaging in any form of nonconformist artistic endeavor" (62).

What I am arguing is that at the core of this cultural tension was a kind of hidden or distant technology, one that had to remain inviolate—if not invisible—if it was to propel the culture into a Communist future. So while the tractor may have been the key icon of the new Soviet society, the Revolution itself became the real, if unspecified, technology, the true machine at work reshaping Russian culture, and the one technology that had to be properly constructed for the state to prosper. Yet unlike the farm machinery, which was emblazoned on posters, stamps, and public signs, and recurred in the movies as an emblem of the modern, collectivist spirit, and unlike the motion picture, which helped spread that message of reform, the Revolution was a machine that propelled everything while remaining itself invisible, secret, safe from interrogation. In the process it became, in a way, a kind of anti-technology.

II

As in the case of the more thoroughly industrialized countries, Soviet science fiction literature finds only a weak reflection among the country's state-controlled film productions. Yet two films stand out in their development of the link between technological and revolutionary development—Yakov Protazanov's *Aelita* (1924) and Lev Kuleshov's *The Death Ray* (1925). In both we find an engineer protagonist whose commitment to the Revolution becomes the central focus. And both place the most advanced technology at the service of a struggling revolutionary spirit. Despite these politically appropriate elements, both films were seen to be at odds with the ideals of the Revolution and were quickly attacked for their supposed political transgressions. The following discussion draws on both films to contextualize this attitude in Soviet cinema, before going on to explore the "technology" of the Revolution more specifically in Protazanov's film.[3]

When we think of Kuleshov's pivotal role in early Soviet film history, the negative reaction to his film seems especially surprising, for as one of the first generation of truly *Soviet* filmmakers, as someone who, through his workshop and theoretical writings, influenced practically every Soviet filmmaker of the next generation, and as a cinematic experimenter who, as David Bordwell sums up, consistently sought "to reveal the laws of socialist art" (235) through his cinematic techniques, Kuleshov was thoroughly committed to a historical-materialist style of narrative. Yet while *The Death Ray*, which premiered in March 1925, apparently proved fairly popular and showcased the talents of a number of future stars of Soviet cinema, its collaborators, as Kuleshov himself notes, "were persecuted for our film. Especially for its lack of a firm ideology, and for its experimentalism" (quoted in Leyda 173). In later years, even Pudovkin, who authored *The Death Ray*'s scenario, would acknowledge the work's shortcomings, although he typically—and quite politically—shifted attention to its technical rather than ideological failings, noting the "constantly confusing rhythm of that film."[4]

But perhaps more to the point of this critical response were the film's fantasy trappings, that is, the manner in which it very clearly mimicked popular Western cinema of the period, particularly the vein of the serials and fantastic adventure films, in their fascination with the features of modern technology. In his story of a Russian inventor who develops a laser-like ray, which is stolen by Fascist forces and which, after various feats of daring, he recovers, Kuleshov admittedly tried "to give the filmed 'bills of fare' the kind of form that would insure their financial solvency" (Kuleshov 142); in effect, he imitated popular Western narrative models. What he accomplished in this way can be measured in Leyda's description of *The Death*

Ray as an "effort to condense all of Pearl White, Harry Piel, and Fantomas within one film" (174). And while that condensation of various serial figures and their respective techniques could be seen as an appropriate response to the call of NEP for works that might rival, both at home and abroad, the most popular Western films, it also contained the contradictions with which Soviet cinema—and indeed the entire new Soviet society—was then contending: a desire to compete with Western cinema and society without being *like* Western cinema or society; an impulse to *use* art in support of the Revolution, but a suspicion of art's ideological impurities, and especially of the impulse toward art for art's sake, which might undermine its ideological message; a need to embrace the latest technological advances—in order to industrialize what remained a largely peasant society—but a fear of what Western-style changes that technology could bring with it; ultimately, a desire both to bridge the distance between the Soviet Union and its more technologically advanced neighbors, and to assert, as unambiguously as possible, the crucial ideological distance that still separated those cultures.

If the official response to *The Death Ray*, seen in these contexts, is at least understandable, the reaction to *Aelita* may be a bit less so. While it too manifests a fantasy lineage, that lineage could be traced right to the popular science fiction literature of the period (as an adaptation of Tolstoi's recently published popular novel), much of which, as we have noted, pointedly espoused a revolutionary vantage. While the film demonstrates a marked consciousness of style (which could indeed be interpreted as *l'art pour l'art*), it is rather obviously the constructivist style, which was then in vogue and specifically linked to progressive—if at times politically suspect—movements throughout modern culture.[5] And while several of its creators had ties with the pre-revolutionary regime and were even initially at odds with the Revolution, the film itself, at least superficially, embraces the spirit of the Revolution, and criticizes those forces that might draw the people away from a commitment to the changes it was trying to institute. As Ian Christie has well summarized, *Aelita* might well be viewed as "*the* key film of the early NEP period, born of a unique moment in post-Revolutionary Soviet society, reflecting its realities as well as its aspirations in a complex and original form, and linking its hitherto isolated cinema with important currents in world cinema" (101). It is as well, I would suggest, the key film for understanding Soviet culture's difficulty in constructing a technology appropriate to the Revolution.

Generally, *Aelita* has fared little better than Kuleshov's film, either in historical appraisals of the burgeoning Soviet cinema or in assessments of early science fiction film.[6] Though the project brought together one of pre-revolutionary Russia's top directors, a major writer, and substantial resources, as Denise Youngblood notes in her survey of Soviet popular cinema, "no other film . . . was attacked as consistently or over so long a period as *Aelita*. From 1924 to 1928, it was a regular target for film critics and for the many social activists who felt that the film industry was not supporting Soviet interests" (110). That native response might at least be partly to blame for the film's absence from most histories of the science fiction film. For in the light of that reputation—one which might have made suspect any efforts to rehabilitate the work—Soviet authorities seem to have been reluctant to maintain the film's availability or in any way add to its place in film history. Consequently, *Aelita* has seldom been seen in the West until recent years, and has drawn little comment, even though it precedes, traverses much the same thematic ground as, and is in many ways a more complicated narrative than Fritz Lang's landmark work *Metropolis* (1926). While Christie has tried to explore the implications of this absence for Soviet cinematic history, we need to focus more specifically on *Aelita*'s missing place in the science fiction film canon and on its pointedly Machine Age response to technological development.

Aelita appeared at a most difficult ideological moment for the Soviet film industry. In 1924, as Youngblood explains, approximately ninety-five percent of the films in distribution were foreign, and most of the successful indigenous productions imitated the popular American and German pictures —those of Douglas Fairbanks, Harry Piel, and so on. Indeed, the state-supported film studios, such as Sovkino and Mezhrabpom-Rus (International Workers' Aid), in a mandated effort to make Soviet cinema self-sufficient and ultimately profitable, consciously tried to produce films that would attract a wide audience and thereby pay for themselves.[7] Aware of the ideological problems involved in such an emphasis, they sought to do so not simply by imitating the plots and characters of those popular foreign offerings, but also by exploring themes that were linked to the Revolution and to the lives of the people, motifs such as "contemporary everyday life" and utopian glimpses of "a happier future" (Christie 85).

Seen in this context, *Aelita* does not seem to justify the contemporary criticism leveled at it. With its central emphasis on ordinary people and on the ways in which they tried to contribute to or profit from the Revolution, it nicely captures the tenor of the times. And with its final emphasis on the need for a personal commitment to constructing the new Soviet society, it seems at first glance a thoroughly revolutionary work, certainly in comparison to the Tolstoi novel on which it was based. At the same time, apart from its depiction of interplanetary travel, it proves to be a rather unsatisfying effort at science fiction, offering a dim view of the science and technology with which the Revolution had initially allied itself and hardly suggesting the sort of "admiration for machines" that Petric observes in a number of other Soviet films of the era (6).

Perhaps some measure of *Aelita's* problematic status can be traced to a reaction against its director Yakov Protazanov, sometimes referred to as the Russian D. W. Griffith. One of the most successful filmmakers in the pre-revolutionary era, Protazanov began working in the Russian film industry in 1907, quickly moved into feature film production, and established a reputation for big-budget adaptations of literary classics, such as his *War and Peace* (1915). Following the October Revolution, he embarked with the rest of the Ermolev studio on a series of moves that would lead him to make films first in Berlin and then in Paris, where he directed six features before eventually returning to the Soviet Union in 1923. While Protazanov was, as Youngblood notes, easily "the most bankable director of the pre-revolutionary Russian cinema" (18), his connections to the old regime and to a popular cinema anchored in the adventure, comedy, and melodrama formulas of Western filmmaking left him suspect. Critics quickly accused the work of Protazanov and his fellow pre-Revolution filmmakers of reflecting a "'petty bourgeois' culture," one that was not believed "to be fully 'Russian.'"[8]

In spite of such attacks, *Aelita*, with its Constructivist costumes and sets, bloated budget, massive cast, and year-long production schedule, still proved to be one of the "major hits" of the Mezhrabpom studio (Youngblood 109). It played in two major Moscow theaters simultaneously, was named on many moviegoers' favorite films lists, and proved one of the most popular export movies of the period. Indeed, as Leyda notes, it "received more publicity abroad than any other Soviet film until the international success of *Potemkin*" (186). However, at home *Aelita* was also, as Youngblood reminds, "excoriated on ideological, economic, class, and national grounds," attacked at every turn for being "too Western" (110). The film was, in effect, a "hit" that was also a "scandal" (Youngblood 118), and thus, finally, a most curious—and revealing—thing. That strange status speaks to a tension implicit in the film, one that follows partly from the double dictates of politics and entertainment, and partly from the very distance at which the real technology here—the technology of the Revolution—remained from the people.

III

Getting beyond appearances is an impossible task: inevitably every discourse is revealed in its own appearance, and is hence subject to the stakes
imposed by seduction, and consequently to *its own failure as discourse*.
—B A U D R I L L A R D , *Selected Writings* (150)

From the outset, *Aelita*, along with its director, faced a
nearly impossible task: helping to establish economic self-sufficiency in the
Soviet film industry, creating an export potential for its productions, winning back the interest of pre-Revolution audiences, and being at all costs
ideologically correct. In trying to do so much, in offering images that might
address each of these impulses within a revolutionary context, it inevitably
laid itself open to the sort of seductive trap that Baudrillard attributes to all
discourse. Here a manifest discourse—that which is trying to be all things
to all viewers—seduces and undermines any possibility for a latent and
truly revolutionary discourse (149). But more than simply an illustration of
the traps to which discourse is prey, *Aelita* is also a narrative *about* seduction, about how the individual too is subject to what Baudrillard terms "the
charms and traps of appearances" (149). Through this narrative development, it illustrates the dangers inherent in moving too close to the era's machine technology—a closeness that can render the individual ever more
distant and detached from what came to be seen as the most necessary
technology, the technology of the Revolution.

Aelita begins on a most telling note, as shots of telephone wires and a
telegraph key—images of distant communication—lead up to a title card
indicating that "a strange signal" is being received at the Moscow radio station. We might well read this opening self-referentially, as a suggestion of
the extent to which the film was itself a rather unconventional "signal" to
emerge from the Soviet film industry, one more in keeping with the genres
of comedy, adventure, and melodrama that typified the popular American
and German film imports of the period. Yet its true "strange"-ness probably
lies more in *Aelita*'s attitude toward that signal—a signal that suggests both
the allure of advanced civilizations and technology (for which we might
read America and its gospels of consumerism and technological development), and the threatening or seductive aspects of those lures, the vague
sense of what might come along with that envied lifestyle and the advanced
technology that was making it possible.

This "attitude" develops through a pattern of seductions that operates at practically every level in the narrative. In its larger framework, *Aelita* offers a very human illustration of how easily we are lured by the "traps of appearances," as it describes the engineer Los's troubled marriage to Natasha and his encounter with the bourgeois Victor Erlich and his wife, Elena. In its embedded tale, set on a constructivist-styled Mars, the film recounts the seductive actions of Aelita, the queen of Mars, as she schemes to take control of the planet. Linking these two narratives is Los himself, the engineer hero of the sort that was so prominent in the era's literature, here reduced to little more than an object of seduction, as he is taken in by Erlich's attentions to Natasha and then lured to assist Aelita's rebellion on Mars. With its interweaving of these different seductive activities, *Aelita* casts the engineer and his technological preoccupations into a most vulnerable light, but only to emphasize all the more the function of the Revolution itself within the new Soviet society.

As part of the narrative's effort at addressing that prescribed theme of "contemporary everyday life," *Aelita* describes the cultural ferment of Russia in the immediate post-Revolution period. It is a time when fighting still rages with reactionary White Russian forces; the convalescing soldier Gusev, who becomes Los's companion in a trip to Mars, reminds us of that situation. And many in the population have embraced revolutionary society only superficially, while still subversively clinging to their bourgeois values, as Victor Erlich and his wife Elena demonstrate. To establish this cultural context, the narrative depicts the activities around the Moscow central radio station where Los works, trains loaded with refugees arriving in Moscow, soldiers recuperating from wounds suffered in the ongoing fighting, a checkpoint in Moscow where his wife, Natasha, processes refugees and newcomers, such as the Erlichs, and various elements of everyday life: the food shortages, the housing problems, the relatively primitive conditions with which the people of Moscow had to cope. While such scenes are precisely the sort that most likely generated a negative response to the film—suggesting, as they do, the many problems of everyday life that the Revolution left untouched—they are necessary to prepare for the central human conflict here, as individuals struggle to reconcile their personal dreams with the discomforts that accompany the building of a new society.

The narrative emphasizes in particular the problems of integrating the bourgeoisie into this new world, especially through the predatory actions of Erlich and Elena. Seeking a preferential housing assignment at the Moscow checkpoint, Erlich tries bribing Natasha and, when rebuffed, begins flirting with her and sends a note praising her "charm." Later, after obtaining an

6. *Seduction in a constructivist context:* Aelita.

apartment in the same building with Los and Natasha, he becomes a constant visitor to their apartment—painting with her, offering her scarce chocolates, taking her dancing. He makes every effort to seduce her, and Los, largely because of his own preoccupation with distant concerns—his fascination with Mars—believes Erlich has succeeded. Elena, for her part, tries to ease the couple's way into Moscow society by looking up her old sweetheart, Los's colleague engineer Spiridov, and feigning a renewed interest in him. Claiming that Erlich is simply her brother, Elena easily seduces the engineer, first wrangling a gold ring from him, and later, after learning where he keeps his valuables, robbing him of all that he owns. Erlich and Elena seem almost to compete to see who can garner the most booty through their personal predations. Thus in one scene Erlich brings home a sack of sugar he has stolen from the Food Distribution Center where he works, only to be trumped by Elena who displays Spiridov's gold ring. Together, these two not only illustrate a lack of commitment to the Revolution—one resulting from a primary concern with the self and individual comforts—but also demonstrate how easily one can be seduced by such selfish concerns, be turned away from the more important goal of constructing the new Soviet society.

Because so much of the narrative focuses on these exaggerated characters, *Aelita* often seems more a conventional social satire than a work of science fiction. Yet much of its narrative strength comes from the way it parallels these figures and their actions with events on the technologically advanced world of Mars. For in following up another of those thematic suggestions for the Soviet film industry, to provide images of a different, "happier future," *Aelita* locates the same problems of selfish concern and the same impulse to seduction emerging in this distant, futuristic society, ruled by the dictator Tuskub and his queen Aelita. Tuskub, we quickly learn, rules with an iron hand, while Aelita, in her desire for power, repeatedly uses her wiles to circumvent his restrictions. She seduces Gor, Tuskub's chief engineer, in order to gain access to his device for viewing distant worlds. Using it to watch life on Earth, she observes Los kissing Natasha and then practices kissing Gor, even as she becomes fascinated with the Earth man she has distantly observed. That fascination prompts her to set about seducing Los after his rocket reaches Mars. However, her efforts only thinly disguise the true trajectory of her desire, which is to rule Mars alone. This plot development points toward a recurring pattern in the science fiction films of this period, in which the world of modern technology becomes linked to the feminine and to woman's dangerously seductive power, and the technological and the feminine become linked assaults on the male status quo. Thus when Gusev and Los ferment a Soviet-style uprising among the Martian workers, Aelita quickly exercises her seductive power over them, offering to lead the rebels against her husband; in response, the workers rally to her and carry her along, like the robot Maria of *Metropolis*,[9] as a kind of revolutionary fetish. And true to the spirit of seduction—with its "charms and traps"—Aelita quickly shifts personality once the revolt succeeds, convincing the rebels to lay down their weapons, calling the leader of the Martian army to her side, and then convincing him to fire on the workers and drive them back to their underground lair. Through this round of seductions, she finally achieves her goal of ruling Mars alone.

What brings these various human and Martian seductions, as well as their revolutionary implications, into sharp focus is the connecting story, that of Los himself, the victim of multiple seductions. For he is easily distracted from his work for the Revolution, as is illustrated by his obsession with a strange signal received at the radio station—"Anta . . . Odeli . . . Uta"—a message one of his co-workers jokingly suggests might "come from Mars." His subsequent fixation on this mysterious message and fascination with the possibility of life on Mars grow along with his unfounded suspicions of Natasha's infidelity, and help to suggest how distant Los is from the

7. *Aelita performs under the stern eye of her husband, the master of Mars.* (Museum of Modern Art/Film Stills Archives.)

everyday life of revolutionary Russia. Eventually, Mars, along with the technological problems involved in reaching it, becomes his own seductive downfall; as a title card notes, "All of Los' energy was devoted to finding a way to reach Mars," instead of serving the very real needs of the Revolution. Distracted in this way, Los leaves Moscow for six months to work on a new power plant, returns to find Natasha with Erlich and shoots her, disguises himself as his old friend Spiridov and sets about constructing a Mars rocket, and upon reaching the Red Planet easily falls prey to the seductions of Aelita. As this summary of Los's story suggests, he seems very much a figure of distance and detachment, lacking commitment to his wife, his colleagues, and the Revolution. It is the sort of attitude, the narrative literally suggests through Los's transformation into Spiridov, that can easily lead us to abandon our true selves, as well as any commitment to social change.

Yet it is also, as the film belatedly reveals, largely a dream, a fantasy: for Los never shoots Natasha, flies to Mars, or encounters Aelita. These have all been the imaginings of an individual on the verge of leaving behind all that is meaningful—all a dangerous daydream as Los stood at the train station, preparing to flee Moscow. Much of *Aelita*'s narrative thus becomes literally what Romanyshyn would term a "dream of distance," a revery about, as he puts it, "a self separated and isolated from the world" (67), primed for departure from it. Framing that "dream" and propelling its seductions are two sorts of withdrawal: first, the bourgeois desire for the past and its values, seen especially in the opportunist Erlich and his wife; and second, Los's own fascination with technology, rocketry, and Mars, rather than with the problems of society and his own marriage. Both lead away from the Revolution and the world it is building.

Appropriately, then, *Aelita* concludes with a "return": to the real world of the present, to human relationships, and to the Revolution itself. Los finds that the mysterious message from Mars was nothing more than an American-style publicity campaign for tires—a capitalist ploy that has seduced him away from his engineering work. Subsequently, he tells Natasha "I was out of my mind," burns his plans for a Mars rocket, and announces, "Enough daydreaming; we have different work to worry about." With Erlich and Elena arrested in connection with the disappearance of Spiridov, an element of obstruction and corruption has been rooted out. And with Los now pledged to this "different work," that is, the work of the Revolution, those fantasies of detachment and escape disappear. In their place, the film promises, comes a commitment to the one technology that might indeed construct a happier future for all Soviet citizens, the Revolution itself.

IV

In this turn from the world of science and technology to the Revolution, *Aelita* is surely a rather problematic science fiction narrative. It retreats from the technological embrace of the original Tolsoi novel, a story that exalts "the stream of reason" and "the power of directed knowledge" (106, 111). In the novel, Los's very real experiences on Mars provide him with knowledge needed to further the promise of the Soviet revolution. Thus, when he returns to Russia, he begins building a Martian-style power plant with which he hopes, as we have noted, to "solve all the problems of the world's economic systems" (173). Of course, that rational, technological solution to class struggle, that almost magical infusion of knowledge, is an all-too-easy answer to the very real problems facing the Revolution. The film's elimination of this resolution, as it turns the Martian experience into nothing more than a daydream, seems to testify to *Aelita's* efforts at confronting those problems. But in this shift in narrative trajectory, the film also recasts technology itself, constituting it less as a potential tool of the Revolution than as a competitor, even a possible distraction from its real work.

Of course, this turn might only be expected if we accept Vivian Sobchack's general view of the science fiction genre, which she sees as a form "born with the culture of late capitalism and the genre most symbolic of it" (300). Thanks to this historical genesis and basic connection, she suggests, we should expect to find a level of contradiction built into the form as a kind of characteristic birthmark. For while science fiction often offers a progressive fantasy, it is one that most typically aims at "locating the future in an imagined past" (as in *Star Wars'* famous invocation of "A long time ago, in a galaxy far, far away"), or conversely, at "celebrating it as 'here' and 'now'" (300). In either case, she argues, its progressive vision, the imagined otherness or alternative society it often holds up for our inspection, entertainment, and ideological satisfaction can never really interrogate the status quo; it leaves it largely unchallenged and intact. In the case of *Aelita*, that other world, the world of Mars and its advanced technology, does seem to strike a bit close to home. The seductive machinations there, as we have seen, form a narrative match to those seen even in the post-Revolution society. At the same time, the advanced technology that marks this obviously corrupt Martian world wields, as Baudrillard reminds us, its own seductive influence on viewers, a sense of fascination and awe that must have been rendered all the more powerful by the rather bleak images of everyday Soviet life that the film offers. As a consequence, a film like *Aelita* became an inevitably conflicted text for Russian audiences of the era.[10]

Yet those involved with science fiction in revolutionary-era Russia certainly had a more progressive hope for the form. As we have seen, figures like Bogdanov and Zamyatin believed that the cultural images they offered might, on the one hand, help in the radical transformation of society and, on the other, call attention to some of the abuses that seem to attend every effort at engineering society. At the very least, their visions might make that ongoing transformation more understandable to the general populace, particularly by articulating a connection between the scientific and technological developments underway throughout Western culture, and those political and economic changes that the Revolution was putting into effect.

Yet as the reactions to films like *Aelita* and *The Death Ray* indicate, that link was not easily made. The future toward which, as Bogdanov suggests, all Russians looked, the future promised by the Revolution, remained distant, only dimly perceived or understood. Certainly, one of the major weaknesses of *Aelita* is its inability to articulate any real *goals* for the new social order whose struggles it so neatly chronicles. In the absence of that ideological articulation, the technological becomes a problematic subject, since it might come to seem separate from the Revolution, another, even competing force for effecting a vaguely conceived social change. Given this situation, there seems to have been a felt need for the Soviet film industry to be about, as Los puts it, "different work." Narratives about technology's ability to overcome distance, to bring people together, were less important—and more problematic—than those that emphasized the Revolution's ability to overcome distance: to dispel social and economic gaps, to produce a classless society, to render alienation an outmoded concept. As a film like *Aelita* illustrates, an effort first had to be made to construct something other than the technological—the Revolution itself as a kind of social machine, capable of powerfully propelling this world into the future.

3

The Picture of Distance

German Science Fiction Film

I

In describing the impact of modern technology, particularly modern machine technology, on human culture, Martin Heidegger described its hegemony as marking our entrance into the era of "the modern world picture," that is, a period when the world "in its entirety" is "conceived and grasped as a picture" (129). It is so conceived because our technology, in its detachment from and "objectification of whatever is" (126), along with the ability it grants us to manipulate those objectifications, transformed our sense of the world from something that powerfully and definitively acts upon us to something we act upon—that which "comes into being in and through representedness" (130), a "representedness" we effect through our technological prowess. Yet this "age of the world picture" confronts us with a momentous task, he suggests; for in designating ourselves as the viewers or creators of that picture, in emphasizing our determining point of view, we all too easily leave ourselves, leave Being itself, out of the picture. The modern human task, then, becomes one of finding ways to bridge that distance, to "get into the picture" (129), to "enframe" ourselves in this new world of our own technological design. The alternative is to remain ever at a remove from our world, like stranded astronauts, to remain little more than spectators, lost in what Romanyshyn, in his more recent assessment of technological culture, terms a "dream of distance"—ultimately, to become the products rather than the producers of our own technology.

During the Machine Age, at the height of his popularity in Germany, Fritz Lang produced a series of science fiction films that directly address this problem built into the modern, technologically driven world, and that draw on this trope of the "world picture." The most famous of these, of course, is *Metropolis* (1926), probably the definitive dystopian science fiction film. It describes a future world of technological estrangement in which the ruling class and the working class inhabit different realms, in which humans have all forgotten—or literally buried, within the catacombs beneath the great city of *Metropolis*—their spiritual roots, in which people, in their conflicted attitudes towards technology, nearly destroy their world and their children. Lang's later science fiction film, *Die Frau im Mond* (*Woman in the Moon*, 1929), in some ways even more starkly schematizes this pattern of distance and estrangement, as it explores the problem of "getting into the picture" through its narrative of *escape from* this world through a rocket to the moon. While seldom discussed or even seen today, *Die Frau im Mond*, described by one critic as "the epic apogee of the German silent film" (Gifford 106), seems to complete Lang's commentary on the "modern world picture" and its "dream of distance," suggesting how in this period we appeared in imminent danger of falling out of the picture, of losing our place in the world, of becoming little more than its distant spectators.

Before looking at these films and their place in that larger "picture" of German Machine Age science fiction, though, we need to sketch the cultural context in which Lang was working—and in which Heidegger first articulated his critique of technology—specifically the nature of this period in Germany. Certainly, science fiction literature had already established a strong position in German culture of the era. While distinguished novelists such as Bernhard Kellermann and Alfred Doblin turned their hands to the genre, a number of writers also appeared who specialized in this relatively new form and saw science fiction as a way to explore the latest ideas in science, politics, and social organization, writers like Otto Gail, Hans Dominik, and Edmund Kiss. At the same time, as in the United States, there flourished a trememdously popular pulp fiction, represented by such series titles as *Kapitän Mors* and *Jan Mayen, Lord of Atomic Power*.[1] This body of literary work—in which we should include the novels of Lang's wife and collaborator, Thea von Harbou—helped establish the climate for a developing cinematic exploration of the age's salient characteristic, its fascination with machines and technology and their potential impact on the political, economic, and social issues of the day.

As we have often noted, the features of the machine pervaded Western culture in this era and, as Richard Guy Wilson writes, "seemed to mandate an art and culture with similar outlines," that is, with characteristics reflecting those of the machine— its simplicity, functionality, power, and cleanness of line (53). For as Cecilia Tichi offers, "the machine-age text does not just contain *representations* of the machine—it too *is* the machine," and as such abides by machine technology's fundamental "design rules" (16). Paul Frankl, for example, who came to the United States just prior to World War I, began producing designs for a "streamlined" furniture, fixtures that enthroned an aesthetic of motion where no motion was possible, and "skyscraper" pieces, such as his famous bookcases, which translated the fascination with flight and the outline of the modern skyline to the earthbound limits of interior living space. A fellow Austrian expatriate, Richard Neutra, created architecture with high technology metal siding and aluminum paint (such as the San Fernando Valley house of the German-American director, Joseph Von Sternberg), which recalled aircraft and factory design. The most prominent and successful examples of a German-developed machine aesthetics, though, probably come from the Bauhaus school, which, under the leadership first of Walter Gropius and later of Mies van der Rohe, eventually gave birth to what is termed the International Style in architecture. With its emphasis on rectilinear shapes, geometric regularity, and functionality, as demonstrated in its famous Am Horn model house, the Bauhaus school suggested how our human constructs might, as Gropius put it, "become commensurate with the energy and economy of modern life" (quoted in Hardison 95). As Wilson sums it up, the very model of the "art in industry or industrial arts movement of the 1910s and 1920s" can be found in the various German movements of this era: the Bauhaus, Austrian Wiener Werkstatte, and Deutsche Werkbund (87).[2]

But perhaps more important than these popular images, these surface characteristics, is the sense of distance and detachment that seems built into the machine aesthetic. For underlying the pervasive and easily observable concern with streamlining, mechanical regularity, and functionalism, underlying the very "dream" of a machine-like world of "energy and economy" which would become appropriated and exaggerated by the National Socialist movement, is the distancing perspective that drives the aesthetic and produces its seductive "world picture." We can readily note this effect in the era's popular setback skyscraper style of architecture—extrapolated to a dizzying extreme in *Metropolis's* two hundred-story buildings—in its cubist paintings with their freezing and dissection of motion, and in the efforts to create abstract images by photographing simple mechanisms from unusual angles and distances—an approach that estranged viewers from everyday objects precisely in order to refigure them as objects of art or aesthetic interest. By placing us at some distance from the object of attention,

8. Metropolis *and the setback skyscraper style of the future.*

by framing it in an unfamiliar way, by recasting our point of view and thereby allowing (or forcing) us to grasp the thing "as a picture," it was thought, we might begin to recognize a deeper sense of order, regularity, and even purpose in our world. In the wake of the cataclysm of World War I and in the face of the dizzying political, economic, and cultural changes it had brought—including the near collapse of the economy in 1922—such a sense of purpose must have seemed appealing to a demoralized and unstable German culture. As the eventual embrace of Nazism suggests, suddenly to find the world resembling a machine—orderly, predictable, functional—could prove a welcome relief, even if it required the people to reconceive their traditional place in and relationship to that world, even to surrender some of the traditional sense of self.

In postwar Germany, as we have noted, that machine aesthetic found some of its most effective embodiments, if also some predictable difficulties. The various movements noted above could flourish, in part, because of the very unsettled conditions of German culture in this era, which allowed, at least for a short time, a new degree of freedom, a liberation from former political, social, and artistic restraints, and from a single, traditional way of seeing the world. These conditions made possible not only the architectural and artistic achievements of the Bauhaus, but also the visual revolution in film, on the stage, and in the graphic arts that we associate with expressionism, as well as with its realist counterpoint, the Die Neue Sachlichkeit movement. As its name indicates, this latter development, associated with an increasing emphasis on the scientific, championed a "new objectivity," a new perspective on German culture that, proponents hoped, might bring with it a clearer focus on social problems. Films like G. W. Pabst's *Joyless Street* (1925) and *Westfront 1918* (1930) typify this development, while Pabst's association with Brecht in the production of his *Threepenny Opera* (1931) points as well towards the flourishing avant-garde dimension of film and the theater in this period. It was, simply enough, a time of great cultural ferment, one in which a machine aesthetic and sensibility vied with and often seemed naturally allied to a variety of other aesthetic developments.

However, the cultural climate of Weimar Germany—and even more so that of Nazi Germany—never managed to embrace that industrial and machine aesthetic without some difficulty. As the historian Jeffrey Herf convincingly argues, German culture between the wars was characterized by a kind of "reactionary modernism," that is, a nearly paradoxical effort to accommodate the latest technological advances within the traditional German culture and its values, meshing the thorough rationalism of the former with the latter's "romantic and antirational aspects" (2). So even as a kind of "miracle" of industrialization helped lift Germany out of its postwar collapse, there remained, as Carroll Pursell puts it, a "kernel of irrationality at the heart of" that miracle (112), a paradox on which the Nazis would build and one neatly summed up in Joseph Goebbels' call for an era of "stahlende Romantik" or steel-like romanticism (Herf 3).

While it would come to seem the very embodiment of radical ideas and would eventually be purged under Nazism, even the Bauhaus school was not quite free from this sort of paradoxical attitude. The Bauhaus was originally linked to the arts and crafts movement which flourished in Europe prior to and immediately following World War I, and as Hardison reminds us, that crafts movement was essentially directed "*against* the impersonal forces of mass production" (95)—forces that had helped produce the war's massive destruction. And yet, points out Elodie Vitale, in the face of "the pressures of social and economic developments" in the postwar era, this emphasis on crafting simple, regular forms and on the nearly mathematical precision that could be achieved by the human hand shifted easily into an interest in industrial design and manufacture that embraced these same features, and eventually into a focus on "forms reproducible by machine" (164). The Bauhaus, in effect, did share in that "reactionary modernism"

Herf observes in German culture of the period; even so it could not survive the worst excesses of that special German brand of modernism. This cultural tension between the rational and irrational, between the pragmatic and the romantic, and the sense of social instability that tension promoted set the stage for the ascension of National Socialism, with its promises of order, control, and social engineering—carefully framed in the traditional context favored by Goebbels. This atmosphere eventually pressured the Bauhaus group to shift its location from Weimar to Dessau to Berlin before disbanding, just as it ultimately spurred many artists and intellectuals—among them Gropius, Mies van der Rohe, and Lang—to flee their homeland.

II

Together let us desire, conceive, and create the new structure of the future, which will embrace architecture and sculpture and painting in one unity and which will one day rise toward the heaven from the hands of a million workers like a crystal symbol of a new faith. —WALTER GROPIUS[3]

This dedication, offered by Gropius at the opening of the Bauhaus in 1919, resounds with the sort of utopian promise that was often echoed in the Machine Age—and eventually aped and compromised by the Nazis. Certainly, in the grandiose vision it offers, it is a fitting start for that visionary school of artists, craftsmen, architects, and designers who, Hardison contends, represented "a watershed in the development of modern consciousness fully as significant as the publication of Einstein's paper on general relativity in 1905" (94). By bringing together in common cause the many different skills of its members, the Bauhaus was intended to foster a new vision, not only of the unity of the arts, all gathered under the broad rubric of architecture, but also of a united human aspiration, of the potential for human progress in an emerging technological culture. The key image Gropius seizes upon, that of a million "hands" reaching upward, reflects that sense of common striving toward a utopian goal which, the Machine Age suggested, was technologically attainable. At the same time it also reminds us of that tension between crafts and technology built into the Bauhaus origins and points in an evocative way towards Lang's landmark utopian commentary, *Metropolis*.

I emphasize this image of the reaching hands because it is one that Lang, who was himself educated as an architect, draws on several times in *Metropolis*, and one with which he addresses the sort of paradoxes at work

in the futuristic culture he envisions, as well as in the present German culture to which he alludes. The film specifically appropriates this image in its
narrative about a failed "structure of the future," the utopian city of Metropolis. We first encounter this image embedded in the film's parable of the
Tower of Babel, which recalls earlier efforts at creating a towering assertion
of human power, a picture of "unity," a "crystal symbol of a new faith" —
specifically a faith in human technological ability. As the "million workers"
assembled for that task become ever more estranged from the dreams of its
designers and little more than slaves of the project, Lang offers us images of
their hands raised in fists of protest and revolt, in a destructive disunity that
heralds Babel's final collapse. Prophetically, that pattern recurs in the futuristic world of Metropolis, where workers and managers have become so
distant from one another that there follows a near-calamitous revolt—one
that Lang again figures in the image of "the hands of a million workers"
raised against their oppressors. What *Metropolis* suggests, through this almost archetypal image, is an essentially age-old pattern of tensions at the
heart of human technological aspiration—tensions that, as we shall see, derive largely from the sort of cultural "picture" the Machine Age was fostering in Germany.

The story of *Metropolis*'s genesis has often been recounted. Lang traces
his vision of this futuristic world to his first encounter with America, as he sat
on a steamship in New York harbor, staring at the city's brightly lit skyline:

> In 1924 I travelled with Erich Pommer to New York f or the UFA. We had to stay
> at the harbor on board ship for a whole night as we still were "enemy aliens."
> There I saw across from the ship a street lit as if in full daylight by neon lights and
> topping them oversized luminous advertisements moving, turning, flashing on
> and off, spiraling . . . something which was completely new and nearly fairly-tale-
> like for a European in those days, and this gave me the first thought of an idea for
> a town of the future. (Johnson 161–62)

Those distantly glimpsed images of the prototypic Machine Age city, as well
as his subsequent impressions of the American cultural landscape, certainly
provided Lang with a visual model or picture of his futuristic city. And indeed *Metropolis*'s images of towering skyscrapers, intertwined highways,
streamlined cars, and a sky filled with airplanes and airships were not that
far removed from the reality of Machine Age America. More important,
with its emphasis on the machinery that powers this world—seen in the
early montage of pumping cylinders and dynamos—and its efficient operation, the film promises a potential for reworking society along the lines suggested by then-current industrial practice, as in the giant Ford factory of

River Rouge that had lately opened. That promise played to what Carroll Pursell has termed "a very human . . . urge" that underlies most of our technological strivings: "for complete control, total self-sufficiency, utter predictability and extreme standardization" (117).

By evoking the distance built into these technological developments, by visualizing the dynamics of this world picture, though, Lang manages to deconstruct that promise. For *Metropolis* suggests how this "urge" can distance us from our very humanity, as it translates that effort at engineering society into a vision of the *human* reworked according to mechanical precepts. It does so literally through one of its most famous images, that of the robot created by the mad scientist Rotwang. Yet its more important representation of that vision, as I have already suggested, is probably the Tower of Babel sequence—a sequence presented precisely as a kind of dominant "world picture." As Maria, the spiritual conscience of the workers, preaches to them, trying to reshape their point of view and thereby to help them understand and endure their current plight, she recalls that ancient legend of an effort to dominate the landscape with human technological accomplishment. In effect, she traces the machine culture of this futuristic city back to that ancient dream of what we might consider a proto-setback-skyscraper world—a dream not of distance, but of the human ambition to bridge the most formidable of distances, that between god and humanity. As Maria explains, the tower began as a kind of consuming image in the minds of Babel's wise men. This image then appears on the screen with a legend inscribed above it—"Great is the world and its creator. And great is man"—a legend that spells out both the motivation for this project and the seed of its failure, its tendency to lose sight of human nature and human limits. We then see a constructed model of this projected tower. However, these neat projections then give way to the reality of the tower's construction, complete with multiple views of the masses of workers marshaled for the task, who have become, it seems, slaves of the tower and of its designers, and who eventually revolt. That initial schematic image of united human striving thus produces precisely its opposite: an enduring image of human disunity and cultural self-destruction.

Fittingly, this sequence concludes with another imaginary picture, this time of the tower's ruins, above which we still see, as if in mockery, that legend of aspiration inscribed. The technological effort to conquer distance literally collapses upon itself, precisely because its technologists could not see their own appropriate position nor properly place their fellow humans, the workers, "in the picture." Instead, their project to bridge the distance between the human and divine fashions only a destructive distance from

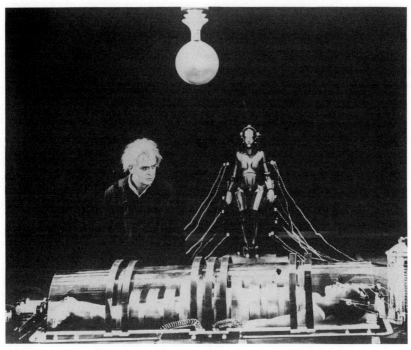

9. *Rendering the human as technology—the scientist and the robot of* Metropolis.

the masses of their fellow men who have been left out of the picture—left to raise their hands in protest, then their fists in violent revolt.

This allegory neatly fits the larger circumstances of *Metropolis*, as the film sets about suggesting how much this age's technological thrust was inscribed with, as Pursell simply puts it, "an agenda for social policies" (108), particularly repressive social policies that would reinscribe a stifling class structure. Like Babel, the futuristic city of Metropolis suffers from a debilitating "world picture," a dominant philosophy that has fashioned a glittering and grimly efficient society, but one that seems fundamentally at odds with itself, in which workers and managers rarely even glimpse each other. The dominating point of view here is that of Joh Fredersen, the master of Metropolis, and it is typified by our first view of him, as he looks out from his tower office onto the city skyline. That panorama of setback skyscrapers, streamlined buildings, and connecting vaulted highways—a panorama that includes virtually no people, save for a shot of masses marching mechanically in several rectangular groups—suggests the manner in which he sees and rules this world. From his distant perch, Fredersen quite literally "monitors" Metropolis and its people: reading a teletype, noting mysterious

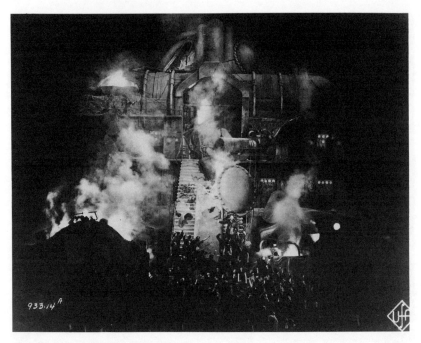

10. *The Luddite spirit unleashed as the workers of* Metropolis *revolt.*

numbers that appear on an electronic board, and viewing his managers —
for example, the foreman of the Central Dynamo plant — on a television
screen. When his son Freder asks about the plight of the workers who built
and operate the machines of Metropolis, he simply declares that they
should remain "in the depths" — below the surface of the city, out of sight
and out of mind. And he punctuates that assertion by closing the curtains
on the panoramic windows that look out over all the city. When the workers
become unruly, he tries to cope with them by a kind of telepresence, by
employing his scientist-advisor Rotwang's new robot, crafted in the shape of
the trusted Maria, to lure the people into self-destructive acts. It is a ruth-
lessly rational approach, however, that provokes a calamitously irrational
reaction, as the workers set about destroying, in Luddite fashion, the very
machines that keep this world running and their own homes free from
flooding. And that end predictably recalls the fate of Babylon, as Lang depicts a world which, in large part because of its very technological accomplishments, has lost perspective on itself and become set at odds with its
own best interests.

This futurisic realm avoids the total collapse that was Babel's fate only by
beginning to fashion a new picture, one that tries to counter the distance

11. *The robotic Maria displays the seductive powers of technology in* Metropolis.

created by the technology that drives this world. That picture comes into focus through young Freder who, after encountering Maria and a group of workers' children, insists on going down among the machines that power the city to see "what my brothers and sisters look like." That impulse to overcome the distances that separate the classes here, along with the shifted point of view it heralds, forecasts the conclusion of the film in which Freder becomes the meeting point between a wedge-shaped group of workers, marching in orderly, machine-like fashion, and his solitary father. This meeting takes place as if on a stage that already brings both past and present into "the picture," as Fredersen stands just outside the city's crumbling Gothic cathedral. Here young Freder physically clasps the two (leader and workers) together, uniting, as a title card emphasizes, "head and hands," and, in the process, suggests—albeit a bit too easily and im-probably—that a new "picture" might emerge of the city's make-up. Still, the subservient position of the people in this last scene, along with their near-mechanical movement in the expressionistically styled, wedge-like mass, which clearly echoes their earlier movements to and from their numbing tasks, calls this simple resolution into question, hinting how diffi-cult it will be to construct a different pattern.[4]

More generally, Lang's film evokes a fascinating, attractive, yet also deceptive world, one made possible by the technology that most of Western culture seemed to be rushing to embrace. As Romanyshyn suggests, that technology typically fosters a distancing effect that makes it easy for us to accept most of its surface lures, everything that its glossy "picture" appears to offer, and for us to *fail* to see clearly—just as the workers mistake the robot for the real Maria and the young men of the city, gathered in the Yoshiwara brothel, take her for a real and powerfully seductive woman. The power of that technological world is such that, the film argues, only with great difficulty can we see it for what it is. Only through the near death of Freder as he fights with Rotwang, the flooding of the workers' homes, and the loss of power to the upperworld, for example, can the workers and especially their children be brought up from the depths and admitted to the surface world, where there is a *possibility* they might participate fully in the future. Only through these events can the human disguise of the robotic Maria be burned away and her—and technology's—seductive manipulations be seen; only through near calamities can the workers and their leaders be reunited perhaps to work for a better society. *Metropolis* helps us see that modern world better by holding the very conditions of our seeing up for inspection, allowing us to gauge the very "dream of distance" to which the technological world picture apparently makes us prone.

III

If *Die Frau im Mond* is never quite as schematic—or as heavy-handed—as *Metropolis*, that may be because it comes out of a more personal interest on Lang's part. In 1923 the German rocket pioneer Hermann Oberth published his treatise *Die Rakete zu den Planteraumen*, an argument for the possibility of space travel using the rocket technology he and others were then developing. One of the founding members of the Verein fur Raumschiffahrt (Society for Space Travel), Oberth was soon joined in that group by Lang (Noblet 171), who would later help finance some of Oberth's rocket experiments and hire him as a consultant for *Die Frau im Mond*. Along with that element of personal interest we might credit some sensitivity for public relations, for which Lang was well known in his later, Hollywood years. As Carlos Clarens suggests, Lang may have turned to such experts in part because in Germany *Metropolis* "had raised violent criticism for its unscientific . . . vision of the future" (34).[5] Whichever the case, the later film certainly bears witness to another dimension of Machine Age technology that was especially marked in German culture of the era—a fascination with rocketry—which, with the state development of the V1 and V2 weapons, would pay nightmarish dividends in World War II.

The resulting film, like *Metropolis* and so many subsequent science fiction tales, centers around futuristic technology and the sense of distance that seems phenomenologically bound up within that technology. The narrative takes as its start a scheme analogous to that proposed by the elders of Babel: Professor Manfeldt's dream of reaching the moon, where he believes large deposits of gold will be found. Achieving that dream depends on the technological genius of the engineer Wolf Helius and the backing of a financial group represented by Walter Turner. While this combination produces a rocket that, like the glittering city of Metropolis and its various technological attainments, becomes the key attraction for much of the narrative, it also promises ill, again because of the motivations activated by this dream of distance, because of the other, human distances it creates. Manfeldt seeks gold, glory, and revenge on those who mocked his theories about the moon; as a title card notes, Turner and his syndicate plan to use the moon's wealth in a plot to gain "absolute control over all the gold on Earth"; and Helius seems to be using the moon project to escape from a failed romance, as his former love Friede Velten has just announced her engagement to his assistant engineer Hans Windegger.[6] In each case, technology is being turned to pointedly nontechnological ends; but what Lang leaves unclear, as he does in the earlier film, is whether the problem lies in the technology itself and its promise of power and escape, or in the people who all too easily turn it to their own self-serving and distance-fostering goals.

That ambiguity lingers in *Die Frau im Mond*'s vision of what is accomplished through technological prowess. For while Helius's rocket technology relatively easily spans the distance from Earth to the moon, the effort ultimately initiates a series of disasters whose outlines recall those in *Metropolis*: Manfeldt discovers his gold but, in hoisting a huge chunk of it, loses his balance and falls to his death in a chasm; Turner nearly dies in the initial take-off, and is later shot when he tries to steal the rocket and abandon the others on the moon; when half of the expedition's oxygen supply is lost in the struggle with Turner, Helius decides to stay on the moon—and face almost certain death—so that the others might return to Earth. In their fascination with rocket technology and efforts to use it to span great distances, each of these characters seems to have left something of himself behind, out of the picture. The result of that single-minded adherence to the trajectory of technology, the film implies, is a kind of lost balance, a lost

12. *The space explorers at cross purposes in* Die Frau im Mond.

contact with our full humanity, ultimately a debilitating sort of distance to which, under the influence of a Machine Age spirit, Western culture seemed quite prone.

Still, in leading up to the disasters that attend this rocket voyage, *Die Frau im Mond,* like *Metropolis,* seems almost fetishistically focused on the technological. As Baudrillard might suggest, it is a narrative seduced by its own possibilities.[7] We should note, in this context, that the German film historian Siegfried Kracauer had scored the earlier film precisely for its fixation on technical details, its emphasis on decor and extreme "concern with ornamentation" (149). Commentators on the later work similarly note its fascination with such details and the nearly "documentary aspect" (Jensen 85) of its treatment of the rocket, its launching, and the flight to the moon. Indeed, for much of the film, "things" seem to dominate: images of the rocket under construction, the preparations for launch, diagrams of the flight, the slow roll-out of the rocket to its water-covered launching pad, the various particulars of the ship's interior, and the different mechanisms for coping with the shock of take-off and the experience of weightlessness. While these many details and impressive images attest to Lang's own interests in space flight, his consultations with the leading rocket experts of the day—Oberth, Willy Ley, and others—and his commitment (apparently a first for the film genre) to rendering the science fiction believable, they also have a telling impact on the narrative. They produce a kind of technical ellipsis in the middle of the narrative that echoes those character motivations noted above, as they largely nudge the human voyagers and the drama of their interactions out of the picture, set them seemingly at a distance from the film's own fascination with technical details. In effect, they demonstrate how easily the lures of technology—even cinematic versions of technology—can make us lose sight of or concern for the human, how our "world picture" can become so intently focused on things and procedures that it loses its focus on a human subject.

That drawing of an almost overly detailed picture, though, is linked to this film's shaping a particular point of view, one from which we can better see its "world picture." We might note that, for an extended portion of the narrative, our views of the rocket, its occupants, and the elaborate preparations for its launch are mediated through a radio announcer who describes the event to an eager audience. The very presence of such a figure should seem a bit curious in a silent film made after the coming of sound, since it invariably calls attention to the film's own technological hesitations.[8] But Lang obviously wants to suggest a widespread enthusiasm for this endeavor by repeatedly cutting to the figure of the announcer, with whom, and with the details that surround him, he accurately forecasts the sort of media event the first real moon landing would be forty years later. But what seems more significant is the way this figure helps evoke our own position *as audience*, as inevitably removed from the event, as spectators engaged in our own mediated "dream of distance," as Romanyshyn would put it. We might say that, with the figure of the announcer, Lang announces his concern with holding our own conditions of "seeing" this world up for inspection.

Indeed, everywhere we turn in the first half of this film we can find a sense of audience and image production at work, and thus an emphasis on the sort of spectatorial stance that, as Anne Friedberg explains, was a natural outgrowth of modern technological culture. *Die Frau im Mond* opens with Manfeldt's addressing an audience of fellow scientists, presenting his latest conclusions about the moon—all of them greeted derisively. Done in a series of reverse angle shots that alternate from the professor to his audience, this scene eventually places *us* in the audience position, as Manfeldt stares directly into the camera and inveighs against his skeptics. In effect, he challenges us to see as he does. After the narrative leaps to the present, we see Turner making a presentation to his finance group about the advisability of backing a moon flight. The group looks at a model of the rocket,

13. *The rocket launch in* Die Frau im Mond: *Spaceship as spectacle.*

cutaway drawings, plans for its construction, a flight plan, and photographs of the moon. Turner then moves to a projection booth where he shows a film about the proposed flight—a film that, we learn, includes stolen footage from Helius's experimental H-32 rocket which has already crash-landed on the moon. The result is one of the more striking images in the film, as we see Turner, like some diabolical filmmaker, staring out from the darkness of the projection booth, trying to gauge the effect of his work on these viewers. The audience is so convinced by the presentation that they unanimously agree to take "the risk" in financing the voyage. Lang handles similarly the ensuing work on the rocket and preparations for its launch, with a constant emphasis on the effort as a kind of public show, culminating in a popular frenzy. We see images of an audience in a grandstand, a crush of photographers gathering around the rocket and its occupants, cheering crowds, the announcer on the radio, throngs being held back by a police cordon, and searchlights playing on the building that houses the rocket and on the voyagers—now media celebrities—as they enter it. When the rocket finally emerges from its hangar, spotlights converge on it as the doors slowly open like the curtains on a great stage. Even inside the rocket, the adventurers recognize the performative dimension of this event, as one notes, "The eyes of the whole world are watching. The ears of the whole world are listening." To underscore this notion, Lang superimposes those words on a montage of eager faces and a radio tower. At every point leading up to the moon flight, the film frames the expedition as a picture, a show, a representation—or more to our point, as an increasingly convincing and captivating, even seductive, dream of distance made possible by technology.

The precise dangers that attend to this dream become apparent only with the rocket's flight and arrival on the moon. Interestingly, the film emphasizes less the physical danger involved—the body's ability to endure the rigors of space flight, for example—than a kind of psychic threat attending the very distance these people are traveling. As Helius prepares his comrades for take-off, Windegger seems less troubled by his description of the pressures on the body than on the possibility that a miscalculation might send them off course; as he notes, "all will be lost—no more . . . no more . . . to be able to return to Earth." And the film repeatedly emphasizes that world they have left behind, as when, after all have recovered from the shock of take-off, Friede suddenly and sadly calls out, "Earth. Where is our Earth?" That reminder brings them all running to a view-port from which they stare wistfully at the Earth as the sun rises behind the planet. In a series of subjective shots, we share that quite novel, distanced point of view of the Earth from space, a unique sort of spectatorship. In the process, we confront several of the consequences of that embrace of distance: first, the appearance of a new, different sort of distance, as a measure of separation; and second, the emergence of a new awareness of the self as, in Romanyshyn's warning words, "a spectator too distant from a world that has become only a spectacle" (228). In a shift that underscores the consequences of this technologically attained point of view, we then see Manfeldt, under the sway of that spectator mentality, steal away from the others to train his telescope on his consuming goal, the moon. In that shift from the common point of view, in that separating of the self from his companions, the professor points up the problem of *human* distance that attends this technological separation.

What we begin to see is the extent to which this technological flight, much like that effort to rise via the Tower of Babel, becomes symptomatic of a flight away from a part of our humanity. Obsessed with the moon, Manfeldt repeatedly ignores orders to close the rocket's viewing port in preparation for landing, despite the risk it poses to the ship and his fellow travelers. After landing on the moon, and in a way that compromises his very status as scientist, Manfeldt refuses to bother with carrying out the necessary scientific tests on the atmosphere. He simply rushes out, strikes a match to see if the atmosphere contains any oxygen, and then hurries off to search the surface. That search quickly proves self-destructive, as he begins acting "lunatic" upon finding his predicted gold and, in his distraction, stumbles into a chasm and falls to his death. His science, like that of the leaders of Metropolis, paradoxically makes him act in very unscientific ways; his single-minded point of view leads him to see so narrowly, focused, as he is, on only his dream of moon gold, that he endangers the others and precipitates his own death.

That pattern recurs in several of the other characters, most notably Turner and Windegger. The former, of course, views the entire expedition simply as a logical use of the latest technology to produce wealth — even if it necessitates sacrificing his fellow travelers. Once assured of the moon's gold deposits, he has no further use for the others and tries to abandon them to their deaths. Windegger, an engineer who has helped design and run the rocket, is so obsessed with his own survival that all he can think about is returning to Earth; as he tells Friede upon their arrival on the moon, he is "more interested in getting away from here" than in exploring the place. And when faced with the prospect of remaining on the moon so that others, including his fiancée, might escape, he dissolves in terror. These characters seem to suggest that our technological abilities, even as they allow us to bridge the great gap between Earth and moon, might lay open more fundamental gaps, such as the psychic and emotional distances between humans. Even as they seem to suggest our capacity for moving toward what we desire, they become flights *away from* what we need. In these other, human distances, Lang illustrates that "kernal of irrationality," which, in German culture at least, seems paradoxically linked to our rational and technological capacities, as well as to the sort of "picture" of our world they help shape.

And yet Lang's vision here is far from cynical or truly dystopian. Just as *Metropolis* manages a rather forced compromise between the workers and managers, suggesting that this thoroughly technologized society might possibly be made to work for all, so *Die Frau im Mond* holds out its own small hope. Helius, the engineer who has brought his fellows across such an enormous distance and removed them from their normal world, is also willing to sacrifice himself so that they might return to Earth, bringing with them the knowledge that might help others to make such flights in the future. While the technological dream might well endanger their lives, their very humanity, the film implies, it also has the potential, if at some cost, to erase that threat and restore the natural human state. It can, we see, "enframe" the human at the center of the "world picture," even "engineer" that proper positioning.

Rather than just retreat from that dream of distance, though, Lang offers a more complex potential resolution for our consideration, even a kind of challenge for his audience. For as Helius resigns himself to staying on the moon and probably dying, while the survivors rocket back to Earth, Friede appears and casts her future with his. The film closes, in fact, with a close-up of their embrace, with an image of what has been gained in human relationship, rather than with the technical victory of the rocket heading to home and safety. The point Lang wants to make is one of human hope, of what this modern age need not lose even as it embraces that distancing technology. While he fled a great distance from a love he thought irrevocably lost, Helius has found that human distance suddenly dissolved. Now he and Freida must wait to see if the technology might be employed for further human ends, if they will remain "in the picture" of those back on Earth who might yet return to save them.

In his discussion of Lang's visual style, Raymond Bellour has observed a constant "play on distance" throughout his films, a recurring "impression of distance" that he simply notes as a key auteurist marker (32). Yet in the case of Lang's science fiction films this "impression" seems far more than just a stylistic issue. Certainly his architectural training prepared Lang to see space and distance in more complex ways than many other filmmakers—in terms of lived human experience—and to consider how they might be conceptualized. And as we have noted, the work of the Bauhaus school had already foregrounded these same concerns, suggesting that the "things" of our world could only be properly understood "in relation to the space" they occupied (Hardison 95). In *Die Frau im Mond* Lang's characters tend to conceptualize their world, see it at a distance, treat it—and their fellow humans—with detachment, view it as a kind of representation or "world picture" in which they have little real stake. By standing apart from their world and from others, by supposing they might manipulate it and their fellow beings, his characters slip into a nearly self-destructive sort of distance, as they effectively remove themselves from the human picture. But they also pose a challenge to that picture, to refocus it in such a way that the human is never quite obscured by the seductive, ruling patterns of the technological or by the desires it might set in motion.

This larger "picture" obscures or renders less significant that challenge implicit in another seductive—and for some, more problematic—element of Lang's films, namely, his treatment of the feminine. We might recall *Metropolis*'s emphasis on the seductive powers of the robotic Maria: how Fredersen emphasizes those powers in order to test the human appearance of Rotwang's creation, and then uses them to mislead and undermine the workers. Giving technology a feminine shape seems the ultimate disguise or denial of the technological, and reminds us how the two have often been seen as opposed. Mary Ann Doane, for example, describes a lingering "fear" throughout modern technological culture that the feminine, especially in maternal form, "will contaminate the technological" (170). And Evelyn Fox Keller has argued that, with the scientific method, modern science essentially "invented a strategy for dealing with" and "asserting power over" what she terms "nature's secrets," including the secrets of "female power" (178). It is a "power" we see evoked in the very title *Die Frau im Mond*, as well as in the lure that Friede exercises over both Wolf and Windegger—a lure that at various points seems to jeopardize the moon mission by spurring conflict and suspicion between the men. Both films thus locate a potentially destabilizing power in the feminine, yet neither finally places that power in opposition to the technological. Indeed, it is the technological world here that seems intent on asserting this opposition, on using the potential of opposition in order to solidify its own claims to order and control. While never quite challenging that notion of opposition, then, Lang's films at least open it up for our inspection, and in so doing they also suggest the extent to which the feminine, as in the case of the real Maria of *Metropolis*, might prove essential to coping with an unbalanced world—whether it be a technological dystopia or the barren wastes of the moon.[9]

IV

Despite these challenges to the way we see our world, Lang's science fiction films always seem primarily to insist on the power of technology and the Machine Age's fascination with that technology. Like so many other science fiction films of the Machine Age—most notably *Just Imagine* (1930) and *Things to Come* (1936), of which we shall later speak, or a subsequent German effort in this vein, *Gold* (1934), noteworthy for its depiction of an underwater nuclear reactor—they tend to be remembered mainly for their visualizations of what might be, of how an ever-advancing technology might fulfill our fantasies, change our lives, alter the very trajectory of cultural development. And in the context of Lang's larger canon, *Metropolis* and *Die Frau im Mond* suggest a recurring fascination with the powers that compel us to act in both constructive and destructive ways: powers of technology, economics, and psychology. That fascination would continue to occupy Lang's attention, particularly in his various Dr. Mabuse films, the last of which, *Die Tausend Augen des Dr. Mabuse* (*The Thousand*

Eyes of Dr. Mabuse, 1960), would have its master criminal using television cameras panoptically to reduce everyone to a distant picture, to frame everyone in a spectator-spectacle relationship, and thereby to insinuate Mabuse's pervasive influence and control.

Yet beyond the surface lures of the technological and resonances of other films of the period, we can see in Lang's science fiction work an exploration of what would become perhaps the central struggle of the modern world: the struggle to determine whether power resides in the humans who create technology or in the technology itself, more specifically, the struggle over how we see our world and our place in it, given the perspective afforded by our technology. To return to Heidegger's metaphor, it is a struggle over the sort of "world picture" we create—a picture in which we might have a central place or one from which we might remain ever distant, as expressed by the image in a later film in this vein, *F.P. 1 Antwortet Nicht (F.P. 1 Does Not Answer,* 1933), of a pilot with no place to land his plane. It is with that complex question—and at least the hope for a positive answer, a return to a humanly hospitable Earth—that Lang leaves us, along with his stranded astronauts, at the end of *Die Frau im Mond.*

Of course, Lang may have already been feeling some of the alienation from his culture that his lost space travelers exemplified; his films became ever darker before he finally fled Nazi Germany in 1933 to work first in France and then in America. The science fiction works that emerged in his wake seem rather less alert to the "reactionary modernism" Herf describes, less interested in questioning technology, and far less willing to raise questions about the reshaping of society associated with the new National Socialist agenda. Of the handful of science fiction films produced in Germany in this later era, *F.P. 1* and *Gold* are easily the most prominent and most pointedly at home within that "dream of distance," and within the politics of the new Germany.

Both of these films are essentially about dreams and dreamers. *F.P. 1,* produced simultaneously in German, English, and French versions, focuses on the scheme of the engineer Droste to create a floating aviation platform in the middle of the Atlantic to facilitate regular ocean-spanning air traffic, thereby opening the world up to easy commerce. *Gold* explores the age-old alchemical dream, to create gold from baser metals, this time through the action of a massive atomic reactor designed by Professor Achenbach. In both cases the films evoke the same sense of distance we observe in Lang's science fiction efforts, but they use it less to suggest the human alienation bound up in those technological developments than to limn the massive scale of the efforts involved, and thus to indicate, in a manner common to many of the National Socialist architectural projects of the era, the scope and difficulty of those achievements.

Certainly *F.P. 1*, like *Der Tunnel*, also of 1933, foregrounds the colossal engineering effort on which its narrative turns—the construction of a massive floating airport. The elaborate sets and model work, much as in *Metropolis*, place the human in stark contrast to the technological creations depicted—dwarfing the humans with their size or isolating them amid the masses who are involved in the projects. One might argue that stylistically the film suffers from its own elaborate design, as all too frequently the narrative resorts to long takes of the model work involved, offering repeated shots of pumps, flooding ballast tanks, or outsized sections of the platform under construction.[10] The combination of subject and style in this and other German films looks toward a similar "monumentalist" approach to technology that we shall see in British films of the era, and it suggests, as William Johnson notes, that science and technology were often coming to mean simply "more and bigger machines and engineering" (6).

Yet even while enthroning such monumental machinery, *F.P. 1* observes some of the same problems of distance and detachment we have observed in earlier films. It does so partly by embodying that sense of distance in its key image, a floating aircraft platform isolated in the middle of the Atlantic, but more by exploring its central characters, Droste and his old friend Major Ellissen. A noted aviator and explorer, Ellissen has taken a hand in interesting the Lennartz shipbuilders in Droste's dream of an aircraft port, and in the process has fallen in love with one of the firm's owners, Claire Lennartz. But as a reporter friend of Ellissen warns her, he is prone to vigorously pursuing every new project he fancies—much as he has suddenly taken an interest in the F.P. 1—and then to disappearing for years at a time in pursuit of some new interest. While Droste in his single-minded concern with the platform seems just as unstable at first, he is the one who encourages Ellissen to quit "rushing around the globe" and "settle down." Yet when Ellissen is asked to test a new long-range aircraft, the Meteor Plane, he drops everything—including Claire—for the chance to pilot the aircraft. In his absence, Droste becomes the image of stability with his commitment, despite numerous production problems and outright sabotage, to building the platform. That Claire eventually falls in love with the responsible and dedicated Droste in the absence of the "flighty" flier points up the film's key development, its transformation of the technological problem of distance and detachment. The narrative translates the issue into a largely personal problem, an instability in human nature, while the technological issue—the massive feat of engineering Droste has accomplished—

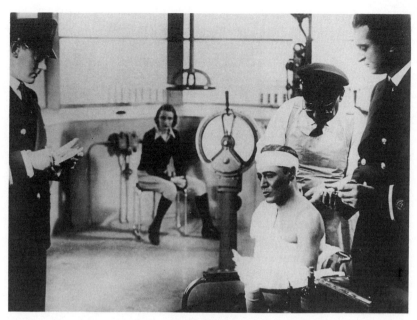

14. *F.P. 1: Coping with sabotage to the mid-Atlantic flying platform.*

becomes an image of stability and connection, one that marks a new era of international ties and potentially peaceful relations. A final shot shows the platform in full operation, a great floating city with planes all around it, while Droste and Claire, arm in arm, look on. That image almost literally illustrates the link between romanticism and technology of which Herf speaks, and pointedly frames the individuals who have devoted themselves to this monumental technology "in the picture."

Gold, which, like *F.P. 1*, was directed by Karl Hartl and stars Hans Albers, initially strikes a similar note with its opening title cards describing humanity's age-old pursuit of gold and noting how that pursuit has led us to "cheat," "persecute," and "kill" one another. That initial sense of a deeply-rooted, almost instinctual drive that sets people against each other, that inevitably alienates and distances, sets the stage for a kind of narrative displacement, a shift in focus from the technological to human nature. The plot line follows this shift: an early emphasis on the creation of an elaborate atomic-powered device for transmuting metals gives way, following a fatal explosion, to the engineer Werner Holt's detective-like efforts to locate those who sabotaged his colleague Professor Achenbach's experiments. Transported to a distant, underwater facility where a far larger version of Achenbach's machine is being completed, Holt must then reverse the process, sabotage this new device before it produces enough artificial gold to wreck the world's economy. In effect, much of *Gold* more closely resembles Lang's stories of international criminals and intrigue—*Spione* (1928) or *The Fatal Passion of Dr. Mabuse* (1932)—than it does hard science fiction in the vein of *Metropolis*. And while the film's massive atomic reactor set, designed by Otto Hunte, recalls the sort of "monumental" approach to technology and fascination with ever larger machines that we noted in *F.P. 1*, the narrative does little to exploit or explore this vantage. Instead, it often settles into what we might term a mundane "industrial" look, emphasizing drab workers dressed in overalls—much as in many of the underground scenes of *Metropolis*—all moving busily around the periphery of this one large set. The film's Moloch-like mysterious machine thus becomes less a focal point for an examination of the technological than an intersection of competing human desires and a rather distant warning of where, in an increasingly technological world, those desires might lead.

Still, *Gold*'s narrative offers an interesting take on the role of the scientist and of technology, one that recalls Heidegger's analysis with which we began this chapter. Fittingly, the atomic device with which the cartel plans to make artificial gold is situated far offshore and, in fact, under the ocean. At this great distance from the mainland, the group intends to manipulate the world's monetary system—in much the way Lang dramatized in *Die Frau im Mond*.[11] It is a threat that, given Germany's devastating experience with hyperinflation in the previous decade, must have had a very real and unsettling ring to it. But the film taps another, perhaps subtler level of menace here. We might say the cartel intends to use the power of technology to create a *representation* of gold, a simulacrum indistinguishable from the real thing, that is, one which allows it to appropriate the power of what Heidegger terms "representedness." Thwarting that scheme is the engineer Holt's ability to get "into the picture," to insinuate himself among those working on this project, awaken his co-workers to the dangers it poses, and eventually cause the machinery to self-destruct. He is, consequently, not simply the engineer-hero whom Tichi sees as commonplace in this era, but the scientist who stubbornly refuses to accept his technological fate: to relish what he can produce with his machinery, to manipulate his world for his own profit, to remain ever at a distance, detached from that world and his fellow humans.

Of course, in *Gold*, as in the other films discussed here, the technological spirit of the Machine Age still wields its power. The most memorable scenes in the film remain those of the massive atomic transmuter—scenes that have, in fact, lived on by being cut into the final reel of Curt Siodmak's

The Magnetic Monster (1953). In keeping with what we have termed a "reactionary modernism," then, this film, much like Lang's works, illustrates a paradoxical pattern common to the era, as it locates much of its attraction in the images of those forces it ultimately critiques. In those very appealing images, German Machine Age science fiction underscores the strength of that emerging "world picture," a view of the world as essentially a production of the technological, even as it offers something of a skeptical recoil. For those images—even in the case of the nearly sabotaged and thus fragile air base of *F.P. 1*—never stand unchallenged, never go unquestioned. Rather, they foreground the relationship between the human and the technological, and at least explore the terms under which the German people might better insert themselves "into the picture" that was then developing.

4

A Remote Power

French Science Fiction Film

I

What was a mere distinction is sharpened into a total separation, a Coperni-
can Revolution. Things-in-themselves become inaccessible while, symmet-
rically, the transcendental subject becomes infinitely remote from the
world. —BRUNO LATOUR (56)

In trying to describe the nature of the modernist attitude,
the sociologist of science Bruno Latour has offered his own diagnosis of
distance or "remote"-ness. In his study *We Have Never Been Modern*, Latour traces the development of an attitude that has rendered us almost "infinitely remote from the world" we inhabit. Its source, he suggests, is a
pointedly modernist desire for what he terms "purification," for categoriz-
ing all elements of the world, compartmentalizing everything, and in the
process separating the human from the rest of the "natural world," thereby
"establishing a great gap between objects and subjects" (55–56). This tendency depends on (or "distils," as he terms it [66]), yet also seems to repudi-
ate another set of practices, "translation" or "hybridization," activities that
trace out the mixture "of nature and culture," of the human and the world
(10), that describe the networks in which we live and in which our science
and technology inevitably must function. This attempt to sketch the background to what has become an abiding postmodern paradox can be useful
in looking at French science fiction in the Machine Age, for Latour reminds us that every effort to understand the workings of "science, technology and society" (3) should begin by acknowledging that very "remote"

posture, by accounting for the detached mind-set or attitude that has helped construct a certain limited view of the technological and its function.

In Latour's eyes, the key modern problem has never been technology itself, the advent of a machine-oriented culture, or anxieties about the human place—or *lack* thereof—within such a culture. Rather, it was what we might term a machine-like consciousness that enthrones difference and distance, and in the process subtly contributes to what Romanyshyn has called our "broken connection with the world" (132), a detachment from the environment it has become our task to learn about and manipulate. Paving the way for the sort of "society of the spectacle" of which Guy Debord speaks (and which we shall explore in more detail in our discussion of American film), this modern attitude mimics the machine in its emphasis on distinct categories, on discrete actions, on differentials, while abstracting the self from the networks of relationship within which we move.

It is an attitude that echoes in much French avant-garde art and design in the early Machine Age, as evidenced by the famous Paris Exposition Internationale des Arts Decoritifs et Industriels Modernes of 1925. That exhibition of art and industrial design, which is the source of such key conceptions as "art moderne" and "art deco," also exhibits the impact of a technological mindset in this era. As Richard Guy Wilson notes, while few of the exhibits offered there "were really machine produced or machine styled . . . the exposition did serve as a source for machine age aesthetics," not only by the way it linked the very notions of industry and modern art,[1] but also by its emphasis on new materials such as reinforced concrete, its pervasive use of stylized and geometrical figures, and the "explicit machine motifs" (49) in most of the exhibits. The world it depicted was pointedly a crafted—or machine-tooled—one that seemed to offer few points of reference to the natural world. The work of such participants as Le Corbusier, Fernand Léger, and Amédée Ozenfant, as well as the exhibit halls themselves and the advertising posters, consistently emphasized an angular geometry, abstract patterns, and a machine-as-parts aesthetic—elements that came to define the moderne style.

That exposition, though, only made more visible a certain attitude towards the technological already prevalent in the avant-garde. Prior to World War I, for example, Marcel Duchamp in a work like *Nude Descending a Staircase* was already fragmenting his central figure into a series of overlapping images, each suggestive of a discrete movement in time, and together shifting focus from a figural depiction—from simple representation—to the *mechanics* of representation. Similarly, Fernand Léger, in such paintings as *City* and *Soldier with Pipe*, as well as in his experimental film *Le Ballet mécanique* (1924), would reinterpret the world around him as an assemblage of cylinders, spheres, and cones, as he set about championing a new way of seeing the world, one in which "trees cease to be trees, a shadow cuts across the hand placed on the counter, an eye deformed by the light, the changing silhouettes of the passers-by. The life of fragments" (quoted in Reed 88). In that effort to "fragment" the moment, the event, the patterns of life—even the theoretical statement—while neglecting or partitioning off their "hybrid" nature, Latour suggests, we can see a problematic character in modern art and modern thought—and I would add, in the construction of the technological at the start of this modern period. To illustrate this issue in French science fiction film, I want to focus primarily on two films closely related to the avant-garde of the Machine Age, René Clair's *Paris qui dort* (aka *The Crazy Ray*, 1924) and Abel Gance's *La Fin du monde* (1930), the former a work that literalizes the effort to freeze the moment in its tale of a stop-motion ray, and the latter one that uses the advent of a comet about to strike the earth to reaffirm a sense of human relationship.

Before turning to these films, we first need to sketch briefly the context, particularly the science fictional context, from which they emerged. The chief figure of note in this context is Jules Verne, whose work signals for many the very beginning of modern science fiction. As Edward James notes, though, Verne's work might more properly be thought of as a *scientific* fiction (16), which places science or technology in a featured role, even if their implications or concerns are not its prime focus. Thus James suggests that in his fiction Verne typically emphasized less the characters or their societies than his engineers' and scientists' creations, discoveries, and inventions. Thanks to that emphasis, he offers, usually "it is the machine that is the hero" (25), inspiring his characters to traverse vast distances or set out on great quests. Among the many obvious examples are the submarine of *20,000 Leagues Under the Sea* (1870), the great flying ship of *The Clipper of the Clouds* and *The Master of the World* (1886, 1904), or the massive gun and spaceship of *From the Earth to the Moon* (1865).

I emphasize this foregrounding of the scientific or technological object in Verne's various *Voyages extra-ordinaires*, as his fantastic novels were called, because it points in two important directions. First, it seems symptomatic of an ongoing fascination with the mechanical contrivance and a pride in the accomplishments of French science. The latter part of the nineteenth century, for example, had seen the development of the new Parisian sewer system, what Carroll Pursell describes as a model of "rational engineering construction" (171), providing not only pipes for waste removal, but also lines for drinking and for cleaning water, pipes for carrying compressed air, telephone and telegraph lines, and electrical wiring, and even a pneumatic mail tube. If the sewer system, in its hidden utility, suggests almost literally a deep-rooted commitment to modern technology, another project, the famed Eiffel Tower, almost literally projects French culture's pride in those technological accomplishments. Designed as a centerpiece for the 1889 World's Fair, the tower suggests, according to O. B. Hardison, Jr., "a work of pure engineering, a magnificent representation that represents only itself" (90). More precisely, it stands as "one of the first examples of large-scale industrialized construction" (Harris 62), with its seemingly delicate iron girders, design of lattice-trussed piers, and ingenious hydraulic support system together fashioning a monument to the power of French technology—or to affirm Hardison's view, to the very idea of the technological.

The Vernian emphasis on the technological artifact has a second implication for the early science fiction films, which would emerge with the development of that key technology, film itself. For the work of Verne seems almost inevitably to dovetail with the fantastic films that Georges Méliès would produce as he set about exploring the technology of cinema, and especially its capacity for fragmenting the world. In fact, Verne's works would inspire a number of Méliès's most ambitious—and among his best-known—projects at the beginning of this century, works such as *Le Voyage dans la lune* (1902, based on Verne's *De la terre à la lune*), *Le Voyage à travers l'impossible* (1904, from the novel of the same name), *20000 lieues sous les mers* (1907, from the novel of that title), and *A la conquête du pôle* (1912, from *Voyages et aventures du Capitaine Hatteras*). In these one- and two-reel adaptations, Méliès's development of a specifically cinematic space and time through the starting and stopping of the camera neatly meshes with his narratives about efforts to overcome the normal constraints of time and space through the creation of fantastic mechanisms—airships, submarines, spacecraft, and so on—for exploring distant places. In effect, the cinematic apparatus and the technologies it depicts both transport us to another, categorically different realm, one from which we invariably seem distant, detached, and at which we thus feel free to wonder and, in many cases, even to laugh.

Albert LaValley precisely measures our own time's response to Méliès's various transformations, appearances, disappearances, and fantastic flights, as well as their similarity to the effect of Verne's works, when he suggests how they prompt us to give "as much or more wonder to the machine which can produce this illusion and of which we are highly conscious. The machine acts as an extension of our senses, delighting us in much the same way children are delighted when they make a new discovery in the real world. But unlike children, we . . . transfer our wonder ultimately to the machine" (147). If Méliès was never really concerned with depicting the real world—as evidenced by his animated severed heads, heavenly bodies that become quite literally *human* bodies, or exploding selenites—he was certainly interested in exploring and exploiting the potentials of his cinematic apparatus. And at the root of that interest is a particular attitude towards both his machinery and the world, one that delighted in a new-found plasticity and fragmentability, a sense that our technologies were making it possible to compartmentalize, rework, and reshape our world.

That sensibility seems particularly prominent in the small body of French science fiction films that began appearing in the 1920s. Among them we should note a largely forgotten feature by Luitz Morat, *La Cité foudroyée* (1922). It focuses on a figure soon to become commonplace in science fiction film, the mad scientist; this one develops a ray gun, which he turns on Paris. His madness is well measured by his actions, as the scientist, in order to demonstrate the power of his technology, sets out to destroy Paris. In particular, he turns his ray on the Eiffel Tower, deploys this advanced technology against what was for this time probably the supreme emblem of French technological achievement. A rather different sort of twist characterizes an effort by the master of French cinema, Jean Renoir. In his short *Charleston* (*Sur un air de Charleston*, 1926), Renoir envisions a world culturally turned upside down, with Europe beset by a new ice age that has reduced it to barbarism and made Africa the home of a cultured, scientific people. His protagonist is an African explorer who descends in a rocket ship to explore Europe and there encounters a white woman (Catherine Hessling, Renoir's wife) who demonstrates the latest barbaric dance, the Charleston. After learning to communicate with her through this dance and completing his "anthropological" research, the African scientist invites her to join him, and together they leave Europe in his ship.[2] It is hardly a conventional narrative film, more a bit of playful avant-garde filmmaking along the lines of Léger's *Le Ballet mécanique*, perhaps a nod in the direction of the surrealist influence of the time. Yet it is a work that pointedly explores the distances between cultures, races, and even the sexes, and in this respect briefly limns the extent to which associations of the technological with a sense of distance and detachment would begin to mesh with other cultural impressions of distance and difference in this period—evidence of the sort of "total separation" of which Latour speaks and with which modern culture was just beginning to grapple.

Certainly, the most important of these early science fiction productions is René Clair's *Paris qui dort*, which similarly explores this distancing effect that has come to seem an inevitable accompaniment to our experience of modern technology. The trope it uses for that exploration suggests something of a paradox, for it focuses on a ray that stills all motion, a new technology that seems to work against the very spirit of the technological, at least against that emphasis on speed, efficiency, and predictability that was associated with the Machine Age. In so doing, Clair's film suggests a developing critique of that highly mechanized world, one rooted in technology's alterations of human society. Yet the film does so in a comic way that also hints at our ability to cope with the often unpredictable effects of science and technology, to live in and with a world from which we are invariably distanced and detached.

II

Romanyshyn sketches just such a possibility as he describes technology's double impact and our potential response. On the one hand, he suggests, our experience of technology has become a sort of dream "of domination, mastery, and control of nature" (211). On the other, it measures our own potential plight, the extent to which this particular dream—including the dream of the movies—controls and masters us, and ultimately suggests our need to regain control. In this respect, the technological points toward what Jean Baudrillard, speaking of the contemporary scene, describes as our "private telematics," the situation in which "each individual sees himself promoted to the controls of a hypothetical machine, isolated in a position of perfect sovereignty, at an infinite distance from his original universe" (*Ecstasy* 15). That "sovereignty," he reminds us, comes at a price, as the technological self becomes like an astronaut in "perpetual orbital flight," weightless—that is, lacking in substance or real power—and struggling to avoid at all costs "crashing into his planet of origin" (*Ecstasy* 15–16). For Romanyshyn, though, "return" or "re-entry" (200) is a real possibility, as we come to find through the technological a new sense of our place in the world and a renewed relationship to it.

We can see an early gauge of this doubled sense of distance, along with its implicit critique of modern technological society in Clair's *Paris qui dort*, especially with its central conceit of a mechanism that stops all motion. The scientist, Dr. Crase, has developed a remote control ray with the capacity for freezing all human activity. When he tests it on an unsuspecting world, apparently the only people who escape its effect are those who have been in some way airborn when the ray struck, in effect, those who were already essentially detached from this world: Albert, the night watchman atop the Eiffel Tower (still the tallest man-made structure at this time), five people who were aboard a plane approaching Paris, as well as Crase and his niece, who were in a room shielded from the ray's effects, the detached observers of this ill-considered "experiment." The ensuing narrative explores the extent to which this technological "event" seems to grant these figures power, while really leaving them largely powerless—like the machine itself which produces the absence of productivity. In their plight we see both the difficulty and the danger in remaining aloof from this world—weightless—in the face of a technology that seems, invisibly and inevitably, to reach everywhere. In Clair's film this trope of an "invisible ray" helps to sketch the perceived reach of technology, the sense of distance it involves, as well as our human ability to confront and live with its seemingly unpredictable influences.

With this central effect, *Paris qui dort* stands midway between two traditions in the early science fiction film. On the one hand, it recalls the Vernian flights of fancy with which, as we have noted, Georges Méliès and his many imitators amazed early film audiences, particularly the startling appearances, disappearances, and transformations that were always central to his work—effects achieved very simply, by stopping the camera and with it the action. Méliès's discovery of the very plastic nature of cinematic time and space, and his exploitation of that plasticity for amusing and at times stunning effects anticipate and provide the basis for much of Clair's narrative about the ray that stops all motion. In this respect, the film is essentially, writes Denis Gifford, an "affectionate look backward at the early French trick film" (67), as well as, in what Garrett Stewart terms its "petrifying implementation of filmic options," its "virtual *decinematizing* of the world's continuous action" (166), a winking acknowledgment of the very nature of the movies. It reminds us that the cinema is by nature a great assemblage of tricks, one of which is the ability to wield seeming control over the very fabric of reality, to manipulate technologically space and time from a safe—directorial—distance, to produce the real and to deny it almost simultaneously. It thus situates cinema as a kind of ultimate machine, granting an amusing mastery over our sense of reality.

At the same time, Clair's conception of a machine that could halt the tumult of everyday reality seems particularly prescient for the development of this genre, and especially its troubled construction of the technological. For the 1930s would see an array of works that moved in an at least superficially similar direction, films about fantastic rays, about devices designed to stop machines, about anti-machine machines, as it were. Such a device becomes another sort of ultimate machine, one which would give its possessor control over all other machines, and thus a sense of freedom from one of the central anxieties of the period: the nearly apocalyptic sense of a total loss of human control, the surrender of sovereignty to the machine. The narratives of works like *Shadow of the Eagle* (1932), *The Mystery Squadron* (1933), *Air Hawks* (1935), *The Fighting Marines* (1935), *The Ghost Patrol* (1936), *Ace Drummond* (1936), *Flight to Fame* (1938), and *Q Planes* (1939), among others, would turn on the fight against these ray-projecting devices that literally rendered planes or other machinery inoperable. That struggle, however, seems to evoke another, nearly postmodern anxiety. For in fighting against a technology that brought every other technology and thus the modern world to a standstill, the individual confronted a possibly paralyzing paradox: the fact that one was thoroughly mired in the modern technological environment, virtually helpless without machines, but potentially helpless even with them. In *Paris qui dort*, then, we see both an early development of what proved to be a recurring fascination of Machine Age science fiction, and the genre's difficulty with fashioning a version of this technological world audiences could accept. It tells of both our own fascination with using technology to manipulate reality, and technology's ability to manipulate us, to reconstruct us as powerless inhabitants of the technological world—to deny us motion, effectively to freeze us in uselessness.

In keeping with the first of these traditions, *Paris qui dort* invokes one sort of distance; in its very playfulness the film distances itself from a serious cinema in order to revisit the spirit of Méliès and early French comedies, including Abel Gance's effort in this vein, *La Folie du Docteur Tube* (1916). Clair's eccentric and absent-minded inventor, Dr. Crase, who develops the stop-motion ray; the figures caught in the midst of their everyday actions (a suicide, trashman, pickpocket, and a policeman, all frozen in their relationships and often in absurd positions); the easily bored characters, faced with a world of new and seemingly unlimited possibility; and the romantic wrangle, as five men confront the possibility that there might be only one woman left in the entire world—all suggest a comic climate, a realm where unpredictability holds absolute sway and the rules of society show their flimsy nature. With a satirist's eye, Clair places us at a distance from his characters and their world, allowing us to see in their sudden rigidity, as if caught in a snapshot, the whole culture: how people dress, how they stand and move, how they go about their daily actions—or *would* if they could. It is, writes Richard Abel, "a wittily satirical social vision" (377)

15. Paris qui dort: *The carefree but precarious life of distance and detachment.* (Museum of Modern Art/Film Stills Archives.)

that results when Clair's one-trick film deploys a simple machine as a lever to pry open the workings of this world.[3]

The central thrust of that satiric vision is clearly the rather fragile structure on which this Machine Age culture is built. Repeatedly, Clair films his characters on the Eiffel Tower, the camera looking out to a blank sky beyond, emphasizing a bit of railing behind, or offering a dim glimpse of vague structures far below. The effect is that these people seem abstracted from the real world, lacking all of the cultural supports on which we commonly and unconsciously rely. They have been effectively transported by this great piece of technology, much as if it were one of Verne's fantastic devices. As a result, they begin acting in ways that suggest their distance from society and the fragility of our acculturation. In this context, values easily turn topsy-turvy. The thief, for his ability to pick any lock and thus open any door to the group, becomes a valued colleague, especially when he offers to "unlock every shop, every museum . . . yes, even the National Bank." The all-too-sober detective, once plied with a bit of cadged wine, quickly becomes a happy drunk and back-slapping supporter of the thief and his proposal. The group appropriates any cars that are handy, and quickly takes to looting the city—in the window of one of their newly acquired cars we even glimpse the *Mona Lisa*—in order to make their tower home more comfortable. And they gather enough banknotes from the pockets of that frozen world to fill a dresser drawer. Albert the night watchman initially resists this impulse—upon encountering the frozen cop and pickpocket on the first morning, he lifts the stolen watch from the thief and places it in his pocket, but then resists the temptation and replaces it, acceding to the earlier, "natural" order of things. Yet by film's end his need for money prompts him to return to Dr. Crase's laboratory to restart that "crazy ray" and refreeze Paris so he might again take whatever he needs. That regression quickly suggests how tenuously rooted are the rules that govern our social behavior, as well as how easily and unconscionably we might embrace the power technology offers us.

In this regression, though, the police step in—as they apparently have had to with the other members of Albert's party, who have similarly been caught acting as they did during the "freeze." Obviously, the problem with society's rules is not Albert's alone, not a *personal* regression but a group affliction, and as such underscores the ease with which we might all distance ourselves from the rights and needs of others, as we construct new values to accord with a "new" society. This comic world metes out no real punishment for such violations, only a temporary confinement, as the police decide that Albert and the others are crazy but harmless, sufferers of a common delusion. The film essentially takes the same tack, hinting that these too are victims of the ray, which has temporarily stripped them of their ability to make appropriate social decisions, left them in orbit around this world rather than part of it, rendered them culturally "crazy."

At the same time, and with an eye to that other, later pattern of science fiction, *Paris qui dort* draws on another sort of distance to present a rather more serious vantage on the technological itself. For the film's central "trick" points up a misuse or thoughtless application of technology that poses another kind of danger to society. As in so many subsequent films, Dr. Crase's mechanism strikes at the very heart of the Machine Age, the era's increasing reliance on machines and its embrace of an ethos of functional regularity, efficiency, and speed. In this respect, much like Fritz Lang's *Metropolis* with its machinery viewed as a devouring god, the Soviet *Aelita* and its communiqués from Mars that lure a young engineer away from rebuilding revolutionary Russia, or the American effort *The Mysterious Island* (1929), with its dangerous submarines with which, we are told, one could easily "rule the world," Clair's film illustrates Cecelia Tichi's observation, that even amid Western culture's embrace of machines and technology in this era, "machine symbols of anxiety and menace" also would "become prominent" (52).

But what precisely is the anxiety onto which *Paris qui dort* opens? Certainly one element of it is a rather commonplace fear of the period, the notion that the widespread use of machines would effectively render humans obsolete, leave them with nothing to do. The year before, we should note, had seen the first staging of Karel Çapek's landmark play on this theme, *R.U.R.*, in which robot workers eventually rebel and replace their human creators. The freezing application of Dr. Crase's ray evokes that same fear. Humans, rendered motionless statues, become little more than amusing elements of the mise-en-scene, as in the case of the thief and cop who are rigidified in the midst of flight and chase, or the suicide, poised to jump into the Seine, while holding a note that blames his fate on an inability to "stand the rush and roar of this city." These and the many other figures frozen by technology have no purpose any longer, save as curiosity pieces or jokes. As lifeless, pointless characters, they effectively metaphorize one potential danger of an increasingly technological society.

Yet perhaps more telling are those who have managed to survive the actions of the ray: Albert and the five others he encounters as he explores a suddenly still and quiet Paris. What the film details is a marked shift in these figures as they set about living in a world without motion. After the initial curiosity wears off, they begin to enjoy having the run of the city—taking a car when needed, drinking all they want at a local cafe, enjoying a morning dip in the pools of the Trocadero, taking money and jewels from those "statues" who have no further use for them, indeed, treating Paris as if it were a vast, free shopping mall and carting off various valuables to decorate the tower onto which they have all moved. But after a few days of such machine-contrived leisure and high life and the excitement of breaking social taboos, they become bored. Many shots show these survivors walking aimlessly about the tower, sitting and talking, playing cards with money that means nothing anymore—as we see when, having been cleaned out by the thief, who is apparently also a cardsharp, two of the men go to replenish their "stock" from a chest stuffed with franc notes. The lone remaining woman amuses herself by unstringing her pearl necklace and dropping the beads from the tower's top platform, while one of the men makes a paper plane from a banknote and sends it flying into space. And finally, all begin arguing and fighting over their interests in the woman. All of these effects obviously send up a capitalist and materialist society, one whose promise of wealth and happiness proves all too empty once realized. However, that society's technological underpinnings are also deeply implicated, for perhaps worse than being rendered a "still life," a meaningless piece of the background, is having all purpose drained from your life, all value removed from things by the operation of technology.

Clair's contemporary, the architect Le Corbusier, glimpsed the dim shadow of this problem as he set about planning a city that would make maximum use of the latest technological developments. Once machine production becomes the order of the day, and once society effectively taps the power of the machine, he suggested, "the leisure time made available by the machine age will suddenly emerge as a social danger: an imminent threat" (64) for which we would have to plan our communities of the future. While our machines will certainly provide us with extra time, he cautioned, it could prove to be time in which we have nothing to do, time in which life might well seem to stand still. *Paris qui dort* underscores that potential emptiness, both with its quickly bored survivors, and with the ease with which Dr. Crase can reverse the effect of his ray. By applying its reversing effects at approximately the same time of day as when he originally applied it, he offers, people will not even notice that they have lost four days of their lives.

As a counter to this realized threat, the film offers a kind of humanistic solution, not far removed from Le Corbusier's suggestions. The architect championed "the harmonious grouping of creative impulses directed towards the public good" (67). For Clair the answer is a bit simpler—and far more concrete. His survivors awake from their lethargy at the faint sound of a call for help on the radio; as a title card underscores, "At last there was someone else to live for." In a sudden "grouping of . . . impulses," they rush off to rescue the caller, Crase's niece, and then to force the scientist to reconsider his actions, bringing him back to Earth, as it were. After breaking into his laboratory, they pose a question that would become archetypal for the science fiction film: "Do you know what you've done to the world?" His admission, that safely distanced from the world in his insulated laboratory—like the scientists we see in such films as *Frankenstein, The Mysterious Island,* and *The Invisible Ray*—he "hadn't thought" of the impact his invention might have, reminds us of a constant need to ask that question. We must, the film argues, guard against a tendency of the technological to transform, as Romanyshyn puts it, "the self into a spectator, the world into a spectacle" (33), the detached object of our experimentations.

One of the primary ways in which the film underscores this particular tendency is in the manner it has, up to this point, characterized its survivors. For they remind us of how the modern self was, as Anne Friedberg has argued, in the process of being redefined as a spectator of reality, or as Vanessa Schwarz more recently offers in her look at turn-of-the-century Paris, of "the way that reality was spectacularized" (110) in the early modern era. Albert, we should note, begins his day by peering out from atop the tower, noting all of Paris below. His view is his measure of the world, as we quickly gather when he sees no one, presumes his clock is wrong, and returns to bed. His subsequent stroll through a frozen Paris provides him with the pleasures of various entertaining tableaux. And his eventual encounter with the others who escaped the ray's influence leads to an auto tour of Paris, as they survey the amusing and curious sights the stilled city provides. The spectatorial stance they take suggests a kind of power they seem to wield—a power they have not just because they are spared from the ray, but also because of their very detachment from all that they view. Separated from the rest of this world by the power of the ray, able to deploy what Friedberg terms the "mobilized virtual gaze" (60) on the curiosities around them, they become "spectacularly" empowered, virtually like the scientist who has brought the world to this pass: detached, isolated, in orbit around a kind of alien world.

The narrative movement sketched out in *Paris qui dort*, though, demonstrates the necessity for some sort of reentry from this orbit. For while the film begins with the isolated individual, the watchman whose life is always set at a distance from others, it ends with a joined couple, as Albert, back at his job, again encounters Crase's niece, takes her onto the tower, and there places around her finger a ring—"the only souvenir" of this crazy episode, as a title card notes—and proposes. The boy who had seemingly been left alone in the world and the girl who had been locked in a room by her crazy uncle unite, but not in any rejection of the modern, technological world. Rather, they remain atop the tower, sharing in that spectator's view it affords, but sharing as well in a more intimate view, as they look each at the other.

This conclusion moves at least tentatively in the direction of the sort of return or bridging of distance that Romanyshyn describes. It is pointedly an alternative to the crashing reentry that, Baudrillard suggests, we all implicitly fear, a reentry which in any case seems practically impossible in the post–Machine Age world of today. It reminds us that, for the modern age, compromise and reconciliation between man and machine, between the distancing perspective and human nearness, still seemed possible. In contrast, the postmodern era confronts us with "the absolute distance of the real," and in that distance the virtual "disappearance" of the self (Baudrillard, *Forget* 76). In the Machine Age that Clair's characters inhabit, that

16. *The Eiffel Tower as a measure of distance in* Paris qui dort. (Museum of Modern Art/Film Stills Archives.)

"distance" was not quite the unbridgeable gap it seems today, the "disappearance" of the people commonly seen milling about the Eiffel Tower only a brief aberration, the self still solidly there, detachment not yet the terrible future that technological power seems to hold out for us. In fact, the problems technology brings are fairly easily reversed, and those who wield that power quickly set back on a proper path.

In light of this easy shift, we should recall that the film begins and ends with characters perched on the Eiffel Tower, which, as Gustave Eiffel's biographer Joseph Harris emphasizes, "was one of the first examples of large-scale industrialized construction" and "the inevitable technical apotheosis" of the nineteenth century (62, 18). As the main setting, the tower evokes an impressive sense of distance, but it is hardly ominous or threatening. While not as awesome as when it opened at the 1889 Paris Exposition, the tower had by this time become, like so many other technological developments, part of the fabric of everyday life: a tourist mecca, a place from which the beauties of the "city of light" might be appreciated, a radio tower sending its signals to all of Paris and beyond. More than just a technological icon, it was a sign that technology might occupy a comfortable place in our world, might even prove a refuge of sorts from its modern hustle and bustle. As Roland Barthes writes, it became another sort of "dream," one evoking not just technology but art, not just science but "the irrational," not just distance but a means of connection or communication with others (28). As he would find, it escapes easy interpretation—just as it escapes the power of Crase's ray—because it apparently "means everything" (27), binds together so much of human culture, bridges so many gaps, constructs a world. The tower thus merits O. B. Hardison, Jr.'s, description of it as a "bridge rotated from horizontal to vertical" (90),[4] and seems a fitting emblem for *Paris qui dort* in its effort to explore the distances that attend the modern, technological world view. With this framing dream image, the film suggests at least a possibility for coping with that other "dream of distance," for living with that often paradoxical technological spirit.

III

For all we might strive to forget the problem of the end . . . or circumvent it by artificial technical solutions, the end does not forget us.

—JEAN BAUDRILLARD (*Illusion* 91)

In her famous essay "The Imagination of Disaster," Susan Sontag has offered one of the most influential and compelling overviews of the science fiction film. Drawing on the great body of films of the 1950s and 1960s with their recurring tales of alien invasion and apocalyptic interventions in nature, she suggests that the genre is fundamentally *about disaster*, about the sort of destructive powers humanity, through its science and technology, has unleashed on the world. Moreover, she offers that the calamities these films envision represent little more than an "inadequate response" (221) by our culture to the various social pressures that instigated these films: problems of the Cold War, the threat of nuclear destruction, anxieties about what our atomic testing and space explorations might produce. Yet, as Baudrillard offers, we have almost no choice, since humans "cannot accept being confronted with an end which is uncertain or governed by fate" (*Illusion* 71), a possible end out of our control—or at any rate, beyond the reach of the technology by which we try to manipulate our world. Thus we narratize the end, "pretend to be the author" (71) of the unthinkable, and in the process distance ourselves from an end that "does not forget us."

We might think of this notion of "the end," though, as denoting something more than just the many images of apocalypse or calamitous disaster that such films offer us—images that continue to exercise a great power over audiences, as we see in such narratives as *Independence Day* (1996) and *Deep Impact* (1998). It seems, as Sontag intuited, a central element of the genre, one that underscores the very role of science and technology, or more precisely the technological attitude on which the genre in its many variations inevitably focuses. In effect, "the end" names the function of science and technology as seen in many of these films: the work by which we try to gain distance from and power over the contingencies of our world, as well as the very power lodged in those contingencies with which we contend.

Because of the different, yet complementary focus on distance that it offers, this sense of "disaster," of "the end," can provide a revealing framework for considering Abel Gance's major effort in the genre, his apocalyptic film *La Fin du monde* (1930). Based on a novel by the French astronomer Camille Flammarion, Gance's film is less concerned with technology per se than with the sort of attitudes that we see in *Paris qui dort*—attitudes which are eventually brought into focus by an event that almost literalizes that "orbital" stance Baudrillard describes: the appearance of a comet apparently on a collision course with the Earth. As humanity faces a seemingly inevitable end, one that, the film emphasizes, no technology can deter, we witness a major transformation in human culture, a "return" of the sort Romanyshyn suggests, when he reminds us that "technology is every bit as much a dream of return as it is of departure" or "distance" (202).

To put Gance's film, as well as its seemingly paradoxical character, into context, we should once again place it within a pattern of films released in this era, works both within and outside the orbit of the science fiction genre, which speak of the sort of technological attitude that was being constructed. Obviously influenced by World War I and the massive devastation and loss of life it wrought, a number of novels appeared in the postwar period recounting calamitous events, works like Jose Moselli's *La Fin d'Illa* (1925), Jacques Spitz's *L'Agonie du globe* (1935), and Regis Messac's *Quinzinzinzili* (1935). In the wake of these works, all mirroring European political anxieties, came a series of what we would today term "disaster films," works that depict a disastrous, even apocalyptic event, attributable either to some natural phenomenon or to humanity's own, often technologically driven misdeeds. Of course, given the worldwide depression, as well as other economic cataclysms and the dress rehearsals for another world war already underway, we should hardly be surprised that the cinema of an era which paid such lip service to the powers of technology, which looked toward, as the World's Fairs suggested, a "Century of Progress" and "The World of Tomorrow,"[5] should also have repeatedly envisioned disaster, calamity, and collapse: earthquakes, volcanic eruptions, collisions with comets, futuristic wars. Through such images, our films could fashion objective correlatives for those real world problems and, in effect, offer resolutions for or at least model responses to them. Thus it becomes seductively easy to read a film like John Ford's *The Hurricane* (1937) simply as an affirmation of our innate human ability to "ride out" the storms of life, even while much of our prized modern civilization tumbles down around us. And, too, the disastrous has always provided inviting images, just the stuff for a spectator-oriented form like the movies. Early in this period, we might recall, Cecil B. DeMille had already parted the Red Sea and then shown it closing, destroying the entire Egyptian army (*The Ten Commandments*, 1923), and Fritz Lang in *Metropolis* depicted the near destruction of a future civilization due to the forces of cultural oppression.

But persistence of "the problem of the end" has to be laid at the door of more than just cultural anxiety or the lure of audience-drawing special effects. On the one hand, the Machine Age saw a variety of films devoted to natural disasters—besides *The Hurricane* we might note works like *Deluge* (1933), *The Last Days of Pompeii* (1935), *San Francisco* (1935), and *SOS Tidal Wave* (1937)—most set in the past, focusing mainly on the unsuspected local furies of nature, and emphasizing, as Maurice Yacowar puts it, "people's helplessness against the forces of nature" (262). On the other hand, it produced a variety of science fiction films that frame "the end" in a pointedly technological context, which speaks to the nature of the genre in this era. Among the films we might include in this category are works like Morat's *La Cité foudroyée*, Maurice Elvey's *High Treason* (1929), Edgar Selwyn's *Men Must Fight* (1933), *Things to Come* (1936), a great variety of serials (most notably the first two *Flash Gordon* serials of 1936 and 1938), and most obviously Gance's *La Fin du monde*.[6]

What is most noteworthy about this latter group of apocalyptic films, apart from the way they capitalize on cinema's own technology through their elaborate special effects, is a single recurring theme: rupture with the old world and the advent of a new order. In *Deluge* and *SOS Tidal Wave* we focus on the unexpected and unavoidable ravages of nature, although on a much larger scale than we see in the first group of films. *Deluge*, for example, involves a solar eclipse and massive tidal wave that together wipe out much of the world's population and leave the few survivors struggling to start civilization anew. Both *High Treason* and *Things to Come* evoke human-inspired apocalypse, as their plots turn on worldwide warfare and its effects. In the latter film, the war, along with the pestilence that follows it, kills off more than half of humanity, but that result clears the way for, as one character puts it, "the brotherhood of efficiency, the freemasonry of science"—the engineers—to step in and take charge of society, to begin constructing "a new life for mankind," based on the rule of a technocratic elite. While the apocalyptic moment on which these films all make such spectacular capital[7] is clearly their centerpiece and would seem to confirm Yacowar's belief that such films cater to an "appetite for disaster" (265), that sense of a "new life" is ultimately much more significant. For it suggests, most obviously, a rather typical bit of genre work, as those apocalyptic elements evoke the broken world of the Great Depression, while their note of renewal reassures us about the possibility of recovery from that metaphorized social calamity. Thus Yacowar notes that, even amid the disasters, there has always seemed "an optimism in the genre. The center holds" (272). At the same time, that hope for "new life" foregrounds the Machine Age's fundamental call to, as Ezra Pound said, "make it new," affirms its faith in technology, or at least in the technological spirit to reshape our world.

Yet that "faith," as I term it, holds within it a sort of paradox that recalls *Paris qui dort*'s double view of the technological. Certainly, it speaks to our capacity for responding to nature's unpredictability with scientific and technological accomplishment. A film like *Things to Come* drives home this point with sledgehammer blows, ponderously reminding us of "the immense task" involved. Yet it also suggests a level of uncertainty and insecurity, even in our technological power. Thus in describing the disaster film's chief characteristics, Yacowar notes its tendency to fall back upon "the tradition of punishment for . . . hubris" (263), for the pride we too eagerly take in our accomplishments. And indeed, that attitude seems particularly prominent in *La Fin du monde*.

By the time he made *La Fin du monde*, Abel Gance was a firmly established figure in the French cinema. He had been writing and directing films since 1911 and, as his comic science fiction piece *La Folie du Docteur Tube* suggests, he had relatively early on demonstrated his interest in exploring the technical possibilities of film. In that 1915 work about a shape-changing powder, Gance used mirrors to distort the shapes of his human players, evoking laughs and a Méliès-like wonder, but also suggesting in the process the current cubist emphasis on perspective and geometricization, seen most spectacularly in the work of Picasso and Georges Braque, as well as the most recent reactions against representationalism, such as the plastic reality of Marcel Duchamp. Thus Steven Kramer and James Welsh historically situate this science fiction/comedy as a first "appearance of the avant-garde in French cinema" (29) and argue that we should view Gance's early work within this very specific "cultural and intellectual context," that of the various artists and intellectuals who helped shape the modern moment (13)[8] and found the technological—especially the technology of film—both a key metaphor and a useful tool in that shaping.

While the early effort of *Dr. Tube* represents little more than a formal—and not particularly well-received—experiment, it points toward Gance's fascination (like that of many of his modernist contemporaries) with technologies of representation and his later efforts at exploring the technical limits of the cinema: his work in radical montage, in varying the size and uses of the screen (Polyvision), and in the expressive use of sound (Perspective Sound). In films such as *J'accuse* (1919), *La Roue* (1921), and the monumental *Napoléon* (1926), he had moved to the forefront of the French cinema, working to discover, as Kramer and Welsh put it, the "grammar" of that "new language" of film (40). More to the point, though, it establishes a key trajectory for his work, an ongoing effort at interrogating perspective itself. This effort is one that Norman King recognizes in his study of Gance's work, which he describes as "a politics of spectacle." He suggests that Gance's films are constantly exploring how the position from which we see determines an ideology, how "a play of looks" can "construct positions" (212) from which we interpret and judge the world. In Gance's films, and especially in *La Fin du monde*, that same "play" becomes the measure of his efforts at remodeling our world, at suggesting the need to move beyond our common "habit of mind," a habit which easily leads us, as Romanyshyn suggests, to become a self "behind the window . . . distant and detached, a self separated and isolated from the world" (67).

While with *Napoléon* Gance had looked back, through the focal point of the French leader, to celebrate an epochal breaking out from the Old World and its ways of seeing, with *La Fin du monde* he turned toward the present and a possible future. Specifically, the film focuses on the attitudes of the present age, the Machine Age, and a new need to break out, to move beyond the conceptions that had become commonplace and culturally stultifying—or, as he suggests in his two *J'accuse* films (1919, 1937), self-destructive—to establish a "new life" for Western culture. Here, though, the catalyst is not the advent of revolution with its inevitable chaos—out of which a Napoleon would fashion a new political order—but a science fiction scenario in which a comet, during its unsuspected orbit through our solar system, hurtles towards the Earth, instigating near-universal panic and social chaos. Faced with the possibility of an apocalypse, Jean and Martial Novalic—the one an actor, poet, and mystic, the other a noted scientist and astronomer—work in their different, even opposite ways to bring about a new perspective on being human. As humanity faces an apocalyptic situation for which, we are assured, there are no "technological solutions," a major transformation occurs in human culture, a "return" from that orbital stance of a sort Romanyshyn suggests. That return is effected by a union of the different vantages the Novalics represent, and it is rewarded when the comet just misses the Earth, affording humanity a last-minute reprieve from its seemingly inevitable "end."

The film, like those before it, evidences Gance's efforts at advancing the language of cinema, as he developed and patented a special sound system, Perspective Sound, for this, the first French talking picture. And while most early sound films tended to be static and given to long takes, he managed to employ the same sort of rapid-fire editing and fluid camera work used in *Napoléon*. Apparently, the project was one for which he had a long enthusiasm; as he notes in an interview, the film "had been taking shape in my mind for ten years" (quoted in King 106).[9] And as a mark of that enthusiasm, Gance reserved one of the key roles, that of the prophet Jean Novalic, for himself. When finally released, advertising for the film would bill it as *La Fin du monde . . . vue, entendue et interprete par Abel Gance (The end of the world . . . as seen, heard, and interpreted by Abel Gance)*, which firmly established the very personal and ambitious nature of the project.

The film as eventually released hardly measured up to those ambitions; King describes *La Fin du monde* as "a critical and commercial disaster" (51). Perhaps responding in part to the rather grandiose billing of Gance in the title (*"vue, entendue et interprete . . ."*), the contemporary reviewer Philippe Soupault blasted it as "portentously naive" and "blatantly unrealistic" (King 52). Yet those problems can be attributed to Gance only with some difficulty, for the film as it first played—and in at least one of its later incarnations—apparently swerves quite a bit from his initial design as reconstructed from Gance's script. In an interview with Kramer and Welsh, Gance termed it "an abortive work" effectively "ruined" by the producer's decision to take the film away from Gance and edit it himself (165). What could have been an early science fiction epic, on the order of Lang's *Metropolis* or the American *Mysterious Island*, became instead a truncated narrative ("fragments of what I intended" [165]); as Kramer and Welsh offer, "a philosophic statement about man and divinity" had been "distorted beyond recognition" (71). In another revision that further obscures much of its science fiction framework, the American distributor Harold Auten in 1934 again cut the narrative from approximately 105 minutes to 54 minutes and, after the fashion of various exploitation films of this period,[10] added an "educational" prologue, a talk by the astronomer Clyde Fisher of the American Museum of Natural History, in which he briefly

outlines a history of comet collisions and explains the point (recently ham-
mered home in graphic detail by the 1997 television movie *Asteroid*) that
science could do "absolutely nothing" if faced with the sort of calamitous
encounter with a comet depicted in the film. As a final indignity, this version of Gance's film received the misleadingly salacious title *Paris After
Dark*.[11]

Yet as implied above, the film was already a bit at odds with itself, bound
as much by paradox as by any sort of misleading packaging or title. As with
the other films we have examined, the idea of "distance" provides a telling
vantage. The menacing comet, which furnishes the disastrous dimension of
this narrative is, after all, a distant menace, something that has gone unnoticed until the astronomer Martial Novalic observes it while scanning the
skies from his observatory—the opening images in the final, shortened version of the film. Even upon its discovery, the world of science initially dis-
counts its approach, identifying it simply as the Lexell Comet, which had,
in its regular orbit, passed through our solar system before in 1770, when it
came within two million kilometers of Earth before harmlessly continuing
on its way. Thus catalogued, the comet is, despite the later warnings of Novalic and an international group of scientists he calls in to confer on its dangers, generally ignored. The modern world, as Gance shows in a repeated
montage of daily activities, simply goes about its business: the stock exchange remains busy, cars are in the streets, people hurry to their jobs. In
fact, the world Gance depicts on the verge of catastrophe offers quite the
contrast to that which we see in *Paris qui dort*. Here everything is hustle and
bustle rather than quiet and stillness; here to be stopped even momentarily
from the constant business of buying and selling, from production, from
grasping after wealth (the image of hands grabbing for franc notes recurs
several times in the film's montages) because of something so distant is unthinkable—or tantamount to "treason," of which Novalic is eventually accused. Distance and detachment from reality remain the order of the day.

In that retreat from truth we can see the film's strange representation of
the spirit of this age. The attitude of the mass of people here suggests the
sort of "window seat" perspective on the world of which Romanyshyn
writes: a distant, detached vantage that allows them to separate their individual fates from that of the world they inhabit or the manner in which they
inhabit it, to continue their efforts to accumulate wealth and power until
destruction becomes imminent. In this psychological symptom of the new
technological age, the culture, as Gance depicts it, not only denies the possibility of death and disaster, but also finally stands against the very truths
that technology holds out.

In fact, Martial Novalic at first shared this self-centered view; he recoiled and withdrew as his mystic brother, like some Old Testament prophet, preached of apocalypse and urged a change in human attitudes. But Jean was pointing not so much to the approaching comet, whose dangers Martial belatedly discerns through his technology, but to the psychological symptom of the new technological age, which, as Gance depicts it, not only distances itself from and thus denies the possibility of death and disaster, but also finally stands against the very truths that its own technology holds out. It is, in effect, an attitude at odds with itself, as we see when the media Novalic turns to in an effort to spread his warning turn against him, as the newspapers and radio report that he is out to achieve world domination for a group of internationalists. Fittingly, that monument to technological achievement, the Eiffel Tower, becomes the source of those propagandistic messages, beamed throughout France—and appropriately, as in *La Cité foudroyée*, it is eventually destroyed by the comet's effects.

In "The Ecstasy of Communication," Baudrillard calls attention to another sort of paradox bound up in that technological spirit, as we experience it today. He describes the contemporary world as marked by the sort of widespread and instantaneous communication the Eiffel Tower, through its use as a broadcast station, had come to suggest and by a ghostly, electronic omnipresence. Baudrillard suggests that because of these effects, thanks to what he terms the pervasive "obscenity of our culture" (35), we are constantly involved in a "desperate attempt" to assert the reality of things and to reinsert ourselves into that reality (32). As Gance's film suggests, the Machine Age was beginning to glimpse the possibilities of such an "obscene" situation, here cast into relief by the comet's approach. For as the possibility of apocalypse becomes more obvious, the end apparently unavoidable, many people turn to literal obscenity, as debauchery and looting become the order of the day. Recalling his treatment of the Convention Hall debate in *Napoléon*, in which he placed his camera on a pendulum and swung it above the scene, Gance here moves the camera in drunken arcs and turns, making it seem a part of this mad frenzy, bringing us up close to those who party in the face of doom, participants in a world that seems to have lost all balance. In this paradoxical context, pleasure, much like leisure in *Paris qui dort*, becomes a most frightening image, an emblem—and admission—of humanity's loss of control, as well as its last desperate effort to retreat from a vantage that seems somehow bound up with this disaster.

In contrast, and repeatedly intercut with these orgiastic images, the film offers another sort of vantage on the Earth's predicament, one far removed from any technological spirit. As the script and Gance's comments recall, the original *La Fin du monde* begins with a passion play, in which Jean Novalic plays the role of Christ. While his performance inspires many of those in the audience, we also sense how much the religious spirit here has become a kind of performance, a public display of values in which practically no one, including Martial, truly invests. But the comet's approach sets off a rush to religion throughout the world, as images of destruction (including the collapse of the Eiffel Tower, from which the government has been broadcasting denials of Martial Novalic's warning) are intercut with a montage of praying crowds, church services, monks in procession, as well as various other religious practices around the world. Branded as "the heavenly destroyer," the comet thus becomes something more than a natural phenomenon; it suggests the failure of the technological attitude, a calamitous visitation of the sort of power, regularity, and predictability associated with the machine world. It also becomes emblematic of a divine wrath at the "obscene" nature of the modern world, and like the Old Testament flood, something sent to wipe out this decadent world so that life might start anew.

    And yet for all of Jean's Christ-like presentiments and prophecies, for all of the world populace's prayers—again depicted in montage, intercut with images of worldwide panic and destruction—the film finally offers no second coming or new spiritual age. While the comet at the last moment deviates from its apocalyptic path and a title card suggests "some supernatural force" at work, *La Fin du monde* emphasizes, much in the fashion of *Things to Come*, the necessary advent of a new secular order, a technocratic renaissance. Even as Jean Novalic wanders among the people, his scientist brother Martial convenes scientists from throughout the world to pledge themselves to rebuild whatever might remain after the comet strikes; sounding much like Oswald Cabal, the technocratic leader in *Things to Come*, he tells the assembly, "We, the scientists, are in command. The fate of the world rests with us. Out of the ruins, we can build a better world." Pledging to "refashion this world on the basis of a new law," a code of "peace and brotherhood," the scientists then proclaim a "Universal Republic." Of course, this turning of the world's scientists in a political and even moral direction is quite in keeping with the Machine Age's widespread technocratic spirit, with what Andrew Ross describes as a kind of "religion" that was then being fashioned "out of the progressive uses of science and technology" (117). But it is a rather peculiar, even paradoxical sort of "religion" the film envisions: a spiritual realm that can only be created by scientists—not by a religious visionary like Jean—and a scientific authority that can only assume its proper position of power once all science and technology have been proven powerless in the face of natural might. It is a technological attitude at whose core remains the phantom of "the end."

Thus *La Fin du monde*, like the comet, finally veers from its apocalyptic promise, allows the people to "circumvent" if not "forget" what Baudrillard terms that "end which does not forget us." It does so by following the orbital logic of the comet, by translating the technological vantage into what Romanyshyn terms a "path of re-entry" (202). Early in the film, as we have noted, the scientist Martial has little use for his brother Jean, the prophet of love and human brotherhood. He prefers to view this world and its inhabitants from his distant, detached, spectator's position, just as he studies space through his astronomer's telescope. Yet that same distant, scientific vision eventually leads him, along the trajectory of the comet, back to earth and a human spirit that, in the modern age, seems to have been all but displaced. As in Clair's *Paris qui dort*, scientific detachment and the distant vision it implies do not prove to be the terrible legacy we might expect, despite initial narrative suggestions. Certainly, when we first see Martial's telescope, it seems a bit threatening, like a canon, at any rate a great mechanical object that dwarfs the astronomer as it rises toward the sky.[12] But that same device, which defines his distant perspective and which has turned his view away from humanity, once it is properly directed, refocuses his vision to the problems of this world. In that redirected point of view—and the radical break with the past it implies—the film holds out a possibility for coping with that detached attitude that was coming to seem a nearly inevitable circumstance of both the modernist moment and the Machine Age.

Regardless of the many cuts and alterations to which *La Fin du monde* has been subjected, then, what remains at its narrative center is a rather curious sort of apocalyptic vision, a reminder of the way that we are, regardless of our technologies, and in some ways because of them, "encircled by our own end" (Baudrillard, *Illusion* 119). That warning—Baudrillard's no less than the film's—is important because of our cultural investment, today even more so than in the Machine Age, in the technological, as well as in a particularly technological way of thinking. In fact, while *La Fin du monde* actually offers but a small sense of the period's technology and spends much of its time suggesting that the true visionaries of the age are like voices crying out in the wilderness, it effectively dramatizes the problematic character of that technological vantage. For in the tradition of so many other apocalyptic visions, including the spate of recent technologically inflected disaster epics (*Twister* [1996], *Independence Day, Dante's Peak* [1997], *Volcano* [1997], among others), it points up another version of the sense of "helplessness" Yacowar observes, another way in we already harbor "the end" in our world, a way in which all of our technological accomplishments can still prove unavailing insofar as they consign us, unreflectingly, to that all-too-familiar distant vantage. Yet at the same time, it finds in that techno-logical stance our best hope for dealing with our fragile human situation.

III

In his recent *Aramis*, a study of the failure of a futuristic French transit system, Bruno Latour reminds us that both technicians and the technological objects they set about creating must always face a daunt-ing issue. They must take into account "the mass of human beings with all their passions, politics and pitiful calculations" (viii), the attitudes that in-evitably attend and inflect our feelings about technology—in effect, the "hybrid" of relationships in which the human and the technological exist. As both *Paris qui dort* and *La Fin du monde* suggest, for the French, in the Machine Age as well, the problem never quite seemed to be technology it-self. In a culture that willingly accepted the Eiffel Tower, a monument to engineering and machine technology, as a proud national symbol, in a country that celebrated Lindbergh's pioneering flight as much as his home-land did, in a land that fundamentally contributed to the creation and status of science fiction literature, science and technology had already found a relatively comfortable place. In fact, as the 1925 Paris Exposition Internationale and the avant-garde films of Fernand Léger and René Claire, such as *Ballet mécanique* and *Entr'act* (both 1924) underscore, technological themes and a machine aesthetic had almost too easily se-cured a place in the mainstream of French art.

However, the attitudes—or "passions . . . and pitiful calculations"—that helped constitute the technological remained open to interrogation. In fact, those attitudes were themselves firmly enough entrenched in French culture, so much a part of the modern spirit, that they hardly seemed lim-ited to science fiction, as if that genre could in no way encompass the breadth and depth of their reach. This may be why we find relatively few cinematic examples of the genre in a culture that effectively gave it birth with the writings of Jules Verne and Georges Méliès's fantastic, Vernian flights of fancy. And yet a questioning of the technological attitude, espe-cially of the personal and cultural distances it seems to engender, appears throughout a range of non–science fiction films in this period. As an exam-ple, we might think of Jean Renoir's films of the 1930s, particularly his two masterworks of the era, *La Grande Illusion* (1937) and *La Règle du jeu*

(1939). The former, in its critique of the attitudes that promote and prolong war, deflates the image of the pilot as a distant and chivalrous combatant. Maréchal's apparent ability to soar above the fray in his machine dissolves as he is shot down and thrown into the squalor of prison-camp life, thrust into a reality from which there is no easy escape. In the latter, the great pilot André Jurieu can fly the Atlantic alone, duplicating Lindbergh's feat,[13] but he becomes helpless and near suicidal once on the ground, while Robert de La Chesnaye is so focused on his mechanical toys and music boxes that he cannot see the fatal chaos afflicting the very unmechanical people in his house. Such films strike right to the core—and uncomfortably so, as evidenced by the hostile reception French audiences gave to *La Règle du jeu*—of a culture that would invest much of its cultural energy and wealth in fashioning a technological defense against aggression, the vaunted Maginot line, a massive work designed to provide safety by forcing the ancient enemy, Germany, to keep its "distance." But as *La Règle du jeu* shows, distance leaves us prone to misunderstanding—as when Christine through a telescope spies her husband kissing Geneviève and assumes he is still having an affair with her; and distance can make it all too easy to release our destructive impulses—as when Robert's gamekeeper Schumacher shoots André Jurieu, whom, at a distance, he has mistaken for someone else.

In Renoir's films, as in the straightforward science fiction works of Clair or Gance, we find no easy embrace of the world of science and technology, and yet finally no repudiation either. In fact, French films of the Machine Age seem rather more attuned to the complexity of the situation than their counterparts in many of the other industrialized, machine-oriented nations. For the French, the machine and all that it seemed to represent— order, regularity, efficiency, power, perhaps even national defense—were an undeniable part of modern life and of the modern spirit. The Eiffel Tower constantly reminded them of that fact, even as its envisioned destruction in *La Cité foudroyée* and *La Fin du monde* and its status as a safe haven in *Paris qui dort* spoke of a troubled attitude towards that presence. A similarly problematic view marks the larger body of French film in both its flights of fancy and its sobering confrontations with reality. Of crucial importance was the attitude driving the technological. In French science fiction, then, we see an ongoing effort to interrogate the distancing vantage that was part of the cultural construction of technology in which film was involved, and a troubled awareness of the modern mind-set, which already seemed well along in the process of "purifying"—separating, differentiating, standardizing—our world.

5

A Cinema of Spectacle

American Science Fiction Film

The whole life of those societies in which modern conditions of production
prevail presents itself as an immense accumulation of *spectacles*. All that
once was directly lived has become mere representation.
—GUY DEBORD (12)

I

When Debord speaks about modern technological soci-
eties, he might as well be describing their cinematic reflections, and particularly the science fiction film. For in its dependence on science and technology, this genre invariably seems committed to spectacle. Certainly, as
contemporary film production especially suggests, the genre has often emphasized the big-budget, high-technology spectacle. But more to our point
is the way it extrapolates from the technological reality of the day, visualizes
what has only been dreamt, images what might lie outside our world—or as
Vivian Sobchack offers, "'real-izes' the imaginary and the speculative in
the visible spectacle of a concrete image" ("Cities" 4). In such spectacular
turns the genre finds its great attraction, indeed, its very reason. Yet as
Debord's comment might suggest, in them as well lies a potential problem.
For the spectacle also tends to reduce our world and its inhabitants to, as he
puts it, "mere representation," encouraging us to see them as something
less than they actually are: less real, less substantial, less human. In
American Machine Age science fiction we can see our cinema engaging
this problem early on, trying by turns to explore the spectacular promise of
technology, to embrace it, and to find some compromise with its implications—implications that are especially daunting since they challenge an

American cultural emphasis on the centrality of the individual. In this very struggle, moreover, we might begin to see why our science fiction films, with their emphasis on visual spectacle, took something of a generic back seat to the popular literature of the period.

In his definitive history of late silent-era cinema, Richard Koszarski observes a relative absence of films in the science fiction genre, despite the fact that "pulp fiction of this kind was already prevalent" (184). Indeed, the period between the two world wars is often described as a kind of golden age of science fiction literature—a period in which it first began to reach a broad popular audience, in which a number of its major authors first began publishing, and in which its major conventions and concerns were developed. Emanating from magazines like Hugo Gernsback's *Amazing Stories* and *Science Wonder Stories*, and John W. Campbell, Jr.'s *Astounding*, this pulp literature brought the genre to a mass audience. In fact, by 1930 there were three monthly American magazines devoted to science fiction, two of them with quarterly companion volumes. While the pulps established a forum for writers like Campbell, E. E. "Doc" Smith, and Jack Williamson, they also helped develop a larger audience for the space romances of Edgar Rice Burroughs and the various utopian writings of the era, what would rapidly become a hard-core "sf fandom."[1] What that fandom came to enjoy was not simply charming romances laced with technological details, but rather fiction of a more speculative nature—focusing on space travel, possibilities for immortality, artificial life/robotics, the superhero, the world of tomorrow, and so on. Moreover, this literary fandom suggested that there was a definite audience for the genre in general, an audience that we would expect a genre-oriented film industry to try to reach.

We might, therefore, qualify Koszarski's assessment, for the science fiction film was only *relatively* absent from American screens in the first three decades of this century. In fact, it achieved a far greater presence here than in the cinema of any other industrialized country in this period, although the number of films hardly approaches that which flooded the industry in the post–World War II era. That number includes a variety of early Méliès-like shorts, works we might generally categorize as part of the "cinema of attractions," films in which mechanisms transform people, animals, and objects, or in which devices allow for fantastic travels or aid in future warfare. It was a time when the attraction of the cinematic mechanism itself and the wonder at what unimaginable things that machinery might offer were often enough to lure an audience.

With the solidification of the production/distribution/exhibition system centering around a few major Hollywood studios, a more ambitious product followed. That product emphasized what David Bordwell has termed certain "preferred practices" (4) of narration and production—practices that drew upon the star, popular genres, and well-known literature, among other things. They resulted in such early science fiction efforts as 1916's *20,000 Leagues Under the Sea* (Universal) and *The Flying Torpedo* (Fine Arts), 1917's *The Mystery Ship* (Universal), and the 1918 Harry Houdini serial, *The Master Mystery* (Octagon), which contained a prototype of the menacing robot that would become such a central feature of serials in the 1930s and 1940s. While often based in fact or in spirit on science fiction literature—most often the work of Jules Verne—our films, particularly in the later stages of the Machine Age, began to find their own vantage, one that tapped into what we might think of as the very nature of film; that is, they are concerned with how we see our world and the sort of spectacular way in which it was presented in America.

One way in which Hollywood aimed at the science fiction audience was by resorting to spectacle in a most traditional way, that is, with such big-budget productions as *The Mysterious Island* (1929) and *Just Imagine* (1930). Later, as science fiction became largely the province of the serial or lower-budget efforts by studios such as Universal, the films became more a matter of spectacular *context*, that is, of a backdrop shaped by Machine Age styles or filled with various technological icons—rockets, television, ray guns, robots, and so on. In what we might see as a transitional tactic, one not unusual in Hollywood, footage and props were even lifted from one production to enhance another—and from one type of film to another. *Just Imagine*, for example, contributed both footage and props—especially its rocket ship—to several of the Flash Gordon serials and to *Buck Rogers* (1939); the big-budget studio production thus helped to beget what many see as its near antithesis, the cheaply made and quickly shot serial. In such circumstances, the visual spectacle shifts easily into the realm of milieu or context and becomes less striking in itself than merely the signifier of a particular situation. In another shift, some of the lower-budget efforts, such as *The Invisible Ray* (1936), scaled their technology to the sort of personal conflicts that typified the era's pulp fiction. Still, as Koszarski's comment implies, cinematic science fiction, rather curiously, was never as popular or as prevalent as the explosion of pulp and utopian writing in the period would seem to predict. Part of the answer, as I mentioned, lies in the nature of American cinema and culture, a kind of nascent "society of the spectacle," already identified with the new and the technological almost in spite of itself, and, as some of our non–science fiction films, such as Chaplin's *Modern Times* (1936), would suggest, at least a little uncertain about that identity.

Thanks to its enormous achievements in technology and industrialization, American culture of the time seemed fundamentally linked to the developments of the Machine Age. As the most famous industrial designer of
the period, Norman Bel Geddes, argued, America seemed more "imbued
with the spirit of the machine . . . than any other nation" (4). And yet as Cecelia Tichi points out, we also harbored a problematic attitude towards that
science and technology. On the one hand, there seemed a shared identity
between machine technology and the spirit of modern America; as she offers, "speed and the belief in cultural acceleration were proclaimed from
every quarter to be, for better or worse, *the* defining characteristics of the
United States" (240). On the other, there was an increasing sense that our
machine technology was contributing to a kind of dynamic anarchy, one
that was ripping us away from our deep roots in an older, more stable Euro-
centric culture. Hence Tichi notes how throughout American culture in
this period "machine symbols of anxiety and menace become prominent"
(52); Henry Adams' awed confrontation with the dynamo in his *The Educa-
tion of Henry Adams* (1918) is probably the most famous example. John Jordan sketches this tension more simply when he describes how Machine
Age America "idolized technology while chronically worrying about its implications" (1). Of course, that pattern of worried embrace, of resisted allure, is hardly unique to America — or to the period we are here considering. As we have seen in the case of *Metropolis* and its seductive robot,
which might free the future society's workers from their drudgery but
which nearly leads them to destruction, the German Machine Age ideology was hardly less conflicted. Yet America, it seems, invested more as a
culture in that ideology, embraced it more readily as identity — even idolized it on the screen, as the energetic characters portrayed by Harold Lloyd
and Douglas Fairbanks suggest — particularly since we did not have a time-
sanctioned alternative, such as the Teutonic mythology in which even such
seeming opposites as Lang and Hitler could find some common ground.[2]

While Jordan attributes much of this technological identification to a
"progressive atmosphere" that seemed to surround the calls for efficiency,
productivity, and machine-like organization, part of it derives from the
very "spectacular" effects that the Machine Age was rapidly bringing in —
effects that promised to transform not only the "look" of American culture,
but also its physical substance. Certainly, spectacular technological accomplishments were part of that transformation — Lindbergh's flight,
Amelia Earhart's achievements, the first television transmissions, the development of the radiotelescope, the invention of the gyrocopter and helicopter. And a number of science fiction films pointedly played off these

cultural spectacles: *Murder by Television* (1935), *Air Hawks* (1935), and *The Invisible Ray* (1935). But more to the point there is a kind of doubleness bound up in some of the most fundamental developments of the period and eventually reflected in our films. The new machine technology had ushered in mass production, and along with that came spectacular *sites* of production, such as Henry Ford's two thousand-acre project at River Rouge, which, as Carroll Pursell notes, was in its time "the single largest and most integrated production plant in existence" (99), a showplace of Machine Age energy. That emphasis on energy shows up especially in the monumental project of Hoover Dam, which was not only in its day the largest dam ever built, but was also seen as, according to Joseph E. Stevens' history of its construction, "a monument to twentieth-century technology, a symbol of man's triumph over nature and his ability to shape and control his environment" (30). The new technology that made the dam possible, as well as the general turn to steel and glass as structural components, had also created the possibility for the skyscraper, which in its "setback" style, as typified by New York's Chrysler, McGraw-Hill, and Empire State Buildings, soon became the icon of the modern urban skyline. Some measure of the visual impact of these creations and their heroic scale shows up in Fritz Lang's crediting the inspiration for *Metropolis* to his first glimpse of the brightly illuminated New York skyline, as if the cities we were then building were already monuments both to the future and to the cinema's own spectacular view of that future.

A correlative machine aesthetic was also beginning to inform the broader American cultural landscape. Probably the most popular example was the new and pervasive visual style of streamlining, seen not only in the era's cars, trains, and airplanes, as might be expected, but also in its buildings, interior designs, and even everyday appliances. As Jeffrey Meikle explains, this style "reflected not perceived reality but a vision of a smooth, frictionless, machine age future" (182). It was a vision readily embraced and rapidly publicized by a figure who typified the new link between art and technology—the industrial designer. Figures such as Norman Bel Geddes, Walter Dorwin Teague, Raymond Loewy, and Henry Dreyfuss, aware that mass production also entailed mass consumption, fashioned a Machine Age "look" that not only captured the spirit or "vision" of which Meikle speaks, but also *sold* it to the public. By fashioning streamlined, thoroughly modern, and alluring spectacles, they encouraged the public to embrace Machine Age products, even in the face of a worldwide depression, and to see those products in the context of an imagined world rather than in the grim situation of the present economic reality.

Some measure of this power, as well as of the link between machine design, spectacle, and public consumption, can be seen in the famous *Art in
Trade* exhibition of 1927. Staged at the Macy's Department Store in New
York, this exhibition sought to demonstrate to the consuming public a new
and appealing link between the artist and machine production. Covered by
the press and radio, featuring daily talks by such speakers as the German
furniture designer Paul Frankl and the president of the Metropolitan Museum of Art, Robert W. de Forest, the exhibit brought approximately forty
thousand spectators to Macy's in only five days (Wilson 65). No isolated
event, though, it merely extended the concept previously explored by
Louis Lozowick's machine-themed fashion show at Lord & Taylor's and
Norman Bel Geddes's two-year stint doing similar designs for Franklin
Simon store windows, and was so successful in promoting the links between
the art world and consumer products that it precipitated a sequel in 1928,
the *International Exposition of Art in Industry*. In this context, we should
hardly be surprised at Richard Guy Wilson's argument that "any understanding of the machine age must be based on an understanding of the
interrelatedness of consumption, the image of business, advertising, and
the emergence of the industrial designer" (66). To this formula we need
also add a sense of *how* this congery of effects was perceived, how they
played spectacularly upon what Anne Friedberg has termed the "mobilized virtual gaze," what we might think of as a new consumerist perspective that she sees as fundamental to both modernism and the rise of the cinema itself (60–61).

What I want to suggest is that, not unlike the movies themselves,
American Machine Age culture, drawing upon that "gaze," packaged its
technology in an especially pleasing manner, crafted and sold spectacle,
and indeed helped to fashion an early version of what Debord has termed a
"society of the spectacle"—even though the entire package was never without its "strings." Certainly, in the work of the most famous industrial designers that effort often proceeded from a solid theoretical foundation. Thus
Teague, for example, based his designs for the Kodak camera, gas range,
and his "bluebird" radio on what he termed the "visible rightness" of things
(15), a principle whereby the design visualized what he perceived to be the
mechanical essence of the object. And Bel Geddes sought to visualize the
energy and motion of the times, noting that "speed is the cry of our era"
(24). But such theoretical pronouncements are themselves symptomatic of
a concern with shaping the image, creating the spectacle, and testimony to
Miles Orvell's assertion—which anticipates Friedberg's work on the vision
of the consumer—that the period was characterized by "a discovery of new

ways of looking at objects" (*Real Thing* 222), by a kind of detached vantage from which one might best appreciate the spectacle that was the rapidly unfolding modern American culture.

When we turn to American science fiction films of the era, we do indeed find a number of what we might loosely term "spectacular" films. Of course, that term seems nearly synomynous with much of contemporary science fiction, as typified by such mega-budget efforts as *The Abyss* (1989), *Total Recall* (1990), *Independence Day* (1996), or *Starship Troopers* (1997). And in this sense of the term, spectacle equally describes such costly and involved earlier efforts as *The Mysterious Island* and *Just Imagine*. But I want to use it to suggest something more, a *narrative* emphasis on spectacle and its implications, a manner in which this period's films drew upon our developing "perceptual patterns" (Friedberg 62) or "new ways of looking," and in the process reveal how our technological "dreams" inflected, often problematically, how Americans were coming to see (and consume) their world. In the best tradition of the larger genre, American Machine Age science fiction films not only try to visualize what *might be*, they also pose questions about those possibilities, speculate on the effects of the spectacles they envision, often by foregrounding the very nature of their spectacles. In some cases, the spectacle seems to overpower the speculation, but in every instance they provide us with a telling measure of the cultural impact of technology in this era, and an ever sharper view of that "dream of distance" in which it—and our films—engaged viewers.

As focal points for examining American Machine Age science fiction, I want to use films that emphasize the most intense period of genre activity, that represent both high- and low-budget approaches to the genre, and that suggest the range of technological concerns found in this period. To these ends the following discussion will concentrate primarily on *The Mysterious Island*, *Just Imagine*, and *The Invisible Ray*, although it will also visit a variety of better- and lesser-known films, such as *Frankenstein* (1931) and *Six Hours to Live* (1932). *The Mysterious Island* seems particularly appropriate to this discussion, not because it is one of our earliest science fiction films, but because of the way in which it connects an older, Jules Verne tradition to the progressive attitudes of this era. While *Just Imagine* extrapolates some of those same progressive concerns in its depiction of a future America, and is clearly linked to Lang's more famous *Metropolis* in its vision of the city of 1980, it seems practically seduced by its own spectacular images and intent on denying the distancing effects of our technology. The low-budget *Invisible Ray* takes as its very subject the seemingly "invisible" effects of our spectacular technology, as it couches its rather mundane "mad scientist" story in terms of devices that affect how we see—and in turn shape—our world. These films, along with the many other science fiction efforts that American studios produced in this era, show the extent to which a particular sort of cinema of spectacle emerged, one reflecting and subtly commenting upon the conflicted attitudes towards science and technology circulating throughout our culture.

II

The Mysterious Island is a fitting starting point to this discussion because of the way it looks back to earlier traditions in the genre, because of the particular historical intersection of art and technology it represents, and because of the very spectacular nature of the production. Like the earlier and more primitive American adaptation of *20,000 Leagues Under the Sea*, it recalls the preeminent influence of Verne on the genre, as well as Méliès's many early efforts involving spectacular journeys or voyages and encounters with the unusual or the monstrous—efforts often mimicked in the earliest American films. And while it hardly follows the plot of the Verne novel on which it is ostensibly based, it does retain much of its spirit. In addition to the sort of technologically driven explorations Verne had made popular, the film offered audiences a correlative experience with cinema's latest developments in color and sound. For to enhance the movie's "spectacular" effect, MGM used the relatively new two-strip technicolor process and, thanks to long delays in the production, which began in 1926 and straddled the introduction of sound in 1927, added a number of dialogue scenes so that it would not seem too dated by the time of its release in 1929. The few interpolated and rather stodgy "talkie" scenes, though, do tend to stop the film's action "dead in the water" and remind us today of the difficulty involved in marrying sound technology to the silent screen. More successful are the spectacular special effects, which include underwater photography, elaborate model work, and scenes combining models with live action. In fact, these elements led effects legend Ray Harryhausen to cite the seldom-seen *The Mysterious Island* as one of his favorite science fiction films (Johnson 161). Yet this spectacular product attests to more than just MGM's reputation for lavish efforts. For the film was nearly three years in production, went through the hands of three directors, and lost much of a second unit in the course of a hurricane while shooting location footage in the Bahamas in 1927.[3] As these new technologies, production problems, and directorial shifts might suggest, the final

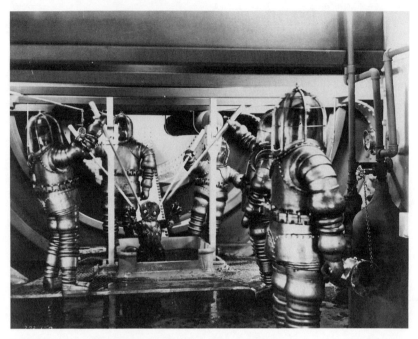

17. *Divers repel an underwater creature in* The Mysterious Island.

product betrays something of that same conflicted attitude previously described—an attitude that speaks to the nature of the spectacular science fiction films that would follow in its wake.

I want to apply the term "spectacle" in several ways as we explore *The Mysterious Island* and its contributions to the construction of a technological sensibility. While the technological culture it envisions seems almost conventionally grounded in Verne's late-nineteenth-century world, the film's images are anything but conventional, even for a period that had already seen such spectacular special effects showcases as DeMille's *The Ten Commandments* (1923) and Fairbanks' *The Thief of Bagdad* (1924). *The Mysterious Island* offered viewers a fully realized underwater world, complete with an aquatic version of the setback skyscraper, populated by dwarfish gill-people; two Vernian submarines engaging in pitched battles, both above and below the sea; fights with a giant octopus and a horned sea serpent; ancient sea wrecks; a bloody revolution and counterrevolution, complete with close-ups of several victims being tortured; and the destruction of a fleet of wooden warships by one of the submarines. This catalogue of images and effects already suggests the more superficial level of spectacle at which the film aims—as well as the direct line of descent to

18. The Mysterious Island: *Count Dakkar's submarine encounters an underwater civilization.*

today's big-budget, special effects efforts. But more to the point is the way the film thematizes the very lure of spectacle, a "way of looking." For it takes as one of its central impulses the possibility that our technological advances might enable us to see things hardly imagined, specifically, those that exist deep within the ocean's depths. The aristocratic scientist Count André Dakkar has been studying various fossils and artifacts brought up to the surface world by the hot water currents circulating around his volcanic island, and he has pieced together bone fragments that suggest an undiscovered humanoid species might exist on the ocean floor. To test that hypothesis, he "build[s] a boat that will descend to the bottom of the ocean" where he might search for that species. Much of the film is, consequently, given over to these scientific and pointedly exploratory efforts at plumbing this tremendous depth to see this quite speculative spectacle.

And yet the film also compromises with its spectacular promise, pulls back from the possibilities of the technology it envisions, looks but then stops looking. It sets the stage for that movement by contrasting the happy peasants/workers who inhabit Count Dakkar's island—introduced in a montage of shots detailing their simple tasks—with the fantastic and seemingly advanced underwater civilization he discovers. The film presents that fantastic civilization as fundamentally primitive, almost animal-like, as we see when they are driven into a collective frenzy by the scent of human blood. Less a wonder than a menace, the ocean dwellers are a group from which the explorers must escape and with which all contact must be severed. This conflict and various others, including a revolution and counter-revolution on the Count's island, find their opposite in the love relationship between Dakkar's sister, Sonia, and his foreman, Nikolai. In keeping with classical narrative practice, the story seems as intent on bringing these two lovers together, despite all obstacles, as on exploring the unknown or displaying technology. The advanced science involved in creating the submarines gives way to a simplistic, almost primitive technology, as a montage of shots designed to show the work of building them depicts lathes, a blacksmithy, and an old-fashioned machine shop. And when the technology Dakkar has developed for exploration becomes a potential tool for repression and warfare, he abandons his work, sinking his last remaining submarine, and himself with it, because of the uses to which others might put his knowledge; as he offers in a dying farewell, "I do not wish to be remembered as one who brought into this world an instrument of death and destruction." By coincidence, it is an instrument of spectacle, a device for seeing this world in a different way, that he abjures in order to keep his own world from being transformed into one of those modern societies of which Debord speaks.

Glimpsed in this light, *The Mysterious Island* is thoroughly in line with one of the most compelling commentaries on the genre. Vivian Sobchack in her *Screening Space: The American Science Fiction Film* asserts that "the science fiction film . . . is concerned with social chaos, the disruption of social order (man-made), and the threat to the harmony of civilized society going about its business" (86). And the self-destructive reaction to this social threat looks toward a long line of similar sacrificial climactic actions in the genre, as seen in such films as *Forbidden Planet* (1956) *Terminator 2* (1991), and *Alien 3* (1993). Moreover, Sobchack's view is essentially congruent with the other most significant commentary on the genre, Susan Sontag's often quoted "The Imagination of Disaster," in which she suggests that American science fiction films are practically obsessed with the potential for cultural catastrophe. What makes *The Mysterious Island* particularly noteworthy in this context is the peculiar way in which it positions its narrative of an advanced science and technology vis-à-vis the question of social chaos or disorder, the maintenance or disruption of society—key concerns in an era that had lately witnessed the Russian revolution. Drawing on Verne's model, the film envisions a technology that is almost too tempting in the power it offers, yet, in keeping with the Machine Age ethos, it suggests the great promise, even the social potential of that technology. It is, consequently, a film that helps us begin to measure the difficult accommodations American culture would have to make with science and technology in this era, difficulties that have much to do with the sort of society that was emerging from or seen as linked to these developments.

We might more easily glimpse this social dimension of the technological in another narrative development of the film, one that parallels Count Dakkar's denial of his technology, his climactic pulling back from its spectacular potential. The first images of *The Mysterious Island* actually echo one of the most famous revolutionary films of this period, Eisenstein's *Battleship Potemkin* (1925), which had premiered in America in 1926 to critical acclaim, just as *The Mysterious Island* was about to be made. As in Eisenstein's film, we initially see images of waves breaking upon a rocky coast, images that are quickly established as a visual trope for the "natural" forces of unrest; thus a title card notes that "oppression has roused disorder in the kingdom" of Hetvia. The following shots depict small groups of people shouting and arguing, some armed, and all dressed in identifiably Russian peasant garb. When Baron Falon visits his old friend Dakkar, he confides that a revolution on the mainland will shortly depose the old king and his corrupt administration and place him in authority. All that we see suggests a necessary and inevitable revolution, one that could not but evoke the recent events in the Soviet Union and the emergence of worldwide class struggles in this era, even though such parallels at first seem a bit curious given the general American attitude towards the Soviet revolution and the notoriously conservative stance of the American film industry.

Yet as we have noted, the technological developments of this period, as well as the burgeoning literature of science fiction, were often linked to progressive social concerns. And as our discussion of *Aelita* has suggested, revolution itself might well have been perceived as a kind of technology, or at least as closely allied to that embrace of positive change and "futurism" that was becoming identified with the Machine Age. Consequently, the initial parallels between the revolution depicted here and the presentation of science and technology become all the more striking—and signposts of another sort of retreat that will occur in the narrative. For in a tradition of isolated scientists depicted in the Machine Age—Victor Frankenstein, Dr. Moreau (of H. G. Wells's novel *The Island of Dr. Moreau* and the Paramount film *Island of Lost Souls* [1933]), Janos Rukh of *The Invisible Ray*—Count Dakkar inhabits an island that is pointedly isolated, a "stronghold" separated from the rest of the kingdom and, by virtue of that separation,

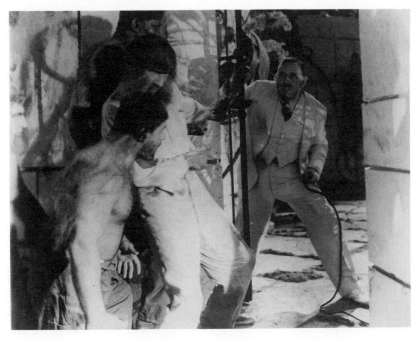

19. The mad scientist fashions human life from animal life in Island of Lost Souls.

free from those conditions and oppressions that have apparently spurred the revolution on the mainland. On his island we see no disenchanted groups or rabble-rousing speakers, no signs of class struggle. In fact, several times the Count notes that, in contrast to those on the mainland, all of his people are treated as "equals." When a jealous Falon sees the commoner Nikolai kissing Sonia and demands that this "servant" be beaten for such affrontery, Dakkar only smiles and again reminds the Baron that "here—on this island—all men are equal." It is, simply enough, a place untouched by the social problems of the kingdom, a land where everyone can, as Dakkar explains, "work with but one end: to study, to learn, to be free, to seek happiness each in his own way," all under the benevolent rule of an aristocratic scientist who knows "nothing of politics" and would "ask nothing but to be left alone." On this happy and industrious island, in this seeming cognate for an early industrial America, which in 1929 had just inaugurated its own scientist-leader, the engineer-President Herbert Hoover, the film clearly implies, there is no class struggle, no need for the revolutions that might develop elsewhere.

Indeed, when Falon brings his revolution to the island it is not to free the inhabitants from tyranny but to subjugate them, gain control of Dakkar's scientific secrets, and garner a position of power for himself. Consequently, the film carefully avoids attributing any particular ideology to the revolt, and Falon's sudden attack with his soldiers—echoing the brutal Odessa steps sequence of *Potemkin* and thereby reversing the film's original alliance with the Soviet film—demonstrates that his real motivation is less the people's plight than his own desire for control. At one point he notes admiringly of Dakkar's submarines that with them one might well "rule the world." With that context established, the narrative effectively transforms its initial images of a workers' uprising—images that might have been lifted from any number of Soviet films of the period—into their near-opposite, a military attack on the contented workers of Dakkar's island and, by film's end, a counterrevolution, as the Count's loyal followers (the good serfs, as it were), with the aid of his submarines, overthrow the revolutionaries and restore the dying aristocrat to power. It is certainly a curious shift, and probably in some part testimony to the film's production problems, particularly to having gone through the hands of three directors, each of whom may have brought a different impetus to the story. But more important, it is a shift that reins in the impulse for social action which was becoming linked to technological development, a shift that questions the very forces that drive social change, and one that finally embraces both the political and technologically status quo. As in so many science fiction films that would follow, this plot turn both caters to our fascination with spectacle, and finally seems to disown it, as the film leaves us with another, lingering shot of the now quieted waters surrounding the "mysterious island," waters that cover all trace of Dakkar and his now sunken submarines.

While *The Mysterious Island* abjures the spectacle, denies the revolutionary, and makes an elaborate display of destroying its advanced technology, it can still hardly be described as technophobic—unlikely, in any case, at a time when, as Richard Guy Wilson notes, "machines and their products increasingly pervaded all aspects of American life" in ways that had already begun "to challenge perceptions of the self and the world" (23). In this film, we see the result of a truly dialogic text, one that speaks simultaneously of many dimensions of Machine Age culture: of the excitement surrounding the Russian revolution and its collective action, coupled with American suspicion of social disorder and a classical Hollywood emphasis on individual rather than group action; of our cultural enthronement of the solitary scientist/entrepreneur, such as Edison or Ford, along with our cultural fear of the unregulated robber barons of industry; of Verne's romantic elevation of technology and its often unstable masters (such as his Captain Nemo or Robur the Conqueror), with recent experience of what the latest technology had wrought in the Great War.⁴ Even amid these multiple voices, we can also hear something of the spirit that Andrew Ross labels "critical technocracy" (105), that is, the tendency of our science fiction culture in this period to challenge "the rules of the game that have governed" the establishment's "idea of technological progress" (131). In this instance, we might consider the manner in which the individual inventor/entrepreneur (Dakkar) stands opposed to the figure of monolithic power (Falon), just as those who have benefited from Dakkar's technological developments readily fight against Falon's attempt at appropriating them. In this respect, the film plays out an ongoing struggle of the Machine Age over who would control and who most directly benefit from technological development. The destruction of Dakkar's work at the narrative's conclusion, we should recall, is not some Luddite action, but rather the considered effort of the inventor/entrepreneur/benevolent leader himself, who, upon careful reflection, decides he does not want his work to be turned to an oppressive use.

At the same time, this retreat also entails a critique of that distancing effect Romanyshyn describes. For Dakkar has been able to carry out his research in part because, in the tradition of those other fictional scientists mentioned above, he has isolated himself on his island—distancing himself from the mainland kingdom and from the conditions of his fellow citizens there, ignoring the ongoing class struggle. It is a pattern that typically suggests human pride rather than concern for others, madness rather than rationality, the realm of horror rather than science fiction. When Falon first informs him of the impending revolution, Dakkar dismisses such issues with a wave of the hand, offering, "All this is out of my knowledge," and, in a phrase that would echo in *Frankenstein*, "asks nothing but to be left alone." In this situation the film not only links science and technology with distance, presenting them as a kind of retreat from the world and its troubles, but also explores the lure of that distant stance. Here the intent is to evoke not the distance of horror—a place of isolation, vulnerability, and otherness—but that of science fiction—a place of speculation. It is distance as dispensation, as imagined freedom from social concern and from the possible cultural consequences of technological development. But it is also the sort of dispensation—what Romanyshyn terms our "broken connection with the world" (132)—that underlies many of our misguided scientific efforts, and indeed our more recent tendency, as chronicled by David Lavery in *Late for the Sky*, to forget about our connection to and need for our own planet and its limited resources. Here that sense of dispensation ultimately costs Dakkar his life, and his people the isolated utopia he feels he has created.

While the spectacles *Mysterious Island* offers are indeed impressive and look toward more recent trends in science fiction, its *treatment* of spectacle is most telling for Machine Age America. For it emphasizes how our technology might enable us to see our world more fully, to penetrate into its unexplored "depths." Yet at the same time it cautions against the isolation and tunnel vision that technology could foster—the truly destructive potential it might harbor. In its double movement, its embrace and relinquishing of advanced technology, the film clearly suggests a kind of cultural hesitancy that, for all of our fascination with the new, still marked America's relationship with science and technology.

III

> The world the spectacle holds up to view is at once *here* and *elsewhere* . . . its logic is one with men's estrangement from one another and from the sum total of what they produce.—G U Y D E B O R D (26)

In contrast to *The Mysterious Island*, rooted in Verne's nineteenth-century science fiction, *Just Imagine* seems pointedly aimed at the *"here* and *elsewhere,"* that is, the present and future, with its story that flashes forward to a barely imaginable America of 1980. At the same time, it evokes what Debord more fully implies in that phrase, a sense of detachment and estrangement, which, he suggests, seems built into the modern technological society. In both instances the film takes its cue less from any American work than from Lang's *Metropolis*, to which it bears a striking and often-noted visual resemblance. That general likeness, as well as its pointedly American character, derives from what Sobchack terms its "selective" borrowings from Lang's film ("Cities" 7). For while *Just Imagine* pictures the same sort of towering cityscape, the same congestion of autos and airships, the same human-dwarfing environment as does its German predecessor, it pointedly omits the "oppressive and negatively affective" ("Cities" 7) elements of Lang's world, and particularly the nether region, the below-ground realm to which workers are consigned. In the process, it thus omits the structural representation of that machine-induced class struggle (the literal *under*class) on which much of the German film turns. Instead, it emphasizes, as Sobchack puts it, "the ideal of highness," its great vertical city becoming "the site of human aspiration" ("Cities" 11, 9), albeit an aspiration that eventually takes a rather conventionally romantic shape.

Moreover, its tone differs markedly, thanks to its incorporation of various song-and-dance numbers and the comedy routines of its star, El Brendel. That shift especially has made it easier to view this film as a parody of Lang's than as a straightforward work of science fiction. Yet the compromises it works on *Metropolis*'s "dream of distance" help sketch an interesting competing view of the technological, one that, even in the dismal context of the Great Depression, managed to inform much of American culture in the 1930s.

What I would suggest is that we approach *Just Imagine*'s musical-comedy version of the future as less a parody of *Metropolis* than an "adjustment," its own images of "aspiration" offering a thoroughly American take on what our technological future might bring. Its vision of 1980 is, in many respects, quite serious; a number of its predictions are right on target; and its elaborate and costly sets look forward to such serious visualizations of tomorrow as Norman Bel Geddes's famous Futurama exhibit at the New York World's Fair as much as they look back to Lang's film.[5] Still, its musical-comedy elements, and especially the casting of El Brendel, who brought to the film his slow-witted Swedish immigrant persona, honed in vaudeville, inflect that technological vision in an intriguing way. As a contemporary reviewer noted, here "fantasy, fun and melody are shrewdly linked" (M. Hall), priming us to "see" this film's world in a far less "distant" manner than we do Lang's, and to find its advanced trappings and future ways more in keeping with some thoroughly familiar and nonthreatening sorts of "aspiration."

Of course, the technological is abundantly evident; in fact, it is probably more pervasive and humanly accommodating in *Just Imagine*'s America of 1980 than in the *Metropolis* of 2015, and certainly more so than in any previous American science fiction film. But the work disguises most traces of that distancing effect of which Romanyshyn speaks, and tries to mine Debord's sense of "estrangement" for comic capital. As a result, the technological in all its manifestations—videophones, rockets, personal airplanes, rooftop landing pads, television screens, light-activated alarms, remote controls, mechanical hand-dryers—seems reinscribed with a rather different set of values. In some cases those developments appear little more than silly; in others they seem extensions of the "entertainment" dimension of this musical-comedy narrative, spectacle as spectacle; and in others they take the form of simple and quite practical developments, the sort of realistic proposals that we might find championed by editor Joseph W. Campbell, Jr., in the pages of *Astounding*. But in almost no instance do these elements appear menacing or betray a kind of hard-wired social agenda. They

20. Just Imagine's *vision of to-morrow: New York in 1980.*

are precisely the sort of dream stuff that a "dream factory" like Hollywood might offer for its customers' pleasurable consumption, nothing that, like *Mysterious Island*'s mighty submarines, might make them feel uncomfortable or estranged from a rapidly changing world—hardly an easy task in an America rocked by the onset of the Great Depression.

As in *Metropolis*, here too we find an effort to evoke a historical context, to "place" this film's future, although in a far more specific way than *Metropolis*'s broad references to Western cultural history ever manage. Brief prologue images of New York in 1880 and 1930, as well as the character "Single O" or Ole Peterson (El Brendel), struck by lightning in 1930 and revived by 1980's advanced science, fashion that particular frame. While the film's rhetoric suggests vast differences on the order of those *Metropolis* visualizes—"If the last fifty years made such a change, just imagine the New York of 1980 . . . where everyone has a number instead of a name, and the government tells you whom you should marry! Just imagine . . . 1980!" a narrator intones—its images and plot make that temporal distance appear almost inconsequential. While the film's prologue offers comparative images of 1880s and 1930s "traffic problems," the futuristic segment begins with a kind of transcendent vision: a sky full of personal aircraft, speeding people to various parts of the great city below. But that vision is hardly unproblematic, as a new kind of traffic jam ensues, with the crowd of planes stopped by a hovering policeman and floating traffic signal. If the government, through the State Marriage Tribunal, now interferes in the choice of a marriage partner, that problem, the film also reminds us, simply reworks the age-old difficulty of parental interference. Moreover, it is apparently doomed to failure: one of the characters sarcastically describes it as just "another noble experiment," like the highly unpopular Prohibition, quickly situating it as far from practical or workable. And if Single O repeatedly refrains "Give me the good old days," or the protagonist J21 sings of his desire for "an old-fashioned girl," those longings carry little real weight, as we readily recognize in them the stock laments of comic and love-struck characters throughout history. These are simply figures who inhabit a world that *looks* different from our own, that has strange, even appealing technological details, but that embraces our values, is driven by our common desires, and seeks as the goal of its "aspirations" the same basic human satisfactions.[6] People here continue to fall in love, drink, long for children, and try to achieve something in their lives. Despite all of its technological trappings, then, that 1980s world seems—and, thanks to its pop tunes, sounds—very much like the contemporary America of 1930.

The film's efforts at engineering or reshaping the world seem equally intent on evoking continuities as on suggesting a sense of distance or an "elsewhere." Certainly, the vision of a New York of massive setback skyscrapers, broad elevated avenues and bridges, and crowded skies was not that far removed from New York of the 1930s, as Fritz Lang's *Metropolis*-inspiring vision of the city's skyline would imply. In fact, as Richard Guy Wilson points out, in the late 1920s there "swept the country" a vogue for such large setback buildings and broad avenues, for a "metropolitanism," as the style was sometimes called (165). Moreover, *Just Imagine* emphasizes that this stylish and rather grander-scale New York is hardly inhospitable. In contrast to the class-segregated situation depicted in *Metropolis* and more in keeping with the egalitarian ethic repeatedly espoused in *The Mysterious Island*, the common people live in these buildings and walk the broad, attractive boulevards here. His hosts J21 and RT42 take Single O on a walking tour of the city, so that he becomes a kind of contemporary *flaneur*, his mobilized gaze taking the measure of this world's "newness." In exercising this new way of looking, Single O and his friends stop at a sidewalk automat for food pills, watch a young couple window-shop, and then climb up to the balcony of J21's girlfriend, LN18. The impression we get is that, for all of its massive size, this technological city—in which a high-rise apartment can appear no less accessible than a contemporary "walk-up"—is easily navigable, inviting, almost familiar.

21. *Aerial courtship amid a traffic jam in* Just Imagine.

In fact, the film becomes largely an illustration of the beneficial effects of technological reshaping. As earlier noted, the future sequences start with a vision of rapid transit, as personal aircraft carry people to every part of the city. When a traffic jam occurs in the sky, we see how technology might let one cope with such "new" difficulties: by simply putting planes in hover mode, casually wing-walking over to a neighboring plane, and carrying on a conversation—or in this instance a courtship. That opening effectively establishes a pattern for the rest of the narrative, as the film recalls how things "used to be," offers a futuristic updating of those "old days," and then demonstrates how our technological developments might address such "timeless" problems. In effect, it seems intent on bringing the "here" and "elsewhere" into alignment. Consequently, its many technical innovations, as well as its thoroughly technologized environment, come to seem less a cause for anxiety than, in the best utopian tradition, something to which we might look forward, and less something that distances us from the material conditions of our world than an easy way to obliterate any bothersome distances with which we currently struggle. Inscribed in all of these wonders are promises of comfort, convenience, and accessibility, even a common ability to exercise some control over our world rather than to be controlled by it and its technology's implicit agenda for change, speed, and order.

22. *Single O notes welcome changes from "the good old days" in* Just Imagine.

While *Just Imagine* does not push its interrogation of technological re-shaping into the same arena of human artifice as does *Metropolis*, it does address the human impact of the technological via Single O. Killed by a bolt of lightning in 1930, Ole Peterson has been restored to life as part of a scientific experiment[7]—a demonstration offered as public spectacle. While acknowledging how much this Rip Van Winkle–like figure has lost—his wife, family, friends—in order to emphasize how estranged he must feel from this future world, the film uses him mainly as a comic foil who must learn to cope with the new world, and in the process demonstrate its many wonders and illustrate how easily one can become accommodated to it. And it does offer some payback, as the film concludes with a comic restoration of that lost family when Single O's son, now an old man, appears and happily accepts his father's invitation to "climb up on my knee, sonny boy." Still, in the manner of the later *Six Hours to Live* (1932), the film does raise the issue of whether such technological developments are entirely wel-come, as the scientist Dr. X10 responds to Ole's initial bewilderment at this brave new world of the future with a simple offer, "If you're unhappy, I can kill you again." Not surprisingly, Single O turns down that proposition, which underlines the sort of miracles this world offers, miracles that excuse small discomforts such as cultural disorientation and the shots O must take until he becomes acclimated to life once again. The doctor's offer simply foregrounds the easy and indeed inevitable choice in favor of the technological that *Just Imagine* consistently holds out to its viewers, which perhaps most distinguishes it from *The Mysterious Island* and the half-hearted retreat from technology on which that film concludes.

A further indication of the ease of that choice can be seen in the way that Single O, once acclimated to this world, becomes like his futuristic friends. In fact, he begins to carry around a hip flask holding his alcohol-in-a-pill, and is eager enough for technologically inspired adventures that he stows away on their rocket trip to Mars. But more to the point is the way this film, particularly with that "Jules Vernesque journey to Mars" (M. Hall), as a contemporary reviewer described it, offers its own take on distance and difference. Here the "dream of distance" dissolves into a technologically impelled nearness, a cosmic *flanerie*, as Mars proves to be just a short and simple rocket flight away—hardly the sort of dangerous and momentous undertaking Lang, thanks to his technical advisors, imagined space flight to be in *Die Frau im Mond*. Analogously, the future itself seems, much as the New York World's Fair would style it, as near as "tomorrow."

On Mars, however, this group of planetary sightseers finally confronts a real challenge of difference; for the Martians are mainly female, idol worshipers, and apparently technologically bereft. Given the link that a film like *Metropolis* draws between female sexuality and technology, as well as the abiding tension that Evelyn Fox Keller notes between the scientific world and the feminine, this situation seems particularly significant. Bathed, pampered, and enticed by beautiful female attendants, the three Earthmen recall the situation of Odysseus and Circe. Seduced not only from thoughts of home, though, these futuristic voyagers are also being lured away from the technological world. As a substitute, they are offered pure physical pleasure—a bargain that suggests how the feminine might be seen as a potentially dangerous and distractive force, even at odds with the technological and its promises.

To emphasize that bargain and the darker side of this seductive power, the narrative then reveals a more subtle, because initially invisible, sense of difference that marks this planet. As J21 discovers, "Everybody on Mars has a twin, one of them good, one of them bad," and those opposites are constantly in conflict. In this strange and primitive world, it seems that the *absence* of technology, along with a mainly feminine populace, goes hand in hand with a fundamental and dangerous sort of "estrangement." The comic misadventures of Single O, J21, and RT42 as they negotiate this strange and estranged world, constantly trying to sort out the "good" and "bad" Martians, show how different the Americans are from such aliens, as well as how similar they are to each other, despite the different time periods from which they come.

This use of distance as a mechanism for dissolving and denying distance springs from J21's desire to "find some way to distinguish" himself, and so prove he is as worthy a suitor for LN18 as the newspaper publisher MT3, who also seeks her hand. The "great inventor" Z4's rocket offers several avenues for such distinction, as a series of testimonials affirms. By piloting the ship to Mars and back, J21 can go where no one has gone before; the rocket's speed insures that "no one ever went this fast before"; and the vantage it offers, from out in space, is of "a sight no one's ever seen before." Such repeatedly noted singularities, achieved through technology, along with the relative ease with which they are managed (even the "old-fashioned" Single O can fly the ship back to Earth), both testify to the power of modern science, and debunk that sense of distance, helping to overcome a rather old-fashioned "estrangement" from technology itself. Thus the film suggests that, despite its spectacular appearance, technology does not so much set us apart from our world and others as it does obliterate distance, by opening doorways that link our world with others, the past with the future, or even one person with another—in this instance, J21 with the girl of his dreams, whose hand he wins through this technological passage. Even with names reduced to random numbers and letters, the film implies, technology never really denies individuality and difference; rather, it holds out new possibilities for distinction and success. Seen in this context, even a flight to Mars becomes only a springboard to what remains our most important goal— human connection.

This brief overview might imply that *Just Imagine* is little more than a naive and fanciful view of technological society, a utopian alternative to *Metropolis*'s darkly dystopic vision and a light-hearted embrace of what *The Mysterious Island* first capitalizes on and then finally retreats from. While the uncomplicated sort of seeing it offers might support such a view (indeed, the only deceptive images offered here are those strange twins encountered on Mars), that reading hardly tells the full story. In his discussion of the era's upwelling of science fiction pulp literature, Andrew Ross cautions against seeing such visions simply as "the North American vulgarization of the high-minded and socially critical European SF tradition created by respectable intellectuals" (104) like Lang or *The Mysterious Island*'s dismissed European directors Maurice Tourneur and Benjamin Christensen. *Just Imagine*, we might recall, also appears amid a revival of technological-utopian literature, a body of work that, as Howard P. Segal explains, tended to see technology as "a far sturdier and more efficacious instrument of progress than the various panaceas proposed by" traditional social activists: "taxes, socialism, religion, communitarianism, or revolution" (122). While *Just Imagine*, with the exception of its comic swipe at Prohibition, seems little impelled by a desire to *change* society, as in the case of so many of those utopian works, it does articulate a distinct attitude toward change, particularly toward the changes that naturally accompany technological development and are even eased by such development. It offers them as neither distant nor as distancing us from our world or each other. In the best ideological tradition, it celebrates such changes while denying that they represent *any real change at all.*

In effect, the film tries to walk a fine line between our ongoing cultural embrace of the technological and the distancing, alienating effect that Romanyshyn and others have seen as part of the inevitable baggage of our technology, as well as between the issue of progressive, social engineering versus natural, evolutionary change. Certainly, at every turn it stresses the values typically associated with the Machine Age—speed, functionality, efficiency, stability. More pointedly, it emphasizes those traits that marked American culture's identification with the age's spirit—a break with the past, a fascination with reshaping our world, a sense of cultural difference, and a new way of seeing. It seems to evoke a world that, in Debord's words, is "at once *here* and *elsewhere.*" Yet it also works narratively to contextualize such circumstances, to help us set them apart from that estranging effect that is typically thought to attend technological culture, to imagine them as just the next, even natural step, not some fanciful Mars-like flight.

That *Just Imagine* was not quite successful in this effort, as evidenced by its weak reviews, may speak to the larger difficulties faced by the movies in this era. We might recall Cecelia Tichi's assertion that the Machine Age text does not simply "contain *representations* of the machine—it too *is* the machine" (16), and as such demonstrates the same basic characteristics as the technology it depicts. Since it is itself a technological art, and one that had recently undergone the great technical alteration from silent narrative to a talking—in this case, an "all talking, singing, and dancing"—medium, film had a special stake in reassuring audiences about any technologically driven change. After all, the cinema too generally set us at a distance from our world, let us view it through a technological window, while trying to make us feel comfortable with this view of the world. A science fiction subject matter, because of the way it invariably thematized these very issues, may have made that cinematic task all the more difficult. At any rate, directly addressing that Machine Age ethos, particularly in the midst of the Great Depression with its implicit message of cultural limitation and individual alienation, had to be troublesome, as *The Mysterious Island*'s halting use of sound and problematic attitude toward technology also suggest.

Carroll Pursell has suggested that we think of our various technological developments as "only social relations materialized" (194), as "something we have imagined to better define ourselves" (219). At a time when our "social relations" were already a site of debate and reformulation, when our imaginings were daily confronted by a stark and seemingly intractable reality, when classes seemed ever more distant from and set against each other, and when many already felt removed from the technology that was rapidly reworking our world, *Just Imagine*'s efforts at a technological dream drained of most of technology's social implications, of a distant view that involved no real distance at all, was probably too great a reach. For most Americans caught in the early throes of the Depression, that sort of vision, no matter how near the film tried to make it seem, must still have appeared too far off, too removed from their everyday lives to be easily imagined, even in the movies.

IV

As the epigraph to this chapter suggests, and as the films we have so far discussed begin to illustrate, we might well place American science fiction films of the late Machine Age within the context of a developing "society of the spectacle," as Debord terms it. While he is speaking primarily of the larger impact of technological culture on human experience in this century, and particularly of the alienating effects of commodification on society, this sort of cultural development seems quite near the surface in the movies that appeared in the late Machine Age. For the vision of technology they offer may generally be described as an "accumulation of spectacles," albeit spectacles that more obviously carry a problematic residue, that hint of a kind of reduction of our world to the level of what Debord terms "representation," that begin to gauge the dark shadow that our technology, even in its implicit sense of distance, could cast.

In this late-Depression period, the serials with their spectacular cliff-hanger irresolutions offer us one new take on the notion of spectacle. As a mainstay of the era's cinematic science fiction, they closely parallel the pulp literature in its less ambitious manifestations. But whereas magazine

editors like Gernsback and Campbell tended to insist on scientific prob-
ability, on a soundly rational basis for all of their fiction's flights of fancy, on
a clear continuity with the world of normal experience,[8] the serials generally labored under no such burden. Death rays, rocket ships, flying wings,
interplanetary travel, and menacing robots were the stuff around which
their unfailingly frenetic action was built.[9] Their settings ranged from outer
space (particularly the planets Mongo and Mars in the *Flash Gordon* serials) to futuristic cities lodged in primitive places (as in *The Lost City*
[1935]), to advanced civilizations far below the Earth's surface (*The Phantom Empire* [1935] and *Undersea Kingdom* [1936]). And any explanation
for the creation of these devices or the heretofore unsuspected existence of
these futuristic cultures was hardly attempted. Far more important was the
very fact of such technological cultures and their technologies, their spectacular self-assertion. These elements simply *stood for* the technological,
representing within the narrative the values conventionally associated with
it: speed, efficiency, organization, precision, power—what we might term,
extrapolating from Romanyshyn, the deep psychology of our "cultural
dream."

Throughout the serials, consequently, audiences simply took a technological presence for granted as milieu, part of the form's expected "attractions." Even those films not specifically in the science fiction vein, such as
the Marine adventure *Fighting Devil Dogs* (1938), the crime story *The Van-
ishing Shadow* (1934), and adaptations of popular radio shows or comic
strips, such as *The Shadow* (1940) or the many *Dick Tracy* films, were typically given a spectacular technological context through the presence of robots, deadly rays, futuristic airships and rockets, "wrist radios," and a pervasive "moderne" style. In these works technology could as easily be
presented in the service of evil as of good; it might be the invention of a scientific genius, hoping to aid humankind, or the offspring of a madman,
aiming for world conquest. The three *Flash Gordon* serials produced by
Universal (1936, 1938, 1940) are an obvious case in point. Each takes as its
premise the plotting of the Emperor Ming the Merciless to control or destroy the Earth and other planets through the power of various special rays,
a force of ray-equipped rocket ships, or robotic bombs. That "black science," as we might term it, in every instance meets its equal in the "white
science" of Earth's Dr. Zarkov, whose rocket ship and other inventions
allow Flash Gordon to thwart Ming's plans and save the universe. Yet pointedly, the crucial edge in each serial is not so much the "good" technology,
in fact, not technology at all, but rather Flash himself, the muscular protagonist whose *physical* prowess—he is, as the first serial establishes, a famous

23. *Flash Gordon, Dale, and Dr. Zarkov captured by Emperor Ming's warriors in* Flash Gordon.

athlete—decides the issue and frustrates all of Ming's rational calculations. With much of the action actually played out, in keeping with the larger serial tradition, as a series of fistfights, swordfights, wrestling matches, or other physical contests between Flash and Ming's minions, the strange yet obviously powerful technology everywhere on display becomes, as I have elsewhere described it, a kind of "charming" backdrop (90), a spectacle that carries neither a particularly positive nor a decidedly negative value. It is simply one more challenge for a physically vigorous American—or America—to overcome.

Probably the more important technological influence—and, as the serials' makers well understood, their chief lure—was the mechanism of the serial itself. While serial literature was already well established in the nineteenth century, as evidenced by the work of Charles Dickens, the movies would give this industrial era form a pointedly Machine Age inflection. The serialized presentation of narrative, often with the recurring pattern of exposition, rising action, and climactic event, all centered around a single developing character, evolves in the movie serials into a fairly rigid formula, one in which characterization becomes incidental (much as individualism becomes irrelevant on the assembly line), narrative development gives way to the sheer power of repetition, and the cliff hanger ending that

24. Buck Rogers: *Buck loses control of his dirigible in the serial's first episode.*

is never a real ending predictably manufactures thrills. With each episode of the "chapter play" closing in much the same way, with the protagonist, his or her helper, or a love interest placed in harm's way, and with each succeeding episode reprising the deadly circumstances only to reveal an unforeseen escape, audiences were treated to a fast-paced, predictable, and precise experience that underscored the films' seriality, their efficient, machine-like, yet compelling workings. Along with their typically spectacular displays of the technological, then, the serials' narrative mechanism emphasizes the technological influence and thus the Machine Age values informing the films. Yet even seriality had to find a compromise with narrative trajectory and conclusion, with a classical predilection for closure. The technological, serial effect had to be framed within a traditional narrative context, anchored in a conventional way of seeing our world.[10]

In our more ambitious narratives, such as Universal's *Frankenstein* (1931) or Fox's *Six Hours to Live* (1932), something of this same pattern lingers, but along with it a sharpening vision of the cultural implications of the technological. In such films technology often provides a spectacular context, a backdrop against which other concerns are played out, even though those other concerns always seem to circle back to the spectacular implications of our technology. Of course, *Frankenstein*, as well as its sequel *The*

25. *Science and technology meet the thriller in the serial* The Phantom Creeps.

Bride of Frankenstein (1935), may seem a rather problematic example, since it is typically claimed by genre students as both a science fiction and a horror film. That blurring of genre boundaries occurs in part because of the very manner in which it separates science and technology from its elements of horror, and indeed from much of the narrative—a separation that is one of the crucial alterations of Mary Shelley's novel. As we might expect from its early-nineteenth-century origins, Shelley's *Frankenstein* is far less concerned with machinery than with viscera, far less interested in the science of creation than in the creative mind and the excesses to which it is prone, far less intrigued by the ability to make an artificial being than by the nature of life itself. While Shelley situated her scientist protagonist in a context of "vaults and charnel houses," surrounded by human "decay" (52), as he set about his "unnatural" researches into the secrets of life and death, the Universal film offers us a Dr. Frankenstein who, early on, displays a pointedly technological bent. In fact, he seems to have spent far more time crafting machines than bodies. Fittingly, the famous creation scene in this film—probably due in some part to the influence of *Metropolis*'s robot-creation scene—is given over more to the pops, flashes, and sparks of the life-giving machinery than to the monster itself. Yet after

26. Science creates life from death in Frankenstein.

the monster's creation and the demonstration of Frankenstein's own imbalance, the science fiction aspect of the film shifts to the background, as the film focuses primarily on human failings rather than on scientific accomplishment, on revenge rather than the search for knowledge. Science and technology, consequently, contribute primarily a visual context and impulse for the narrative, both of which ultimately seem at odds with the horrific trajectory that takes over—a trajectory that is almost too neatly summed up in the narrative shift from the modern technological scene in which the monster is created to the ancient windmill in which it is apparently destroyed. And yet that windmill is, after all, just another machine and, in that respect, an appropriate site for the destruction of this machine-created menace, particularly since it reminds us that there are ancient urges—for power and mastery—latent in all our technological creations.

In like fashion, *Six Hours to Live* provides us with a technology that is primarily spectacle, almost grafted on (Frankenstein-like) to a rather un–science fiction narrative, yet the implications of that technology resurface at the last, almost as a kind of narrative afterthought. A romantic melodrama with a scientific twist, *Six Hours to Live* interweaves the conflict surrounding an International Trade Conference with the arrival of Professor

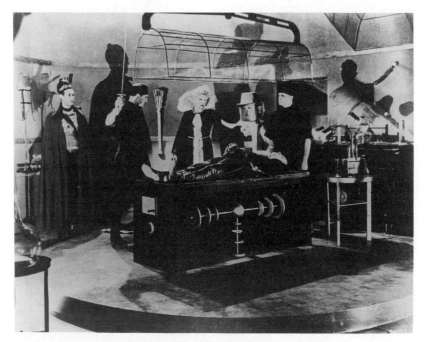

27. *Life wrested from death in* The Phantom Empire's *Radium Reviving Chamber.*

Otto Bauer, bringing his latest invention to show his colleagues at the university. He describes the device only as "something that science will shout about." When the Sylvarian diplomat, Captain Paul Onslow, is assassinated because he opposes a treaty that would deliver his country "helpless into the hands of those who covet her," Professor Bauer uses his device, a rejuvenator, to revive Onslow. However, the effect lasts only six hours, and in this time he must locate his murderer, help various individuals overcome personal problems, and cast his deciding vote against the unfair treaty. The film thus focuses less on this amazing technology than on the sort of ripple effect it produces, as in his last six hours Onslow works a kind of rejuvenation in others and in his homeland.

As in *Frankenstein* and *Metropolis*, the centerpiece of this otherwise simple narrative of international intrigue and individual awakening is the spectacular *re*-creation scene, a surprising and visually striking intervention of the technological in an old world setting and amidst age-old political wranglings. The rejuvenator, like the device that brings Single O of *Just Imagine* back to life or the revitalizing chamber that restores Gene Autry in *The Phantom Empire*, would seem an unqualified boon, which at the very least offers an affirmation—certainly a welcome one in the darkest times of the

28. *The singing cowboy turns technology against itself in* The Phantom Empire.

Depression—that, as Bauer says, "in the sphere of modern science, nothing is impossible." Yet Onslow, returned from the dead, qualifies that triumph, as well as our view of the technological here, not only with his inevitable death six hours later, but with his knowledge of what lies beyond death, and his assertion, in what has become a stock lament of the genre, that there are some things humankind should not know. His newfound religious faith, the calm way he accepts his fate, and finally, almost as an afterthought, his destruction of the spectacular device that has brought him back to life cast that seemingly beneficial invention in a new light. The technological spectacle, even in what would seem its most beneficial form, can set the self at an unbridgeable distance from the world, can create an almost unimaginable sort of alienation, as life longs for the natural release of death.

Onslow's problem is that, in his new status as a temporarily living dead man (a technological zombie), he has no real place in this world. If technology has delivered him—for a time—from humanity's oldest and greatest fear, it has also, as Romanyshyn's analysis of technology would predict, distanced him from everyone around him, made him into a kind of imitation of life, turned him into, as Debord might put it, a "representation": of death, of resistance, and of both the power and limitations of our technology. And while developed only slightly with early scenes of Onslow's being villified in the press and on the radio, the larger implications are that the spectacle culture itself is at the root of the very problems that this technology helps spectacularly (if belatedly) to resolve. The technology of the mass media is, after all, what the other industrialized nations have been using to turn public opinion toward their predatory designs and against Onslow. So while that great technological boon serves mainly as a mechanism for resolving this narrative—finding the murderer, ensuring peace, and so on—Onslow's final destruction of the device suggests the problems and contradictions implicit in technology as spectacle, and more generally in an increasingly technological culture.[11]

To illustrate this developing concern with technology as spectacle and the human tensions technology was increasingly seen as instigating, I want to turn to a film that more clearly situates itself as science fiction and seems especially symptomatic of the genre in the later 1930s, Lambert Hillyer's *The Invisible Ray*. Long considered one of the more accomplished science fiction films of the time, this "tight and visually inventive" work (43), as John Baxter calls it, would be imitated by a number of films in the next few years, notably, *The Man They Could Not Hang* (1939) and *Man-Made Monster* (1941).[12] It provided its star, Boris Karloff, with a complex role that speaks to the changing cultural perceptions of science. No longer simply the monstrous offspring of a misused science, as in *Frankenstein*, here he is both scientist and monster: the long-suffering genius Janos Rukh, ignored by the scientific establishment, and a radioactive killer, the victim of his own researches. Another version of this doubleness marks Rukh's opposite here, the representative of traditional science, Dr. Felix Benet, fittingly played by Karloff's cinematic competitor Bela Lugosi. He embodies a kind of establishment science, blind to much of what falls outside its limited perspective, and thus in its own callous way monstrous; yet he also suggests the benevolent potential of that science, as he appropriates Rukh's discovery of "Radium X" to cure blindness in his Paris clinic. In the conflict between these two figures and the tensions each embodies, *The Invisible Ray* limns the far more complex and problematic position occupied by science and the technology it produced in the later stages of the Machine Age—in which they serve less as a spectacular context for action than as an agent of spectacle, an agent that seems inextricably linked to both boons and bane.

Like *The Mysterious Island*, *Frankenstein*, and *Six Hours to Live*, *The Invisible Ray* begins by conjuring up physical distance, setting its science at some remove from the American situation and its key scientist isolated from much of the humanity he would hope to serve. The film opens, in

29. The Invisible Ray's *Rukh sets up a telescopic view for his skeptical guests.*

fact, with shots of a castle-like structure in the midst of the Carpathian Mountains on a stormy night, a scene that better evokes medieval Europe and vampires than the world of modern science, better suited to a horror film than a science fiction one. This ancestral home of the scientist Rukh, though, is hardly as detached from the modern world as those initial images, or even the foreign setting, would imply, for with the coming of his guests—Dr. Benet, his wealthy patrons Sir Francis and Lady Arabella Stevens, and their nephew the explorer Ronald Drake—a tracking camera follows Rukh's wife, Diana, as she walks from the ancient house across an open and airy portico, to his metal-ceilinged modern laboratory, and then to his observatory to announce their arrival. The shifting visual icons here—stone walls, stately columns, classical statuary, and then gleaming metal surfaces and various electronic devices—abruptly suture the ancient and the modern, the Gothic and the Machine Age, while preparing us for another link Rukh wants to make for his guests, one that points up his own fascination with distance and spectacle.

Much as *Just Imagine* invites us to see the future as not so far removed from the present or past, Rukh, working on the thesis that "everything that has ever happened has left its record on nature's film," proceeds to evoke visions of the past for these members of the scientific establishment. His

30. *The scientist Rukh protects himself against the dangers of his spectacular show in* The Invisible Ray.

demonstration draws spectacularly on a recent technological development, the radiotelescope, which was introduced in 1932. With his own telescope, Rukh captures a beam of light observed from the nebula in Andromeda, "three-quarters of a million light years distant," and then transfers it to a projector and shows it on his laboratory's ceiling, effectively transforming his guests into viewers of a special sort of "film" he has drawn out of nature. It is a quite spectacular "movie" they see, one in which their own point of view is shifted five hundred light years distant from Earth, which shows them the record of an asteroid that struck our planet thousands of years ago, bringing with it an element "far more powerful than radium." This "tour in time," as Drake describes it, serves ostensibly to prove Rukh's theory, rejected by the scientific establishment, of the astral source of this rare element. Yet more to the point, it spectacularly demonstrates his technological mastery over time and space, his ability to demolish distance with science rather than be bound by it. And that point is reinforced when he immediately agrees to fly off to Africa on an expedition his guests have mounted, so that he might locate and bring back that theorized Radium X.

As the narrative proceeds, however, that distancing effect we have observed in so many other science fiction films quickly resurfaces, as Rukh becomes seduced by the very spectacle he has used to overcome his skeptics.

31. Benet (left) crafts a technology that can restore sight from Rukh's discovery of Radium X in The Invisible Ray.

For on the African expedition, as a close-up of a news report notes, he physically separates himself from the others, including his wife, as well as from their research in "astro-chemistry," when he goes off alone in search of his element. At the expedition's base camp, we learn that they have heard nothing from Rukh for many weeks, and Sir Francis comments that "he's elected to desert us"—as well as his beautiful young wife. The parallel cuts between scenes of Rukh's single-minded, self-obsessed quest through the jungle and Benet's medical ministrations to save a sick child underscore the different attitudes at work here, as the former's scientific obsession distances him from everyone, while the latter puts aside his research and uses his knowledge to help others. This sequence models one of the central questions of the film, reiterated several times after the expedition returns from Africa: how might we best *use* our science and technology? Or as Benet asks Rukh about his element, "you have harnessed its power to destroy. Have you harnessed it to heal?"

The full impact of that distancing effect appears only when Rukh finally locates Radium X. The discovery is another spectacular scene, as Rukh comes upon a pit belching smoke and flame in the middle of the jungle. Dressed in a metallic radiation suit, he descends into the pit and there retrieves samples that glow and emit sparks. When his native bearers become frightened, he loads a sample of Radium X into another sort of projection device, one that, in an elaborate display of power, emits a beam that disintegrates a nearby rock. In contrast to that earlier instance of projection, in which Rukh offered a compelling visual spectacle to his fellow scientists, quelling their skepticism, this scene, played as an overt effort to intimidate and subjugate the natives, points up the destructive power he has unleashed. It also links him to those European powers that were then using the latest advances in military technology to subdue parts of Africa and extend colonial empires. Separated from its potential human values, the power of technology seems to have quickly seduced him. In effect, Rukh's scientific discovery becomes a tool with which to avenge his years of neglect by the establishment and to gain hegemony over others; as he notes with a smile of satisfaction, Radium X offers him "power, more power than man has ever known."

Predictably, that technological power brings with it further estrangements. Because of his work with the element, Rukh contracts a kind of radiation poisoning that makes his body glow, literally turning him into a spectacle, a representation of the very thing he has been searching for, as well as a sign of alien-ation—a model of the alienating effect of the colonial impulse. On first sighting him in this spectacular state, his native servant flees in fear. When his faithful dog comes to comfort him, Rukh pets the animal and it immediately dies from his touch. As Diana appears at his camp, he refuses to see her and dismisses her with the warning, "I don't want to be bothered with anyone." He becomes both physically and psychologically alienated—a condition neatly summed up in his complaint to Benet, "I can't touch anyone." Eventually, that sense of distance, exacerbated by radiation sickness, which is slowly eating away at his mind, destroys his efforts at research, his marriage, and what promised to be his new status in the scientific world. Driven mad by his sickness, Rukh fantasizes that his colleagues are stealing the credit for discovering Radium X, that his wife is unfaithful, and that everyone is plotting against him. He has become a model citizen of a "society of the spectacle"—inhabiting this world, seeing all it has to offer, but thoroughly estranged from it, save for his role as potential master.

As Romanyshyn suggests, one effect of the technological vantage and its distancing is that, for all of the power the individual appears to wield, he finally seems to have no real place in this world. Since Rukh has come to see the world as excluding him, then, he removes himself from it definitively—by faking his own death. Once officially "absent" from that world, he can become what the trajectory of his technology has all along implied, simply a spectator of the spectacles around him, just as "invisible" and just as deadly as his "ray." Hence, he sets about eliminating the five other people involved in the fateful African expedition, who, he feels, have wronged him, but he does this in a way that suggests a kind of spectatorial dehumanization, that shows he has come to see them as little more than "representations" of the forces arrayed against him — and of his own alienation. Above the church where the now-free Diana has married Drake stand six statues, which Rukh immediately associates with himself and the others. Renting a room facing the church, he uses his Radium X ray to destroy the statues one by one, with each mysterious destruction marking his murder of one of his supposed betrayors. The result is not simply a mystery to the authorities, but a public spectacle, as is underscored by the close-ups of newspaper headlines, such as, "Sacred Image Mysteriously Disappears in Sight of Throng as Onlookers Faint and Pray." It is a spectacular process that again recalls his first action, when he visualized the cataclysmic collision of a meteor with the Earth. In this case, Rukh has recast all of Paris as spectators for his destructive visualization and, like his native bearers in Africa, as frightened witnesses to and potential subjects of his power.

As *The Invisible Ray* makes clear, though, in a society reduced to spectacle, no one is immune from being recast as "representation," from being reduced to the same sort of distantly observed — and vulnerable — object as Rukh has made of the others. Consequently, the film offers a parallel scene, in which Dr. Benet discovers Rukh's murderous actions by applying the same sort of technology in reverse: he uses a special device to photograph the eyes of the latest victim, Sir Francis. There he discovers a lingering image — a latent spectacle, a fitting artifact for a world of spectacle — that of the murderer, Rukh. Armed with this knowledge, Benet and the police arrange a trap in which Rukh will himself become the central spectacle — a farewell lecture on Radium X at Benet's home. By extinguishing all the lights at midnight, they plan to use the darkness to reveal Rukh's glowing body in their midst, but Rukh foils that scheme when he surprises Benet and kills him. Still, he too dies spectacularly as, with the police closing in, the radiation poisoning overcomes him and he bursts into flames before them. That ending seems most appropriate, given the film's constant focus on visual spectacle. For Rukh has tried to use his science to master the "society of the spectacle," to turn his world into a series of "representations" of his power. In his death we witness the danger in that construction of the technological: the purveyor of spectacle becomes the final spectacle; the one who has denied the distancing effect of his science literally disappears from this world.

While *The Invisible Ray* repeatedly develops a tension between two pos-sibilities of science—"the power to heal, the power to destroy"—it offers more than simple moralizing about the proper uses of the technological. As John Jordan explains, during the period of World War I America had seen "the creation of a technicopolitical ethos in which technique, moralism, and self-interest jostled for primacy" (65). In the wake of the war's great dev-astation, that jostling tended to produce a "preoccupation with technique, with best methods as opposed to best purposes" (67), as calls sounded for a more rational, more scientific approach to government, for applying engineering's methods and principles to the operation of the state, for a lit-eral social engineering. Certainly, the election of Herbert Hoover, the engineer-President, attests to this attitude. However, the eventual recogni-tion that, in the process of engineering society, "values could be subordi-nated to technique" (83), sparked a national debate in the pages of such magazines as the *New Republic*. It is in this context, of a national dialogue about values and technology, rendered all the more politically charged by the impact of the Depression, that we need to see *The Invisible Ray*'s cen-tral conflict.

At the same time, we should keep in mind how this conflict is framed. For the key manifestations of science and technology here are all what we have termed spectacular devices, technologies that produce or facilitate spectacle, that emphasize our ways of seeing: Rukh's observatory and the special projector with which he shows the light beams from Andromeda; his destructive projectile beam of Radium X, used to inspire fear and awe; his modified healing beam that restores his mother's sight; Benet's healing rays, projected onto the eyes of his patients; and Benet's special camera that allows him to "see" what the dead have seen. More than just tapping into the fundamentally reflexive dimension of all fantasy narratives,[13] this spec-tacular element of *The Invisible Ray* attests to what Miles Orvell has dem-onstrated in both *The Real Thing* and *After the Machine*, that the Machine Age was particularly fascinated by our many technologies of representation and reproduction—the movies, radio, photography—as well as by a set of complementary cultural practices—waxworks, panoramas, arcades, peep shows, and so on.[14] As Orvell offers, our "newly arising technological civil-ization . . . thrived on a traffic in representations and replications of every possible sort" (*Real Thing* 33–34). His argument is that these developments not only catered to a tremendous cultural appetite for reproduction or imi-tation, but also suggested that the technological might provide us with "new ways of looking at objects," ways of seeing "more than would nor-mally be seen" (*Real Thing* 222), perhaps even ways of seeing *through* our conflicted attitudes toward technology. Viewed in this context, *The Invisible Ray* suggests both the problems and possibilities bound up in such "new ways," an anxiety about the manner in which the technological world might influence our seeing, as well as hope for what it might help us to see.

The hope, we might recall, is articulated in a very forthright way here. Put to a *moral* use, Radium X restores eyesight; it lets people see, as in the case of Rukh's mother, a young girl we observe in Benet's clinic, and many others whom, we learn through the newspapers, he has miraculously cured. Used in this way, it does not create a "society of the spectacle" but, as do our very best movies, enables us to see our world more clearly, to overcome an estrangement like that which Debord describes. In this respect the film speaks directly of the potential the Machine Age found in technology, even in the movies, a potential that would soon be celebrated in a kind of living science fiction film, the New York World's Fair of 1939–1940. There we would be allowed to see our world precisely as the "World of Tomorrow," to see the technological not as a spectacle but as a threshold to, as Richard Guy Wilson puts it, "blessings and benefits and a way of life free from want" (40).

And yet, as we have noted, *The Invisible Ray* and its late–Machine Age kin—films like *Murder by Television, The Return of Dr. X* (1939), *Man-Made Monster*, and others—still seem bound to the horrific, determined to reveal a monstrous aspect in that technological embrace. When Benet tries to help Rukh with his radiation poisoning by preparing a "counteractive" drug, he warns Rukh to take the drug regularly lest "your body again becomes the deadly machine it was." Later, when he informs the police that Rukh is behind the mysterious killings, Benet echoes this note, warning that "his body is an engine of destruction." That notion of the body as transformed into a "machine" or "engine," and particularly a "deadly" one, seems a telling development for this period, and more than just an interesting way of bridging the genre boundaries between horror and science fiction. It is a motif that would be repeated a few years later in Universal's *Man-Made Monster* when Lon Chaney, Jr., receives such a massive dose of electricity that he becomes literally capable of shocking people to death.[15] And it would surface in a number of Cold War–era science fiction films depicting scientific advances that produce deadly side effects, most notably *The 4-D Man* (1959) and Roger Corman's *X: The Man with X-Ray Eyes* (1963). Herbert Marcuse has suggested that one of the consequences of industrial civilization, of a world designed by science and propelled by technology, is that it "transforms the object world into an extension of man's mind and body" (9) so that we can better control and manipulate that world. Yet as *The Invisible Ray* and its cousins seem to imply, that "benefit" may come at some reciprocal cost—that the "mind and body" might take on the character of the "object world," or at least of the mechanisms by which we deal with that world. We might become little more than machines—or spectacles—ourselves, and perhaps even more disconcertingly, those machine characteristics might displace our sense of values and even prove deadly.

As we moved toward the later years of the Machine Age, and as signs of another possible cataclysm like the Great War began to appear, American science fiction films seem far more attuned to such deadly possibilities latent in our science and technology. While technology might enable us to see our world differently, might even *compel* us to do so, they suggest, that shift in perspective might be dangerous. For as attractive and compelling as a "society of the spectacle" might appear, the spectacle relationship fostered by the technological—that relationship of distance, detachment, objectification, estrangement, even colonialization—had to give us pause. For the conditions of production fostered by the technological could also *produce us*, remake us as something other than we thought we were. In the very distance we fashion by situating ourselves as spectators and the world as spectacle, in coming to see both the world and ourselves from the standpoint of the machine, we risk fully displacing ourselves, becoming the sort of simulations of the real, which Jean Baudrillard would find symptomatic of that later, technologically shaped, postmodern world we now inhabit.

6

A Monumental Event

British Science Fiction Film

I

It's so big. It won't be too big for us, will it? —*The Tunnel* (1935)

The underlying Machine Age concern with distance takes a rather special character in British science fiction films of the era. In describing efforts in the other arts to convey and interpret the impact of technology during the period, Dickran Tashjian has noted a trend toward what he terms "monumentalization," a tendency "to monumentalize the machine" (257): by depicting it in extreme close-up, by accentuating its aesthetic dimensions, by emphasizing extraordinarily large constructs. We might think of Paul Strand's close-up photographs of various machine parts, Paul Frankl's skyscraper-inspired furniture, or Norman Bel Geddes's designs for outsized planes and ocean liners. Beyond simply emphasizing our machinery's size and power—while trying to suggest a human power unleashed through it—this approach drew the technological out of its everyday context, detached it "from any past that it might have had" (258), and hinted of an independent, inspiring power at work in these human creations. In other words, its very "big"-ness became emblematic of technology's distance from us, its sovereignty, and by extension our own rather uncertain ability to manipulate or control it. The line cited above from the film *The Tunnel* (aka *Transatlantic Tunnel*) neatly articulates this effect. For here a character responds with both awe and anxiety to one of the many "monumental" subjects found in British films of the period, in this case an effort in a relatively near but unspecified future to span the Atlantic Ocean with an underwater tunnel. As this tentative response suggests, such monumental objects or events—in part because of the way they became mingled in the public mind with other unavoidable facts of modern life, such as the Depression, international conflicts, the quickening pace of everyday existence—reflect both the culture's uncertain embrace of the technological, and its desire to be reassured that it could deal with what that "brave new world" would bring.

If British science fiction films of this period seem characterized by their "big" concerns, they hardly outdo the literary efforts in the genre which, in comparison to the pulp product that has become identified with the early upsurge in American science fiction literature, is characterized by intellectual seriousness and respectability. While the literature of science fiction in early Victorian England went through its own "penny dreadful" period, by the second decade of this century it had taken on a more substantial and creditable status, thanks in part to the standing of the writers who tried their hand at the form and their willingness to use it for tackling big issues. If American science fiction was largely restricted to pulp publication, in Britain it typically appeared in hardback. Serious writers such as Aldous Huxley, C. S. Lewis, and J. B. Priestley took turns at the genre and produced well-accepted works (Huxley's *Brave New World* of 1932 is probably the most notable example), which thereby helped confirm the genre's "respectability." And there was already a precedent for taking on important social issues in a science fiction context, thanks to the early efforts of H. G. Wells who, by the late Machine Age, had already earned the sobriquet many have since bestowed on him—Father of Science Fiction[1]—and had also become something of a canonical figure in world literature. Given the model of Wells and others, then, it is no wonder that, as Brian Stableford describes them, the many British science fiction novels that appeared in the period between the wars were largely "serious in intent, ambitious in their attempts to analyze genuine human problems, and frequently subtle in their development of ideas. They were written in—and made a contribution to—an intellectual climate where concern for the future prospects of society had a certain urgency" (55).

That urgency, Stableford argues, derives from a slightly more pessimistic climate in England than was to be found in the United States, even in the midst of the Great Depression. Thanks to the effects of that worldwide depression, increasing class consciousness, a restiveness and in some cases outright rebellion in the colonial empire, and increasing political pressures on the continent, anxiety about the future was running high in British intellectual circles. We can easily detect the shape of that anxiety in the types of literature that dominated Machine Age Britain: future war stories, tales of what Stableford terms "apocalyptic anxiety" (51), dystopian narratives (again, most notably Huxley's *Brave New World*), and a large body of speculative nonfiction (such as the "Today and Tomorrow" series of pamphlets[2]), all of which suggest a greater suspicion of technological accomplishment than appears in American and German writing of the era, and a more active debate on the subject, as is suggested by Bertrand Russell's pamphlet *Icarus, or The Future of Science*. Responding to a similar pamphlet by J. B. S. Haldane, entitled *Daedalus*, which sketched the positive changes science was expected to bring by the turn of the century, Russell cautions against a possibly catastrophic result from giving ever greater technological power to elite groups—the possibility of an Icarus-like fall for Western culture. While the body of speculative fiction and nonfiction is certainly large and influential, then, the shape of that influence is noteworthy. For these writings consistently probe beneath the technological atmosphere that was extending across the industrial countries and express doubt "about the certainty of progress" (Stableford 54) linked to Western culture's grand march into the Machine Age.

More to the point here are the effects of this literary attitude on the British cinema—or rather, its apparent *lack* of major effect. Despite a growing public interest in science fiction literature, the acceptance fostered by major writers, and even that sense of cultural "urgency" of which Stableford speaks, the cinematic genre never attained great popularity in this era. While the period saw little serious market research in England on which we might draw for explanation, Sidney Bernstein, owner of the Granada theater chain, conducted a series of highly publicized polls among his patrons in the mid-1930s which reflects tellingly on the genre's popularity. In trying to determine what sort of product filmgoers would prefer, the Bernstein surveys polled respondents on their favorite stars, directors, and story types. A question about the narrative preferences of various age groups did not elicit a single top vote for science fiction; rather, the poll favorites were consistently the "society drama," "thriller adventure," and "musical comedy" (Wood 132). Corroborating these results, the trade paper *Kine Weekly*, which compiled a listing, both by year and month, of the "most popular" films as determined by box office receipts, included no science fiction films in any of its tabulations of the top films between 1936 and 1940 (Wood 133–34).

Still, the general respect for the literary genre, as well as the tenor of the times, helped to argue for a number of significant efforts in the genre—films that suggest how that same "dream of distance" noted in other cinemas haunted British film as well. In the same mold as the literature about future warfare and apocalypse were such early films as *The Airship Destroyer* (aka *Battle in the Clouds*, 1909), *The Aerial Anarchists*, and *The Pirates of 1920* (both 1911). The one ambitious work in this vein, though, appears only much later, *High Treason* (1929, remade in 1952), a late-silent-era film directed by one of the top British filmmakers of the period, Maurice Elvey, and based on a play by Pemberton Billing. Along with a model of London that recalls *Metropolis*'s famous cityscape, *High Treason* offered a host of images that would become commonplace in science fiction of the period, such as a giant videoscreen, television phones, helitaxis, and a tunnel under the English Channel. But qualifying all of these images of future progress, speaking to that ongoing debate about the uncertain potential of technology, and thus testifying to the difficulty involved in constructing an acceptable view of the technological was the film's prescient depiction of a cataclysmic war in 1940. This war between two great confederations of nations culminates in a gas attack on New York and the destruction of that Channel tunnel. (This general scenario, we might note, recurs in an analogous American production, the aptly titled *Men Must Fight* [1933], which also projects into the year 1940 a great war pitting Western nations against the Confederation of Eurasian States, and depicts the destruction of one of the foremost emblems of Machine Age culture, the Empire State Building.)

In the later Machine Age this imagery of a monumental disaster and apocalypse not so much disappears as takes a backseat to technological possibility—although that possibility almost invariably shows its darker side as well. Appropriately, the narrative pattern that dominates in the key films of this period is that of a technological effort to bridge vast distances. *F.P. 1* (1933, better known under its German title, *F.P. 1 Antwortet Nicht*), as we noted in an earlier chapter, is a German-English-French co-production that details the creation of a massive floating platform in the middle of the Atlantic and its near destruction by a foreign power. That film's vision of regular air activity between Europe and the Americas rematerialized in the science fiction murder mystery, *Non-Stop New York* (1937), which visualized fast intercontinental air travel as a normal event. A far better known, if seldom seen film, *The Tunnel*, as we have noted, offered a different approach to the conquest of distance. It details a future international effort to tunnel under the Atlantic, thereby linking England and America in an effort to improve international relations and promote peace. The most famous science fiction film of the period, though, is certainly *Things to Come* (aka *The Shape of Things to Come*, 1936), based on H. G. Wells's book and written for the screen by Wells. It too looks toward a near-future war of cataclysmic proportions, describes the efforts of a group of elite engineers to come to the rescue of a war-ravaged humanity that is quickly slipping back into primitivism, and depicts the construction of a future world, one in which a humanity, finally free from want and from class struggle, begins to push into outer space. Its climactic image, of a human-occupied projectile being shot into space by the latest monumental project, a massive "space gun," reasserts a fascination with distance and our technological ability to conquer it, which consistently informs British science fiction of this period.

As this brief overview suggests, a kind of monumentalism, as I have termed it, a fascination with the outsized in both style and subject, inflects most British science fiction cinema of the period and intimates how that cinema sought to locate a kind of heroic proportion and agenda in — and, perhaps, to ascribe a kind of irresistible power to — the age's technological influences. With that sense of proportion, the cinema could emphasize, in the serious vein of British science fiction literature, the importance and the impact of technology on the culture, while with that agenda it might also locate these concerns in a narrative mode — such as the adventure tale — that audiences might more readily embrace.

And yet, as we have noted, relatively few films exploited these possibilities, a paucity with a variety of causes quite apart from the more general notion of public taste. In part it directly reflects the era's economics. For the British film industry, this period was, after all, largely that of the "quota quickie,"[3] the low-budget indigenous production designed to balance the dominance of American or other foreign cinematic imports. Films like *The Tunnel* and *Things to Come* simply required too large a share of the available cinematic resources — both financial and technical — to proliferate in number. This economic imperative helps explain why we find a number of films in this genre being made as cooperative ventures. *F.P. 1*, for example, could be made by adding the resources of the Gaumont British studio and the French branch of Fox to the German giant UFA. The result was that three versions of the film were shot, each with a cast of the appropriate nationals and in the language of the releasing country, but sharing the same sets and special effects processes[4] — and pointing, I suggest, to certain shared attitudes. Other European co-productions in this vein include *L'Atlantide* (aka *Lost Atlantis*, 1932, German, French, and English versions), an earlier *The Tunnel* (1933, German and French versions), and *Gold* (1934, German and French versions). Interestingly, upon their American release, these alternate national versions were often treated as quite different films. For instance, in the case of *F.P. 1* the *Variety* reviewer lauded the German version, calling it UFA's "greatest picture of this year," largely on the basis of its technical effects, and yet scored the English version, which arrived eight months later and boasted an American star, for its too "frequent recourse to machinery in motion,"[5] in effect, for its over-reliance on special effects and model work.

Marcia Landy has offered another and intriguing thesis to help account for the rather slight number of British science fiction films in the period.[6] Extrapolating from a sense of the era's rising social consciousness, she suggests that the genre had a difficult time conveying "social meaning" (389), particularly since that "element of rationality" endemic to all science fiction tended to stand "in the way of their developing a complicated treatment and critique of power" (391). In support of her contention, we should note that both *The Tunnel* and *Things to Come* do seem all too ready to evoke the specter of a monolithic power wielded by a select few and then have that dark potential simply evaporate in the light of the monumental accomplishments the films chronicle—accomplishments that derive largely from the great efforts of common people. However, Landy's charge might then apply equally to the literature of the genre, but as Stableford and others have shown, it does not. Perhaps more important, given film's technological basis,[7] was the lingering suspicion of technological reforms in England, which were not only seen as contributing to the slaughter of World War I, but which had also introduced labor practices, such as the assembly line, which labor unions viewed as threatening and as increasing unemployment in the Depression, and which they at times even violently resisted.[8] The very "monumentalism" to which British science fiction in this era gravitated, consequently, tended to evoke conflicted reactions. Certainly, in an era when the colonial empire was beginning to crumble, the massive projects envisioned in films like *F.P. 1*, *The Tunnel*, the docudrama *The Conquest of the Air* (1935), and *Things to Come* held out the prospect of other, technological potentials for cultural accomplishment and greatness—another sort of empire awaiting exploitation. At the same time, those monumental undertakings always seem qualified, careful to acknowledge the potential for disaster built into their efforts, and at least on some level self-conscious about the relationship between technology and class, if not that between technology and gender.

To illustrate this monumentalist approach to the technological and its at times contradictory implications, I want to focus on what are arguably the most famous British science fiction efforts of the Machine Age, *The Tunnel* and *Things to Come*. While both tend to be weak in their narrative development—long on dialogue and explanation, light on action—they are quite revealing about their culture's "distant" attitude vis-à-vis the technological.

In the first of these, the monumental effort to span the Atlantic by tunnel ends in a kind of cultural glory, with Britain leading the world to peace, but only at great individual cost; that cost underscores the level of technological anxiety with which these films all had to deal. In the second, technological devastation gives way to a complete technological transformation of world culture, although the restiveness that results, even in the midst of an apparent utopian society, produces yet another monumental effort, the creation of a "space gun" to shoot humans off into outer space — to escape the problems that still and may always plague us here on Earth.

II

There's a certain charm about a dreamer, even if he dreams of iron and steel. — *The Tunnel*

Despite Landy's assessment that British science fiction films of this period are "more didactic than dramatic" (391), there is a definite dream-like quality about them, much as we noted in the later German films of the era. While invariably warning about the potential for international conflict — and in that regard, looking back to the nightmare of World War I, as well as at the ominous political climate of the 1930s — they are more generally dreams of glory, of what might still be achieved through the country's technological prowess. Consequently, much like the protagonist of *The Tunnel*, the famous engineer McAllan, these films have "a certain charm," even as they propose, elaborately explain the difficulties involved in, and carry out the most monumental technological projects: spanning oceans and continents by air, tunneling under the Atlantic, rebuilding world civilization, launching humans into space.

Much of that charm derives from the manner in which they set about constructing the technological, as both films emphasize, alongside the monumental, the small human scale, thereby reaching for some humanization of the technological, and at least a human measure of its impact. In this regard, the opening scene of *The Tunnel* is exemplary. It begins with a long shot of an orchestra, offering an uninspiring version of a Beethoven overture. An elaborate tracking shot pulls back from that initial vantage to distance us from the performance, to emphasize that distance by framing our view of the orchestra with an elaborate, art deco archway that leads into another room, and then to anchor that framed image in the points of view of several, obviously bored onlookers: the powerful industrialist Mr. Lloyd and his daughter, various representatives of the oil, steel, aircraft, and armaments industries, the famous engineer McAllan, his wife, and others. With the conclusion of the music, a panel shuts the orchestra off from this audience, as Lloyd rises, announces that "I expect you're glad that's over," and then beckons the assembled industry representatives into a meeting to discuss his proposal to tunnel under the Atlantic. The key point here is not so much the visual distance with which the film begins—a distance that looks toward the larger project Lloyd then describes and the immense distances it concerns—but rather the way in which it uses that distance to help set off and measure individuality, as that elaborate track ends in a series of reaction shots that identify and characterize each of the major figures. Unpretentious, uninterested in supposedly "high art," these people, for all of their wealth, are generally simple and practical types, not bothered by class distinctions, only concerned with what the latest technology might accomplish and, more important, what profit it might bring them.

The most important of these figures is the key "dreamer," McAllan, who "dreams of iron and steel" and, we quickly learn, has already constructed a tunnel under the English Channel. He becomes the anchor for the larger narrative about spanning the Atlantic, as his personal problems interweave with those besetting the project, while his technological abilities represent the prowess on which Western culture—here, most pointedly England and America—can confidently rely. Although Mac (as he prefers to be known) works with and at the behest of the great industrialists, the film carefully establishes his simple, down-to-earth nature; he is the prototype of the engineer hero that Cecelia Tichi observes in a variety of the period's literature. McAllan calls himself "a sort of human mole," "just a mechanic," someone who is ill at ease in such social gatherings because he has always been "better at doing things than I am talking about them." He has no pretensions, no imposing personality; he is the common man, and the small human anchor for this monumental undertaking. Through Mac the film implies that even a simple man, given the appropriate technological resources, might accomplish the most formidable project.

Appropriately, then, the narrative focuses as much on the conflict between the technologist and his monumental project as it does on the task of building the tunnel itself. Even before the project gets underway, Mac's wife Ruth voices that concern we have previously cited: "It's so big. It won't be too big for us will it?" Following his reassurances, the rest of the film emphasizes the effects of this "big"-ness through his personal experience. A narrative ellipsis of three years introduces us to a project still far from finished,

32. The Tunnel: *Friends at odds over the imperatives of technology.*

a public that is losing interest in the task, difficulties in funding the project, and most important, strains on the family relationship. After coping with a problem in the tunnel, Mac surfaces to meet Ruth and his young son Geoffrey for an all-too-rare dinner together and a party for the boy's birthday. Even before he can give his son the present that his assistant Robbie has picked out for him, though, Mac is called away by a long-distance summons from Lloyd, who demands he immediately fly to New York to save the project from ruin. The videophone on which they speak, the gyroplane that then whisks Mac swiftly across the Atlantic and onto a rooftop heliport, the international television broadcasts and news media that show Mac with Lloyd's daughter as they try to gain publicity for and renew public interest in the project, the tunnel itself, and even the toy plane that is Mac's forgotten gift to his son—all devices dedicated to helping us overcome vast physical distances—become technological measures of the great personal distances that the project has produced, examples of what Romanyshyn describes as the almost inevitable consequence of the technological spirit, humanity's "broken connection with the world" (132). More particularly, they are measures of Mac's own failing marriage and his inability even to see how his single-minded effort is causing the family to disintegrate.

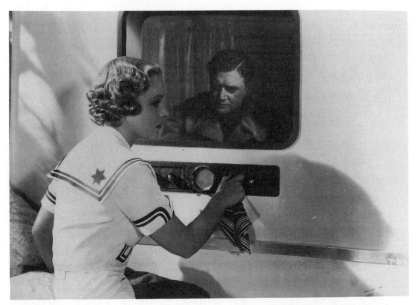

33. *Technology as a force of separation and alienation of husband and wife in* The Tunnel.

That sense of a "broken connection" then becomes the key motif for much of the film. As Mac tries to call his wife and explain his absences, she refuses to speak to him; at one point, Mac complains to the videophone operator that he must have a "bad connection." To protect against the total destruction of the project in case of an accident, Mac designs and tests massive steel doors that can shut off—or disconnect—parts of the tunnel. Gasses seeping into the construction produce what is called "tunnel disease," a permanent blindness that temporarily halts the project (even as it metaphorizes the blindness of Mac's own self-absorption). And Mac's family breaks up when his wife runs off with their son after she, too, in a final effort to join this monumental effort, goes to work in the tunnel only to contract the blinding disease. The monumental task, the film seems to imply in a way that suggests a gender bias built into the technological, is still not woman's work. After another narrative ellipsis, one we measure mainly by the advanced age of Geoffrey who reappears, now old enough to work on the tunnel, we witness a final "broken connection," an explosion and collapse that requires Mac to order the massive protective doors to be shut, even though it means leaving his son to die with the others trapped in the disaster. Much of *The Tunnel*, consequently, seems dedicated to demonstrating not that this monumental project is "too big" for the individual, but rather that in dedicating himself to such a massive technological effort, the individual can become like the project itself, cut off from the everyday world, from other humans, even from family and friends.

Yet in an effort to weigh these many broken connections against what might be gained, to ideologically redeem the technological here, *The Tunnel* reaches for a greater payback. We might recall that visions of apocalyptic warfare figure prominently in British science fiction literature, as well as in some of the era's films, especially in *Things to Come*. In its own way, *The Tunnel* too addresses these concerns, for it repeatedly suggests that the connections this project promises might ease international tensions and thus help avoid future wars. When Mac is asked if his work "must . . . take everything," all of his energy and concern, he answers without hesitation, "I believe my work will bring peace to the world." And indeed, the major subversive threat to the project's promise proves to be someone for whom peace is bad business—one of the original backers, the world's leading munitions maker, who wants to control the tunnel for his own ends. In contrast to this effort at co-opting the tunnel's power, the film offers us inspirational speeches by the British prime minister and the American president,[9] each of whom strikes the same note of international accord. In a television address, beamed around the world, the prime minister states that "the Atlantic tunnel will be greater than any treaty" in helping to ensure peace and "understanding" between people, while the president, in reply, strikes a similar, if more precise note, predicting that, with the tunnel's completion, "sums of money hitherto wasted on wages of soldiers and munitions of war will be diverted into useful and peaceful channels." The final images of mutual celebrations in New York and London upon the tunnel's completion, presided over by those same leaders, reaffirm this dream of a new era of peace and understanding among peoples, and emphasize the tunnel's status as a kind of monument to this new age.

Just as much to the point is the way in which the various threats to the tunnel simply disappear amid this harmonious conclusion. With the exception of Lloyd, who had conceived the tunnel project, the various industrialists who backed it in hopes of making vast profits drop out of the narrative with no explanation. The munitions maker's plot to secure control of the tunnel apparently never comes to fruition, thanks, we suppose, to Mac's determination. And public apathy, which had threatened to dry up support and funding for the project, gives way to worldwide celebration. Whatever questions of social power and control the narrative had raised with its very conception of such a massive, international technological project, dissolve in the cultural embrace with which the film concludes. A monumental effort has reached completion but, as a concluding montage of the proud faces of the principals in the construction asserts, it is essentially the achieved dream of these determined individuals: Lloyd and his daughter, Varia, Robbie, Mac and his wife, Ruth. Determined dreamers, it seems, can control even the mightiest technological efforts, and with the aid of that technology, the film implies, the individual can bridge any distance.

III

At its ultimate stage the pathology of utopia conceals under its traits of futurism the nostalgia for some paradise lost, if not a regressive yearning for the maternal womb.—P A U L   R I C O E U R (122)

Ricoeur's commentary on utopian projections reminds us that every effort to conceptualize the utopian or perfect society entails a kind of paradox. In our designs of what has not yet come into being, he says, we typically evoke that which we have already "lost"—or *believe* we have lost; as we move into the future, we recall, even "yearn" for the past as a kind of anchor, a point of stability from which we might cope with the distancing effects of rapid and dizzying change. It is a principle that seems quite close to the surface of the H. G. Wells–Alexander Korda collaboration *Things to Come*. For this most noted British science fiction film of the period seems torn between future and past, a newly designed world and a lost one, a monumental approach to visual design and a more intimate, human focus, much as in the fashion of *The Tunnel*. And in that very tension we can see the difficult task it faced in constructing the technological attitude that Wells might have envisioned.

Of course, *Things to Come* was from the start informed by an element of this tension implicit in the very partnership that brought it into being. For Wells and Korda brought rather different perspectives to the task. The former had established his reputation as a master of science fiction literature at the turn of the century, with such novels as *The Time Machine* (1895), *The Invisible Man* (1897), and *The War of the Worlds* (1898). Indeed, most of the works that would establish his reputation as the father of British science fiction appeared well before World War I, while in the postwar era his work became more polemical, aimed, as Brian Stableford offers, at telling his readers "how desperate their contemporary historical situation really was" (51), and thus emphasizing the need for a technologically driven social reform. Korda, in contrast, was a figure of another time and place, a filmmaker who had established himself in the postwar Hungarian cinema. Upon shifting his operations to England in 1930, he directed and produced a string of popular comedies, including *The Prince and the Plumber* (1930), *Marius* (1931), and *The Wedding Rehearsal* (1932), before turning to historical epics, such as *The Private Life of Henry VIII* (1933), *The Private Life of Don Juan* (1934), and *Catherine the Great* (1934). With this latter group of films, Korda fashioned a reputation for ambitious and high-quality works that helped him lure Wells into a collaboration on his most recent utopian novel, *The Shape of Things to Come*, assuring him that the film would be adequately financed to achieve Wells's vison of the future and that, as Christopher Frayling notes, he "would be guaranteed a say in all aspects of the property's translation to the screen" (20).

But *Things to Come* was more than just adequately done; it was the single most expensive British film to date, costing approximately three-hundred-thousand dollars (Frayling 16) and proved to be one of the more visually impressive films of its time. In fact, Frayling credits it with having a "significant" visual impact, one extending beyond the bounds of the science fiction community, as he notes that the film's "look . . . entered the bloodstream of contemporary visual culture through the work of countless graphic, fashion and product designers" (11). That influence, though, seems less unique to the film than testimony to the way it drew on—and drew together—some of the most forward-looking figures at work in the Machine Age, figures who were already trying to forge new links between everyday human life and the emerging machine culture. For example, Walter Gropius, late of the Bauhaus group, had "informally advised" Alexander Korda on the design of his elaborate Denham Studios. Another former member of the Bauhaus, László Moholy-Nagy, was brought in to design sets for *Things to Come*, although none of his work made it into the finished film. The final "look" of the film, though, seems essentially modeled on the popular and Bauhaus-influenced "moderne" style. While Wells's initial script treatment included his own "design suggestions," he also approached the French avant-garde artist and filmmaker Fernand Léger to provide "concept sketches and costume ideas" for the film's futuristic city and its inhabitants (Frayling 62). Another important influence on the look of the town of the future was the French architect and city planner Le Corbusier, whose work was well known to both Wells and Korda. His emphasis on the need to "recuperate" living space, especially that given over to "our sentimental needs" for open places and views of the sky (Le Corbusier 52), obviously echoes in the images of the film's burrowed Everytown of the future. Finally, the most famous of the American industrial designers, Norman Bel Geddes, contributed to the film's futuristic look through his "Air Liner #4" design that was adapted to the film's Basra Bombers, as Wells named them.[10] In much the way Bel Geddes might have hoped, the sudden appearance of these planes on the horizon heralds the coming of a new age, in this instance, one embodied in the irresistible power of the Wings Over the World organization. The resulting "Age of the Airmen," as the central character John Cabal terms it, is at least in conception far removed from the everyday world of 1930s England, although it distills the visions of many of the most important figures of the Machine Age art world.

The movie draws most heavily on the visual design I have termed the monumental, which seems to speak especially to the interests of its creators—Wells's in the great power of technology, Korda's in the elaborate cinematic spectacle—as it sets about constructing the technological attitude needed to move society into a new age. Of course, the film actually begins on a rather small scale, on the individual concerns of a small group of friends—John Cabal and his wife, their friends Passworthy, Harding, their children—all gathered together for an intimate Christmas Eve celebration. As the children unwrap and play with their presents, one adult appraises their many toys and, grasping a miniature cannon, wonders "if perhaps all these new toys aren't a bit too much for them." That remark recalls an earlier street montage in which a child admires the toys displayed in a store window, particularly the toy soldiers and guns, while all around the newspaper headlines forecast war. These early scenes not only place the miniature in ironic contrast to the monumental event of impending war, and thus child's play to adult folly; they also prepare us for the film's larger comment on current attitudes towards the technological. For as we watch Passworthy playing on the floor with the children and their toys—acting quite like another child—and listen to his laughing dismissal of the last war as "not as bad as some people make out," we recognize how the technologies of warfare, the planes, tanks, and cannons, become for many people little more than toys, devices that might well be "a bit too much for" us after all. The miniature, in effect, underscores a kind of cultural trivializing of the technological, a distance from its real power at which most people, even in the late Machine Age, seem to stand.

Thus the film sets about illustrating how technology, placed in the hands of childish adults, might have the most monumental consequences. It begins that turn in a style reminiscent of German expressionist films, by contrasting a shot of one of the children, playing soldier, against a background of giant shadows of marching soldiers. In a lengthy and powerful montage, punctuated by brief illustrative scenes, we see the massive destruction wrought by the life-size versions of these toys: formations of tanks charging across a wasteland, squadrons of planes dropping bombs and poison gas, ranks of cannons firing. It is, in effect, that distanced, detached vision brought up close, brought home to produce massive consequences — not only worldwide destruction but also, after twenty-four years of such warfare, the "wandering sickness," a variation on the bubonic plague that, a title card notes, kills off more than half of the human race. By the time the sickness runs its course, everything is in ruins, petty warlords rule, the machines of modern society have all stopped working; as one character sums up, "Civilization's dead." That result speaks not only to the enormous power of the machines humanity has created and then toyed with, but also to the need for an attitutude other than the childish detachment of Passworthy and his like who see technology, like war itself, as having little serious consequence, or of the Boss who now rules over Everytown, who views technology simply as a tool of conquest and domination.

This total breakdown further suggests the need for the sort of radical social agenda Wells had advocated: a new system of social engineering, overseen by a technical elite who understand the power and capacity of technology. Thus, coincident with the film's shift from the miniature to the monumental comes an enthronement of a technocracy suited to direct that technology, along with the assertion that, as *The Tunnel* argues, no technological project is "too big" for human control. In this narrative turn we can see Wells's belief in the saving powers of science and technology dovetailing with the era's many other efforts towards a technological utopia: the production efficiency of Henry Ford ("Fordism"), which had already made significant inroads into British manufacturing and especially the automotive industry, the principles of scientific management popularized by Frederick Winslow Taylor ("Taylorism"), Howard Scott's "Technocracy Crusade," and the social engineering championed by a variety of European intellectuals.[11]

The film heralds this development with the reappearance of John Cabal, who represents a new order, "all that are left of the old engineers and mechanics" who have "pledged ourselves to salvage the world." As part of what he calls "the brotherhood of efficiency, the freemasonry of science," Cabal extends the hand of technological aid in exchange for the renunciation of conflict, an offer that the Boss of Everytown rejects precisely because of the small, childish way in which he continues to see technology. In response to that rejection, Cabal's Wings Over the World organization offers a monumental display of power: squadrons of its massive Basra

34. *The monumental lesson of* Things to Come, *as Cabal points to the future.*

Bombers drop sleeping gas that knocks out the entire population of Everytown and hordes of black-clad paratroopers then descend, disarm, and subjugate the people. This sort of violent and even retrograde response in the name of peace echoes in Stableford's reminder that Wells in this period seemed to believe that war "might be a good thing if it could clear away the old social order and make way for the construction of a Socialist world state" (51). What Cabal terms "the rule of the airmen" thus begins with a new kind of conquest, not just the triumph of reason over a destructive insanity, but the powerful and massive display of technological might. While that "rule" marks the film's turn in a utopian direction, toward a construction of a truly technological society, it is one that, for late-1930s Europe, must have sounded a disturbingly dictatorial note, as Cabal outlines his "plan of operation" that begins with "a round-up of brigands" before proceeding to "settle, organize, advance" across the world. What he announces is the triumphal march of the technological spirit—no longer a petty activity, producing "toys" for mankind to play with, but a monumental effort at reshaping the world. Yet it is also problematic, for Cabal's description of "an active and aggressive peace" sounds rather like another sort of warfare. It is a note that Leon Stover emphasizes in his interpretation of the film, as he suggests that Cabal seems "no less intolerant than were the religious fanatics of the Moslem conquest" (69).

While that dictatorial stance is indeed troubling, it seems fundamentally bound up with a key substitution the film makes—in the best tradition of generic problem-solving—as it gradually substitutes cultural concerns about the march of technology for far more pressing anxieties about the threat of war. Moreover, the film tries to recuperate this disturbing dimension in a fashion reminiscent of *The Tunnel,* by dissolving our concerns in monumentalism, by offering us the seductive sweep of history and great technological transformation, measured out in grand gestures. Marking the transition, a voice-of-god commentator punctuates Cabal's explanation of "how I conceive our plan" with a seemingly awestruck and rhetorical question: "Do you realize the immense task we shall undertake?" The subsequent montage, illustrating the construction of a great metropolis, a new Everytown, the Utopia of 2036, underscores the monumental impulse driving this plan through its outsized images of great turbines, earth-moving machinery, and massive construction equipment—devices that dwarf people or, thanks to the long shots necessary to frame these elements, render them practically invisible. At the same time, these devices for building the future recall the earlier montage of war machinery to suggest the replacement of those destructive toys by great construction devices, along with the new and apparently inevitable rule of a constructive attitude, even if it serves an unyielding technocratic vision.

However, it is an attitude that, much as Ricoeur predicts for all utopian schemes, turns inward, as that massive machinery is set to work burrowing into the ground, returning to the "maternal womb," reshaping the earth itself. Thus *Things to Come* envisions the underground construction of entire cities, complete with their own setback sky(or earth)scrapers, vaulted walkways, and giant television screens for public gatherings. It is a shift from what one character terms "the age of windows" to one of artificial light and atmosphere, the disappearance of visual variety in favor of an unvarying whiteness and harmony of design that emphasize the massive, fabricated nature of this new world—a design scheme thoroughly in keeping with Wells's notion that the future envisioned here "must not seem contemporary" but rather be "constructed differently" (quoted in Frayling 50). That difference involves a movement forward that is also a retreat within, an embrace of a thoroughly technologized world which also seems a bit simpler and perhaps warier of humanity's misuse of the technological than in the past.[12]

In this shift we also witness the emergence of a new spirit stirring beneath the surface of this peaceful monumentalism. For the introductory

35. *The Great White World of* Things to Come: *The technological utopia.*

montage of the new Everytown's creation eliminates the sort of strenuous, muscular, physical activity that we see in a film like *The Tunnel* or earlier in this narrative, in favor of a fully mechanized operation, an example of the Machine Age's credo of order, efficiency, and speed pushed to an extreme. This montage begins with elaborate model work, with the massive burrowing machines in action. Here too the human disappears from view, as it does in a later montage of wheels, gears, and spinning cylinders—all shot in extreme close-up, like a Ralph Steiner photograph, to emphasize their great size and power. We see, as a final element in this monumental transformation, single humans supervising the great machines, watching from the foreground while massive gears and dynamos turn in the background. The cumulative effect is clear: in the creation of this new world the human practically vanishes or assumes a small supervisory role as machines set about accomplishing their great task of reconstruction.

The "subjective consequences" of this technological takeover, though, resurface in the film's final conflict, which centers directly on this crowding out, on the way in which the human again seems distanced from the world. The new conflict is between those who have become restive in and suspicious of this "great white world," as one character calls it, and all its technological accomplishments, and those who, like the new leader, Cabal's great-grandson Oswald, envision a future of perpetual human striving. While scientific progress has apparently made life easier, provided a cleaner environment and numerous conveniences, many feel that something has been lost. We recall the earlier Christmas scene in which a grandfather evaluates children's "new toys," when a young girl tells how this technologically ordered world seems to have made "life lovelier and lovelier," even as her great-grandfather cautions that it often "seems like it's going too far." In the same vein, the sculptor Theotocopolus, at work on a massive stone carving, suddenly stops his work and speaks out to a colleague against "all this progress" and what it has done to the quality of life, to human happiness. Of course, the film carefully calculates our reactions by depicting him as a thoroughly morose type, prideful, given to bombast, the artist who will always be at odds with the scientist. And in a European climate conditioned by the emergence of Hitler, the relish with which he seizes on the opportunity for rabble rousing shows him in an even more disturbing light, while helping to balance the earlier image of John Cabal as technocratic dictator. Still, he helps draw the thematic lines here quite starkly. Should he be a slave to this great monument, should people be slaves to their monumental world, a world driven by technology and the constant push for progress, or should he and the others resist, "make an end to this progress now," as he puts it?

Seeing *Things to Come* as typical of "the remoteness of British 1930s cinema from" its audience's concerns, Roy Armes scores the film for its "refusal to face up to the reality" of the time (123), for a kind of "regressive" attitude. Yet in this question—and Theotocopolus's media-assisted crusade against the "evil god" of "progress"—we can easily see this film confronting many of the realities of its day. For what Theotocopolus crystalizes is not just the question about human striving, about "progress" in its various forms and the multiple effects it brings, but also the issue of humanity's own seeming "smallness" when viewed from outside our individual desires, from the sweep of world change, from a distance. Indeed, too many of the people here seem *small-minded*, easily led by a Theotocopolus, a Boss—or a Hitler. Yet at the same time, it becomes obvious that technology itself can often play a role in fostering a certain "small" way of thinking through the monumental nature of its creations and the great power over human destiny it seems to exercise. Thus technology's very greatness, its *monumental impact*, might be seen as constructing a diminished role for and view of the human, leaving us all the more open to demagoguery. In response to this

36. *The revolt against a monumental technology: The people attack the space gun in* Things to Come.

possibility, *Things to Come* acknowledges both the small and the monumental, human and technological nature, and embraces them as inevitable elements of a tension that will mark the future—elements with which we shall continually have to struggle.

The way the film frames this response centers around another monumental creation of this new society, the "space gun" with which Everytown's leaders plan to begin human space exploration. Cabal argues that this undertaking is not simply a grandiose technological scheme, but part of the inevitable destiny of the race, and the gun is thus a monument to humanity itself. In opposition, Theotocopolus turns the massive gun into a towering symbol of technology's problematic role, as he urges the people, "Make this space gun an image of all that drives us and destroy it now." While his call for rebellion against progress fails to stop the gun's firing, the film acknowledges the power of this reactionary small-mindedness by reframing the argument in a final debate between Cabal and Passworthy's great-grandson, who in the same timid spirit as his ancestor, complains that humans "are such little creatures . . . so fragile, so weak," while Cabal argues for what such "little creatures" might accomplish, how even in their smallness, they might grasp for "all the universe." For him, and for the film, the issue of technology is ultimately one of recognizing and embracing the monumental capacity of the human spirit. In this move, in equating the outsize technology with our own great potential, the film suggests, as it concludes with a shot of the gun "shell" carrying two of those "fragile" creatures toward the moon, we might hope to bridge even the greatest of distances.

IV

While *Things to Come* was the most expensive British film of its time, enjoyed the personal attention of the father of science fiction, and unflinchingly espoused the technocratic philosophy that science and technology could save humanity, it did seem to regress in at least one part of its technological vision. That central image of a "space gun" on which the conclusion focuses drew some harsh commentary for the very *un*scientific conception of space travel it offered. A commentator in the *Journal of the British Interplanetary Society* expressed amazement that the film "actually suggests that the scientific world of 2036 will revert to the fantastic, nineteenth-century, Vernian idea of space travel . . . by means of a gun-fired projectile" (Johnson 41), and after calculating muzzle velocity, capsule acceleration, and the impossible forces that would crush the astronauts, admonished Wells and Korda to "play the game" properly (42) with an audience that was rather technologically literate.

Of course, Wells was a novelist first and foremost, and for a novelist an image or metaphor might well convey a truth far more important than any literal or factual representation. While scientifically unsound, this monumental image seems, in another way, most apt for the vision of technology that is being offered up. Noting a pattern of visual rhymes in the film, Christopher Frayling suggests that the gun serves to "balance the destructive technology of the opening air raid, with its smaller-scale anti-aircraft gun pointing toward the stars" (66). Seen in this light, the space gun seems an effective metaphor, suggesting a shift from a fearful humanity that for too long has turned its technology against itself, to an aspiring humanity, shifting that destructive technology to the service of knowledge and exploration, using it to reach outward, beyond our ken.

But a more telling narrative "rhyme" here is between this monumental gun and that earlier, miniature, toy cannon, which together frame the entire film. Taken together, they suggest a kind of growth, a maturation of the technological spirit, a development we should surely embrace. While the space gun, like those Bel Geddes–inspired Basra bombers, is so massive as to be frightening, it is also so large that it transcends any destructive connotations. Its power will send projectiles not arcing a few miles to fall destructively on other humans, but millions of miles into space in a measure of human aspiration. Of course, Cabal admits the shell's occupants might not survive, might not even return—they might become the prototypes of Baudrillard's postmodern astronauts. For the narrative, this symbol of our monumental technological growth is enough. But the distance to which those in the shell are consigned should sound a warning, much like Cabal's threat to bomb the people of Everytown with the "gas of peace" in order to protect the gun.[13] This distance is, finally, not so very different from the detached view that Passworthy, toying with his miniature canon, offered about World War I or that Cabal takes to his fellow citizens. Though they evoke the very spirit of the Machine Age, at least as Wells might have viewed it, that massive gun and its monumental effort also, if unwittingly, speak of an anxiety bound up in this spirit, in our seemingly inevitable embrace of a technological age.

That image also seems particularly telling for British Machine Age culture as we have seen it reflected in these films. For that culture the technological clearly held out the potential for great accomplishment, for matching the Americans with their monumental technological projects, such as the Hoover Dam and the Empire State Building, for achieving another sort of cultural greatness at a time when the British colonial empire was beginning to come apart. The space gun, with its capacity for bridging those great distances to the moon and the stars, only slightly exaggerated the impulse already bound up in the notion of a transatlantic tunnel and the various efforts at intercontinental flight we have seen envisioned in these films. At the same time, as suggested above, that gun is not simply a massive sword turned into a scientific plowshare. It remains a gun, freighted with all the destructive potential and fears—as well as the distancing potential—attached to such devices. Those concerns surge to the foreground with the calamitous conflicts envisioned in films like *High Treason* and *Things to Come*, but they never stand at that far a remove in any of the films mentioned here, as evidenced by the many references to foreign powers, saboteurs, munitions makers, and an unstable world situation. Thanks to a tense international situation and changing social conditions at home, technology had become linked to a general unease, even a fear, in the face of the many other changes it accompanied.

The British science fiction film, consequently, became a rather problematic site for the construction of technology in this era. I would suggest that it was never quite, as Marcia Landy argues, an "unthreatening" form (391). If it had been, we might well have seen, despite the economic considerations, far more examples of the genre, since it spoke to and of contemporary cultural concerns, particularly of political instability and ongoing class conflict. It thus might have provided, in the best generic tradition, a vehicle for imaginatively addressing and resolving those issues. Instead, British Machine Age science fiction became a site where a variety of those concerns all constellated, where they found a rather uneasy expression, and where the embrace of a new, technologically driven world, even one offered under a "monumental" imprimatur, was always tentative. For all of their elevation of the technological, these narratives retain an aura of "distance" linked to the technological, a wariness of its promises and supposed potentials that is a fundamental critique of real power. Perhaps the issues at hand were, in the end, just too "monumental" to find easy or convincing formulation.

7

"I Have Seen the Future"

The New York World's Fair as Science Fiction

I

All visitors exiting from the General Motors Futurama exhibit at the 1939 New York World's Fair received pins proclaiming, "I have seen the future." To provide that vision, Futurama, what Roland Marchand terms "the unrivaled 'smash hit' among corporate displays" at the fair (II, 103), put six-hundred viewers into easy chairs (approximately twenty-eight thousand per day), mounted on a conveyor belt, running above a thirty-five-thousand-square-foot model of a metropolis of 1960. Here in air-conditioned comfort, while a dramatic voice-over and orchestral accompaniment played in their individually sound-equipped chairs, visitors could glimpse a corporate conception of "the many wonders that may develop in the not-too-distant future" (*Futurama*), all modeled in great detail by the most famous industrial designer of the era, Norman Bel Geddes. Yet more than simply *seeing* the future, visitors, upon arising from their mobile seats, also had the opportunity to enter the world of 1960. For Futurama culminated in a life-size intersection of a city of tomorrow, complete with advanced-model autos (and an auto showroom), an apartment house, a theater, and a department store in which visitors could buy souvenirs—virtual proof of their time travel. If the first part of Futurama resembled a kind of 3-D cinematic experience, this final element must have left visitors feeling as if they had actually entered into a science fiction movie, stepped into an essentially cinematic vision of the future. Like the Universal Studios tour, as well as other theme parks of today, it was a kind of movie world virtually constructed for the fairgoers.

That effect, of course, was hardly accidental. The designer Walter Dorwin Teague, a member of the fair's official design board, announced that this exposition intended to offer exhibits that would "make the best of Hollywood respectful" (Marchand I, 100). And indeed, the seven-million-dollar cost of Futurama far exceeded the average cost of a major Hollywood production of the time, which was typically under four-hundred thousand dollars. But the New York World's Fair was unlike any previous exposition not just because of the great sums spent on its corporate exhibits, its emphasis on spectacle, or its seemingly single-minded focus on our technological entry into the future. Rather, with the talents of the former theatrical designer Bel Geddes, the work of Teague's firm, which, in his own words, specialized in "visual dramatization" (Marchand I, 97), various attempts to "stage" life in the future,[1] and over five-hundred different films which were prepared for this event, the fair was from the start stamped with a kind of cinematic character and inflected with a science fictional atmosphere. In sum, it seems to have been conceived more like a science fiction film of the period than any traditional exposition, and a film with a pointedly international flavor.

I emphasize this characterization because I want to look at the New York World's Fair in the same context as we have previously examined the era's various science fiction films: as a record of the cinematic construction of the technological—and a technological attitude—in the Machine Age. Its appearance at the end of the decade, along with its promise of a soon-to-arrive technological utopia,[2] allows us to see it as a summary of many Machine Age concerns; and its status as a World's Fair, a representation of many national conceptions of the technological, neatly dovetails with our cross-cultural exploration. But the fair's emphatically cinematic nature should also draw our attention: its emphasis on filmic accompaniment, its concern with amusement, and the sense of distance with which it too seems to have struggled make it all the more appropriate an end point for this study. Thus, I want to close this discussion with a look at the fair as science fiction movie, first, by offering an overview of its technological strategies, and, second, by turning to a compendium of its various cinematic artifacts that have been gathered together in a filmic time capsule, the contemporary documentary by Lance Bird and Tom Johnson, *The World of Tomorrow* (1984). Of course, in this turn, in looking almost simultaneously at a cultural artifact and a film about that artifact, I risk conflating the two or trying to reconcile two rather different vantages. However, this double focus might help us better see a shifting view of the technological that the fair put forward, and a developing potential in the films that explore the technological, a potential for what Romanyshyn has termed "return and re-entry" (199) from that distance bound up in our depictions of the technological. It also might help emphasize the extent to which the Machine Age developments we have been chronicling have continued to inflect the contemporary world and its films.

II

Movies about the future tend to be about the future of movies. Science/fiction/film: this is no more the triadic phase for a movie genre than three subjects looking on at their own various conjunctions.

—GARRETT STEWART (159)

Almost exactly midway in its account of the New York World's Fair, the documentary *The World of Tomorrow* interrupts its tour of the many wonders displayed there to offer what seems like a child's confession. Its narrator, recalling the boyhood experience of attending the fair, notes that for all its technological marvels and amazing glimpses of what the future would be like, "the true secret goal of every visit" was the amusement park—the contemporary playground and midway that was attached to this "Eighth Wonder of the World," as the fair had been described. Yet more than just confessing a "guilty pleasure," a childish delight in something other than the edifying, this remark points up a "secret goal" that, this film implies, underlay much of the fair's scientific and futuristic wonders. It hints of a key link that was to be found there between amusement and technology, and more broadly of the way in which, in other contexts throughout our culture, an almost visceral pleasure was being used to sell the comparatively cold, abstract, and at times even unappealing accomplishments of the technological.

Of course, the science fiction film, in the Machine Age and after, is no stranger to this cultural attitude. As we have seen, even as it critiques the excesses of the technological consciousness, warns against a kind of "machining" of the human, a work like *Metropolis* (1926) practically mesmerizes with its images of a futuristic society. In fact, the negative implications of those images of advanced technology largely drain away in such films as *Just Imagine* (1930), *Things to Come* (1936), and the various serial developments of the genre that appeared throughout the 1930s. In the post–World War II era, much as we have seen in the post–World War I period, there is a recoil from the technological, due to wartime experiences and our justifiable fears of what mass destruction our technology, especially the new atomic developments, could bring. Yet balancing that recoil is a cultural fascination with space flight, exploration, and the possibility of encountering alien cultures, as envisioned in such films as *Destination Moon* (1950), *This Island Earth* (1955), *Forbidden Planet* (1956), and, most notably, *2001: A Space Odyssey* (1968). Of course, the *Star Wars* saga (1977, 1980, 1983) managed to further recuperate the technological by making it the necessary context for heroic adventure and its nostalgic, Machine Age trappings—blasters, light sabers, rocket sleds, faithful robots—essential to those adventures' success. But in more recent times we have begun to see another shift, as the technological has found a more intimate arena, has encroached more on our sense of self. In the many films that have followed the path of *Blade Runner* (1982) in exploring the issue of human artifice—focusing on robots, androids, cyborgs, and so on—a more skeptical, even a kind of reflexive attitude surfaces, as works like *Hardware* (1990), *Total Recall* (1990), and *Independence Day* (1996) suggest. What these works present is a kind of double vision, as they, like their generic predecessors, exploit the attractions of the technological—find in it the stuff of amusement—while they also, through a textual reflexivity, interrogate both its effects on us and its very presentation in the media. In so doing they demonstrate how the science fiction genre has often let us indulge our fascinations, while also helping us explore and assess these images that hold such power over us.

But my aim here is not to bring us all the way to the present, only to focus on a way our past has paved the way for this vantage—in effect, a way the modern has always anticipated the postmodern. By bringing into simultaneous focus the New York World's Fair and *The World of Tomorrow*, a documentary named after the fair's initial theme, we can find a revealing gloss on our cultural tendency to sell the pleasures of technology while deferring questions about its nature, to construct an image of the technological that might somehow avoid self-reflection, to bring the technological home yet also hold it at a safe psychological distance. We can also benefit by examining some cultural texts that stand outside of the science fiction tradition on which we have been focusing. For seen from a distance, the fair reveals a cultural agenda or "goal" for the proper consumption of the technological at the close of the Machine Age: a tendency to place in a proper ideological context the possibilities of an other or better world—or self—that might be realized through technology, and even to keep those possibilities *amusing*. At the same time, as its title suggests, *The World of Tomorrow* offers us a kind of science fiction vantage, akin to any of the works we have previously discussed, on this agenda. At least it is a work that well understands the lure of the technological, which such films—and fairs—

usually exploit. It thus both measures well the cultural link between pleasure and technology on which these films draw and offers insight into their uses of this link to pursue their own "true secret," to try to fashion a pleasing cultural construction of the technological.

Certainly, as a record of the fair, *The World of Tomorrow* evokes a number of the semantic conventions we usually associate with science fiction films, and especially those Machine Age texts we have been examining: it offered a robot, futuristic vehicles and architecture, new inventions, a scientist or two (we briefly see Einstein who, the narrator notes, came to the fair "to do something scientific, I forget exactly what"). It also illustrates some of the syntactic elements or plot movements found throughout the genre: the marshaling of great technological forces to transform the earth (the creation of the fair out of an ash dump), efforts by the scientifically informed to convince the skeptical of technology's benefits, and demonstrations of the "better life" that scientific advances will bring. Moreover, both the fair and this film account center on one of the abiding themes of science fiction, the utopian effort to design a different and better world, an effort we have glimpsed in such works as *Just Imagine* and *Things to Come*.

And yet, for all of these elements, it remains a fact film, not traditional science fiction, nostalgically focusing on our cultural past, the closing of the Machine Age in 1939–1940, not the near future trumpeted by the fair. In many ways, it recalls some of our most famous ethnographic films. But it is ethnography with a curious twist, intent not simply on objectively recording an event, but on casting its subject in both a *new* and *authentic* light. We might think of this documentary as supplementing the fair, letting us see not quite what it lacked, but rather what it, like many of this period's science fiction films, was essentially "up to." As the Futurama exhibit suggests, the "movie" that was the fair was intent on "selling" a certain pleasurable experience of science and technology, those elements of modern life that had already begun to define — with more than a bit of corporate and industrial nudging — our future.

The sort of self-consciousness I am attributing to this film, though, represents something more than the typical playfulness of a postmodern text. For all its quotations from the past, its overt display of structure, and its collage approach, *The World of Tomorrow* aims not so much at an ironic evocation of the past or of cultural history, and it seeks no escape or freedom from it or from history itself, as we might associate with someone like Baudrillard, whom I have evoked a number of times already. It is thus never as amused about its subject matter as is a somewhat similar work, *The Atomic Cafe* (1982) with its ironic attitude towards 1950s atomic consciousness and paranoia. Its narrator is no *bricoleur* passing through and snapping up souvenirs of the past for our amused consideration. Rather, the work, like this book, seems intent on reclaiming something of the past, on tracing out a manner of thinking and presentation that still echoes in our present modes of thought about the technological, and in the process reminding us of some of the themes we have teased out of the science fiction films it generically recalls.

In its self-consciousness it echoes a pattern Garrett Stewart sees in many more recent science fiction films and that we have at least glimpsed in several of those treated here. He suggests that the form always carries a potential for demonstrating its *movieness*: for reminding us of film's technological base whenever our films look at technology, and for throwing us back into the present as we glimpse images of a possible future. It is a pattern we have briefly noted in such films as *Die Frau im Mond* (1929) and *The Invisible Ray* (1936), and one that can help us understand the twist in *The World of Tomorrow*'s ethnography. In the best science fiction tradition, both this film and the Fair it chronicles play with "various conjunctions" of film, science, and fiction to evoke that potential. It thereby reveals what I have here termed a distant, detached—even *cinematic*—way Western culture in general, but American culture especially often looks at the technological: a removed, half-serious, and ultimately amused way we have often taken to contemplating these things in our culture. At the same time and in its curiously double way—looking at our past and looking at the present through the past—the film manages an equally double product. While revealing a "secret goal" of amusement in the fair, it also points up the "true secret" of many other science fiction films, a desire to find a better, human measure for the technological.

III

Umberto Eco in his "Theory of Expositions" has tried to account for the peculiar nature and allure of World's Fairs. In Expo '67, the 1967 Montreal World's Fair, he notes a significant shift in approach. Once, he suggests, fairs emphasized displaying things in the context of their cultural history; they inventoried amazing objects and the products of culture in order to trumpet society's accomplishments. But, he says, a rather different impulse seems to propel the modern exposition, one which "does not display goods, or if it does, it uses the goods as a means, as a pretext to present something else. And this something else is the exposition itself" (296). In effect, Eco sees recent expositions as reflexive texts, which talk to their audience about themselves in a way that follows from a new "ideology" of the exposition: the sense that "the packaging is more important than the product, meaning that the building and the objects in it should communicate the value of a culture, the image of a civilization" (299). He thus sees the "new" fair as an offshoot of "show business," offering audiences entertaining and ideologically correct images of cultures that put themselves on display in this way—much like a movie, in the business of selling viewers a predetermined, preapproved view of their culture and of technology's place in it.

Yet as we shall see, both through the fair's history and its representation in *The World of Tomorrow*, this cultural project was already well underway by the time of the 1939 World Fair. The late Machine Age, in fact, saw an explosion of regional, national, and world fairs in which a new approach to exhibiting the latest advances was gradually being developed. Between the 1933 Chicago Century of Progress Exposition and the opening of the New York World's Fair, major expositions were held in San Diego (1935), Dallas (1936), Cleveland (1936), Paris (1937), Miami (1937), and San Francisco (1939). Over the course of this decade of fairs, as Roland Marchand notes, corporate exhibitors not only spent increasing sums of money to promote their technological advances, but they also "began to merge their factory-oriented 'educational' efforts with elements of pure entertainment" (II, 105). Thus figures like Bel Geddes and Teague became ever more important to these events. In fact, Teague's design firm undertook a study of visitor reactions to the exhibits at the Chicago Century of Progress Exposition, and determined that subsequent presentations would have to increase emphasis on "animation and some form of visitor participation" (I, 98). Drawing on this background, his group, throughout discussions for the New York World's Fair, "liberally employed" the expression "hit shows" as a guideline in their planning. Thus, for the Ford exhibit they designed a massive, animated cyclorama, accompanied by a Technicolor film, *Melody in F*, in which the various figures seen in the cyclorama would come to life (Marchand I, 90). In keeping with this attitude, General Motors' Futurama guidebook would proudly proclaim that its display "for sheer entertainment . . . rivals anything on the midway" (*Futurama*).[3]

The larger design of the fair echoed this pursuit of entertainment. Of course, the Amusement Area, with its rides, "girlie shows," and Billy Rose's Aquacade—complete with its movie star headliners (first Johnny Weissmuller, then Buster Crabbe)—immediately strikes this note. But the fair was also a place where celebrities, stars of the movies and of popular culture, appeared frequently in carefully staged events, orchestrated by fair president Grover Whalen for maximum publicity. While not quite a Technicolor production, the fair was color-coded, all of its buildings supposedly conforming to an overall design scheme of complementary colors. And the fair consistently represented itself as a kind of epic production, featuring a cast of thousands, and constantly credited the size of its offerings—its own sort of "monumentalism." The architect who headed the Theme Committee, Robert Kohn, specialized, as David Gelernter offers, in "bigness" (25). Thus the fair announced that it had the longest escalator in the world, the largest sundial ever built, the biggest diorama, and when it staged the massive musical show *American Jubilee*, it did so on "the largest revolving stage ever constructed" (Gelernter 353). The fair simply aimed to be, as *Time* magazine would call it, the "greatest show of all time" ("Curtains" 72).

This point is driven home by *The World of Tomorrow*, which repeatedly links this show business, amusement park element to the fair's technological presentations. Set up like a home movie, as a young boy's view of the fair, the film frames this fictional vantage with its own highly self-conscious view, with a kind of meta-cinematic attitude. Consequently, even as it sets about describing the design and construction of the fairgrounds, surveying the various wonders of today and tomorrow displayed there, and recounting its history, even as it treats the fair like some curious artifact of prewar America, the film also lets us see how much the fair and all its technological wonders were but further extensions of show business, as if the fair were a movie in itself, what I would suggest we think of as the prototypic science fiction film of its day.

While lacking many of the images Stewart, in his discussion of the science fiction genre, terms "videology," *The World of Tomorrow* repeatedly calls to mind "the mechanics of apparition" (161) that were at work at the fair. It unreels entirely through the imagery afforded by films of the fair's era, and thus often seems to be *about* those films. Of course, this effect follows partly from its status as a "compilation film," a work assembled from various bits of "found footage": newsreels, period documentaries, instructional and publicity films, cartoons, and home movies. All of this footage produces an intriguing record of the fair and its era, especially since much of the material is in the dazzling and, for the 1930s, still relatively fresh Technicolor process. Indeed, the very wealth and quality of material that remains of the New York World's Fair create an impression that more attention was paid to creating a visual record of it than of any prior fair. It seems the product of a society nearly as fascinated with the cinematic chronicling of its events and accomplishments as with the events and accomplishments themselves.

But perhaps more to the point is the fact that much of this footage was produced as a kind of self-promotion. In the years leading up to the fair's opening, Grover Whalen often staged and widely disseminated scenes of the planning and development of the various exhibits in order to create a public awareness of and an eagerness for its start. In fact, one piece of footage turned up by filmmakers Bird and Johnson shows Whalen and a few of his aides before the newsreel cameras, doing several versions of a "spontaneous" reaction to one of the many fair-publicizing stunts. In a telling choice of metaphors, the narrator notes that the "working model of tomorrow" they were planning was obviously "always ready for a second take." The fact that many of these "takes" are presented complete with the production companies' credits—Universal, Paramount, Movietone, and so on—attributes a further level of promotion and self-awareness to all of these images.

Besides such publicity material, though, as we have noted, during the fair's two-year run more than five-hundred different films were screened there,[4] including travelogues, instructional and advertising films, and documentaries. So numerous were the fact-based works shown at the fair that one historian has described the exhibition as a veritable "documentary showcase" (Barnouw 122). Among these many works, RCA offered its *The Birth of an Industry*, which described its efforts to develop a new medium of communication, which debuted at the fair: television. Teague's *Rhapsody in Steel*, another short made for the Ford exhibit that his firm designed, depicted pixilated engine parts coming together to produce a powerful engine. Similarly, Chrysler's advertising film, *In Tune with Tomorrow*, was done in the new 3-D process and showed a Plymouth sedan magically assembling itself—technology working its miracles without any human intervention. Such films begin to suggest how a cinematic context was fashioned for the marvels of science and technology displayed at the fair.

Probably the most famous work screened at the fair, and the one Bird and Johnson draw on most heavily for the first third of their film, was a more conventional documentary sponsored by the American Institute of City Planners, Ralph Steiner and Willard Van Dyke's *The City*. A film about the emerging urban crisis, it attests to the tremendous fascination in this period with redesigning the city around the latest technological developments, visions that often culminated in a kind of "Titan City" model, typified by the images in *Metropolis*, *Just Imagine*, and *Things to Come*, and envisioned in the designs of architects like George Howe, Hugh Ferriss, and Francisco Mujica.[5] But while *The City* begins from the same premise adopted by most of these architects and planners, from the argument that

America's population centers were rapidly turning into urban wastelands nearly unfit for human habitation, it envisions a hopeful alternative, based on large-scale, up-to-date urban planning. It offers the model of Greenbelt, Maryland, a planned community designed to exploit rather than be victimized by the many potentials of modern technology that the fair championed; it represents, as Carol Willis suggests, a vision of urban order as "democratic, liberating, harmonious, and hygienic" (184).

From this vantage, we might think of *The City* as representing one view of the fair itself, whose original theme was "Building the World of Tomorrow." Certainly, the contemporary critic Archer Winsten thought so, as he noted that even "if there were nothing else worth seeing at the fair, this picture would justify the trip" (126). After all, *The City* offered a kind of utopian vision of "tomorrow," or at least of what tomorrow might look like for those who could afford to move away from the present-day urban wastelands where most of the factories and jobs were then located. It presented a grand vision of urban planning, or as Howard Segal puts it, a "technological utopia" (133), achieved by glossing over many practical problems—including problems due to the period's technology—that were already making our urban communities undesirable. Yet Winsten's final sober assessment, that for all its fine ideas, *The City* still has "the dreamy aspect of wishful thinking" (128), points up the distance that remained between this documentary and the real world, between the technology for living and its actual application to our lives—and by extension, between the fair and the future it envisioned as already so close at hand.

Yet what makes the footage from *The City* particularly effective in the context of *The World of Tomorrow* is that, like much of the other footage used here, including the advertising films noted above, it reflects so directly on the fair itself. For the fair had from the start presented itself as a model of such urban reclamation and redesign, of ways in which the latest principles of scientific planning and the newest technology might reshape our lives. And that same note was sounded in various exhibits. The Futurama narration, for example, emphasized the "abundant sunshine, fresh air, fine green parkways, recreational and civic centers" that would result from "thoughtful planning and design" (*Futurama*). Sounding a note that recalls the attractions of science fiction, *The World of Tomorrow* offers a clip from a Universal newsreel about the fair which trumpets how, in "the single greatest engineering feat of the century," a "huge ash dump in Flushing" was transformed into a model city that looked "like no place on Earth." In effect, the fair offered itself precisely as one of those model cities of tomorrow, a realization, on a limited scale, of the ideal described in both Futurama and *The*

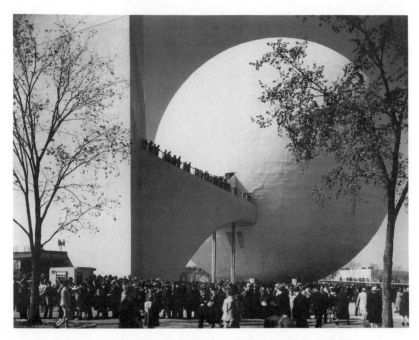

37. *Crowds waiting to view the "Democracity" diorama displayed in the fair's Perisphere.*

City: laid out logically, populated by a democratic mix of nationalities, not only displaying but also *using* the latest scientific advances, and, as a result, free of the waste and ugliness fast becoming typical of modern urban life. And as if to reinforce this impression, it offered as its key exhibit, housed in the central Perisphere structure, another self-image akin to that found in Futurama. Democracity, a diorama of a utopian American city of the year 2039, fashioned by another famous industrial designer, Henry Dreyfuss, let viewers see in a five-and-a-half-minute program—in effect, another miniature science fiction narrative—what a single day would be like in such a futuristic, technologically shaped metropolis. Through these multiple reflections—or what *The World of Tomorrow*'s narrator terms a mix of "razzmatazz and social planning"—the fair implied that such a world "is possible today." And yet, as with *The City*, we also sense a "dreamy" or "wishful" aura in those claims, a great distance between those claims and reality.

That effect results precisely because, as I have suggested, the fair as seen in *The World of Tomorrow* unreels like a series of movies, a collection of the sort of dreamy or wistful images we typically associate with that great "dream factory," Hollywood. In keeping with this pattern, the film notes an interesting historical coincidence, the proximity of the fair's opening to that of a more familiar fantasy narrative, *The Wizard of Oz*. Thus the black and white images we expect to find in a documentary about 1939—as the narrator intones, "the past is black and white"—will suddenly shift to color footage in a way that quotes the similar shift when Dorothy enters Oz. But more than just a brief homage to that film, this shift is repeated and underscored: pointed out to us over and over by the narrator's remarks about the fair being "My own Emerald City of Wisdom and Illusion at the end of a Yellow Brick Road," his "feeling we're not in Kansas anymore," the soundtrack's recurring and even mournful strains of "Somewhere Over the Rainbow" (a fact the film fails to note is that the key road within the fair, one everyone had to cross over as they moved down the central mall, was Rainbow Avenue), footage of, among the many celebrities who came to the fair, Judy Garland, and munchkin-evoking shots of a midway midget show. In all these details the film is more than simply using a most apt trope to suggest the colorful and exciting nature of the fair, even its fantastic, otherworldly (out-of-Kansas) character. Rather, the film is also reminding us of the fair's cinematic spirit, as well as the amusing, even fantastic character of much of the science and technology it put on display—a character that ensured these elements would remain at some distance from the real world in which they were supposed to function.

As we have noted, the film includes many other cinematic resonances. Besides the references to *The Wizard of Oz*, *The World of Tomorrow* takes much of its color footage from a publicity film that was part of the Westinghouse Corporation's exhibit. This film describes the experiences of a typical American family, the Middletons—a father, mother, young son (Bud), and older daughter (Babs)—who come from Indiana to visit grandmother and see the fair and learn all about the "wonders" of "tomorrow"—"those wonders . . . we called science." It recalls, in many ways, MGM's popular Andy Hardy series, with its solidly middle-class family composition and its general homilistic nature. And *The World of Tomorrow* underscores that comparison by intercutting with this footage several scenes that show series star Mickey Rooney and his costar in several of the Hardy films, Judy Garland.

The thrust of the Westinghouse film was clearly two-fold. On the one hand, it offered characters who would stand in for moviegoers as they viewed and marveled at the displays of technological achievement in the Westinghouse exhibit. Through them we could have our own guided tour of such wonders as "Electro, the Westinghouse Motoman"—a robot all too similar to those found in popular serials like *The Phantom Empire* (1935), *Undersea Kingdom* (1936), and *The Phantom Creeps* (1939); the kitchen of the future,

38. Envisioning an "electric" future: The Electrical Products, Westinghouse, and General Electric pavilions at the 1939 World's Fair.

complete with such labor-saving devices as an electric dishwasher; and even a television camera and monitor/receiver. In this regard, it worked as a kind of "Preview of Coming Attractions" for those considering attending the fair.

But on the other hand, through the careful subject-positioning of its viewers in this "typical" family, it sought to convey "naturally" what the narrator terms the fair's "lessons" in the proper understanding and consumption of technology. Particularly, through Bud (the Andy Hardy surrogate), who feels that, with the onset of the Depression, his society holds little hope for the future since its best "opportunities" are all gone, we learn about the many jobs and potentials that science and technology were already opening up for eager minds and willing bodies. Through Babs, her mother, and grandmother, we glimpse the changes technological development was working in the lot of women—a lot, we should note, that still placed them solidly within the home and a thoroughly modern kitchen. And through the family's encounter with an old neighbor, Jim Treadway, now a guide at the Westinghouse exhibit, we glimpse the utopian future that scientific "facts" and industrial effort were making imminent.

If today we stand at a comfortable, even ironic distance from this fictional family—much as we do from the Hardys—easily resisting such subject-positioning and finding the characters' ready acceptance of this technocratic propaganda and sexual stereotyping a bit hard to take,[6] *The World of Tomorrow*'s narrator, like, we would suppose, the typical visitor to the fair, seems to face a more difficult proposition, as another reflexive turn makes clear. Various verbal clues and some home movie images identify the narrator as a boy in his early teens at the time of the fair; he was, we assume, about the same age as the fictive Bud, a nascent Andy Hardy. So Bud's pattern of experiences—first, skeptical of this new world's promise, then awed by all it has to offer, and finally won over to its possibilities—reflects on the narrator's own situation. Yet the narrator backs away from the comparison, reaching for some distance from Bud and, we gather, from Bud's fictive response. As the narrator notes, these characters, "being fictions," could "grasp the lessons of the fair more easily than I did." It is a point that suggests the "lessons" of technology were far from clear, their construction hardly a simple text.

Appropriately enough, as the source of our point of view here, the narrator seems troubled by this discrepancy, by the fact that, in the face of so much that was new and daunting, he never felt like such "a smart fellow," as Electro the Motoman describes himself. So the broader tour of the fair that follows, an alternate version of the Middletons' carefully staged, corporate version of the "edifying experience," explores what lay behind these flashy images of modern science and technology. Thus, the film juxtaposes the wonders of the Westinghouse film and pavilion with that "secret goal," here linked to the famous Amusement Area, which is presented not simply as another sort of attraction, but as the real logic behind these alluring images—an experience of illusion and entertainment, the ultimate movie. In a telling sound bridge, the *Oz* theme again swells on the soundtrack, as we see various circus sideshow attractions: midgets, a fat woman, a fake mermaid (probably from Salvador Dali's "Dream of Venus" show, and thus a hint of the extent to which the avant-garde too had compromised with amusement), and semi-nude models, who, the narrator notes matter-of-factly, "weren't science and they weren't art; they were just there"—all part of the largest amusement park outside of Coney Island.

Of course, the nudes, quickly following on the Westinghouse film's images of and rhetoric about the "new woman" of modern society, point up just how far removed this world is from an "imminent" utopia, at least for women, how little the technological seemed to offer them. For all of the fair's surface appeals and publicity, we remain "there," in the present, in a world ruled by the same old human lures, bound by conventional gender roles—much as we see in the Earth scenes of *Just Imagine*—far distant

39. *The Entertainment Zone—the real attraction of the New York World's Fair?*

from that utopian "tomorrow." With much of the edifying pretense, much of what Eco terms "the packaging"—like the models' clothes—stripped away, the Amusement Area seems at least as revealing as the scientific and technological exhibits that were the fair's supposed raison d'être. In fact, for the adolescent male narrator, the human "secrets" of this area seem more immediately compelling. Armed with this hindsight, he offers a crucial recognition: that the fair was "only superficially" concerned with science and technology; "in the end, it was illusion."

Certainly the fair was illusion, much like the movies themselves, promising, as Hollywood so often did, a perfect life on the near horizon. And like most Hollywood films, it sought to disguise its generally imaginary quality and its attempt to entertain, as well as a kind of ideological indoctrination, behind its technological fantasies. It is only fitting, then, that this recognition of how deceptive the appearances of a utopian future were and how ill they squared with reality introduces a sequence of decidedly realistic texture, albeit one *about* appearances. The sequence is from a Paramount newsreel focusing on a rather different sort of technology, Army Air Corps planes on maneuvers, laying down a smoke screen around Manhattan. The scene reminds us of the fair's broader context, of those world events that, in its pretense at neutrality and isolation, America had been keeping at a distance but that were already conspiring to bring the fair to a close: the looming reality of a world war that would deploy the very forces of technology being celebrated here—streamlined ships and planes, jets and rockets, new types of energy, the latest forms of communication—much as *Things to Come* had prophesied, to help destroy rather than redesign the world. In this strangely juxtaposed scene we recognize how easily the world could shift gears from utopian imaginings to a war footing, how quickly that technology could be turned in a different and more dangerous direction than was suggested by the fair.

Yet this scene may be more important for the way it resonates in the fair's own workings. Like the fair, this newsreel is, after all, a publicity piece, a display of potentially dangerous technology, a *show* staged to reassure the public that America's own technological might could keep it safely distant from that European war. But this scene finally reveals more than it camouflages; even through the wall of smoke partially obscuring the New York skyline—its shrouded skyscrapers recalling the fair's other trademark building, the Trylon—we glimpse the outlines of a strategy that guided the exposition. It too put down a smoke screen of sorts, a nearly impenetrable wall of publicity and images so alluring that, like the movies themselves, we really did not wish to see behind them, to view the mechanism that allowed both their artifice and our dreams to converge and flourish. The display, the show, the amusement—its "there"-ness—seemed enough.

Appropriately, this smoke-screen scene gives way to a series of fantasy images from the covers of pulp magazines, scenes of entertainers promoting the fair, and a complete Max Fleischer cartoon, *All's Fair at the Fair*—all intercut with newsreels of contemporary events, including the German invasion of Czechoslovakia, which further contextualize the fair while also underscoring its distance from reality. From a world of fantasy masquerading as reality, we have moved to the real presented in the context of fantasy, an animated, cartooned version of human experience. Feeding our common cultural desires for a simple, yet pleasurable view of the world, *despite* a pressing reality, the images of entertainment suggest a popular attitude at odds with those other, nonanimated, truly threatening, and utterly real images of the world of 1939–1940. And those real images of mechanized invasion and destruction effectively cast the Machine Age itself in a very different light, not only pushing any notion of a utopian world to a far distant future, such as that typically and fantastically evoked in the pulps, but also reminding us of our uncritical, optimistic, and ultimately detached view of the technological.

We might, moreover, see Fleischer's *All's Fair at the Fair* as completing a narrative movement that began with *The City* and then developed in the Westinghouse publicity film. Viewed in this context, it forms a fitting fictional cap for our double vision of the fair and this documentary about it. For the cartoon brings us clearly and directly into the cinematic/amusement heart of the fair, offers to amuse us just as it did audiences at the end of the Machine Age. As we would certainly expect, *All's Fair at the Fair* never touches on the difficulties of urban life, the just-surfacing issues of class and gender, the problematic potentials of our science, the troubles of the contemporary world—much less the technological menaces that would soon, "tomorrow," be set loose on this world. What cartoons of this era did? Instead, it tells a simple story of amusement and personal change, as two "hayseeds," Elmer and Mirandy, come to the fair in a wagon drawn by their horse Dog Biscuit.[7] They glimpse a few wonders—instantly grown and squeezed orange juice, prefabricated houses, various automated conveniences—but the real focus is an individual transformation wrought by their visit to the fair. Elmer enters a roboticized barbershop and Mirandy an automatic beauty parlor, from which both emerge as "beautiful people"—Elmer even has a piece of straw plucked from his teeth. Thoroughly modernized, they go dancing and then drive off into the sunset in a streamlined auto, dispensed from a vending machine, along with their now useless but—since relieved of its drudgery—thoroughly happy horse. In this brief piece, the technological shifts its focus from the world to the individual, promising not so much a utopian realm in some distant future as a machine-worked, happy life right now.

This shift in focus, like *The World of Tomorrow*'s larger shift from *The City*'s serious propositions to the cartoon's humorous transformations, can help us see the fair's own altered focus. For after its first year, with attention turning from the future to the present, to a world in crisis, and with attendance dropping drastically, the fair's organizers tried to rekindle interest by shifting emphasis more overtly toward entertainment. They not only lowered admission prices, but also eliminated many of the "educational" exhibits, changed the fair's official theme from one emphasizing our proximity to utopia ("The World of Tomorrow") to one suggesting American isolationism and detachment from world events ("For Peace and Freedom"), and expanded the Amusement Area—which, after all, made no pretense at remaking the world. Scenes of the fair's final night suggest it had become something of a party, a moment of escape, one in which that cartoon essentially comes to life, with revelers—many in costume, as if themselves animated figures—dancing away as the sun sets on the fair and on the Machine

Age which it trumpeted. The wonders and attractions of the future have here been reconfigured—or *revealed*—as the pleasures of the present, and our cultural interest in science and technology shown as something of a cartoonish fascination, better glimpsed from a distance, enjoyed much as spectators do the movies themselves.

With both *The World of Tomorrow* and the World's Fair it documents, then, we could well be watching conventional Machine Age science fiction films. For they display advanced technologies of the era as a key, almost generic allure, while, on another level, they help us see the very nature of that allure, the distance built into the technology they chronicle. The fair in its movement from "Tomorrow" to today (our desired "Peace and Freedom") and the film in its shifts from technological exhibition to entertainment cast the technological in a new light, one forecast by our examination of the era's science fiction films. Both illustrate how our technological artifacts have so often appealed to us precisely insofar as they distance us from the real, from the everyday, in their ability to amuse or distract us from the very problems to which they seem to offer some solution.

And just as the fair's organizers worried about its being seen as too educational, so too does this film retreat from the didactic. In fact, it ends on a wistful note; even its oddly melancholy revelation of the fair's "secret goal" leaves a curious residue of sadness, incompleteness, and dissatisfaction that bears further consideration. In this context, we might recall Susan Sontag's famous discussion of the science fiction genre. Focusing primarily on films of the 1950s and 1960s, she describes the genre's fantastic imagery as "above all the emblem of an *inadequate response*" (227) to our human problems. She refers not to our own world's shortcomings, to how incomplete our realm is without those developments the films put so showily on display, but rather to a certain inadequacy in the images themselves—their clearly fictive and ultimately unsatisfying nature. In the science fiction realm, she implies, we always want more—more convincing "special effects," more elaborate sets and models, more compelling action. We want those images to fit seamlessly into our world, to work not only as fascinating illusions but as very near and real possibilities—much as the fair sought to suggest—and thus to eliminate that sense of distance with which the science fiction film, almost in spite of itself, has always seemed to contend. Yet that inadequacy remains, here as elsewhere, and with it a bit of self-consciousness at how easily those images draw us in, and even a measure of wistfulness for a world of the non-imaginary, a real and workable world where such transparent lures do not so readily colonize our consciousness.[8]

Here is a key, if often overlooked struggle that our science fiction films, from the Machine Age to the present, have continued to play out, and that both the fair and *The World of Tomorrow*—our world is, of course, that "Tomorrow"—might help us see. It is a struggle not simply between the forward-looking forces of science and a stubbornly conservative, nonvisionary, timid humanity, here embodied in a narrator who recalls his youthful and even disappointed response to the fair's displays. Rather, it is a struggle to hold both those forces and our own natures in focus, to grasp both our distant *potential* and our present *reality*, and to find some way of squaring these two. It is, in effect, a struggle to see our own reflection in those wondrous technological images—a goal at which the trajectories of this documentary about the Machine Age and the science fiction films of the period clearly intersect.

Our best science fiction films, from their earliest formulations in Méliès' magic transformations to recent big-budget spectacles such as *Total Recall*, *Terminator 2* (1991), and *Independence Day*, try to resolve this struggle by offering mutually reflective images of film and technology, by fashioning a dynamic that, in the best fantasy tradition, forces us to see—our films, their subjects, and eventually ourselves—in a different way. The result is a reflexive pattern that ranges widely: from a focus on robotics and technological reproduction (the sort of reproduction to which film, the art form of what Benjamin terms the "Age of Mechanical Reproduction," seems dedicated) found in most recent science fiction films, including *Blade Runner, Making Mr. Right* (1987), and *Hardware*; to the self-conscious advertising, even self-advertising of the three *Back to the Future* (1985, 1989, 1990) films, which constantly acknowledge their dimension as popular culture hucksters through the appearance, in nearly every scene, of easily identified product tie-ins;[9] to the "videology" Garrett Stewart describes, the omnipresent video screens, computer terminals, holographic forms, and mass media images that abound in works like *Star Wars, E.T.* (1982), *The Last Starfighter* (1984), and *The Fifth Element* (1997), and remind us of the movieness of these technologically based stories about the possible roles of science and technology in our lives. Such elements have seemed nearly omnipresent in our science fiction films from the time of the Machine Age and, I am suggesting, for good reason.

This reflexive dimension holds a special potential on which the best examples of the genre have learned to capitalize. Such films try to do more than just fascinate us with images of science, technology, and technological potential, or warn of the dangers we might risk. In their more successful moments, their reflexive elements emphasize this fascination, reveal the genre's "secret goal" of amusing us as, finally, no great secret at all. The sci-

40. *The trademark Trylon and Perisphere seen from Rainbow Avenue at the New York World's Fair.*

ence fiction film can thus become a special kind of amusement park—or fair—in which our postmodern culture, far more than that of the Machine Age, takes a curious pleasure. For our movies exhibit a view of tomorrow, at least of tomorrow's gadgets, of various bits of technology that promise to make us suitable occupants of another era, even as the contexts of those exhibits—the arid Martian wastes of *Total Recall*, a war-devastated, robot-ruled future in the *Terminator* films, the acid-rain bleakness and urban decay of *Blade Runner* and *Hardware*, or the grotesque alternate future of *Back to the Future, Part II*—qualify the experience and give us pause. What they leave us with is a kind of self-deconstructing "world of tomorrow," which challenges us to design—or film—a better one, that effects the sort of "return trajectory" Romanyshyn sees as the real hope of the technological.

Moving through such expositions, we can suddenly round a corner and find ourselves facing a kind of funhouse mirror, something that brings us up short, as we see reflected there our own images surrounded by these bits and pieces of an imaginary tomorrow. It is a slightly embarrassing encounter, partly because that momentary experience reminds us just how easily we opt for the fair over the real world, for an imaginary rather than true sense of self, for a transparent tomorrow—or perhaps "a long time ago in a galaxy far, far away"—over today, and for the distant over the near at hand.

It is embarrassing also because it suggests how lightly we often take the very elements—science and technology—that can work such transformations. Those glittering images, because of the ways they have been culturally constructed and obligingly consumed, all too easily distract us from the practical problems of development and application, just as a fascination with what we *can* do too often seems to distract us from what we *should* do.

Yet this moment of embarrassment can serve us well. As *The World of Tomorrow*'s narrator realizes, if the fair, like many Machine Age science fiction films, "was unwilling to imagine" the *real* future, it did manage, both then and now, to reveal much about the present. It crystalized a moment "when you can see the world turning from what it is into what it will be," and thus offered any who looked carefully enough, who could see its own cinematic nature, a striking image of its own day, of the distance that still had to be traveled in order to reach these tantalizing dreams of that near time, 1960. While the tall spire of the Trylon drew the eye skyward, away from this world, the arc of the Perisphere's dome led it back to Earth, along a trajectory of return. This is the "secret" behind our best work in the science fiction genre, including many of those films discussed here. These films, these cinematic fairs, these varied "worlds of tomorrow," try to catch us up in that web of pleasurable fascination and recoil, take us along the paths of what Romanyshyn terms "departure" and "re-entry" (202). In their reflexive turns they try to counter the danger he describes, a danger bound up in the allure of the technological image that heralds "a false optimism concerning technology and . . . an uncritical acceptance of its style and its claims" (202). They accomplish that feat by reminding us of distance, making us step back, if but briefly, to reconsider our sense of self and our ability to tell what is real and what only a fair-like amusement.

8

Conclusion

Science must enter into the consciousness of the people.
—ALBERT EINSTEIN

Addressing the opening-night crowd at the 1939 New York World's Fair, Albert Einstein offered the above remark as a guiding principle for the modern age. Yet as David Gelernter reports, the speech that followed was largely garbled due to a combination of Einstein's thick German accent and a malfunctioning sound system, making it practically "impossible for the crowds to hear anything past his opening words" (349), much less to understand how they were supposed to bring this science of which he spoke into their lives. Moreover, the dramatic nighttime illumination of the fairgrounds that he was then to turn on also refused to function as the fair's designers had planned. Einstein's talk thus proved a rather inauspicious start for the fair's own effort at bringing science into the public consciousness.

In this regard too, the fair proved a fitting analogue for the sort of rendition of the technological that we have observed in the movies of the Machine Age. For in film after film and across international boundaries, we have traced an effort, generally congruent with modernism itself, to construct a technological sensibility, to bring science into the common consciousness, to exploit its exciting potential, which always fell a bit short of the mark or seemed somewhat garbled. Even as these films tried to offer viewers strategies for coping with and overcoming any technophobia of the times, for at least easing suspicions of all that the Machine Age's accomplishments held out, they also invariably imposed a kind of distance, typically left viewers feeling like, as Romanyshyn offers, some "spectator self behind his or her window" (186)—a version of Anne Friedberg's "window shopper" or Miles Orvell's photographer paradigm for the inhabitant of modern technological society.

Yet if science and technology never quite managed to dominate modern consciousness in the way Einstein might have hoped or even to have articulated their message in the most understandable way, their images did persist, colonizing our culture despite that distancing effect we have described. In fact, even the coming of World War II did little to dispel the Machine Age's most compelling cinematic images. Footage from *Just Imagine* continued to show up elsewhere. The *Buck Rogers* serial of 1939, for example, used the earlier film's images of New York in 1980 to suggest a truly far-off future, the world of the twenty-fifth century. The rockets from *Just Imagine* and the *Flash Gordon* films would continue to appear in serials into the early 1950s. Similarly, the clanking tin-can robots prototyped in the serials of the 1930s, as well as the Westinghouse exhibit at the New York World's Fair, would linger in both serials and feature films well into the 1950s. And the atomic reactor and various special effects footage from *Gold* would resurface decades later in *The Magnetic Monster* (1957). More recently, the era's aesthetics, particularly the emphasis on streamlining, have been central to the design scheme of a series of fantasy films, largely based on comic strip and radio figures of the period: *The Rocketeer* (1992), *The Shadow* (1994), and *The Phantom* (1996), among others. And the urban vision of *Metropolis* and *Just Imagine*, particularly that of massive setback-skyscraper canyons navigated by flying cars, has influenced Ridley Scott's *Blade Runner* (1982), Tim Burton's *Batman* (1990), and received extended homage in Luc Besson's pastiche of science fiction conventions *The Fifth Element* (1997). In sum, the imagery of the era's films has continued to haunt our cinematic consciousness, testifying to both the continuing evocative power of those Machine Age images and their felt connection to our own technological age.

Still, what they evoke is a kind of distant technology—machinery, a machine style, a machine attitude of an earlier, seemingly simpler time. Undeniably, a nostalgic lure is involved here, but the nostalgia serves, I would suggest, not simply to escape from the present and to avoid the many cultural implications we have come to see as inevitably bound up in a technological world. These images call to mind a period when we were beginning to understand how dramatically we could shape our world through the technological, how we might fashion all sorts of worlds of tomorrow—before we fully understood the problems and complexities involved in that shaping. For most people of the era, technology was something that, as

Gelernter offers, "dealt in the tangible and the everyday, not in strange stuff like software and silicon" (262). And typically, it was something that physically involved us. Thus in the films discussed here, we less often saw someone push a button than pull a lever, and usually with great muscular exertion. Perhaps the lingering feeling is that in those distant images we might trace out a trajectory of return—to the common, to the knowable, to a kind of human control over, and through, our technology, which often seems to have gotten a bit out of control, or at least out of the common person's ability to understand it.

And such an evocative potential already suggests an important level of cultural connection. For that anxiety about our human control of the technological is commonplace today. The increasing sophistication of our robotics and bioengineering could well lead to the production of beings physically superior to humans, as a film like *Blade Runner* suggests. The never-ending effort at reengineering urban space might lead to nearly uninhabitable places, as *The Fifth Element* offers in its vision of the setback skyscraper impulse run amuck. In an age of thinking machines, we debate how long it will be before those machines start to think just as we do, as the famous Turing Test suggests—and then begin to think us out of the equation, as *The Demon Seed* (1977), *2001: A Space Odyssey* (1968), and the *Terminator* films (1984, 1991) all posit. In such circumstances we inevitably draw back, try to distance ourselves a bit from the full force of a technological vision, as so often did the science fiction films of the Machine Age.

Of more importance to us today, though, is another sort of model or lesson that we have often encountered in the images, concerns, and themes of this era's films. As a final example, let me return briefly to one of its non–science fiction films, Chaplin's *The Great Dictator*, which appeared in 1940, when World War II had already staggered Europe and was looming unmistakably on the American horizon. This end-of-an-era film, Chaplin's first true talkie and final surrender to the technology of sound, tolls a loud warning about the period's "sensibility." The little tramp figure is here reincarnated as the Jewish barber mistaken for the German dictator. Forced to impersonate Hynkel on an international radio broadcast or be discovered, the barber turns the dictator's expected bombastic address into a passionate warning not to "give yourselves to these unnatural men—machine men with machine minds and machine hearts." Of course, Chaplin himself had effectively been forced, by the tide of film history, to speak, to give his tramp a voice or disappear from the screen. And he had chosen in various halting ways—first with music in *City Lights* (1931); then with the sound effects, recorded voices, and gibberish speech of *Modern Times*; and finally

with *The Great Dictator's* bombastic speeches—to accept that technological imperative in order to continue to address a wide audience. With this
final speech in *The Great Dictator*, then, Chaplin addresses both his own
situation as filmmaker and that of a world on the brink of destruction, a destruction largely wrought, he implies, by a certain machine sensibility that
has been thoroughly absorbed but also corrupted by those in power, the
"machine men."

And yet like Chaplin with sound film, the Jewish barber, almost in spite
of himself, manages to use technology—a radio broadcast being beamed
throughout Europe—against the technological spirit, at least against those
who would twist it to subjugate and systematize life itself. It is an act that
suggests the necessity for compromise, a reluctant accommodation that
points toward the uneasy relationship between the human and the technological that was emerging towards the end of the Machine Age. In fact, we
should note that Chaplin would further demonstrate that spirit of accommodation in the next two years, as he resurrected his finest silent film, *The
Gold Rush* (1925), reedited it, appended sound effects and specially com-
posed music, and added his own voice-over narration in an attempt to let it
"speak" to a new generation. But this posture is one that the science fiction
film had already conceptually worked through. As we have seen, *The Invisible Ray* suggests how we might turn a deadly force into one that could cure
blindness, both *The Tunnel* and *Things to Come* posit the work of engineers
as an antidote to humanity's warlike tendencies, and the serials of the late
Machine Age would repeatedly position a good science against a bad one, a
technology of protection against one of destruction.

Of course, the struggle itself is also telling, reminding us today of just
how difficult it was, even in a period that had supposedly embraced the
technological as no age before it, to construct a view of technology that
could be easily accepted. The "World of Tomorrow" was, almost throughout the Machine Age, being shadowed by the warfare and mechanized destruction of the present: America's "Banana Wars," the Italian conquest of
Ethiopia, the Spanish Civil War, the repeated Japanese annexations and attacks on China, German predations on the heart of Europe, and so on. In
the films discussed here, we have noted an increasing effort to accept the
technological and the values typically attached to it—speed, efficiency,
predictability, power—particularly as World War I began to recede from
the common experience, if not quite from memory. For all of its troubling
implications, for example, the technoculture depicted in *Things to Come*
still seems far more beneficent and humane, suggesting a much more acceptable relationship between the human and the technological than we

find in Lang's *Metropolis* of a decade before. And yet even here, the cloud of what might come from that relationship never really disappears from the horizon; the gun still looms large.

That ongoing tension points up the extent to which distance and difference were coming to be felt—and envisioned—as inevitable components of the modern age. And it hints as well of technology's implication in a variety of cultural differences which were just beginning to come into view in this period—especially differences between classes (as in *The Mysterious Island*), genders *(Metropolis)*, and races *(The Invisible Ray)*—all of which would only become more obvious as the distancing effect of technology itself came more into focus. Despite its seemingly egalitarian promise, our technology would provide no easy antidote to the distances that separated us in these areas, and insofar as the technological was invariably involved in those distances, often contributing to rather than diminishing them, it seems rather appropriate that our science fiction films—our visions of the connections between science, technology, and culture—would largely disappear from movie screens until the Cold War provided us with new boundaries and relationships on which to focus.

But in the films of this period we can already glimpse the outlines of this development, already make out the frame of that "window" behind which we were being positioned. And in the process we can begin to see the sort of accommodations toward which modern culture would have to work. If machine culture seemed to make possible escape (in the form of rocket flights to the moon, Mars, Mongo, and elsewhere depicted in the era's films), it did not mandate that move. While it produced powerful, often destructive forces (seen in our cinematic submarines, airships, and various sorts of death rays), it hardly required that we deploy them against less sophisticated peoples. If it could create a kind of technocratic elite, an upper class of knowledge (against which a film like *Metropolis* especially warned), it never stood against a democratic impulse. Certainly, there was a great distance between these different potentials, but that sense of distance was itself the challenge of our technology, the challenge to what Einstein termed "the consciousness of the people." And it is a challenge we are still trying to work out in our post–Machine Age science fiction films.

Notes

1. Introduction: Technology and Distance (pp. 1–27)

1. For a brief background on the development of color technology and its impact on film narrative, I recommend Richard Neupert's excellent article, "Exercising Color Restraint."

2. Bazin argued that the cinema represented an effort at satisfying "our obsession with realism" (12). That obsession begins, he says, with a myth, "the myth of total cinema" (22), a dream that we might perfectly reproduce "the world in its own image" (21). This dream or "myth" is one that Walter Benjamin, Miles Orvell, and other commentators have linked specifically to modernism and especially to the Machine Age, with its emphasis on mechanical reproduction.

3. While the appellation "science fiction" first appears in 1851 in a work by William Wilson, this genre was long known under a variety of terms. As Edward James explains, in the late nineteenth century the American publisher of dime novels, Frank Tousey, used the phrase "invention stories," a widely adopted term which was replaced in the next century by such titles as "pseudo-scientific stories," "scientific fiction," and, as popularized in the subtitle of the famous pulp *Amazing*, "scientifiction" (9). Hugo Gernsback, publisher of *Amazing*, is credited with finally establishing the current appellation "science fiction" in 1929, although a phrase like "scientification" lingers well into the 1930s in some of the pulps.

4. Throughout his discussion of the causes of laughter and ultimately his generalizations about comedy, Bergson refers to "mechanical inelasticity" as the fundamental factor. His oft-cited formula, the "mechanical encrusted on the living" (84), offers a useful way of seeing and thinking about the most basic appeal of silent comedy in which the human often becomes machine-like, while the machines—cars, planes, boats—repeatedly exhibit human characteristics.

5. Of course, at this point in his career, Chaplin did feel that he was being menaced by cinematic technology, that he was being forced to radically alter his films and especially his tramp portrayal due to the popular demand for "talkies." In *Modern Times*, as he literally does in the opening sequence of the earlier *City Lights* (1931), he essentially thumbs his nose at the vogue of talking pictures by having several of his characters speak not normally but through mechanisms: a television speaker, a phonograph record, a radio. And in the final scene, when the little tramp is forced to sing, he forgets the words of his song and sings gibberish instead, while miming actions that convey the song's implications and thereby wringing laughter from his audience. It is a final, fleeting moment of triumph for the strategies of silent comedy before Chaplin fully succumbs to

the sound imperative—and in the process says goodbye to his little tramp persona—with *The Great Dictator* in 1940.

6. Many stories about Keaton attest to his personal fascination with the technological. As Rudi Blesh describes Keaton's first meeting with Fatty Arbuckle, Keaton's primary interest was not so much in the work of his fellow comedian as in the film apparatus, the camera, which he proceeded to disassemble and inspect in great detail (88). And as a reflection of that fascination, Blesh sees the abiding story in the Keaton films as always "man at the mercy of both chance and The Machine" (xi).

7. The several serious injuries and close calls Keaton suffered while making his films—including a broken neck in *Sherlock, Jr.* (1924)—attest to a certain level of unpredictability that attended the technology of filmmaking itself. In the case of *The Electric House*, though, that element reflects on the larger thrust of the film, for the unpredictable escalator was in fact just as depicted. In early shooting, Keaton caught his foot in the mechanism and suffered a broken ankle that shut down work on the film for several months. See Blesh's account of this dangerous machine encounter in his biography of Keaton (154).

8. *Wings* used more than thirty-five hundred active-duty troops and sixty Army Air Corps airplanes, as well as various other government resources. As Wellman biographer Frank Thompson notes, the director "was given orders by the War Department that granted him authority to request whatever assistance he needed . . . No other military film ever made was to have such complete cooperation by the Armed Forces" (61). That cooperation was apparently due in large part to the public's turning away from the military in this time of peace and prosperity, which the military hoped to counter by its own sort of cultural construction, that is, by encouraging a view of the military that melded the heroic efforts of the Great War to the Machine Age's fascination with the technologies of flight and speed.

9. Since the late 1920s, an active science fiction fandom has influenced the shape and reception of the literary form. As Edward James notes, this "body of enthusiastic and committed readers . . . has had an appreciable and unique, if unmeasurable, impact upon the evolution of sf, influencing writers, producing the genre's historians, bibliographers, and many of its best critics, and, above all, producing many of the writers themselves" (130). We might also note that the first World Science Fiction Convention was held in New York in 1939, coincident with that watershed of the Machine Age, the New York World's Fair.

10. As an example of that relative neglect, we might note that in her broad-ranging overview of the American science fiction film, *Screening Space*, Vivian Sobchack makes no mention of the films on which we shall focus here: *The Mysterious Island, Just Imagine*, and *The Invisible Ray*. And of these three, only the last receives even a cursory treatment in John Baxter's dated but useful historical account, *Science Fiction in the Cinema*, although he does include brief discussions of several of the foreign works in this period and suggests some intriguing connections between them. For its comparative and cross-cultural focus, his book remains a valuable resource.

11. Sontag's essay, "The Imagination of Disaster," remains one of the most thoughtful and influential pieces on the genre. In it she explores the importance of those images of catastrophe and disaster that so dominated our science fiction films in the 1950s and 1960s, and attempts to link those images to a larger thrust of the genre.

12. For an extended account of this figure's function within the history of both literary and cinematic science fiction, see my *Replications*.

13. In his examination of various strains of "cyberculture," Dery sounds a note very similar to that of Baudrillard's work, as he describes how the latest technology "seduces us with its promise of delivery from human history and mortality" (10).

14. Heidegger's work, especially his key essays "The Question Concerning Technology" and "The Age of the World Picture," provides an important grounding for this notion of the technological as a way of thinking, as a fundamental human attitude. See *The Question Concerning Technology and Other Essays*.

15. This application of the technological clearly runs counter to the thrust of Mark Twain's original novel of 1889. In that work he emphasized the potential for mass destruction that our technology made possible and offered up horrifying images of slaughter, all achieved with the best of intentions by his Yankee protagonist.

16. In her essay "Technophilia," Mary Ann Doane argues that science fiction has always been "obsessed with the issues of the maternal, reproduction, representation, and history" (174). That "obsession," she claims, is rooted in a fundamental opposition between the feminine and the technological, with the latter always promising "to control, supervise, regulate" the former (163). It is an opposition that Romanyshyn sees as implicit in that distancing effect he imputes to the technological, which he reminds us is "not only a dream of escape from matter but also a flight from the feminine" (172).

2. Revolution as Technology: Soviet Science Fiction Film (pp. 28–46)

1. Marinetti's writings, particularly his "Futurist Manifesto" and "The Futurist Cinema," were especially influential. The latter piece, published in 1916, illustrates both the extremes to which the futurist movement went in its glorification of mechanized warfare and its leading role in suggesting the power of a true machine art, the cinema. Even as Marinetti praises the "great hygienic war" then going on for its "renewing power" (130), he also emphasizes the constructive potential of film, particularly its ability to unite "painting, architecture, sculpture, words-in-freedom, music of colors, lines, and forms, a jumble of objects and reality" (131).

2. In her study of American art and culture in the Machine Age, Tichi chronicles the "extraordinary enthusiasm" of American readers for the engineer figure (118), and suggests that this type embodied important lessons of stability, power, and efficiency for a culture "that was trying to surmount its anxieties about instability" (105). A very similar argument could easily be made for Russian culture which, in both the pre- and post-revolutionary eras, was in seemingly constant turmoil.

3. I focus my attentions primarily on *Aelita* because it is readily accessible to any who want to study this period. I have been unable to locate more than a brief clip from *The Death Ray*, and thus have had to rely on the accounts of those associated with the film — Kuleshov, Pudovkin — and historians such as Leyda.

4. Leyda translates and cites Kuleshov's reactions to the film's treatment in his *Kino* (173–74).

5. Christina Lodder suggests that *Aelita*, even in its visual style, already betrayed a certain decadent impulse. She describes its Martian sets as less truly constructivist than "art nouveau" and dismisses the costuming of Alexandra Exter (a figure heavily involved in the realms of futurist and cubist art) as essentially "decorative fripperies" (155).

6. Both *Aelita* and *The Death Ray* receive very brief descriptions in John Baxter's dated but useful overview of the genre, *Science Fiction in the Cinema*. A later, more academic treatment of the genre, Slusser and Rabkin's *Shadows of the Magic Lamp*, mentions neither film, and only *Aelita* appears in the filmography of William Johnson's *Focus on the Science Fiction Film*.

7. In 1923 and 1924 the Mantsev Commission studied the problems of film production plaguing the Soviet Union and recommended to the 13th Party Congress a series of changes, including the abolition of the failed state film company Goskino. See Youngblood's account, pp. 14–16.

8. Youngblood offers a detailed account of this tension in the popular and, as she notes, largely overlooked area of the Soviet cinema in her *Movies for the Masses*. She observes that, as was the case before the Revolution, in the first decade following that social upheaval "popular cinema was defined by models that were labelled 'Western' and seen to be a reflection of a 'bourgeois'" society (7). Still, it was those "bourgeois" films, rather than the more famous works of the revolutionary avant-garde, which were consistently more popular at the Soviet box office.

9. The similarities between *Aelita* and *Metropolis* seem strangely coincidental, particularly in light of Youngblood's note that *Aelita* was among "the most popular films exported to Germany" in the silent era (60). Both films use an avant-garde visual style to suggest the texture of their futuristic/alien civilizations. Both emphasize the distant, detached nature of the civilization's ruler and his repression of the working class. In both films the workers are undifferentiated types, confined to underground quarters. And in both a seductive woman leads them to revolt and nearly to self-destruction. However, Lang's film never wavers in its vision of technological development, drawing all of its power from its analysis of a machine culture and its human effects, while Protazanov's work more conventionally emphasizes the love relationship of its engineer protagonist and his wife.

10. This same conflicted nature seems to mark *Aelita*'s near kin, Lang's *Metropolis*, especially in its problematic conclusion. However, *Metropolis* seems much more conscious of the difficulties in presenting the technological, more aware of the seductive power of technology itself. For a detailed examination of this issue, see my discussion of *Metropolis* in *Replications* (54–71).

3. The Picture of Distance: German Science Film (pp. 47–71)

1. For much of this background on German science fiction literature of the period, I am indebted to Edward James's recent survey, *Science Fiction in the Twentieth Century*. See especially his discussion on pages 10 and 40.

2. We might note several measures of the widespread popularity of German industrial design in this period. The first museum exhibition of modern decorative arts was the Newark Museum's 1912 show, "Werkbund Exhibit of Industrial and Applied Art." From 1922 to 1924 the products of the Wiener Werkstatte were exhibited and made available for purchase through its own New York city showroom. And Paul Frankl operated his own gallery in the city in this same period.

3. Gropius's invocation is taken from the Program of the Staatliches Bauhaus on its opening in Weimar in 1919. The translation is quoted in Noblet (159).

4. I have suggested elsewhere that the more optimistic reading of *Metropolis*'s conclusion is difficult to sustain. Lang's vision of technology's influence, probably colored in great part by his experiences in World War I, seems too cynical for such an easy resolution. We might call to mind the extent to which his master criminal Dr. Mabuse, in several films throughout Lang's career, uses technology to observe others, manipulate them, and insulate himself from danger. See too my treatment of *Metropolis*'s ending in *Replications* (67–70).

5. In America too *Metropolis* was taken to task for its unconvincing vision of the future, although it was, at the same time, praised as a work of cinematic art. Welford Beaton's review for the *Film Spectator* typifies this reaction, as he protests that "None of the things that *Metropolis* says time will do to society seem reasonable to me," and yet lauds the film as "a great intellectual feat as well as an example of the extraordinary possibilities of the screen" (190). According to Jensen, it was in response to this reception that Lang took "pride in the efforts made to keep" *Die Frau im Mond* "as scientifically accurate as possible" (91).

6. It is probably worth noting that *Die Frau im Mond* employs a crude symbology in its character naming. Wolf, after all, hints of a strong, natural creature (der Wolf), while his counterpart Windegger evokes something ephemeral, light, inconstant (der Wind). Both men desire the aptly named Friede Velten, the beautiful or peaceful world.

7. As Baudrillard explains, every discourse, every narrative risks a kind of self-seduction: "inevitably every discourse is revealed in its own appearance, and is hence subject to the stakes imposed by seduction, and consequently to *its own failure as discourse*. Perhaps every discourse is secretly tempted by this failure and by having its objectives put into question" (*Jean Baudrillard* 150). See the discussion of the "seductive" pattern built into the technological display of *Metropolis* and that pattern's connection to the attractions of the science fiction film in my *Replications*.

8. *Die Frau im Mond* is probably the last important silent film to come from Germany, although it achieves that distinction largely as a result of Lang's personal prestige. While every major city in Germany had at least one sound theater by 1929 and while UFA, the company with which Lang was working on this project, had "decided to convert its current pictures to sound," Lang, as Jensen explains, refused to comply on the basis that "his film had not been planned" with sound in mind (79). That reluctance, I would suggest, seems consistent with the rather hesitant embrace of the technological that we find in both of his science fiction films of this period. Lang, it seems, well understood that a filmmaker could not simply retrofit sound to a film. To do so would be treating the new technology as if it were quite neutral, lacking in its own specific problems and possibilities. He preferred to design a film from the beginning around that technology, and with his next film, *M* (1931), one of his greatest successes, he demonstrated the wisdom of that approach.

9. For further discussion of Lang and the feminine, see especially Andreas Huyssens' examination of *Metropolis*, "The Vamp and the Machine."

10. A stylistic emphasis on the sets, model work, and special effects may be at least partly explained by the fact that *F.P. 1* was a cooperative venture, intended for release in at least German, French, and English versions. Like *Der Tunnel* and the earlier *Die Herren von Atlantis* (aka *L'Atlantide*, 1930), the film was shot with German, French, and English casts (and in the case of *L'Atlantide*, shot by a French director), and the character scenes were then intercut with the special effects footage. The result, at least in the case of *F.P. 1*, for which I have been able to examine several different versions, is films that have some distinct national flavor. In fact, the *Variety* reviews of *F.P. 1* suggest something of a qualitative distinction, as the review of the German release glowingly terms it "UFA's greatest picture of the year," while the English version, when it reached America some eight months later, was poorly received and even scored for its dependence on special effects footage.

11. We might lay this recurring concern with monetary manipulation at the feet of the terrible economic experience of the German people in the post–World War I era. In 1922 the country suffered a period of hyperinflation that rendered German currency practically worthless, from which the economy only very slowly recovered. With the National Socialist rise to power, many such cultural ills were typically blamed on outside, manipulative forces.

4. A Remote Power: French Science Fiction Film
(pp. 72–97)

1. It is worth noting that this exhibition, which had such an impact on avant-garde art, was sponsored by the French Ministry of Commerce and Industry.

2. For a more detailed summary of *Charleston*, see Francois Truffaut's commentary appended to Bazin's study *Jean Renoir* (208–209).

3. Appropriately, all that we ever see of this machine is a lever, a handle jutting out of the floor in Crase's laboratory/house. Its very slightness and simplicity point to how easily this ordinary world can be upset, its rules reversed.

4. In this context, we should note that Eiffel achieved his greatest fame up to the time of the tower by building monumental bridges, elaborate cantilevered structures — such as the two hundred-foot-tall Douro River Bridge in Oporto, Portugal, or the four hundred-foot Barabit Viaduct in France — that spanned deep gorges or crossed great distances. For background on Eiffel's various projects, see Harris's *The Tallest Tower*.

5. These were the themes, respectively, for the 1933 Chicago World's Fair and the New York World's Fair of 1939–1940. We shall discuss the role of these and the many other fairs of the era in chapter 7.

6. We should note that the novel from which would come one of the most famous apocalyptic science fiction films, *When Worlds Collide*, was written in this same period by Edwin Balmer and Philip Wylie. Purchased for future production by Cecil B. De-Mille in 1934, that project languished until the "golden age" of film science fiction, the 1950s. In 1951 George Pal resurrected the script and, with director Rudolph Maté, produced the Academy Award–winning film. See John Baxter's *Science Fiction in the Cinema* (149–50).

7. This notion of making capital is very literally the case with *Deluge*, as its footage of New York's destruction was sold for use in a number of other features, most notably *SOS Tidal Wave*. In this respect it follows in a tradition of other works of this period, such as *Just Imagine* and *Gold*, whose special effects footage contributed significantly to later science fiction films, *Flash Gordon* and *The Magnetic Monster* respectively.

8. It might be useful in this context to appropriate the distinction O. B. Hardison, Jr., makes between "modern" and "modernist." "Modern art," he offers, "recognizes a radical discontinuity between past and present and affirms the present," and in doing so it tends "to accept and celebrate technology." In contrast, the modernist view recognizes change but laments "everything that has been lost" in the process, while also betraying a subtle "dislike of technology" (132–33). Among the most notable early moderns would be Gertrude Stein and Hart Crane, while T. S. Eliot typifies the modernist camp. Gance would certainly have placed himself among the former, for even as he focuses on the past in some of his best-known works — for example *Napoléon* and *Un Grande Amour de Beethoven* (1936) — he does so to explore figures who reacted against the conventions and restrictions of their age, who sought in various ways to articulate a new vision.

9. King notes the existence of a scenario dated 1918. In this early version of the narrative there is only one Novalic brother, although he apparently contains the dual attitudes that Gance would later separate for dramatic effect into the figures of Jean and Martial (227).

10. As examples of this sensationalistic approach, barely masked by an "educational" frame, we might note such films as *Reefer Madness* (1936) and *Cocaine Fiends* (1936). In part because of their affected combination of sensationalism and edification, both films have achieved a cult status in recent years.

11. For its recent rerelease on videotape under the dual titles *End of the World/Paris After Dark*, the film was even stamped with an "Adults Only" label.

12. We might compare the equally ambiguous view of the canons in *Napoléon* or, perhaps more to the point, the shifting vision of war in Gance's first *J'accuse*. Begun during World War I, that film paradoxically combines, as Kramer and Welsh offer, "pacifism . . . and a certain amount of French nationalism" (67).

13. In having André Jureau repeat Lindbergh's feat twelve years later in what an aircraft engineer assures us is "a standard Caudron" monoplane, Renoir is pointedly satirizing his culture's seemingly desperate need for a hero in a rather tense and dark time in French history.

5. A Cinema of Spectacle: American Science Fiction Film (pp. 98–138)

1. Edward James stresses the importance of the development of "fandom" in this era, suggesting that it "was to have . . . a pronounced, and unique, effect on the genre" (51). In fact, he asserts that this turn was a key element in the creation of literary science fiction in the twentieth century: "in a sense readers had created a genre before publishers, or even writers, were clear what that genre was" (52). This assertion seems a bit problematic, given the popularity of earlier writers, such as Jules Verne; the illustration of Verne on the nameplate of *Amazing*, peering into his own grave, suggests that both the magazine's editor and contributors were keenly aware of the tradition in which they were working.

2. Jordan's account of the debate surrounding industrial organization during World War I is particularly revealing in this regard. Even as some Americans were calling for "a perfect organization that constitutes a single machine" for purposes of waging the war, that model was being measured against Germany, described by one member of the Taylor Society as "the finest example of the mechanistic idea, fully worked out" (quoted in Jordan 65).

3. While Lucien Hubbard is the director of credit, as well as coauthor of the script, *The Mysterious Island* was initially assigned to Maurice Tourneur, who after only a brief time was replaced by Benjamin Christensen. Tales of the film's production difficulties are widely known and briefly recounted in a number of histories of the genre. See, for example, Parish and Pitts's *The Great Science Fiction Pictures*. Given this study's focus on the images of technology within the films of the era, I have tried to limit such production history material.

4. Andrew Ross observes something of this multivalent attitude in his discussion of the pulp literature of the period and its place in the developing culture of technology. He notes, for example, how "the inventor wizards who starred in the pulp SF stories" were already becoming "anachronisms in the corporate research world of Bell Labs in the thirties" (107).

5. Futurama was the General Motors–sponsored exhibit at the 1939–1940 New York World's Fair. Designed by perhaps the most famous industrial designer of the era, Norman Bel Geddes, it offered audiences a thirty-five-thousand-square-foot model of a planned city of 1960 and an automated "tour" of that future world. Seated in "traveling sound-chairs," 2,150 people per hour moved along a conveyor track above relief maps and models of the metropolis of tomorrow, while a narrator described the "countless . . . wonders of the future" that would be found there (*Futurama*).

6. In fact, initial reviews of *Just Imagine* suggest that not enough attention was given to a sense of futuristic difference. The *Variety* reviewer, for instance, notes the

film's failure in this regard and offers that, in its publicity, the studio, Fox, has "its best chance" at attracting viewers if it places "emphasis upon . . . the amusing appliances of the coming age" (18), rather than upon the rather stock elements of its narrative.

7. This motif of technological resurrection surfaces in a number of films in this period. It takes on monstrous implications in the various *Frankenstein* films, in large part, I would suggest, because Dr. Frankenstein is not simply trying to raise the dead, but to give life to something that, he repeatedly asserts, never really lived before, something he, with nearly divine power, has created from the dead. These films all take the European setting of the Mary Shelley novel, keeping this monstrous use of the technological at a somewhat "safe" geographical remove, as was also the case in another Fox effort about resurrection, *Six Hours to Live*. In contrast, we might consider a thoroughly American rendition of this motif in the famous Mascot serial *The Phantom Empire*. In this film the singing cowboy Gene Autry is killed after stumbling upon the futuristic city of Murania, but its scientists have developed a "radium reviver," which brings him back to life. In this film no dark shadow is attached to that ability to manipulate life and death; there seems to be no suspicious agenda in the technology itself. It simply allows Autry to return to his ranch and his radio show where he might once again sing "That Silver Haired Daddy of Mine."

8. Edward James emphasizes the influence editors like Gernsback and Campbell had on the sense of generic identity that emerged for science fiction in the 1930s. In contrast to those who saw the form as primarily an imaginative exercise and popular entertainment, he offers, "there was a strong feeling that sf *should* be written for scientists, and indeed that sf was part of the scientific discourse which would remake the world, quite as much as the experiments in the laboratories" (61).

9. For an extended discussion of several science fiction serials in this period, particularly as they focused on the image of the mechanical being or robot, see my *Replications: A Robotic History of Science Fiction Film*. For a more general discussion of the form, particularly in the 1920s and 1930s, consult John Baxter's *Science Fiction in the Cinema*.

10. Another, extranarrative way in which the serials found closure was with the very experience of moviegoing, in the ritualistic act of going to see the latest installment each week.

11. While not a science fiction film, *Gabriel Over the White House* (1933) offers a similar plot pattern in which rejuvenation is eventually linked to the technological. A fantasy, this film depicts a crooked President of the United States, similarly attacked by the press, who is nearly killed in a car crash and then mysteriously brought back to life. Following that resurrection he becomes a crusading leader who deploys the country's technological might to impress and intimidate other world leaders, coercing them into paying their debts to the United States. With this nation-saving mission accomplished, the President collapses and dies. Even in a narrative about supernatural intervention in our Depression-induced troubles, the technological once again becomes the means of reaching an important national goal.

12. We should note that this motif was hardly new in *The Invisible Ray*. A 1920 serial of the same title also recounts the search for a powerful, radiation-emitting mineral, and 1921's *Nan of the North* details the discovery of a powerful new source of energy, Titano, similarly found in a meteor. In any case, this notion of a projectable ray does seem a particularly Machine Age conception. One model for Rukh in *The Invisible Ray* is certainly the discoverer of X rays, Wilhelm Roentgen, whose first accidental discovery of the rays dates to 1895, or the early Machine Age.

13. In her study of fantasy literature, Rosemary Jackson emphasizes this visual thrust, as she reminds us that the very term *fantasy* translates as "that which is made visible" (13).

14. For a discussion of various late-nineteenth- and early-twentieth-century cultural activities that typify the development of a kind of culture of spectatorship in line with a

"society of the spectacle," see Anne Friedberg's "Cinema and the Postmodern Condition," as well as her longer investigation of the topic in *Window Shopping*.

15. We might consider in this context Baudrillard's suggestion that contemporary humanity "has *the passion to be object*," an enigmatic "impatience" to achieve "the destiny of objects" (93). If, as many critics imply, Baudrillard's analysis of the postmodern world is clearly echoed in much of our recent science fiction, it should come as little surprise that our late Machine Age science fiction films would anticipate these concerns, would, on a more fundamental level, begin to visualize the sort of "ecstatic" world, as he terms it, that our technology might produce.

6. A Monumental Event: British Science Fiction Film (pp. 139–161)

1. For much of the background on British science fiction I have drawn on James's *Science Fiction in the Twentieth Century* and Stableford's "Science Fiction Between the Wars: 1918–1938."

2. The "Today and Tomorrow" series was comprised of approximately one-hundred pamphlets published by Kegan Paul, Trench, and Trubner, beginning in 1924. Beginning with the text of a lecture by J. B. S. Haldane entitled *Daedalus, or Science and the Future*, it included work by some of the most prominent thinkers of the period, including Bertrand Russell, James Jeans, Andre Maurois, and Robert Graves. See Stableford's discussion of this (54–55).

3. Under the British Cinematographic Film Act of 1927, film exhibitors were required to show a quota of British-made films (initially seven and one-half percent of those exhibited) to balance the predominance of American works and to help stimulate the British film industry. While in effect from 1928 to 1938, the act generally boosted domestic production, but the films were for the most part cheaply made, technically unsophisticated program fillers—hence the term "quota quickies"—and were often financed by American studios, which thus exerted a subtle control over the domestic industry. The dominant narrative types produced under this regime were domestic comedies, musicals, and thrillers. See Landy's discussion of the "quota quickie" in her *British Genres* (24–25).

4. Some accounts indicate that a Spanish version was also produced. While the German and British versions of *F.P. 1* are relatively accessible, the French is much more elusive, and I have found no evidence of a Spanish version.

5. See the reviews for January 17 and September 19, 1933, in *Variety Film Reviews*. Linda Wood, in *British Films*, notes that in the late 1920s and early 1930s "there was a far higher degree of inter-European cooperation" than most histories acknowledge, but also points out that such efforts are difficult to sort out, given the absence of production records for many of the films, as well as the tendency of the films themselves to obscure such involvement: "it was rare to include details of any such" international partnerships on any release prints (62).

6. In fact, in her study of British film genres, Landy lists only three science fiction films for the decade 1930–1940: *The Tunnel*, *Things to Come*, and *The Man Who Could Work Miracles* (1937). The last of these, though, seems nearer pure fantasy, given its narrative about some bored gods who one day decide to bestow on a rather insignificant man miraculous powers. Questions of science and technology, largely absent from that film, are certainly more central to works like *Non-Stop New York* (1937) or the spy drama *Q Planes* (1939).

7. It might be worth noting in this context that even in the cinema technological

change was hardly embraced wholeheartedly. In another one of the period polls Linda Wood cites, seventy percent of British women who were regular filmgoers indicated that they would not welcome the advent of talking pictures (132).

8. The Austin automobile factory, for example, suffered a massive and violent strike in 1929 when it tried to introduce the assembly-line techniques of Henry Ford. See Carroll Pursell's discussion of the reactions of the various craft unions to technological innovation in England in *White Heat* (107–108).

9. Probably as much for their iconic as for their box-office value, the film cast Walter Huston as the American president and George Arliss as the British prime minister. The former had already become rather closely identified with the presidency, thanks to his executive roles in the recent *Gabriel Over the White House* (1933) and *American Madness* (1932), as well as the title role in *Abraham Lincoln* (1930). In the first of these films he had also offered national addresses over the radio that look toward his internationally televised speech in *The Tunnel*. Arliss had played a series of powerful industrialists and historical figures, but was perhaps most noted for his Academy Award–winning performance as the British prime minister in *Disraeli* (1929).

10. See Bel Geddes's *Horizons* (109–21) for his plans for a gigantic flying wing capable of international travel. The design of his "Air Liner #4," done in collaboration with the German aeronautical engineer Otto Koller, describes a plane with a wingspan of 528 feet, a weight of 1,275,300 pounds, a range of 7,500 miles, and a passenger capacity of 606—a kind of airborne ocean liner. In both size and appearance, it was unlike anything that had ever flown; however, it never progressed beyond this design stage.

11. For background on Scott and the other champions of technocratic rule, I have drawn primarily on Segal's "The Technological Utopians" and Ross's *Strange Weather*. As the latter offers, the "rhetoric of unstinting faith in the progressive virtues of science ranged across a wide political spectrum" (105) in both the United States and England, surfacing in pulp science fiction as well as in serious social debate. As part of that social debate and coincident with the shooting of *Things to Come*, we should note, the sixth International Congress for Scientific Management met in England in 1935.

12. Stover, drawing heavily on Wells's writings, including both the source novel— *The Shape of Things to Come*—and his first film treatment of this material—*Whither Mankind?*—reads this transformation in a more troubling light, as representative of Wells's desire to transform the nature of labor and the laboring class, as symbolic of a radical Socialist agenda. That reading, however, seems less an explication of the film itself and more an effort to surmise Wells's original intentions for the film project—a risky business for any critic—and to impose them on the film as it exists.

13. Stover's treatment of this climactic scene again calls for some comment. Drawing on Wells's brief description in his *Whither Mankind?* treatment, particularly the lines indicating how "Theotocopulus and his staff are seen buffeted and torn by the wild rush of air" as the gun fires (176), he concludes that the space gun's firing represents an act of "mass murder," that all of the protesters are "wiped out in one cruel blow by the concussion of the Space Gun" (87–88). Of course, the *film* never offers us such images; the visual narrative simply fails to support this interpretation of Wells's possible intentions in this scene.

7. "I Have Seen The Future": The New York World's Fair as Science Fiction (pp. 139–161)

1. As an example of these efforts to "dramatize" future life, we might consider the various houses that constituted the fair's "Town of Tomorrow." Equipped with the latest

appliances and conveniences, these houses were never simply static displays. During the fair's run, forty families were chosen to stay in the houses for a week at a time. These families not only could enjoy all the conveniences of domestic life of 1960; they also served as a kind of living theater, illustrating to fairgoers the pleasures and comforts our technology would eventually bring to all (see Kihlstedt 110, 114). In this respect, we can all the more clearly see the lineage of the fair and Disney's Epcot, which was originally planned as a similar demonstration community, the "experimental planned community of tomorrow."

2. The argument for seeing both the New York World's Fair and the Chicago Century of Progress Exposition as utopias is advanced in articles by Kihlstedt and Segal.

3. While *The World of Tomorrow* makes great capital from comparing the various technological exhibits to the fair's "Amusement Area," with its more commonplace rides, games, and displays, in fact the corporate exhibits outdrew the Amusement Area by a seven-to-one margin (see Marchand I, 90). As Teague's comments suggest, though, those corporate presentations were themselves designed—much as is today's Epcot Center—as amusements.

4. For a brief discussion of the nature of these films, see Kihlstedt's "Utopia Realized." He cites a contemporary critic, Eugene Raskin, who suggested that the fair itself need not ever be built; rather, that "the best way to build a World's Fair is not to build it at all, but to make a motion picture of it" (110), in effect, a science fiction film. As *The World of Tomorrow* presents the fair, it might be argued that, after a fashion, this is very nearly what happened.

5. I take the term "Titan City" from a famous exhibition held in 1925 entitled, "The Titan City, a Pictorial Pageant of New York, 1926–2026." It featured the designs of Harvey Corbett and Hugh Ferriss, which emphasized the setback skyscraper design, multilevel, interconnecting transit systems, and pedestrian bridges. As Carol Willis offers, the images in this exhibit, much like those seen in many of the films discussed here, seem practically "intoxicated with technology" (179). Ferriss, we might note, along with the architect William Orr Ludlow, designed the layout of the New York World's Fair (see Gelernter 84).

6. It is worth noting that the actor who plays Mr. Middleton, Harry Shannon, would shortly be cast as Charles Foster Kane's father in *Citizen Kane* (1941). It is a role in which he essentially sells his son off, turns him and all the wealth he is to inherit over to the banks and power brokers of modern America. In this earlier instance, of course, Mr. Middleton does not turn his son over to the technocrats, but he certainly seems intent on "selling" him on their philosophy of the future. In retrospect, the chance juxtaposition of this publicity film with *Kane* seems almost as telling as the happy accident of history that linked the fair and *The Wizard of Oz*.

7. The character of "Elmer" was also a centerpiece for a new publicity campaign for the fair in 1940. Designed to balance the first year's emphasis on technological wizardry and accomplishment, this campaign pushed the familiar, the American, the entertainment potential of the fair. Elmer was supposed to represent the average American who might come to the fair—and help overcome its twenty-three-million-dollar debt. Portrayed by an actor, Elmer's likeness appeared on posters, he made public appearances across the country, and finally he became a greeter at the fair, much like the various Disney characters who today move among the crowds at Disneyland and Disneyworld (see Gelernter 352).

8. At this point, my argument intersects with Vivian Sobchack's reading of the science fiction genre through the vantage afforded by Fredric Jameson and his Marxist analysis. See her *Screening Space*, especially the final chapter.

9. Writing about the film industry in general and its pervasive reliance on product

tie-ins, Mark Crispin Miller suggests that "movies now are made deliberately to show us nothing, but to sell us everything" (13). In carrying out this corporate mission, though, the movies risk calling attention to their very mechanism, that is, making viewers aware of their larger status as ideological vehicles, as what we might term "culture commercials."

Filmography

The following is, I must stress, a *select* filmography. The Machine Age, after all, coincides with the formative years of the cinema, and many of the films made during this time no longer exist or have become largely unavailable. The list below, consequently, generally indicates those films that have contributed to my thinking about this era and that should prove useful to those interested in pursuing this study's concerns and exploring the early history of the science fiction genre. Regrettably, in a few cases, notably *The Death Ray* and *High Treason*, I have had to rely on printed accounts, summaries, and reviews of the films. In the case of *La Fin du monde*, I have drawn on the later, American version, as well as script extracts and various accounts of the film.

Aelita (1924). Mezhrabpom-Rus. Dir.: Yakov Protazanov. Scr.: Fyodor Otsep, Alexei Falko. Cin.: Yuri Zhelyabuzhky, E. Schonemann. Design: Victor Simov, Isaac Rabinovitch, Alexandra Exter, Sergei Kozlovsky. Cast: Igor Ilinsky, Yulia Solntseva, Nikolai Tseretelly, Nikolai Batalov. 99 min.

Bride of Frankenstein, The (1935). Universal. Dir.: James Whale. Scr.: John L. Balderston, William Hurlbut. Cin.: John D. Mescall. Music: Franz Waxman. Cast: Boris Karloff, Colin Clive, Ernest Thesiger, Elsa Lanchester. 75 min.

Buck Rogers (1939). Universal. Dir.: Ford Beebe, Saul A. Goodkin. Scr.: Norman S. Hall, Ray Trampe. Cin.: Jerry Ash. Cast: Buster Crabbe, Constance Moore, Jackie Moran, Henry Brandon. A serial in twelve chapters.

Death Ray, The (1925). Goskino. Dir.: Lev Kuleshov. Scr.: Vsevelod Pudovkin. Cin.: Alexander Levitsky. Design: Pudovkin. Cast: Sergei Komarov, Piotr Galadzhev, Alexandra Khokhlova.

Doctor X (1932). First National/Warner Bros. Dir.: Michael Curtiz. Scr.: Earl Baldwin, Robert Tasker. Cin.: Richard Tower, Ray Rennahan. Ed.: George Amy. Music: Leo F. Forbstein. Cast: Lionell Atwill, Fay Wray, Preston Foster, Lee Tracy. 80 min.

F.P. 1 Antwortet Nicht (*F.P. 1 Does Not Answer*, 1933). Gaumont/UFA/Fox. Dir.: Karl Hartl. Prod.: Erich Pommer. Scr.: Walter Reisch, Curt Siodmak. Cin.: Otto Baecker, Gunther Rittau, Konstantin Tschet. Cast: (German) Hans Albers, Paul Hartman, Sibylla Schmitz, Peter Lorre. (English) Conrad Veidt, Leslie Fenton, Jill Esmond, Donald Calthrop. (French) Charles Boyer. 109 min. (Note: English, German, and French versions, all with different casts, were filmed simultaneously.)

Fin du monde, La (aka *Paris After Dark*, 1930). L'Ecran D'Art. Dir.: Abel Gance. Prod.: Ivanoff. Scr.: Abel Gance, André Lang. Cin.: Jules Kreuger, Roger Hubert, Nikolas Roudakoff. Art Dir.: Lazare Meerson. Cast: Abel Gance, Victor Francen, Colette Darfeuil, Samson Fainsilber. 91 min.

Flash Gordon (1936). Universal. Dir.: Frederick Stephani. Scr.: Frederick Stephani,

George Plympton, Basil Dickey, Ella O'Neill. Cin.: Jerry Ash, Richard Fryer. Cast: Buster Crabbe, Jean Rogers, Charles Middleton. A serial in thirteen chapters.

Flash Gordon Conquers the Universe (1940). Universal. Dir.: Ford Beebe, Ray Taylor. Prod.: Henry MacRae. Scr.: George H. Plympton, Basil Dickey, Barry Shipman. Ed.: Joseph Gluck, Saul Goodkind, Louis Sackin, Alvin Todd. Art Dir.: Harold H. MacArthur. Cast: Buster Crabbe, Carol Hughes, Frank Shannon, Charles Middleton. A serial in twelve chapters.

Flash Gordon's Trip to Mars (1938). Universal. Dir.: Ford Beebe, Robert Hill. Scr.: Wyndham Gittens, Norman S. Hall, Ray Trampe, Herbert Dalmas. Cast: Buster Crabbe, Carol Hughes, Charles Middleton. A serial in fifteen chapters.

Frankenstein (1931). Universal. Dir.: James Whale. Scr.: Garrett Fort, Francis Edward Farogh. Cin.: Arthur Edeson. Ed.: Clarence Kolster, Maurice Pivar. Music: Bernhard Kaun. Cast: Boris Karloff, Colin Clive, Mae Clarke, Edward Van Sloan. 71 min.

Frau im Mond, Die (aka *Woman in the Moon, The Girl in the Moon, By Rocket to the Moon*, 1929). UFA. Dir.: Fritz Lang. Scr.: Lang, Thea von Harbou. Cin.: Kurt Kourant, Oskar Fischinger, Otto Kanturek. Design: Otto Hunte, Emil Hasler, Karl Vollbrecht. Technical Consultants: Hermann Oberth, Willy Ley, et al. Cast: Gerda Maurus, Willy Fritsch, Fritz Rasp. 156 min.

Gold (1934). UFA. Dir.: Karl Hartl. Prod.: Alfred Zeisler. Scr.: Rolf E. Vanloo. Cin.: Gunther Rittau, Otto Beacker, Werner Bohne. Design: Otto Hunte. Cast: Brigitte Helm, Hans Albers, Michael Bohmen, Lien Deyers. 102 min. (Note: A French version, directed by Serge de Poligny, was filmed simultaneously.)

High Treason (1929). Gaumont. Dir.: Maurice Elvey. Prod.: L'Estrange Fawcett. Scr.: L'Estrange Fawcett. Cast: Humbertson Wright, Jameson Thomas, Benita Hume, René Ray, Basil Gill. 95 min.

Invisible Man, The (1933). Universal. Dir.: James Whale. Prod.: Carl Laemmle, Jr. Scr.: R. C. Sherriff (based on H. G. Wells's novel). Cin.: Arthur Edeson. Ed.: Ted J. Kent. Music: Heinz Roemheld. Special Effects: John P. Fulton. Cast: Claude Rains, Gloria Stuart, Henry Travers, E. E. Clive. 71 min.

Invisible Ray, The (1935). Universal. Dir.: Lambert Hillyer. Prod.: Edmund Grainger. Scr.: John Colton. Cin.: George Robinson, John P. Fulton. Cast: Boris Karloff, Bela Lugosi, Frances Drake, Frank Lawton. 81 min.

Island of Lost Souls (1933). Paramount. Dir.: Erle C. Kenton. Scr.: Waldemar Young, Philip Wylie. Cin.: Karl Struss. Cast: Charles Laughton, Richard Arlen, Leila Hyams. 70 min.

It's Great to be Alive (aka *The Last Man on Earth*, 1933). Fox. Dir.: Alfred Werker. Scr.: Arthur Kober, Paul Perez. Cin.: Robert Planck. Ed.: Barney Wolf. Cast: Dorothy Burgess, Emma Dunn, Robert Greig, Joan Marsh. 69 min.

Just Imagine (1930). Fox. Dir.: David Butler. Scr.: Butler (from story by Buddy DeSylva, Lew Brown, Ray Henderson). Music: Buddy DeSylva, Lew Brown, Ray Henderson. Cin.: Ernest Palmer. Ed.: Irene Morra. Cast: El Brendel, Maureen O'Sullivan, John Garrick, Frank Albertson. 107 min.

Mad Love (1935). MGM. Dir.: Karl Freund. Scr.: Guy Endore, P. J. Wolfson, John Balderston. Cin.: Chester Lyons, Gregg Toland. Cast: Colin Clive, Peter Lorre, Frances Drake. 83 min.

Men Must Fight (1933). MGM. Dir.: Edgar Selwyn. Scr.: C. Gardner Sullivan. Cin.: George J. Folsey. Ed.: William S. Gray. Cast: Lewis Stone, May Robson, Phillips Holmes. 72 min.

Metropolis (1926). UFA. Dir.: Fritz Lang. Scr.: Fritz Lang, Thea von Harbou. Cin.: Karl Freund, Gunther Rittau. Design: Otto Hunte, Erich Kettelhut, Karl Vollbrecht. Special Effects: Eugene Schufftan. Cast: Brigitte Helm, Alfred Abel, Rudolf Klein-Rogge, Gustav Froelich. 93 min. (Several restored versions are currently available, offering additional footage and, in some cases, production stills to illustrate lost material.)

Murder by Television (1935).Cameo Pictures. Dir.: Clifford Sanforth. Prod.: Clifford Sanforth, Edward M. Spitz. Scr.: Joseph O'Donnell. Cin.: James S. Brown, Jr., Arthur Reed. Ed.: Leslie Wilder. Art Dir.: Lewis J. Rachmil. Cast: Bela Lugosi, June Collyer, George Meeker, Hattie McDaniel. 60 min.

Mysterious Island, The (1929). MGM. Dir.: Lucien Hubbard. Prod.: J. Ernest Williamson. Scr.: Lucien Hubbard, Carl L. Pierson. Cin.: Percy Hilburn. Art Dir.: Cedric Gibbons. Music: Martin Broones, Arthur Lange. Cast: Lionel Barrymore, Jane Daly, Harry Gribbon, Montague Love, Dolores Brinkman. 95 min.

Non-Stop New York (1937). Gaumont. Dir.: Robert Stevenson. Prod.: Michael Balcon. Scr.: Curt Siodmak, Roland Pertwee, J. D. C. Orton, Derek N. Twist, and E. V. H. Emmett (based on the novel *Sky Steward* by Ken Attiwill). Cin.: Mertz Greenbaum. Ed. Al Barnes. Cast: Anna Lee, John Loder, Francis L. Sullivan. 71 min.

Paris qui dort (aka *The Crazy Ray*, 1924). Films Diamant. Dir.: René Clair. Prod.: Henri Diamant-Berger. Scr.: René Clair. Cin.: Maurice Desfassiaux, Paul Guichard. Cast: Henri Rolland, Madeleine Rodrigue, Albert Préjean, Martinelli. 38 min.

Phantom Creeps, The (1939). Universal. Dir.: Ford Beebe, Saul Goodkind. Prod.: Henry MacRae. Scr.: Mildred Barish, Willis Cooper, Basil Dickey, George Plympton. Cin.: Jerry Ash, William Sickner. Art Dir.: Ralph DeLacy. Ed.: Irving Bernbaum, Joseph Gluck, Alvin Todd. Cast: Bela Lugosi, Dorothy Arnold, Regis Toomey, Edward Van Sloan. A serial in twelve chapters.

Phantom Empire, The (1935). Mascot. Dir.: B. Reeves Eason, Otto Brower. Prod.: Armand Schaefer. Scr.: Wallace MacDonald, Gerald Geraghty, H. Freedman. Cast: Gene Autry, Smiley Burnette, Frankie Darro, Betsy Ross King. A serial in twelve chapters.

Six Hours to Live (1932). Fox. Dir.: William Dieterle. Scr.: Bradley King. Cin.: George F. Seitz. Cast: Warner Baxter, Irene Ware, John Boles, George Marion. 78 min.

Things to Come (aka *The Shape of Things to Come*, 1936). United Artists. Dir.: William Cameron Menzies. Prod.: Alexander Korda. Scr.: H. G. Wells. Design: Vincent Korda. Cin.: Georges Perinal. Cast: Raymond Massey, Ralph Richardson, Sophie Stewart, Cedric Hardwicke, Edward Chapman. 92 min.

Tunnel, Der (1933). Wandor Film. Dir.: Kurt (Curtis) Bernhardt. Prod.: Ernst Garden. Scr.: Kurt Bernhardt, Reinhart Steinbicker. Cin.: Carl Hoffman. Cast: Paul Hartmann, Olly von Flint, Max Schreck. 73 min.

Tunnel, The (aka *Transatlantic Tunnel*, 1935). Gaumont. Dir.: Maurice Elvey. Prod.: Michael Balcon. Scr.: Clemence Dane, Dugarde Peach, Curt Siodmak, H. Kellermann. Cin.: Gunther Krampf. Ed.: Charles Frend. Cast: Richard Dix, Leslie Banks, Helen Vinson, C. Aubrey Smith, Madge Evans. 94 min.

20,000 Leagues Under the Sea (1916). Universal. Dir.: Stuart Paton. Prod.: Stuart Paton. Scr.: Stuart Paton (based on Jules Verne's novel). Cin.: Eugene Gaudio, Ernest Williamson, George Williamson. Art Dir.: Frank Ormston. Cast: Lois Alexander, Curtis Benton, Wallis Clark, Howard Crampton. 105 min.

Undersea Kingdom, The (1936). Republic. Dir.: Joseph Kane, B. Reeves Eason. Prod.: Barney Sarecky. Scr.: John Rathmell, Maurice Geraghty, Oliver Drake. Cast: Ray "Crash" Corrigan, Monte Blue, Lon Chaney, Jr. A serial in twelve chapters.

Bibliography

Abel, Richard. *French Cinema: The First Wave, 1915–1929*. Princeton: Princeton UP, 1984.

Armes, Roy. *A Critical History of the British Cinema*. New York: Oxford UP, 1978.

Barnouw, Erik. *Documentary: A History of the Non-fiction Film*. Rev. ed. Oxford: Oxford UP, 1983.

Barthes, Roland. *The Eiffel Tower and Other Mythologies*. New York: Hill and Wang, 1980.

Baudrillard, Jean. *Baudrillard Live: Selected Interviews*. Ed. Mike Gane. London: Routledge, 1993.

——. *The Ecstasy of Communication*. Trans. Bernard and Caroline Schutze. New York: Semiotext(e), 1988.

——. *Forget Foucault and Forget Baudrillard*. New York: Semiotext(e), 1987.

——. *The Illusion of the End*. Trans. Chris Turner. Stanford: Stanford UP, 1994.

——. *Jean Baudrillard: Selected Writings*. Ed. Mark Poster. Stanford: Stanford UP, 1988.

Baxter, John. *Science Fiction in the Cinema*. New York: Paperback Library, 1970.

Bazin, André. *Jean Renoir*. Ed. François Truffaut. New York: Simon and Schuster, 1974.

——. *What is Cinema?* Vol. 1. Ed. and trans. Hugh Gray. Berkeley: U of California P, 1967.

Beaton, Welford. Review of *Metropolis*. Rpt. in *American Film Criticism: From the Beginnings to Citizen Kane*, eds. Stanley Kauffmann and Bruce Henstell, 188–90. New York: Liveright, 1972.

Bel Geddes, Norman. *Horizons*. Boston: Little, Brown, 1932.

Bellour, Raymond. "On Fritz Lang." In *Fritz Lang: The Image and the Look*, ed. Stephen Jenkins, 26–37. London: BFI, 1981.

Benjamin, Walter. "The Work of Art in the Age of Mechanical Reproduction." In *Illuminations*. Trans. Harry Zohn, ed. Hannah Arendt, 217–51. New York: Schocken, 1969.

Bergson, Henri. "Laughter." In *Comedy*, ed. Wylie Sypher, 59–260. Garden City, N.Y.: Doubleday, 1956.

Blesh, Rudi. *Keaton*. New York: Collier, 1966.

Bogdanov, Alexander. *Red Star: The First Bolshevik Utopia*. Eds. Loren E. Graham and Richard Stites. Trans. Charles Rougle. Bloomington: Indiana UP, 1984.

Bordwell, David. *Narration in the Fiction Film*. Madison: U of Wisconsin P, 1985.

Christie, Ian. "Down to Earth: *Aelita* Relocated." In *Inside the Film Factory: New Approaches to Russian and Soviet Cinema*, eds. Richard Taylor and Ian Christie, 80–102. London: Routledge, 1991.

Clarens, Carlos. *An Illustrated History of the Horror Film*. New York: Capricorn, 1967.
Constantine, Mildred, and Alan Fern. *Revolutionary Soviet Film Posters*. Baltimore: Johns Hopkins UP, 1974.
"Curtains." *Time*, 4 Nov., 1940: 72.
Dardis, Tom. *Keaton: The Man Who Wouldn't Lie Down*. New York: Scribner's, 1979.
Debord, Guy. *The Society of the Spectacle*. Trans. Donald Nicholson-Smith. New York: Zone Books, 1995.
Dery, Mark. *Escape Velocity: Cyberculture at the End of the Century*. New York: Grove, 1996.
Doane, Mary Ann. "Technophilia: Technology, Representation, and the Feminine." In *Body/Politics: Women and the Discourse of Science*, eds. Mary Jacobus, Evelyn Fox Keller, and Sally Shuttleworth, 163–76. New York: Routledge, 1990.
Eco, Umberto. *Travels in Hyperreality*. Trans. William Weaver. New York: Harcourt Brace, 1986.
Frayling, Christopher. *Things to Come*. London: BFI, 1995.
Friedberg, Anne. "Cinema and the Postmodern Condition." In *Viewing Positions: Ways of Seeing Film*, ed. Linda Williams, 59–83. New Brunswick: Rutgers UP, 1994.
———. *Window Shopping: Cinema and the Post-Modern Condition*. Berkeley: U of California P, 1993.
Futurama. Official Program. General Motors Corp., 1940.
Gelernter, David. *1939: The Lost World of the Fair*. New York: Avon, 1995.
Gifford, Denis. *Science Fiction Film*. New York: Dutton, 1971.
Grant, Barry Keith. "Experience and Meaning in Genre Films." In *Film Genre Reader II*, ed. Barry Keith Grant, 114–28. Austin: U of Texas P, 1995.
Griffiths, John. *Three Tomorrows: American, British, and Soviet Science Fiction*. Totowa: Barnes & Noble, 1980.
Hall, Mordaunt. "A Trip to Mars." *The New York Times*, Nov. 22, 1930.
Hall, Stuart. " The Television Discourse—Encoding and Decoding." In *Studying Culture*, eds. Ann Gray and Jim McGuigan, 28–34. London: Edward Arnold, 1993.
Hardison, O. B., Jr. *Disappearing through the Skylight: Culture and Technology in the Twentieth Century*. New York: Viking, 1989.
Harris, Joseph. *The Tallest Tower: Eiffel and the Belle Epoque*. Boston: Houghton Mifflin, 1975.
Heidegger, Martin. *The Question Concerning Technology and Other Essays*. Trans. William Lovitt. New York: Harper, 1977.
Herf, Jeffrey. *Reactionary Modernism: Technology, Culture, and Politics in Weimar and the Third Reich*. Cambridge: Cambridge UP, 1984.
Huyssen, Andreas. "The Vamp and the Machine: Technology and Sexuality in Fritz Lang's *Metropolis*." *New German Critique* 24–25 (1981–82): 221–37.
Jackson, Rosemary. *Fantasy: The Literature of Subversion*. London: Methuen, 1981.
Jakobowski, Maxim. "French SF." In *Anatomy of Wonder: A Critical Guide to Science Fiction*. 3d ed., ed. Neil Barron, 405–40. New York: Bowker, 1987.
James, Edward. *Science Fiction in the Twentieth Century*. New York: Oxford UP, 1994.
Jensen, Paul M. *The Cinema of Fritz Lang*. New York: Barnes, 1969.
Johnson, William. "Introduction: Journey into Science Fiction." In *Focus on the Science Fiction Film*, ed. William Johnson, 1–12. Englewood Cliffs: Prentice-Hall, 1972.
Jordan, John M. *Machine-Age Ideology: Social Engineering and American Liberalism, 1911–1939*. Chapel Hill: U of North Carolina P, 1994.
Kawin, Bruce F. "Children of the Light." In *Film Genre Reader II*, ed. Barry Keith Grant, 308–29. Austin: U of Texas P, 1995.
Keller, Evelyn Fox. "From Secrets of Life to Secrets of Death." In *Body/Politics: Women*

and the Discourse of Science, eds. Mary Jacobus, Evelyn Fox Keller, Sally Shuttleworth, 177–91. New York: Routledge, 1990.

Kihlstedt, Folke, T. "Utopia Realized: The World's Fairs of the 1930s." In *Imagining Tomorrow: History, Technology, and the American Future*, ed. Joseph J. Corn, 97–118. Cambridge: MIT Press, 1986.

King, Norman. *Abel Gance: A Politics of Spectacle*. London: BFI, 1984.

Koszarski, Richard. *An Evening's Entertainment: The Age of the Silent Feature Picture, 1915–1928*. Berkeley: U of California P, 1990.

Kracauer, Siegfried. *From Caligari to Hitler: A Psychological History of the German Film*. Princeton: Princteon UP, 1947.

Kramer, Steven Philip, and James Michael Welsh. *Abel Gance*. Boston: Twayne, 1978.

Kuleshov, Lev. *Kuleshov on Film*. Trans. Ronald Levaco. Berkeley: U of California P, 1974.

Landy, Marcia. *British Genres: Cinema and Society, 1930–1960*. Princeton: Princeton UP, 1991.

Latour, Bruno. *We Have Never Been Modern*. Trans. Catherine Porter. Cambridge: Harvard UP, 1993.

LaValley, Albert J. "Traditions of Trickery: The Role of Special Effects in the Science Fiction Film." In *Shadows of the Magic Lamp: Fantasy and Science Fiction in Film*, eds. George E. Slusser and Eric S. Rabkin, 141–58. Carbondale: Southern Illinois UP, 1985.

Lavery, David. *Late for the Sky: The Mentality of the Space Age*. Carbondale: Southern Illinois UP, 1992.

Le Corbusier. *The Radiant City: Elements of a Doctrine of Urbanism to be Used as the Basis of Our Machine-Age Civilization*. Trans. Pamela Knight, Eleanor Levieus, Derek Coltman. New York: Orion Press, 1933, 1967.

Leyda, Jay. *Kino: A History of the Russian and Soviet Film*. New York: Collier, 1973.

Lodder, Christina. *Russian Constructivism*. New Haven: Yale UP, 1983.

Marchand, Roland. "The Designers Go to the Fair, I: Walter Dorwin Teague and the Professionalization of Corporate Industrial Exhibits, 1933–1940," and "The Designers Go to the Fair, II: Norman Bel Geddes, the General Motors 'Futurama,' and the Visit to the Factory Transformed." In *Design History: An Anthology*, ed. Dennis P. Doordan, 89–102, 103–21. Cambridge: MIT Press, 1995.

Marcuse, Herbert. *One Dimensional Man*. Boston: Beacon Press, 1964.

Marinetti, F. T. *Marinetti: Selected Writings*. Ed. R. W. Flint. Trans. R. W. Flint and Arthur A. Coppotelli. New York: Farrar, Straus, 1972.

Meikle, Jeffrey L. "Streamlining: 1930–1955." In *Industrial Design: Reflections of a Century*, ed. Jocelyn de Noblet, 182–92. Paris: Flammarion, 1993.

Miller, Mark Crispin. "The Big Picture." In *Seeing Through the Movies*, ed. Mark Crispin Miller, 3–13. New York: Pantheon, 1990.

Neupert, Richard. "Exercising Color Restraint: Technicolor in Hollywood." *Post Script* 10, no. 1 (1990): 21–29.

Noblet, Jocelyn de, ed. *Industrial Design: Reflections of a Century*. Paris: Flammarion, 1993.

Orvell, Miles. *After the Machine: Visual Arts and the Erasing of Cultural Boundaries*. Jackson: UP of Mississippi, 1995.

———. *The Real Thing: Imitation and Authenticity in American Culture, 1880–1940*. Chapel Hill: U of North Carolina P, 1989.

Parish, James Robert, and Michael R. Pitts. *The Great Science Fiction Pictures*. Metuchen, N.J.: Scarecrow, 1977.

Petric, Vlada. *Constructivism in Film*. Cambridge: Cambridge UP, 1987.

Pursell, Carroll. *White Heat: People and Technology*. Berkeley: U of California P, 1994.

Reed, Herbert. *A Concise History of Modern Painting*. 3d ed. New York: Praeger, 1974.

Review of *Just Imagine*. *Variety*, Nov. 26, 1930: 18.

Ricoeur, Paul. "Ideology and Utopia as Cultural Imagination." In *Being Human in a Technological Age*, eds. Donald M. Borchert and David Stewart, 107–25. Athens: Ohio UP, 1979.

Romanyshyn, Robert D. *Technology as Symptom and Dream*. London: Routledge, 1989.

Ross, Andrew. *Strange Weather: Culture, Science, and Technology in the Age of Limits*. London: Verso, 1991.

Schwartz, Vanessa R. "Cinematic Spectatorship before the Apparatus: The Public Taste for Reality in Fin-de-Siècle Paris." In *Viewing Positions: Ways of Seeing Film*, ed. Linda Williams, 87–113. New Brunswick: Rutgers UP, 1995.

Segal, Howard P. "The Technological Utopians." In *Imagining Tomorrow: History, Technology, and the American Future*, ed. Joseph Corn, 119–36. Cambridge: MIT Press, 1986.

Shelley, Mary W. *Frankenstein, or The Modern Prometheus*. Ed. M. K. Joseph. London: Oxford UP, 1971.

Sobchack, Vivian. "Cities on the Edge of Time: The Urban Science Fiction Film." *East-West Film Journal* 3 (1988): 4–19.

——. *Screening Space: The American Science Fiction Film*. 2d ed. New York: Ungar, 1987.

Sontag, Susan. "The Imagination of Disaster." *Against Interpretation*, 212–28. New York: Dell, 1966.

Stableford, Brian. "Science Fiction Between the Wars: 1918–1938." In *Anatomy of Wonder: A Critical Guide to Science Fiction*, 3d ed., ed. Neil Barron, 49–62. New York: Bowker, 1987.

Stevens, Joseph E. *Hoover Dam: An American Adventure*. Norman: U of Oklahoma P, 1988.

Stewart, Garrett. "The 'Videology' of Science Fiction." In *Shadows of the Magic Lamp: Fantasy and Science Fiction in Film*, eds. George E. Slusser and Eric S. Rabkin, 159–207. Carbondale: Southern Illinois UP, 1985.

Stites, Richard. "Fantasy and Revolution: Alexander Bogdanov and the Origins of Bolshevik Science Fiction." In *Red Star: The First Bolshevik Utopia*, eds. Loren Graham and Richard Stites, 1–16. Bloomington: Indiana UP, 1984.

Stover, Leon. *The Prophetic Soul: A Reading of H. G. Wells's "Things to Come."* London: McFarland, 1987.

Tashjian, Dickran. "Engineering a New Art." In *The Machine Age in America, 1918–1941*, ed. Richard Guy Wilson, Dianne H. Pilgrim, and Dickran Tashjian, 205–69. New York: Abrams, 1986.

Teague, Walter. *Design This Day: The Technique of Order in the Machine Age*. New York: Harcourt, Brace, 1940.

Telotte, J. P. *Replications: A Robotic History of the Science Fiction Film*. Urbana: U of Illinois P, 1995.

Thompson, Frank T. *William A. Wellman*. Metuchen, N.J.: Scarecrow, 1983.

Tichi, Cecelia. *Shifting Gears: Technology, Literature, Culture in Modernist America*. Chapel Hill: U of North Carolina P, 1987.

Tolstoi, Alexei. *Aelita, or The Decline of Mars*. Trans. Leland Fetzer. Ann Arbor: Ardis, 1985.

Variety Film Reviews: 1934–1937. New York: Garland Publishing, 1983.

Vitale, Elodie. "The Bauhaus and the Theory of Form." In *Industrial Design*, ed. Jocelyn de Noblet, 154–65. Paris: Flammarion, 1993.

Willis, Carol. "Skyscraper Utopias: Visionary Urbanism in the 1920s." In *Imagining Tomorrow: History, Technology, and the American Future*, ed. Joseph J. Corn, 164–87. Cambridge: MIT Press, 1986.

Wilson, Richard Guy, Dianne H. Pilgrim, and Dickran Tashjian. *The Machine Age in America: 1918–1941*. New York: Abrams, 1986.

Winsten, Archer. "The City Goes to the Fair." *New York Post*, June 23, 1939. Rpt. in *The Documentary Tradition: From Nanook to Woodstock*, ed. Lewis Jacobs, 126–28. New York: Hopkinson and Blake, 1971.

Wood, Linda, ed. *British Films: 1927–1939*. London: BFI, 1986.

Yacowar, Maurice. "The Bug in the Rug: Notes on the Disaster Genre." In *Film Genre Reader II*, ed. Barry Keith Grant, 261–79. Austin: U of Texas P, 1995.

Youngblood, Denise J. *Movies for the Masses: Popular Cinema and Soviet Society in the 1920s*. Cambridge: Cambridge UP, 1992.

Zamyatin, Yevgeny. *A Soviet Heretic: Essays by Yevgeny Zamyatin*. Ed. Mirra Ginsburg. Chicago: U of Chicago P, 1970.

Index

NATIONAL UNIVERSITY
LIBRARY   SAN DIEGO

UNIVERSITY PRESS OF NEW ENGLAND publishes books under its own imprint and is the publisher for Brandeis University Press, Dartmouth College, Middlebury College Press, University of New Hampshire, Tufts University, and Wesleyan University Press.

About the author: J. P. Telotte is a professor of Literature, Communication, and Culture at the Georgia Institute of Technology. He has written several books on film, including *Replications: A Robotic History of the Science Fiction Film* (1995), *Voices in the Dark: The Narrative Patterns of Film Noir* (1989), and *Dreams of Darkness: Fantasy and the Films of Val Lewton* (1985). He is the editor of *The Cult Film Experience: Beyond All Reason* (1991).

Cataloging-in-Publication Data

Telotte, J. P., 1949–
A distant technology : science fiction film and the machine age /
J. P. Telotte.
    p.   cm.
Filmography: p.
Includes bibliographical references and index.
ISBN 0–8195–6345–5 (cloth : alk. paper). — ISBN
0–8195–6346–3 (pbk. : alk. paper)
1. Science fiction films—History and criticism.   I. Title.
PN1995.9.S26T45   1998
791.43'615—dc21   98–38718